SOLITARY WALKER

A Novel of Mary Wollstonecraft

N.J. Mastro

Black Rose Writing | Texas

ISBN: 978-1-68513-561-4
LIBRARY OF CONGRESS CONTROL NUMBER: 2024945158
PUBLISHED BY BLACK ROSE WRITING
www.blackrosewriting.com

Printed in the United States of America
Suggested Retail Price (SRP) $22.95

Solitary Walker is printed in Garamond Premier Pro

*As a planet-friendly publisher, Black Rose Writing does its best to eliminate unnecessary waste to reduce paper usage and energy costs, while never compromising the reading experience. As a result, the final word count vs. page count may not meet common expectations.

*For my family, whose love and support
has always been unwavering.*

Praise for
SOLITARY WALKER

"A tour de force. *Solitary Walker* brought me totally inside the heart and mind of the extraordinary 18th century feminist icon Mary Wollstonecraft. I wept at the end. Mastro's meticulous research brings to life a heartbreaking tale of a brilliant mind who challenged societal norms. Her writing captures the personal anguish and utter betrayal of a broken heart. An unputdownable novel and more."
–Joan Fernandez, author of *Saving Vincent, A Novel of Jo van Gogh*

"N. J. Mastro writes with tender compassion as she plunges the depths of the complex and often conflicted inner life of the world's first feminist, Mary Wollstonecraft. Using a multi-hued palette of historical details, Mastro paints a beautiful portrait of one of history's earliest female political writers. Highly recommended."
–Debra Borchert, author of *Her Own War, Book three of the Château de Verzat* series

"In *Solitary Walker*, N.J. Mastro presents the remarkable life of a woman of extraordinary courage, stubbornness, and fortitude. Everyday domestic life in 1790s England, the perils of the Terror in revolutionary France, and the rigors of travel in Scandinavia are all rendered in convincing detail. Especially compelling is Mastro's imaginative rendering of the inner life of Mary Wollstonecraft, her choices, tribulations, and moral certainties."
–Carolyn Korsmeyer, author of *Charlotte's Story* and *Riddle of Spirit and Bone*

"... a clear and engaging portrait of a woman whose fierce intellect and strong passions were at odds with society's expectations. The central character comes vividly to life as Mastro effectively delves into Mary's thoughts and emotions while fully revealing her strengths and weaknesses ... daily life in late eighteenth century England, revolutionary France, and mercantile Scandinavia, and the politics of the age are explored with accuracy and finesse."
–Margaret Porter, award-winning best-selling author, *The Myrtle Wand* and *Beautiful Invention*

SOLITARY WALKER

PROLOGUE

Spring 1771
England

A biting wind swept through an open window at the end of the hall where Mary kept vigil outside her mother's bedroom. The month of May had been mean thus far to the rural market town of Beverley in East Yorkshire, and she burrowed deeper into the flimsy linen shift she wore, the one Mamma had passed down to her. The shift was too large for a girl of twelve, but little money remained for new things. The Wollstonecrafts were living on their last supply of borrowed impressions. Before long, they would leave the old Tudor they were renting and move again to escape creditors.

Chimes in the clock that looked like a coffin on the main floor below performed their hourly duty. Half-past midnight. Mary's heart leapt when, moments later, the main door to the house opened.

Papa.

Mary scrambled to her feet.

Uneasiness rose in her as he climbed the stairs, the steady scrape of his boots against the wood a sure sign he had lost at the racetrack. He would be in his cups again, angry at the entire countryside. She readied herself the way she had seen her brothers fight bullies—arms up, two fists.

On the landing Edward Wollstonecraft came to a swift halt, a sliver of moonlight all that separated him from Mary. "You little spy," he said, sneering at her. "Here to protect your mother again, are you?"

The sickening smell of rancid smoke and sour whiskey wafted from him, causing her stomach to flip. Bile rose in her. He looked like a vagrant. His worn frock coat hung on his gaunt frame like a rag pulled from a bin at the almshouse. "You're drunk. Go away." She hated what he had become.

"You've no right to intrude."

Mary spread her arms to block the door, the wood hard against her back. "Stop hurting Mamma."

Papa lunged at her. She charged in return, rage that had been squatting in her turning fierce.

He caught her in his arms midair and thrust her to the floor. "When you become a wife, you'll understand."

Before Mary could regain her footing, he entered Elizabeth Wollstonecraft's bedroom and slammed the door behind him. The lock clicked.

Mary spat at where he had stood. "I shall never marry." The words tasted bitter on her tongue.

PART I

A New Genus
1787–1792

*"I do not wish them [women] to have power
over men but over themselves."*

Mary Wollstonecraft
A Vindication of the Rights of Woman (1792)

ONE

August 1787
Sixteen Years Later
Bristol, England

Strengthen the female mind, Mary Wollstonecraft told the girls on their very first day together, and there would be an end to women's blind obedience. A girl who learned to think for herself grew up to be a self-sufficient woman.

She had arranged a schedule upon becoming governess one year ago that turned out to suit them like a well-tailored frock. Lord and Lady Kingsborough's daughters Margaret, Caroline, and Mairen were intelligent and demonstrated excellent potential, proving Mary's theory that girls were as capable as boys when given the chance to cultivate their minds. She met with them for lessons every morning, except Saturday and Sunday. A walk outdoors after lunch followed, which she expected them to partake of seven days a week, though not on holidays. Afternoons were for exploring individual interests. In return for this delicious freedom, all she required of them was to report back to her what meaningful knowledge they had gleaned.

This particular day, the girls had chosen to read for the afternoon in the sitting room of Mary's small apartment in the family's rented villa at Hotwells Spa. The Kings were spending the summer in Bristol, taking the waters that bubbled from St. Vincent's Rocks in the Avon Gorge below. The apartment lacked fine things but was equipped with serviceable furniture and had ample shelves for books, along with a table for lessons and soft seating for lounging. The walls were bright white on sunny days. But as this was a gray day, the room's color had turned ashen. Outside was hot and drizzly, making a picnic or a river trip out of the question. A storm was brewing. Everyone's clothes felt damp; even the pages of their books had gone limp.

"What are you reading?" Margaret asked, sitting beside Mary on the sofa. "It troubles you."

Mary looked up and blinked. She did not mind the interruption. Questions were a hallmark of the kind of disposition she had dedicated herself to fostering in the girls. "Why do you ask?"

"You've furrowed your brow and have twisted your mouth to one side."

Mary smiled. "Your observation is keen." Margaret was fifteen and perceptive. When Mary had first met her, she thought Margaret like one of the wild Irish living beyond the Pale—restless and feral, a girl with flaming red hair that sprang from an iron will. But they had in common a rebellious temperament. Instead of their fiery spirits dividing them, Mary and Margaret had become allies.

"What observation?" Caroline asked from where she was sitting on a carpet at Mary's feet with Mairen. They wiggled closer to Mary until snuggled against her like kittens. Caroline was twelve, Mairen six. All three of the girls had sunburned cheeks they had failed to protect on yesterday's hike along the river when Mary let them shed their bonnets.

"I'm not troubled," Mary said. "I merely disagree with this author." She held up *Emile* by Jean-Jacques Rousseau. Margaret had been right. Mary was an ardent fan of the Swiss philosopher, but his words left her steaming inside.

Margaret said, "You must tell us more." She laid her head on Mary's shoulder.

Mary's ire at Rousseau's writing softened as Caroline and Mairen closed their books and looked at her with anticipation, their fingers marking their pages. "*Emile* frames Rousseau's views about education. He believes it is best, as do I, for young children to interact naturally with the world through their senses. However, in the fifth book in his treatise, I object to his depiction of Sophie."

"Who's Sophie?" Mairen asked.

"The author's symbol for female development."

Margaret perked at this and sat up straight, her emerald eyes fixed on Mary.

"Rousseau thinks Sophie's education should be for the sole purpose of grooming her to become Emile's wife," Mary said. What he meant, of course, was preparing to become a wife was all any girl's education should entail, and it was this that had made her critical of him.

Margaret frowned. "But that would make Sophie nothing more than a plaything to Emile."

"Precisely," Mary said. "How very often I have heard women bleat opinions they had learned to recite rather than speak from a depth of understanding. All meaning has been lost to them. Which is why I believe girls must receive an education equal to that of boys, or girls' minds will never improve." And tradition would forever hold them hostage, Mary thought.

The girls agreed that Rousseau was, indeed, misguided in his interpretation of how things ought to be, and Mary listened, pleased, as they broke into an enthusiastic debate over what girls must learn and when. She had taught them well. Her affection for all three was as warm and sweet as the milky-white spring water Hotwells visitors drank for their health. Perhaps her reluctant decision to move to Ireland the prior year had not been such a mistake after all. The King girls were on their way to a glorious future, even if she, at twenty-eight, was not.

A sadness that was bittersweet rippled through her as outside lightning flashed, followed by the rumble of thunder. Within moments, rain slicked down the mullioned windowpanes, sealing her and the King girls inside her apartment. Mary enjoyed teaching, but she had never imagined herself a governess, betwixt and between worlds, neither a servant nor a member of the household. What she wanted was to be a thinking woman. A member of a chapter of the Blue Stockings Society and live a quiet life in a little cottage outside some small village. Exposing the King girls to books and the world beyond Mitchelstown Castle where they lived in County Cork, however, would have to do for now. At least she was to visit the Continent soon, where the family planned to travel in September, taking the girls and her with them. All her life she had dreamed of seeing exquisite paintings in Rome, taking in the blue of the Mediterranean Sea, and walking the streets of Paris until dusk.

"There you are," said Lady Kingsborough.

Mary stiffened, as did the girls, at the sudden intrusion of the Viscountess Caroline King, who marched into the sitting room with one of her dozen lapdogs tucked in her arms.

Lady Kingsborough's boots clacked on the marble floor. "Why are you thitting in here?" She spoke with a fake lisp, which was the fashion of the day. Wisps of curls trickled down the sides of her face from hair swept high above her head, adding to her regal veneer, as did three distinct beauty marks (which *were* real) gracing the left side of her long neck. Her usual scowl loomed over them like the shadow of a steep garden wall whose purpose was to keep things out. She was said to be a beauty, though plump at the middle after having given birth to twelve children, nine of whom survived.

The two younger girls inched closer to Mary.

Margaret, however, glared at her mother. "If you looked out the window, you would notice the weather is rainy. Besides, we're too young to promenade or to visit the Pump Room, and we've already toured the colonnade of shops so many times it's no longer a novelty."

"I must speak to Miss Wollstonecraft. Alone," Lady Kingsborough said, ignoring Margaret's saucy tone. She lifted her delicate chin and looked away as if the sight of her daughters and their governess displeased her.

The girls turned in unison to Mary, who wondered what she had done now. If she could quit the room, she would. Instead, she stood and nodded toward the door, a signal for the girls to follow their mother's command. They left, heads bent, shoulders sagging along with Mary's spirits.

"You and I must have consistent aims," Lady Kingsborough said when the girls had gone. "Margaret is almost of age for her own ball. But when I told the ladies at the spa of your curriculum, they warned that my daughters' education has been far too broad. They need not be learning history or the natural sciences. And their French is terrible, which I will not allow. Not a single of their accomplishments, I might add, have improved under your tutelage. Instead, you have them reading entirely too much. Their minds are not built for such stimulation."

Mary discreetly set aside her copy of *Emile*, facing the cover down on a nearby table. Things like fancy needlework, painting, and playing the pianoforte were fine to know. But quietly to the girls, Mary called them *misaccomplishments*. What good were they if girls could not also reason and apply logic? Lady Kingsborough, however, only thought of her daughters finding good matches. As Ireland's largest landowners and its wealthiest Protestant family, the Kings expected their girls to marry well.

"My lady," said Mary, who saw no purpose, let alone dignity, in the way genteel families auctioned their daughters in marriage, "when you hired me, we agreed to a focus on academics." She held the woman's gaze. What had once been an amicable relationship between them had become a tinderbox. The tenor had only worsened in Bristol.

"Of course. We Kings are forward-thinking people." The viscountess stroked her lapdog. "But embroidery is a necessary skill for all young ladies. Yet not one of my girls has stitched anything I'd be proud to show others. It further occurs to me I've never seen a needle in your hand."

Mary simmered inside. "I shall see to it that they spend more time on fancy needlework," she said, knowing she would not.

"That will not be sufficient."

The hair on Mary's neck prickled. "You are being cryptic, my lady."

Caroline King stepped closer, her eyes narrowing. "What I mean is, your work here is finished. Your methods are too liberal. I shall find another governess, one who follows my instructions strictly."

Mary parted her lips, then clamped them shut, her stomach tightening with the maddening feeling of having no power to put a woman of Lady Kingsborough's stature in her place. Nor would it be wise. When Mary started her position, entering Mitchelstown Castle had been like walking into the Bastille. Now another kind of prison flashed before her—the place for debtors. "Surely we can find common ground." She could not afford to be dismissed, not with debts to pay and family members who depended on her.

Margaret rushed into the room. "You cannot release her!" she said to her mother, her gaze frenzied. She must have been standing outside the door. "Miss Wollstonecraft is the finest of governesses. You've said so yourself. You brag of her to all. And she loves us." She sent Mary a desperate look. "Stay. I will talk to Papa."

"Compose yourself, Margaret," Lady Kingsborough said. Her voice had turned to a high pitch, prompting a sharp bark from her lapdog. "Lord Kingsborough has no say in the matter."

"I regret leaving you," Mary said to Margaret, a raw feeling like an old wound breaking open in her from having to give in to Lady Kingsborough's command. She loved the girls like sisters. To desert them meant leaving a piece of herself behind, the part of her that had grown with them and would always be theirs.

Margaret ran to Mary and clutched her hands. "I want to come with you."

"That's quite enough, Margaret," Lady Kingsborough warned.

Margaret sprang at her mother, her fingers stretched and curved like claws threatening to strike. "I will become a wild animal without her!"

"You mustn't say such things," Mary said to Margaret, using a soft voice she had learned calmed the girl. "Your mother is right. It's time for me to go."

Margaret rushed into Mary's arms.

A knot formed in Mary's throat. Lady Kingsborough neglected her children, leaving the servants to raise them, a wrong Mary found impossible to forgive. Children needed their mother, even one who was cold. She stroked Margaret's hair and urged her to be strong in the face of this new adversity. Before pulling away, she whispered in her ear that she would write, then led the girl to the sofa.

"This is your fault," Lady Kingsborough said to Mary, disregarding Margaret, who had collapsed into a sobbing heap. "You have indulged my girls far too much."

"And you, my lady, love them far too little."

Margaret's cries pierced the boom of thunder outside as Mary turned on her heel and retreated to the privacy of her bedroom. She knew the pain of a mother's indifference, the scars it left. Her own mother had barred Mary from affection when Mary was not much younger than Margaret.

Into her worn carpet bag, Mary stuffed what few items of clothing she possessed. She had known this day would come. Earlier that year, she had published *Thoughts on the Education of Daughters*. At first, Lady Kingsborough had treated her with respect for publishing a book, parading Mary in front of visitors when the King family was in Dublin for the winter season. The book was popular there, producing a new kind of thrill in Mary—the satisfaction of being heard, of being valued for her intellect. The electricity produced by scores of accolades lingered still. They had sustained her during times of doubt and helped stave off moments of despair she increasingly faced in Ireland. The same compliments, however, had made Lady Kingsborough jealous. Not knowing what to expect from one so shifting, Mary distanced herself, occupying the same room only when required.

Lady Kingsborough may have been plotting to dismiss her. Mary, however, had been planning her own escape. A sudden feeling of triumph replaced the resignation she had experienced only moments prior. Ireland had been a purgatory, a sideways existence she was glad to put behind her so she could begin what she had always intended—to make her own way in the world as a solitary woman. She retrieved a stack of handwritten pages tied with string from a drawer in her small writing desk. No more speaking only when spoken to or marching to the demands of a mercurial mistress. Mary had no idea where she would rest her head that night, but freedom, even uncertain freedom, was dear. Tomorrow, she would make her way to London.

TWO

August 1787
Three Days Later
London

Towering brick buildings two and three stories high bore down on Mary like
goliaths as the hackney coach lurched to a stop in St. Paul's Churchyard on a street
lined with bookshops and taverns. Without waiting to be handed down, she thrust
the door open and stepped onto the cobblestone.

The driver tossed her dusty bag from up above. "G'day then, miss," and with
nary more than that as a goodbye, he grazed the tip of his tricorn with a leathered
index finger and wheeled away.

The stranger's departure left Mary feeling alone despite streams of people
walking to and fro. Her spirits had grown depressed over the more than one
hundred miles she had traveled from Bristol. Had she been wise to come all this
way when a parcel with a note would have been sufficient? She could not falter
now. The foul stink of the Thames a block away reminded her how, in one small
turn, life could rot. When she spotted St. Paul's Cathedral across the way, she
prayed for more luck than life had thus far granted her.

She turned then, and there it was, No. 72, an odd-shaped corner affair, narrow
at the front, wide at the back, the kind of building that she imagined had stories to
tell and secrets to keep. Books for sale displayed in the front window fanned the
flames of discontent that had delivered her to London. Someday, volumes of her
own work would sit alongside them.

In the glass, Mary peered at her reflection. Plain, gray linen dress. Black worsted stockings. Low-heeled walking shoes. She looked like a milkmaid. But the worn-out beaver riding hat she preferred over something more feminine sat atop her reddish-brown waves, which were free of pins or powder, saying this was who she was. Mary Wollstonecraft, aspiring writer. Here in the heart of England's book trade, she would live by her pen.

It was that or perish.

A bell above the door chimed a cordial welcome when she entered the bookshop. The space was dark despite the large window. The aroma of pristine paper and the unmistakable smell of drying ink bolstered her resolve, and she inquired after the proprietor.

Without glancing her way, a young man hunched over a podium scratched away with his pen. "May I tell him who's calling?"

The man's head jerked to attention when she said her name. His face turned red, and he set down his writing instrument. "Excuse me, miss. I didn't realize one of his writers was calling. Rowland Hunter, at your service." He stood and bowed in proper greeting, telling her he would announce her straight away and scurried off, the sound of his steps a sharp clip echoing down a darkened hall.

That he had even heard of her surprised Mary, having but one advice book to her name. While waiting, she picked up a daily sitting askew on a shelf with others and scanned the front page. Fellow passengers on the coach had warned her London was growing faster than its roads and bridges could handle. She should expect to see a crowded, dirty city. The paper echoed their claims even though William Pitt was busily introducing governmental reforms to improve England's social and economic conditions.

"Politics," an older gentleman sitting across from her on the coach had grumbled. "Discourse is more partisan than ever. Damned radical Whigs. They're going to destroy the whole country."

He was a Tory of the worst kind: pigheaded and unimaginative. Though she knew little of politics, Mary assumed she must align with the so-called radical Whigs. It was time England looked forward.

Rowland Hunter reappeared. "He'll see you now." He reached for her bag, meaning to retrieve it from her like she was a wisp.

Mary maintained her grip. "I can manage. Thank you."

Mr. Hunter looked confused but recovered, as would any good gentleman facing a headstrong woman and led her down the hall past a large printing room on one side, storage rooms on the other, to the end, where light from an open door spilled into the walkway.

A tiny man about her size stepped out to greet Mary. "A pleasure to see you, Miss Wollstonecraft." Joseph Johnson pulled his cuffs from his sleeves after he finished wiggling into a worn frock coat with wrinkles no amount of patting could subdue. He quickly adjusted his lapels to make them lie flat, then he stood straight, looking at her with quiet earnestness. "Back so soon?"

Heat from uncertainty at what he would say to Mary being dismissed crawled the length of her neck. "It appears I am." Would he think differently of her now? Would he see her as a failure?

Mr. Johnson invited her into his office, and she seated herself in the circle of chairs in the center, their leather seats sagging from years of use, their arms worn down to unvarnished wood. He settled in the chair opposite her and crossed his slender legs just as he had done a year earlier when she had paid him a visit, the only time she had met her publisher in person.

He offered Mary a sympathetic half-smile. "I take it things did not improve with your employer." Joseph Johnson was by nature an amiable man, almost fifty, a confirmed bachelor sporting the standard gray wig with two rows of curls just above the ears. His firm jaw and thick eyebrows contradicted his diminutive stature, however; he was a lion in the publishing business. But his body was thin, and he wheezed as he spoke. Asthma. A lone window emitted a single shaft of light, illuminating tiny specks of dust floating in the air.

At a loss over how to explain her new situation despite his warm welcome, Mary avoided looking at Mr. Johnson and glanced about the room. Bookcases lined two of the walls, stuffed with volumes of an array of sizes. Jammed into the rare open space between the books were stacks of paper. Taking up a third wall were portraits, most of them philosophers. Mary spotted Rousseau. Her eyes rested, however, on her beloved John Locke, who seemed to be taking her to task as he peered at her past the tip of his long nose, his stern look reminding her of his famous words, what worries you, masters you. But it was hard not to worry these days.

"Lady Kingsborough relieved me of my duties three days ago," she said, her shame still oozing. She was not just penniless, homeless, and without means of an income; she owed the benefactress of her school in Newington Green nearly two hundred pounds. The school had collapsed prior to Mary going to Ireland. Her work as governess to the Kings was meant to pay off her debt. "I hope in my letters I did not sound too desperate or too critical of my circumstances, which reminded me of all those years ago when I was a companion to an elderly woman in Bath, an observer of other people's lives." Mary and Mr. Johnson had been corresponding the entire time she had been in Ireland.

Mr. Johnson's dark eyes turned solicitous. "Your news does not mystify me, my dear."

Relief swept through Mary, and her shoulders relaxed as she melted into the chair. "I thought you'd be disappointed in me."

"The woman sounded ghastly. People like her are best avoided, which you've accomplished, albeit in a rather ... circuitous way." He smiled his half-smile. "You're here now. Frankly, I scarcely could be more pleased. It's the novel you've been writing that I wish to hear about."

Mary sensed his nose for profit on display. Mr. Johnson, a shrewd businessman, published seventy titles a year, half again as many more than his nearest competitor, making him one of the most successful publishers in all of London. Glad to leave the subject of her dismissal behind, she reached into her bag and handed him her manuscript. "I'm calling it *Mary: A Fiction*."

He propped his spectacles at the end of his nose and untied the thin string holding her handwritten pages together.

She bit her lip as she watched him thumb through the papers with expert speed, his nimble hands those of someone whose life had been spent assessing the potential of drafts presented to him by hopeful writers whose stomachs performed a series of acrobatics, as hers did now, while awaiting his appraisal.

"Autobiographical, is it?" he asked, glancing at her over the top rim of his spectacles.

"The plot and characters are of the imagination. Mostly." Mary folded her hands to keep them from fidgeting. The work was, in fact, based in part on personal experience and reflected the nature of some people she had met, her feckless parents and Lady Kingsborough among them. Though using a false name, she had cast Lady Kingsborough in an especially unflattering manner, revenge she supposed for the way the woman treated her. But it was Mary's first serious work of fiction. Her own life was all she really knew from which to draw. "Mary's story is the tale of a young woman of uncommon humanity," she stammered. "Her parents force her into a loveless marriage. Fortunately, her new husband leaves to study on the Continent, allowing her to be free of him. Meanwhile, Mary's dear friend, Ann, who is living in Lisbon and bereft over a lost love, contracts consumption. Mary leaves England to care for her."

"A take on your relationship with Miss Blood?" Mr. Johnson asked with the kindness of one who knew the answer yet felt compelled to ask, a polite means of expressing sympathy.

At the mention of Fanny, tears pressed behind Mary's eyes, and she fingered the mourning ring on her hand where a lock of Fanny's hair substituted as a stone in the center. A day did not go by when Mary did not long to hear her voice. Three years prior, Fanny, her best friend, had at last married her beau of ten years and had become pregnant within the month. Mary had left her school in Newington Green in the middle of the academic year and sailed to Lisbon to be with her. But consumption, that hated disease, had reduced Fanny to the size of a sparrow. The rigors of delivering a baby were too much, and Fanny died. The child, a boy, went to his eternal resting place two weeks later.

"Miss Wollstonecraft?" Mr. Johnson said, drawing Mary back to the present.

"Ann's story is different," she replied, collecting herself. "While Mary visits Ann, whose consumption has confined her to a sanatorium, Mary falls in love with Henry, one of Ann's fellow consumptives. After Ann's death, Henry follows Mary home to England and dies later in her arms. Mary's husband returns from the Continent, leaving her facing a life she detests, one in which she perceives death as her only escape ..."

Mary's voice trailed off. Mr. Johnson appeared unmoved by the story.

She gulped. "Perhaps you find the book's themes too reformist," she said, her spirit sinking to the bottom of the Thames like a piece of lost cargo. Her views regarding girls' education had landed her in trouble with Lady Kingsborough; she could not afford to offend Mr. Johnson, too.

Another half-smile teased Mr. Johnson's lips. "I hadn't pegged you as a sentimental novelist."

Mary chafed at his assessment of her. *A Fiction* was more than some fantastical tale written to make women's hearts flutter. The female novel was popular, but Mary dismissed the genre as anemic. "Mary is a woman who loves with passion," she said, squaring her shoulders, "but she finds herself trapped in society's expectations. Telling her story, I hope to inspire women to weigh their choices carefully, to caution them about the lure of romantical thinking."

Mr. Johnson's eyes twinkled. "Not a novel of love, you say?"

His dry attempt at humor did not settle her anxiousness over whether the novel interested him. "I'm afraid it's all I have, sir." She did not have time to write a different book. Another failure now would leave her destitute. With London's prices, she would be on the street in a fortnight, after that, catapulted into Fleet Prison.

"Indeed." Mr. Johnson patted the manuscript and stood. "I shall read it with care. The demand for women's novels has never been greater."

His words of encouragement lifted Mary from her chair. "I'm most grateful. Might you be so kind as to recommend a reasonably priced inn nearby?"

"Nonsense." Mr. Johnson removed his spectacles and slipped them into the breast pocket of his frock coat in one fell motion. "I insist you stay with me."

Mary's cheeks flushed. "I would not think to impose." She trusted Mr. Johnson but was wary of the gossip a young woman staying at the home of a bachelor would elicit. As with most publishers, Mr. Johnson's bookshop was home to printing, distribution, and sales on the main level; his residence was on the floors above.

"There's no harm," he said, noticing her hesitation. "You and I are friends and business partners. You need a place to stay; I have plenty of room."

Mary shifted from one foot to the next, weighing Mr. Johnson's proposal. In her already tentative position, she could not end up with her name splattered across

London's broadsheets. But she would be foolhardy to say no. In life, when pressed against circumstances, she had learned to embrace unexpected opportunities.

Mary let out her breath as if she had been holding it in since Bristol. "If you're sure it's not an inconvenience." However improper his invitation, she was a realist. Accepting his kindness was the only sensible thing to do. Sometimes, a woman must make her own rules.

THREE

The next morning, Mary looked forward to her first full day in London. She had lived in the suburbs of Hoxton and Newington Green, but did not feel well acquainted with the city proper and was eager to explore. When she met Mr. Johnson for breakfast at ten, however, an incubus—a demon—in a painting looming over the table in Mr. Johnson's dining room greeted her. The image caused her to shift in her seat. In the painting, draped over the side of a bed, was a woman sleeping, her hair and arms spilling to the floor. Not only did she appear drugged; the incubus crouched upon her torso, staring at the viewer. According to Germanic legend, an incubus laid itself upon a sleeping woman when desirous of having sex with her. Mary wondered, had she made the right decision to stay with Mr. Johnson, or did he entertain certain ... odd proclivities?

"An early rendition of *The Nightmare*," Mr. Johnson said, meaning the painting. If he thought Mary might find its subject matter offensive, he gave no indication. A young woman entered carrying an old scuffed and dented pewter pot, from which the smell of coffee wafted across the table. "My niece Betsy Hunter. Sister to Rowland, the young man whom you met when you arrived."

Betsy chirped a good morn to Mary and curtsied, then went about her business pouring them coffee, filling their cups until steam spiraled from both. Like Rowland, she was small, blonde, and moved with efficient speed. Neither she nor Rowland could have been over twenty years of age.

As Betsy whisked herself away, Mary searched for signs of perversion in Mr. Johnson. He simply asked if she preferred cream or sugar, as if he were a servant. "Both," she said, determining that the man next to her was unlikely to have any hidden secrets. He was too kind, too ordinary, and she set aside any other belief about him.

They sat in silence as he enjoyed his porridge, his spoon scraping now and then against his bowl, while Mary let her own porridge grow cold. Her stomach, a constant bundle of nerves, had gurgled like a brook all night, keeping her awake. She switched her attention to Mr. Johnson's frugality to occupy herself until he finished. His provincial English oak table, nicked and scratched, was a far cry from the luxury at Mitchelstown Castle. The quality of his chairs was hardly superior to those in a tavern. Other than the pleasing aroma of fresh coffee, the room even smelled of spilled liquor that, long prior, had seeped into the worn and uneven floorboards. She realized there were no right angles or straight walls in any room she had been in, including this one. The simplicity of russet-colored walls with dings and missing chips of paint charmed her. Tacked to the walls with pins and nails were an assortment of smaller drawings and paintings, some without frames, and sketches addressed to Mr. Johnson. A fluttering of birds outside drew her attention to the window, where St. Paul's Cathedral loomed like a sentinel.

The Nightmare, however, would not release Mary. "An odd painting," she mused aloud, trying to ascertain its artistic qualities. She had seen few pieces so dark. The savage beast stared at her as if it were alive, ready to shift his pounce to her.

"My good friend Henry Fuseli painted it." Mr. Johnson's voice revealed special appreciation for the work. "The final version, in which he floated a ghostlike horse's head above the bed, caused quite a stir when he showed it at the Royal Academy. The painting brought him fame."

And a bit of notoriety, thought Mary.

"It would please me a great deal to publish your book," Mr. Johnson said after his last spoonful of porridge.

His announcement shocked her. "An answer so soon?"

Mr. Johnson offered her a roll, which she accepted, her appetite now a bear to tame.

"I spent the night reading it."

"Nothing would make me happier, sir." All her worrying had been for naught. He approved of her writing after all, which meant he approved of her, a much-needed boost after Lady Kingsborough's severe treatment.

"I can have it out by January. We'll need to publish it anonymously, of course."

Mary's hand, about to stuff a torn-off piece of roll into her mouth, stopped midair. "But it's my story—"

"It's customary to—"

"Because I am a woman. Yes, we wouldn't want the public judging it based on my sex." Having never been good at hiding her disappointment, Mary slathered her bread with butter, using flying strokes. She wanted to be taken seriously as a writer. How could she if no one knew her identity? Writing under a pen name would be much like being a companion or a governess—a life lived in the shadows.

Mr. Johnson seemed to understand her disappointment. "I suggest we follow what works in publishing," he said with sensitivity. "If sales are strong, we'll publish the second edition under your name."

"If there is no other way, then as you wish." She felt a scowl run across her forehead, but she was in no financial position to argue. And she could reason with herself that it was not Mr. Johnson's fault. Publishing novels anonymously was common. Especially—almost always—for women.

"I don't like it any more than you, this whole business about being anonymous, I can assure you, but I'm a practical man. If the public reacts negatively, it won't tie the work to you. There is great positivity in that, wouldn't you say?"

Mary's back muscles tightened. "Is there something in the book that concerns you?"

He hesitated, and she urged him to be frank.

"It seems the story argues against marriage," he finally said. "Is that your intent?"

His question took her aback. She assumed him a more progressive man given the kind of books he published, books that often pressed beyond the limits of established thought. "The novel only suggests women be free to marry whom they choose. Or to not marry at all." And to show how they gave up their autonomy when they did marry. The title of "missus" meant servitude for women. She withheld her thoughts, waiting to know Mr. Johnson better.

"Hm. Perhaps your premise will resonate with readers. Though we shall see. I've no objection personally to your position, of course. I'm only thinking about who might read such a book. I've seen few women profess to want to forsake marriage entirely."

Mary let out a soft *harrumph*, a snort, almost. What safety or security was there for a woman whose husband beat her and took all her money, as had been the case with her parents? Women had limited options other than marrying, unless they were like Mary, willing to be odd and independent, endure hunger if needed.

"You'll make some money from the sales of *Mary: A Fiction*," he continued, "and I'll soon print a second edition of *Thoughts on the Education of Daughters*, which I'm happy to say is doing reasonably well. Even if you're extremely lucky, however, I doubt the combined royalties on books like these would be enough on which to live. You must pardon me for asking, but for your sake, might you wed one day?"

Mary's body became taut at the typical question women her age faced. Few understood the desire to be single; spinsterhood was unnatural. "I object to tyranny in any form." She would never subject herself to a man's rule. Marriage gave men undue power over women. Under the surface, all men were like her father.

"An inheritance, perhaps?" Mr. Johnson asked.

"None." Mary's voice was flat. In addition to abusing his wife and terrorizing his children, to pay off a portion of his debts, her father had used the money Mary's mother had set aside for annuities and dowries for Mary and her sisters. Her body shook inside, recalling her father's selfish ways. Mary was furious still. She would never forgive him.

"I see." Mr. poured them each coffee, the sound of liquid rising to the brims of their cups.

"Before going to Ireland," Mary said, "I asked you if I had a future in writing."

"As I recall, the larger question was whether you could make a living at it."

"Is your answer the same?" At the time, Mr. Johnson had discouraged Mary, and she had left their meeting disheartened. It was a dream, of course, to become a writer. She had little formal education, only three years of school for girls when she lived in Beverley. Beyond that she was almost entirely self-taught other than what she had gleaned from her mother's instruction for Mary and her sisters. No one would accuse Elizabeth Wollstonecraft of being a born teacher.

Mr. Johnson's brow furrowed. "No woman I know, certainly no single woman, lives solely on her royalties. She relies on the security of prior means, a husband or family money, to supply her bank account."

Mary gripped her cup. "There must be some way." She would rather die than go back into service. And she would not go crawling to her father, who was living like a pauper in Wales.

"I didn't mean to suggest it would be *impossible* to support yourself," Mr. Johnson said, seeming to reconsider. "You've a unique voice and have already shown an interminable strength of will. I'd venture to guess that if any woman could make a living through her literary exertions, it would be you, my dear."

Something Mary had been clenching inside released. "Do you mean it?"

"If you're determined to write for a living, then I have no desire to stop you, only to warn that you'd be embarking on a very difficult venture."

Mary sat up in her chair as if a bolt of energy had charged through her. "I want to steer my own life, no matter how hard or mean it is."

Mr. Johnson shook his head. Another half-smile. "I've discovered many an author, Miss Wollstonecraft, and I must say, I like your style best. You've a fearlessness about you. I admire that." His eyes twinkled again. "If you're going to write for a living, have you something in mind for your next book?"

Mary's answer came with ease. "A collection of educational tales for girls." She was eager to influence girls' education through stories designed to teach important lessons in life. Working as a teacher and as a governess had convinced her of the need for girls to learn the same rigorous curriculum as boys—logic and reason. Latin and Greek and French. Natural sciences, philosophy and the maths, along with history and geography. And literature, including the classics.

"A sound idea," Mr. Johnson said. "In the meantime, regarding employment." He leaned forward and rested his arms on the table. He was keen to circulate more literature from the Continent and needed another translator. "You know some French; I could hire you immediately. If you could learn German and Italian, I have no shortage of text for you to translate there as well."

Mary stared at him, mute. She had taught herself French in a matter of months prior to going to Ireland. Translating, however, was another matter. Her French skills had improved in conversation with the King sisters, but as Lady Kingsborough had pointed out, she was anything but fluent. And to learn German and Italian besides?

"Well then." Mr. Johnson did not wait for Mary to reply. "That settles it. You may begin whenever you're ready." He pulled out his watch and checked the time. "I'm off to the Chapter Coffeehouse. While out, I'll start looking for a house for you to rent."

"A house?" Having difficulty absorbing all that had just occurred, Mary's thoughts became flurried. She could never afford a house, not with her obligations to her former benefactress. "Perhaps I could rent a room from an elderly woman, if you know of someone."

"You needn't worry. I'll front your rent until you're able to manage on your own."

Mary protested. "I couldn't. You're far too generous. What if my translation skills—"

Mr. Johnson held up a hand to interrupt. "It wouldn't be the first time I've paid someone's rent. And I'm sure it won't be the last." He chuckled as he stood and headed toward the door, where he stopped and rested his grip on the handle, then turned to face Mary. "I believe in you, Miss Wollstonecraft. It's time you did, too."

He departed then, leaving Mary bursting inside with hope. Less than twenty-four hours in London, and she was back on her feet. She left the dining room, her step light as a new dawn.

When she reached the stairs to her temporary bedroom, however, her elation plummeted. Her family must soon find out she had returned to London. They could thwart all hopes of becoming a writer. Her father and siblings were incomprehensible to her; she had spent the last ten years trying to escape them.

On a tour of Mr. Johnson's printing shop later that day, the pungent odor of dust and chemicals made Mary lightheaded until she became accustomed to the smell. Sunlight streamed through the row of windows facing the street, illuminating walls of gray and turning them pale yellow. Tables holding stacks of blank paper alongside piles of finished books lined the remaining perimeter. She watched, fascinated, as a compositor selected letters from a wooden case, and with meticulous care, placed them onto a stick.

"I like to keep my books simple in appearance and small in size," Mr. Johnson said as he led her from the typesetting area to one of his presses, a wooden contraption almost as big as Mary. "Plain fonts. Cheap paper. Still of good quality, mind you. Readers these days won't stand for anything less."

Mary held her breath as a printer applied ink to a ready plate and positioned a piece of paper, then pulled a lever, producing a finished page. The process was simple, but to her it was magical. Books had been her salvation since the early days of her hapless childhood. She trailed Mr. Johnson from press to press, flooding him with questions about publishing. He seemed delighted with her interest and responded in detail. He had been in the business for over thirty years after moving from Liverpool to London as a lad of fourteen to work as an apprentice to a bookseller. At twenty-two, he opened his own house on Paternoster Row. According to Rowland and Betsy, who had taken Mary into their confidence, Mr. Johnson conducted business with little more than a handshake.

"A bit too trusting, if you ask me," Rowland had said of their uncle.

"People can take easy advantage of so kind a person," Betsy had added.

Mary doubted anyone fooled Mr. Johnson. She knew a shrewd man when she saw one. His success became apparent in more ways than one as the week unfolded. His dining room, which he used for business more than he did his office, was a rendezvous for writers and artists. They showed up day or night to collect their mail, pick up royalty checks, request an advance, or ask his advice. Others simply dropped by with no apparent aim beyond enjoying Mr. Johnson's liberal hospitality. And once a week, at precisely three p.m., he hosted dinner for them and other thinking men—friends or acquaintances—from various trades and professions.

"You must join us this afternoon," he said to Mary the Sunday after she arrived.

"Oh?" She imagined herself the only female present at a dinner of men who, by her estimation, were among London's rising class of writers, and this made her hesitant to accept his invitation. Among his writers and associates, she had not seen a single woman yet. "Do other women join you?" She did not want to embarrass herself or give Mr. Johnson reason to regret investing in her, or worse, to oust her as Lady Kingsborough had. The woman's brazen treatment was still a fresh wound. Lady Kingsborough had often placed Mary at the center of conversation in her elegant, gilt-edged parlor where Ireland's prominent Protestants and dignitaries gathered day upon day, only to usher her out of the room if Mary gained too much attention. Mary did not want the same to happen with Mr. Johnson, whose calm, easy-going temperament was helping to restore her confidence.

Mr. Johnson offered Mary his customary half-smile. "There's the occasional woman." He listed two female authors who sometimes joined him, women who had written children's books Mary recognized. "Although none will be present tonight, you will always find yourself among friends at my table, I can assure you. Be they men or be they women."

Several hours later, Mary found herself in Mr. Johnson's little dining room with its crooked walls and uneven floor.

"Are you to be the new standing dish?" asked the very tall John Bonnycastle, a mathematician, Mary had learned in their brief exchange during which a half-dozen men filed into the room. Bonnycastle's mouth rose at the corners when he spoke, exposing all his teeth, and his oversized spectacles bulged to the side, his face reminding her of the placid brown gelding her father used for hunting when she was a child.

Mary covered her mouth to stifle a laugh. "What, may I ask, is a standing dish?"

With an air of formality, Bonnycastle gripped the lapels of his brown wool frock coat. "A regular." He tipped his nose in the air and sniffed. "Mine eyes smell onions." Quoting Shakespeare, the man drifted away.

"Be on guard with him." Mr. Johnson's tone was good-natured. "Bonnycastle likes to quote the Bard. Often."

"Don't take the piss out of us yet, Johnson," George Fordyce quipped. "You'll scare the poor maid away." Dr. Fordyce, Mr. Johnson's friend and physician from St. Thomas's Hospital, poured himself a glass of whiskey and held it up in a toast. "Welcome to Sunday dinner, Miss Wollstonecraft."

By then, Mary had captured everyone's interest. She wanted to retreat to the side, feeling no more than a rough outline compared to the men's pedigrees and educational attainments. Most were the products of boarding schools and university training followed by time abroad, society denying women the former and Mary's poverty denying her the latter.

"We call ourselves Johnson's Circle," said Thomas Holcroft, a novelist and playwright, who had edged past others to seek her out. He handed her a glass of wine. "A motley collection of philosophers, theologians, scientists, and artists." He leaned toward her and whispered, "Some so radical they'll corrupt your very soul if you're not careful."

His wink that followed drew a much-needed smile from Mary. She took a hearty gulp of wine. They would not corrupt her, not under Mr. Johnson's watchful eye, who glanced with approval as she talked with Holcroft.

The playwright pulled out a chair for her, to which Mary obliged. "Liking London so far?"

She was, she said. In London, she felt among her own kind again, working men and women with nothing but their wits to guide them.

Mr. Johnson took his seat at the table, continuously glancing towards the door. It was then Mary noticed an empty chair.

As she was about to ask who was missing from dinner, Holcroft said, "I'd be happy to show you some sights." He had a ruddy complexion that gave him a weathered, rugged look, like that of a farmer, except he was dressed in an urban man's clothes, an inexpensive black frock coat and white cravat. He wore his ginger hair back, tied with a leather strap into a queue. His smile was congenial, and he had an easy way about him. He was, he said, the son of a man who was sometimes a shoemaker, more often a peddler. Holcroft was not pensive per se, but Mary noticed a sadness to him beneath his earnestness. She soon learned why. Holcroft was a widower thrice over, yet he could hardly have been much over the age of forty.

In that moment, the door opened, and Mary gasped. "Reverend Price!" She leaped from her chair, stretching her hands out to meet his as she strode toward the elderly gentleman. The moment he grasped them, she experienced yet another unexpected feeling of good fortune.

"I wanted to surprise you," Reverend Price said. "How do you fare, my dear?"

"Very well, thanks to Mr. Johnson. And how is *Le Sage*?" she asked, using the nickname she had given the leading liberal philosopher in all of England.

"Old." He smiled but winced as he walked to a seat. "But quite fine, God willing." Until a year prior, he had preached at the Unitarian Church in Newington Green before retiring and moving to Hackney. Mary listened to his sermons when she lived in Newington Green. The two had become close friends.

"Still angering the powers that be?" she asked with mischief as the men shifted places to allow her to sit next to Reverend Price. The Anglican establishment disliked him for his views on liberty and equality. He, on the other hand, liked nothing more than to annoy church heads and government officials.

"It is the way for us nonconformists," he replied. His brown eyes shone like burnished marbles. Reverend Price was a prominent Dissenter, Protestants who had left the Church of England, people whom Mary now looked to as role models after spending time with them in Newington Green.

With no visible cue from Mr. Johnson, Betsy and Rowland arrived with platters of veal and vegetables, which guests passed around like clockwork to the clink of glasses and the clatter of utensils. Mary nibbled at her vegetables as she listened to the men's banter. Their talk reminded her of Reverend Price's own weekly dinners she had attended in Newington Green. He was in his glory amidst debates regarding politics, government officials and their foibles, and how a just world would look. But he had aged in the year since she had last seen him. The lines on his face had deepened, worrying her. His wife had died months before Mary left for Ireland, so he was alone now. And Reverend Price was no stranger to controversy. Death threats showed up in his post because of his radical views, especially after the American colonists had used his writings as one of many inspirations for their revolution.

Mary hoped he no longer had to deal with such dangers. He had supported the colonists' fight for independence with vigor, which had angered the British government. He now claimed friendships with Benjamin Franklin and George Washington and was on personal terms with John Adams and Thomas Jefferson. When in London, these and other American diplomats attended his services in Newington Green, causing further resentment from those bitter over losing the colonies. Listening to him this evening, however, Mary could tell there was still fight in him.

In time Mary inserted herself into the conversations at the table. The men's welcome of her words was balm for her battered soul after being trivialized by Lady Kingsborough.

When the evening had drawn to a close, Reverend Price looked with fondness upon Mary. "I see you've not changed," he said. "Still brimming with ideas." Before leaving, he extracted a promise from her to visit soon.

"Might I escort you to the theater this week?" Holcroft asked Mary when just he and Bonnycastle remained. *Much Ado About Nothing* was playing at the Haymarket.

She had enjoyed their conversation and found him attractive, but she must do nothing to invite his interest and so declined the invitation. And she did not have a chaperone. While in London she intended to protect her status as a spinster.

"Mr. Johnson's niece could join us if it's a chaperone you are thinking of. Though life in London could get rather dull, if in constant need of one." He raised a brow.

Was he daring her?

Mary despised the old rules of conduct. Such strictures treated women as helpless and kept them infantile. Perhaps the evening's conversation had emboldened her, or perhaps she was tired of living a half-life just because she wore petticoats. A feeling of liberation danced through her. "A chaperone won't be necessary," she said. "On the contrary, I'd be pleased to join you."

Just then Bonnycastle's voice boomed across the table. "I must to the barber's, monsieur, for methinks, I am marvelous hairy about the face, and I am such a tender ass; if my hair do tickle me, I must scratch."

Mary bit down a smile.

"Come with me, Bonnycastle," Holcroft said. Mr. Johnson herded the two out, Bonnycastle's guffaws echoing down the stairs as they disappeared into the night.

"Did you enjoy yourself?" Mr. Johnson asked when they were alone.

"I have been fed and nourished as though after a famine!" Mary said, ebullient still. "Without them, the room is a tomb."

"Good. Tomorrow, there is someone else I'd like you to meet."

Iris Kendall had moved to London from Manchester two years earlier when she and Jason Kendall wed. Mary learned this when Mr. Johnson left her and Iris in his sitting room, a pot of tea steaming between them, proffered by the ever-efficient Betsy Hunter. After introductions, Mr. Johnson and Mr. Kendall had already removed themselves to the dining room to discuss Mr. Kendall's second book of sermons, which Mr. Johnson was soon to publish. Jason Kendall was a Dissenting minister who preached at a progressive Unitarian church in Somers Town, a small but growing suburb on the outskirts of London.

Late afternoon light coming in from two windows facing the street was yellowish brown, making Mr. Johnson's worn furniture look dull. Paintings depicting the English countryside covered walls the same rust color as his dining room, and a large carpet had frayed through to the floor in some patches. An old looking glass hanging over the mantel would have created the illusion of enlarging the room were it not for foxing that blurred images reflected in the glass. But books were always in proximity to Mr. Johnson, and his sitting room was no exception, making it Mary's favorite place to relax in his living quarters.

A familiarity about Iris Kendall enchanted Mary as she assumed the role of hostess. She sensed an attachment already existed between them, as if they had met before, but Mary knew this to be impossible; she had never seen Iris, had never been to Manchester. But when Iris laughed, the reason for Mary's strange sensations became clear: Iris Kendall reminded her of Fanny Blood. Mary's heart tightened like a fist. It was as though Fanny was in the room.

But Fanny was dead. Mary's mind spun like a windmill. She took a desperate sip of tea and focused her eyes on Iris. "Is Somers Town far from here?" she managed to ask after Iris told her the Kendalls rented an apartment near a brickworks factory. Properly speaking, Iris and Fanny did not look alike, but their mannerisms were replicas of one another. Iris had the same heart-shaped face as Fanny. The same delicate hands. Even her earbobs danced when she spoke—just like Fanny's had. It was all too much, and Mary feared being overcome by grief.

"It isn't far at all," Iris said. "You must visit. There are lovely meadows." She leaned toward Mary in a chipper way and added, "It certainly smells less vile than London." Another playful laugh erupted from Iris—Fanny's laugh—a joyful expression of genuine amusement.

Mary offered Iris a weak smile in return. A familiar ache returned, an emptiness she knew would never go away, and her goal suddenly was to disapprove of and oppose everything about Iris to drive her away. Mary could not risk being around someone who reminded her of Fanny. Burying Fanny in Lisbon had made Mary want to quit living. For months afterward, Mary longed to join Fanny on the other side of eternity.

Unaware of the pain she caused Mary, Iris spoke casually as if meeting a new friend was the only unusual thing occurring in the room. How could she know Mary's feelings of sorrow? She appeared very feminine in her blue linen dress and straw bergère hat, situated without fuss on her mass of brunette hair. Iris, like Fanny, possessed a natural beauty and was far from being bland, unlike some ministers' wives. She was livelier and well spoken. Mary found it hard not to be drawn to her; beneath Iris's homespun manner, she detected a supreme intellect.

"You appear to have received an excellent education," Mary said, swallowing hard, her mouth dry as cotton. "To encounter a learned woman is all too rare."

"My widowed father, also a minister, raised me, indulging me with books and affection, much to the dismay of his parishioners, who thought me wild. I have a brother as well, who, along with my father, encourages me to envision a world without limits."

"You've achieved a long list of accomplishments, no doubt," Mary said, envious of Iris having a family that cared for and nurtured her. Mary fought for the simple permission to visit a circulating library weekly.

"Few. A woman's worth exceeds her sewing and drawing abilities, would you not agree? I am better with a soup ladle. I wish to be out in the world assisting Mr. Kendall with his ministry, which is geared toward justice for the poor." The way she looked at Mary, Iris seemed to gauge whether Mary sympathized with Dissenters.

"Indeed." Mary felt herself unable to resist a growing urge to warm toward Iris. Her greatest wish was to join forces with Dissenters in London, as she did in Newington Green. "Your efforts are honorable. My own desire for fairness in society has sharpened over the last decade. Dissenters are, to me, thought leaders on a great many things." She noticed Iris's ink-stained index and middle finger on her left hand. "Do you write as well?"

"Poetry."

"Any you've published?"

Iris let out a cheerful sigh. "I only dabble."

"How unfortunate. Given your way with words, I imagine you write intriguing poems. Children, then?"

A sudden sadness grabbed Iris's expression, and she fixed her gaze on her hands, knotting and unknotting her fingers.

"I'm sorry." Mary worried she had pried. "I didn't mean—"

"I don't mind. We've not been blessed with children ... as yet." Iris lifted her gaze to Mary's. "Though it is my fervent hope."

Alarm mounted quietly in Mary like trouble brewing on a distant horizon, a storm felt before it was seen. "Then it is mine as well." Though by instinct, she feared for Iris's well-being. Iris was petite and slim; carrying a child would be difficult for her. Just as it had been for Fanny.

"Do you know London well?" Iris asked.

"Very little," Mary replied, still aching in for Fanny, but glad for the change in subject, the only thing that could rescue her mind from its downward spiral into the past.

"London is a hundred times the size of Manchester. Or Bristol. It has all the ills that accompany city life, all the dirt and grime cities inevitably possess. Though I must say, I love it, really. London is a vibrant feast. Every street, every corner, offers something new." Iris grinned impishly.

The next two hours passed quickly, Iris telling Mary of the many things she had seen and done in London, whetting Mary's appetite for adventure.

The longer they visited, the more Iris seemed less like Fanny, and Mary's feelings reversed toward Iris. Despite the reminder of Fanny, Mary knew by instinct she wanted to be friends with her. Fanny was shy and reserved, whereas Iris was spirited. And it occurred to Mary, what good was the memory of a friend if one could never revisit it without guarding one's affection? Iris reminded Mary now was a time to live, to let grief find its own resting place.

While Mary and Iris set down plans to sightsee together, Mr. Johnson and Mr. Kendall returned. When they did, Mary noted an immediate change in Iris. She and Iris had many things in common, except one. Iris Kendall was a woman deeply in love. With Jason Kendall in the room, Iris's demeanor shifted. She gazed at him in a way Mary had seen few women look upon their husbands. Iris was completely smitten.

During Mary's visit with Iris, the young woman had spoken with such tenderness regarding her father and brother that she reminded Mary of the importance of family, even one that was imperfect. Mary's memories of her parents—a father who degraded her and a mother who neglected her—were void of happiness. Still in Mr. Johnson's sitting room, but alone now, Mary could picture her mother, the daughter of a wealthy wine merchant from Ballyshannon, standing with her hands on her hips. *Don't be thinking you're special now*, she would say with the lilt of the Irish she never lost, no matter how she tried after marrying a wealthy Englishman. *You're just a girl, and don't forget it. It's a husband you'll be needing, not books or fancy words. Neither pay the rent.* Elizabeth Wollstonecraft had entered her marriage with her own fortune, but Edward Wollstonecraft spent it when his own money dried up, Elizabeth having no avenue to prevent him.

Feeling restless, after filling her cup with the remaining tea, Mary occupied Mr. Johnson's library armchair, an old, battered piece of furniture. It was too big for her, made for a man. Its threadbare damask fabric had seen heartier days. But it was next to the window, where she could observe the bustling Churchyard and the city where she aimed to succeed. It was hard to know who she resented more as she contemplated how to explain to her family she would write for a living—her father for his savage treatment, or her mother for not trying harder to protect herself and her children from him. But Elizabeth Wollstonecraft was dead. When Edward Wollstonecraft married the family's housekeeper days after his wife died six years prior, Mary vowed not to lay eyes on him again. Her brothers and sisters were another matter altogether, and it was them she longed to see. All but one she loved. As the eldest sister, she had tried to fill in where their mother had failed.

Mary put aside her tea, which by now had grown cold, and retired to her room where she wrote letters to her sisters telling them to expect her for a brief visit. She wrote nothing of her change in circumstances, preferring to keep things to herself for now. Her family would pity her if they knew she had been so unceremoniously dismissed. As to her becoming a writer, they would accuse her of deluding herself.

"The school's vulgar," Everina Wollstonecraft said to Mary five days later in Henley-on-Thames. Her sister's school apartment was no more than a bedroom and a small sitting room, furnished with a pitiful sofa, a low table, and a solitary side chair. A poor excuse for a writing desk, stacked with books and papers, occupied a corner. Chalky-blue walls seemed as downcast as Everina. Even the air was stuffy.

"Come now. Things can't be that disagreeable." Mary parted the curtains and opened the window, spilling light into the room.

Everina threw herself onto her sofa and wrapped her long arms around a frayed pillow into which she buried her face. "I miss you. I miss Eliza." Tall and slender as a spoon, she wore her coppery hair in a simple bun. Everything about her was plain, from her shoes to the hand-me-down muslin dress with embroidered edges.

"Everina," Mary said, feeling tenderness for her sister and sitting next to her. She slipped her hand in Everina's, which was rough and coarse like a washerwoman's. "I wish—"

"Why can't we be together?" Everina pushed the spectacles she had worn since childhood up the bridge of her nose.

A lump wedged itself at the top of Mary's throat. Everina rarely asked for anything, and Mary wanted to help. It was hard leaving her stranded. Mary's sisters were like her, daughters of a bankrupt gentleman, left to fend for themselves in the world. Until she got settled in London, Mary could not assist Everina. "For now,

your current position must suffice. Have you heard from our brother James?"
James was nineteen.

"Still at sea." Everina sighed and tossed the pillow aside. "I don't believe he
cares for it, but it provides for his keep and earns him a few shillings. At least it
keeps him out of trouble."

"And Charles?" Charles was the baby of the family, whom Mary had not seen
since their mother died. He would be seventeen by now.

"Articled to Ned to learn the law."

Mary's lips flattened into a thin line upon hearing the name of their oldest
brother. "Ned's an intolerable lout." Everina had lived with him since Mary's
school closed the year prior until he expelled her from his household, insisting it
would be better for her to live on her own. That he could now support Charles was
telling. Certain that he was using the boy as cheap labor, Mary smoldered inside
like a peat fire. As the oldest son, Ned had inherited a third of their Grandpapa
Wollstonecraft's estate, making him a wealthy individual at age six. Thirty now, he
boasted a lucrative law practice and lived with his wife and children behind the
Tower. He could have helped all his siblings escape poverty; it would have been
customary to do so. But he refused.

"At least he sends me a stipend," Everina said in defense of him.

"One that is not enough on which to live. Does Charles like working for Ned?"

"You'd have to ask Charles."

"I suppose Ned's preferable to our drunken father," Mary said, more to herself
than to Everina. And the law was one of the few occupations suitable for a
gentleman. The Wollstonecrafts had fallen from grace because of their penury, but
Edward Wollstonecraft had once owned tracts of land and still held a set of
apartments on Primrose Street, maintaining the family's status as members of the
landed gentry, the only thing that allowed Mary to hold her head high in a room
full of privilege. There was another brother, Henry, whom Mary knew better than
to inquire about; he had disappeared when he was fourteen, never to be heard from
again.

"You should contact Charles," Everina said. "He asks about you."

Mary rose from the sofa. "I'd rather no one in the family knew of my return."
Especially their father, who would soon ask her for money.

"Are you to stay in London, then?" Everina looked confused. "I thought you were on holiday."

"I am," Mary lied. "Though I'm considering not returning to Ireland," she added, to quell a voice inside chastising her for being dishonest.

Everina sat up, hope kindling in her eyes. "Can I live with you?"

"'Twould do neither of us any good." Mary regretted coming. Saying no to her sister felt like committing some grave offense. But she needed time. Further weighing on her was a determination to keep her sisters at arm's length. They had let her down. Mary and her sisters had lived together along with Fanny Blood in Newington Green. Mary hired them to work at her school. Neither sister extended herself beyond a basic level. When Mary went to Lisbon to help Fanny deliver her baby and left her sisters in charge, the school collapsed. Mary could not look past their laziness. The last thing she needed was two helpless women on her hands.

Their conversations during the rest of the week reinforced Mary's desire to evade her sister's questions. Henley's rustic setting, by contrast, allowed her to embrace time alone, a respite after a trying year in Ireland. To Mr. Johnson she wrote:

My Dear Sir,

> *Since I last saw you, I have, literally speaking, enjoyed solitude. I wander alone by the Thames and in the neighboring beautiful fields and pleasure grounds. I caught tranquility while I surveyed them. My mind was still active. I found an old French bible here and amused myself with comparing it to our English translation, then I would listen to the falling leaves, observing the tints autumn gives them. At other times, the singing of a robin or the noise of a watermill engaged my attention. Will you allow me to call this way of passing my days pleasant? Have you found a house for me yet? I often think of my new life. I long for a little peace and independence*
>
> *...*

> *I am, sir, yours, etc.*
> *Mary Wollstonecraft*

A week later in Market Harborough, invigorated after spending a week in nature, Mary's peaceableness dispersed like a flock of blackbirds scattering from the branches.

"I'm miserable," said Eliza. She was four years Mary's junior and working as a companion for an elderly woman. "Mrs. Tew is a dreadful bore."

Mary took sympathy on Eliza. Mrs. Tew was indeed a bore, whereas Eliza was young and vibrant. The two sisters were strolling a path in the woods along the River Welland at sunrise. In the distance, sheep bleated, and cattle sounded morning milking routines. The pastoral surroundings lifted Mary, yet appeared to have no impact on Eliza, who had been out of humor since Mary had arrived the day prior. She treaded with care by saying, "You must bear it for now. Do well, and another opportunity soon will present itself."

The cool breeze washing over them reminded Mary of when they were young and life was easier. Not that she wanted to go back to her youth. Not ever. But autumn's rotting leaves and the moist soil's pungent aroma was a reminder of nature renewing itself through death and rebirth. Much the way Mary and Eliza were trying to restart their own lives, though Mary could see Eliza was finding it harder.

"Surely you can come up with something better for me." Eliza's voice was laced as always with expectation. And resentment. Mary could see the wall of ice separating them had not melted during the year she had been in Ireland.

"I can try to find you a job elsewhere, but your options are few." Eliza was a married woman, a disgraced one at that.

"Who are you to remind me?"

Eliza's words cut like a shard of broken glass. Three years prior, Eliza had left her husband, Meredith Bishop, after suffering a mysterious mental breakdown following the birth of her daughter. At Bishop's request, Mary had stayed with them where they lived in Bermondsey to help nurse Eliza back to health. It was then Eliza accused Bishop of misusing her.

Even now, Mary wondered what had really happened between the young couple. With her assistance, Eliza fled Bishop, leaving her baby behind, fully expecting him to send the child to her along with a living allowance. He refused. Eliza never saw her baby again. Eight months later, the child died.

Still bereft over the loss of her niece, Mary could not imagine how heartbroken Eliza remained. She reached out to comfort her, but Eliza crossed her arms and riveted her gaze at the path ahead.

"I wasn't cut out for teaching or being a companion," Eliza said, drawing the hood of her cloak further down until it covered her face. "It wasn't how I expected things would turn out."

Nor did Mary. Growing up, Eliza had been the beauty among the three sisters. She still was. Her eyes were brown like Mary's, but darker, and her hair was not reddish brown but the color of raven wings and fell to her waist when not pinned. Her life with Meredith Bishop had been a fantasy. The wealthy shipbuilder had fallen in love with her months after Elizabeth Wollstonecraft died. For a year, Eliza lived in a fine house with servants and private carriages. If Mary had not listened or assumed Bishop was like their father, she might have convinced Eliza to stay. In the end, Mary was blamed as the incendiary.

Had she been? She would never know for sure. Eliza's mental state improved after leaving Bishop. The couple was still married, but Eliza gave no hint of wanting to return to him, leading Mary to believe her claims of misuse were true. Eliza's experience proved how treacherous the proposition marriage was for women, cementing Mary's resolve to stay single. How could a woman really know a man before becoming his wife?

"You could take me back to Ireland with you," Eliza said.

Mary slowed her step. "I may not go back."

Eliza looked at her, aghast. "But what will you do? You owe all that money—"

"You're not to worry. The debts are mine."

"Have you another position?"

Mary hesitated, as she had with Everina. She was anxious about her sisters' futures, had always tried to advise them as best she could. But she did not feel in a position to help them. Not yet. Her own quest for peace and independence left Mary with apprehension over whether she would be successful as a writer. That something might be in the works was all she revealed to Eliza.

Eliza's face lit up. "If you're in London, I could live with you there—"

"I don't think it would work." Mary glanced at the river, ashamed again at not telling her sisters the truth about her plans to settle in London. At times like this, the undertow of family obligations threatened to drown her. Her sisters represented all that was wrong with the way society taught women to be dependent. Everina and Eliza could sew and draw and sing, all the usual parlor accomplishments, but between them they had not an ounce of personal ambition. They wanted to be taken care of, to live a life designed by others.

"You must stay here," Mary said. "I shall look for something better for you, I promise. You can help by doing your best so Mrs. Tew will give you a good recommendation. Without one—"

"You don't care about us. Me or Everina." Eliza lifted her skirt and ran toward Mrs. Tew's.

Mary raced after her and caught her arm, but Eliza pulled away, leaving Mary alone at the water's edge.

As Eliza disappeared from view, guilt rose in Mary like steam rising from the river. Crouching low, she dipped her hand in the river, as if washing away the sin of refusing her sisters. Mary's desire to be independent must seem selfish in their eyes. Everina and Eliza could not see what they might do for themselves. They lived in an age when women were not to assert themselves. Mary hoped they would one day forgive her for wanting work to call her own, for seeking a life of purpose created through her own labor. Was it really so much to ask?

FOUR

November 1787
Two Months Later
London

The air was raw this high above the Thames. Mary pulled her beaver hat low to keep the wind from whisking it into the waves below. A month prior, she had moved into a bright yellow, three-story terrace house on George Street in Southwark, a mere ten-minute walk from Mr. Johnson's bookshop on the other side of the Thames by way of Blackfriars Bridge. She was on her way to meet him, and she was late.

The surrounding sights never ceased to leave her in awe no matter how many times she trekked across the bridge. As she made her way toward St. Paul's dome, the wind mercifully swept away the smell of Billingsgate Fish Market as men on the riverbanks loaded and unloaded cargo vessels. To the west was the majestic Westminster Abbey, to the east, the ominous Tower.

Mary had been loath to leave her house that morning. Having a place to call her own made her want to spend each waking minute nestled inside its walls, where she found the sense of belonging she had been looking for, the kind that came from within, not the benevolence of someone else. A growing list of friends stopped by for conversations over subjects that mattered, saying what they thought without fear of censure. As her needs were spartan, she furnished her rooms with items from a secondhand shop: a bed, a table, and three chairs. Mr. Johnson lent her an old bookcase. He also arranged for her to hire a country cousin of his as her single house servant, freeing Mary to write.

Other than Mr. Johnson, Mary's first visitor was Iris Kendall, to whom she served wine from mismatched teacups. Iris and Mary now enjoyed weekly outings together exploring London's labyrinths of shops and bookstores. The city proved to be the feast Iris had promised. With signs to guide them everywhere, they went where they pleased. Adam and Eve symbols on the signs for fruiterers. The horn of a unicorn telling passersby that inside they would find an apothecary, which Mary and Iris liked to visit just so they could see the human skull the shop was always sure to have. Perfumery shops drew Iris in, where she inhaled exotic smells, while bookshops like Mr. Johnson's called to Mary. If they were hungry, they bought potatoes from baked potato men or visited coffee stalls where they dipped pieces of gingerbread purchased from gingerbread ladies roaming the streets. They also attended lectures together, visited galleries, and walked in the park. Evenings, they attended concerts and went to the theater. Life was full.

There remained the nagging issue of Mary's family, however. Prior to today's trip across Blackfriars, she had given in to a gnawing voice that urged her to tell her sisters what had transpired in Ireland and what was in store for her now:

> *Mr. Johnson, whose uncommon kindness, I believe, has saved me from despair, assures me that if I exert my talents in writing I may support myself in a comfortable way. I am then going to be the first of a new genus—I tremble at the attempt, yet if I fail—I only suffer—*

A new genus! The possibility made the November air seem effervescent as it splayed across her face and sent her hair swirling. She would leave it to her sisters to tell the rest of the family.

When Mary arrived at Mr. Johnson's bookshop, the bell overhead announced her arrival with its emphatic clang. Standing next to Mr. Johnson was a fresh-faced young man with an engaging smile. Mr. Johnson introduced him as Thomas Christie. Christie had just arrived from Montrose, up the coast from Edinburgh.

That explained Mr. Christie's Scottish brogue. Mary noticed in him a restlessness she had seen before in men, a palpable sign of a dreamer within that aroused her curiosity. He seemed very unlike the placid Mr. Johnson. His handsome frock coat must have cost three times her publisher's decades-old threadbare coat. Younger than she, by her calculation, Mr. Christie had soft waves of sandy brown hair unencumbered by a queue that fell to his shoulders.

"Mr. Christie and I are starting a new periodical," Mr. Johnson explained, all three settled at the table in the dining room where Betsy Hunter served them coffee. "One aimed at reform. We don't want to offend conservatives, but the more widely circulated publications these days are so," he exchanged a sly look with Mr. Christie, "one-sided."

Mr. Christie slid to the edge of his chair. "Journalists must expose society to a wide range of new ideas, especially when politicians resist progress. The world changes, and so must the British Empire."

Mary noted an impatient urgency to his voice. Johnson and Christie were like the tortoise and the hare from one of Aesop's fables. How the two had formed an alliance puzzled her.

"We're calling it the *Analytical Review,*" Mr. Johnson said. "Our intended audience will be intellectuals."

Mary searched Mr. Johnson's face. "What has this to do with me?"

"We'd like you to be one of our book reviewers."

"Me?" The offer intrigued her, but she sensed a catch. Reviewing, a competitive field, was dominated by men. "What type of books?"

"Those written for women and children," Mr. Christie replied.

Pablum for the mind. Women wrote religious reflections, advice books, and romances. No one considered them serious literature. Mary did not dismiss such books. Women were, after all, an important readership, and she herself was an author of one educational book and another one in progress.

"You'd be the first and only woman in London to earn a majority of your income from reviewing," Mr. Christie said, animated, as if the job was being offered to him.

It was easy for him to assume that the offer would satisfy Mary. She doubted they would limit a male to reviewing books for women and children. And who was Mr. Christie to say her books alone would not support her meager lifestyle? The truth was, the idea of reviewing appealed to her a great deal, but she would have preferred meatier works. "What about commentaries on politics or contemporary literature? Travel journals. Biographies. Could I write those as well?"

The room went silent. Mr. Johnson passed around a plate of biscuits. "Reviewing is tough business, Miss Wollstonecraft. Readers can be callous. No doubt some will characterize our publication as ... radical." He bit into his biscuit, giving Mary time for his meaning to soak in.

He was mistaken if he thought being associated with a radical press intimidated her. The idea of supporting a progressive publication was not the problem. Mary rather liked the idea of shaking up a sleeping populace, especially women, if that was for whom she was to write. Other than politicians, writers could do that best. Perhaps better. However, whose name the periodical would attach to her work was a question that arose in her. "Would I write as myself?" She directed her question at Mr. Johnson, knowing she was needling him. The answer was apparent. She had read her share of periodicals.

Mr. Johnson met her stare. "You'd publish under your initials, of course."

Mary had seen how he could be a force with other writers, and he was being so now with her. He showed no sign of wavering.

"You must trust me," he added, knowing, she assumed, what was going through her mind.

"Using one's initials avoids labels, and above all, consequences for writers," Mr. Christie quickly interjected, worried, it seemed, that she might say no.

"Indeed." Mary bristled at the inevitability of anonymity again. Mr. Johnson knew of her fervent desire for her writing to carry her name. It was not solely about Mary; she wanted to prove what any woman could do when allowed to enter the sphere of men's work. If no one knew the writer was a woman, what did it matter if she was the first of her sex to earn a majority of her income from reviewing?

"I know what you're thinking regarding being an anonymous contributor," Mr. Johnson said. "I urge you to consider it this way. Reviewing will allow you to experiment with your writing, to try your ideas on for size."

How well he already knew her! But Mary did not come to London to be anonymous. "Would my time be better spent on my own writing? My collection of tales is only half complete." And translating was time consuming, at least until her proficiency in French improved. Along with studying German and Italian in the evenings, she already was working day and night.

Mr. Johnson, no stranger to negotiations, sweetened the offer. "We've monthly editions planned; write as much or as little as you prefer."

She could test her literary wings at a pace that met her needs, making Johnson and Christie's proposition more attractive by the minute. Mary had much to learn, not just about reviewing, but about writing as well. She read a wide range of books and publications, but her written grammar and spelling were lacking. One could either spell or not, and she could not. Reviewing could sharpen her writing skills.

"What say you?" Mr. Christie asked, his eyes lit up like fireworks. "What could be more rewarding than helping us launch such an important undertaking?"

"At over one hundred pages per issue, there will be plenty of room for experimentation," Mr. Johnson added.

Mary's publisher was handing her another opportunity. Declining for the sake of pride in having her name in the publication would be foolish. Upon performing a quick mental calculation, she deduced that the income earned reviewing would enable her to send money to her family, softening their disapproval of her decision to join the corps of individuals who wrote for a living.

"Gentlemen, I accept."

Reviewing more than augmented Mary's finances. The act of reading and commenting on the work of brilliant men and women gave her back her soul. Mr. Johnson praised her style as informal. She signed her articles with 'M' or 'W' unless it was an educational piece, in which case, she signed it with a 'T' for teacher. In a matter of months, she progressed beyond women and children's books to literary works and plays.

And, as promised, the following January Mr. Johnson published *Mary: A Fiction* and her third book, the children's collection of stories which Mary wrote in just a little over three months. In *Original Stories from Real Life; With Conversations, Calculated to Regulate the Affections, and Form the Mind to Truth and Goodness,* Mrs. Mason takes in two girls. Through questions, she teaches them valuable moral lessons. Mary again borrowed from personal experience. In effect, the book outlined her signature teaching pedagogy.

Mary's life in London was not only about work. She and Iris devoured the city, two kindred spirits scouting every nook and cranny that piqued their interest. As Mr. Kendall was not a conventional minister, Iris was no conventional pastor's wife. Mary and she paraded about as if they had not a care, Mary in her beaver topper, Iris in a floppy felt hat like Juliet Capulet wore in a Shakespeare production she and Mary had seen together. Iris had gone home and sewed an exact replica.

In this period of financial relief, Mary paid for Everina to study French in Paris so Everina could apply for a better teaching position, and she augmented Eliza's paltry income as a companion. Her father wheedled a monthly stipend out of Mary after calling her high and mighty and accusing her of abandoning her family. Mary relented, just so he would stop writing to her.

"You'll not sustain a living as a writer if you keep this up," Mr. Johnson warned. "You're far too generous. Your family is becoming a liability." Having never been a good money manager—who is when one had never had money to manage?—Mary found it impossible not to help others in need, especially her siblings.

"I see the wild Swiss is here," Thomas Holcroft said to Mary at Sunday dinner the following autumn when a small man with a sweep of white hair stepped through the door and claimed the room in a single lusty glance before handing his greatcoat to Rowland Hunter.

"Who's he?" She and Holcroft had been discussing an Italian translation she had puzzled over earlier that day. If Mr. Johnson had become like a father to her, Holcroft was like a brother. Her friendship with him had evolved into one of mutual admiration and candor.

"Only the most famous among us." Holcroft rolled his eyes and poured himself a whiskey, then wandered away.

"Miss Wollstonecraft," Mr. Johnson said to Mary a moment later, "I present to you Henry Fuseli. Artist, lecturer, and writer."

The artist who had painted *The Nightmare*. He was not the type of individual Mary had pictured producing such a peculiar scene. Fuseli was short, only four or five inches over her own five feet.

"At last, I meet Johnson's newest protégé," Fuseli said, his German accent thick as fresh cream. He reached for her hand and kissed it.

"Mr. Johnson has spoken of you," Mary said, wanting to pull her hand away when Fuseli's lips lingered too long for her sensibilities. Based on his art, she had formed an unfavorable impression of him. Seeing him in the flesh, he seemed slithery.

"My dear Johnson," Fuseli said, looking with fondness at his friend, slapping him on the back. "Had he not taken me in when I first moved to London all those years ago, I would no doubt have died an obscure reprobate."

Dinner guests chuckled at Fuseli's attempt at self-deprecation. Mary suspected it was not his nature to poke at himself. He struck her as irreverent, unlike the humble, self-effacing Mr. Johnson. How the two could be close friends perplexed her.

Mr. Johnson sat at the head of the table, with Fuseli to his right and Mary to his left, opposite the artist. A fire had destroyed Mr. Johnson's first book business on Paternoster Row almost twenty years ago, Fuseli explained, as he smoothed and adjusted his well-tailored blue frock coat with rich silver embroidery. Fuseli was living with him at the time. Both men lost everything. Afterward, Mr. Johnson moved to the Churchyard and Fuseli left for Italy to study art.

"That explains the Italian influence in your painting." Mary nodded at *The Nightmare* hanging across from her. He raised an eyebrow, impressed, it appeared, at her observation. She took a sip of wine, then set her glass on the table and leaned forward. "Though I must admit, I find the subject matter rather grim." She noticed a slight tremor in his hand as Fuseli poured himself port and added water to it. Before taking a drink, his gaze darted around the table as if assessing the disposition of every person in the room.

"The beast," he said, when his biting blue eyes circled back to her, "does it frighten you?"

Mary laughed. "On the contrary. Though I wonder, what inspired such a dark creation?"

"A dream." Fuseli spoke briefly about dreams as fertile soil, an expansive realm of ideas, day, or night.

"But an incubus? You tease me, sir, by not saying more." Mary couldn't stop herself. She had studied the painting and assumed a symbiosis between the artist and his artwork. "I'm curious about your decision to put a phial and a looking glass on the table next to the woman's bedside. And why a book at her side?"

Fuseli's eyes flickered with delight at her string of questions, but he refused to comment.

His reticence to answer what to her seemed like simple questions was dismaying to Mary. "The moral of the painting then. Perhaps you'd be so kind as to share that?"

"There is no moral."

"Am I to believe a painting of an incubus, which, by definition, is a male sexual demon who preys on innocent women, has no moral intent?" She raised her voice without intending to, and the entire table turned their attention to her.

Fuseli's eyes locked with hers, and he shrugged.

"Then I shall assume you are the beast," she said with good humor, to goad him one last time into an explanation. Mr. Johnson's guests erupted into laughter, and she let herself join in the merriment of provoking the artist. But Fuseli refused to share any more thought on the matter, and Mary let the subject go, giving her the final word, a small triumph, but oddly exhilarating.

"What of France, gentlemen?" Fuseli said, ending their repartee just as Betsy and Rowland Hunter brought in boiled cod and vegetables.

Mary, too, was interested in France and welcomed the shift in topic. The past year, everyone had been watching events unfold in Paris. Seismic changes were happening on European soil. France appeared to be inching toward revolution.

"The people are rising," Thomas Christie said, buoyant over what was happening across the Channel. "The king's economic policies have left a starving population desperate for relief. I dare say we'll see real reform soon."

"The possibility of a revolution in France horrifies England's conservatives," Dr. Fordyce said. "Should France adopt a democracy like the United States, there is concern that people will act independently, as the colonists once did."

A pall settled over the diners. Thomas Holcroft held up his glass of whiskey, contemplating the amber liquid in the light. "Tories better prepare themselves. The Bourbon king is a buffoon."

Mary agreed with Holcroft. The French monarchy was oblivious to the plight of its citizens. Louis XVI's regressive tax structure was leading his country to the brink of bankruptcy. He had tried to tamp down unrest by convening France's Estates General in May, an assembly of France's three estates of the realm. Only the Third Estate, which consisted of commoners, paid taxes. The First Estate (the clergy), and the Second Estate (the nobles), paid nothing. It was time for France to distribute wealth fairly and empower its people.

"Lafayette is drafting a declaration of rights with Thomas Jefferson's help," she said, burning inside at the prospect of France becoming a true democracy. Ambassador Jefferson was in a strong position to bend perceptions. If the French could do it, England could too. "The United States' Declaration of Independence is the ideal road map for the French insurgence." And perhaps France could surpass America by granting full citizenship to women, Negroes, and indigenous people not allowed to vote.

For the next several hours, Johnson's Circle discussed all that could go wrong in France—and all of what could go right. Those in attendance held strong views. To a person, they were anti-monarchist, including Mary.

"Imagine, a populace toppling a centuries-old regime," John Bonnycastle said.

All talk came to an abrupt halt. The idea seemed incredible—but possible. England had the House of Lords and the House of Commons, but its age-old constitutional monarchy denied Britons true democratic representation. The king held too much power, while the average citizen possessed none.

"We should all act wisely and with care," Mr. Johnson said, an ominous tone in his voice. "Watch what you write. Pitt's administration could easily view support for a revolution in France as grounds for treason against the British Crown."

"Cry havoc and let slip the dogs of war," Bonnycastle said with another quote from Shakespeare.

Mary's arms and neck tingled. She turned to see Henry Fuseli, his bottomless blue eyes, deep as a dark secret, fixed on her.

Later that evening, on her walk home alone—she always refused the offer of an escort—Mary paused beneath a streetlamp half way across Blackfriars Bridge. The bridge was a massive arched structure nearly a fifth of a mile long, held up by stone piers connected by stone arches. A passing watercraft drifted through the moon's reflection in the Thames. Shivers passed through her, and she pulled her shawl close as water rippled in its wake.

Henry Fuseli. To her surprise, her preconceived opinion about him had proved inaccurate. Various images of the artist floated through her mind, his features as fine as if cut from marble. His arrogant mouth. The snide way he looked at others. He had a caustic wit and an apparent inability to conceal his sentiments. He ranted on certain matters, shouting across the table. He and Bonnycastle had broken into sudden spars throughout the evening, a game between them to see who was more learned, who had the sharper memory. Such qualities, however, gave him a commanding presence. He spoke of the unrest in France with the kind of authority reserved for seasoned orators. When talk turned to the arts, he held the men rapt talking of his connections to the Royal Academy. He could be harsh and judgmental, a sign of his passion.

Mary did not desire marriage, but she valued male friendships. Her attraction to a person stemmed from their scholarly mind and eloquent expression, and men's education made them interesting. Fuseli was a prime example. He had a profound intellect despite his outsized ego.

She thought of the painting. It must have personal meaning for him. Why else would he be so cryptic about it? People, Mary had learned, often refused to talk of things too close to the source of their deepest sorrows. She was determined to find out what inspired a man like Henry Fuseli.

FIVE

July 1789
One Year Later

Mr. Johnson handed Mary a copy of the latest *New Annual Register* when she arrived at his office one summer afternoon. "Read this."

Advice is received from Paris of a great revolution in France ...

"The French have done it!" Mary raced through the article. On July 14, an angry mob of French citizens stormed the Bastille. Its military leader, Governor De Launay, surrendered. When he did, the mob executed him.

"King Louis's plan to calm the waters by convening the Estates General failed," Mr. Johnson said, his gaze flashing his approval of the mob's actions. "A democracy is all but assured!"

It appeared so. Days prior to the attack on the Bastille, the Estates General had converted itself to the National Assembly—against the king's wishes—launching France on its way to abolishing feudalism, the Catholic Church's control of state matters, and extending the right to vote to the masses. "Though I hope the bloodshed ends at the Bastille." The image of De Launay's head being carried around on a pike sickened her. After growing up with a vicious father, she abhorred violence of any kind, even in the name of revolution. "What will happen now?"

"It's anyone's guess, though I dare say, the flame of democracy is alive and well on French soil."

Mr. Christie burst into the room, full of jubilation. "A revolution is born, one that will mark the end of the *Ancien Régime*! Monarchies are finally becoming a relic of the past!"

"Where are you going?" Mr. Johnson asked, shocked to see Christie carrying a packed bag.

"Miss seeing democracy unfold?" Mr. Christie said. "Never."

He was on his way to Paris. How Mary wished she could go with him! What better pursuit existed for mankind than to give power to the people? She wondered to herself how would Reverend Price perceive this new development. Surely he would be as pleased as she.

Mary navigated between piles of books and papers that had multiplied since her last visit to Mr. Johnson's sitting room.

"Good evening, gentlemen," she said. After her walk across Blackfriars Bridge, her cheeks tingled from the warmth shooting from a fire blazing in the hearth. November's night air had energized her, as did the happenings in France, which was making steady progress toward becoming a nation ruled by men instead of the dictates of a negligent king. News was flying across the Channel. A new renaissance was underway. Even from a distance, Mary considered herself part of events that were sure to prove historic.

Mr. Johnson poured wine for her. "Fuseli and I were beginning to think you might snub us tonight and stay at home engrossed in a book."

Mary smiled. "I would never think to neglect my two favorite gentlemen." She tossed aside her beaver hat. Flames cast a radiant glow across Johnson's and Fuseli's faces. The men occupied two shabby, mismatched wingback chairs flanking the fireplace. Since meeting Fuseli, Mary spent evenings with him and Mr. Johnson each week. Tonight, as always, she looked forward to formulating new perspectives informed by their common introspection. The three also enjoyed frequent social outings taking in London's cultural scene. Sometimes Fuseli's wife, Sophia, joined them, along with Iris and Mr. Kendall and often Thomas Holcroft. Sophia, a former artist's model, whom Mary found agreeable as well as beautiful, was stylish, like her husband. The flamboyant couple turned heads wherever they went and seemed to like the attention their presence garnered.

Mary seated herself opposite Mr. Johnson and Fuseli. A low table stacked with books and papers separated her from the men. Wax dripped from the flames of three flickering tapers and collected in the basins of their bronze candle holders.

Fuseli held up the Declaration of the Rights of Man and of the Citizen. "A crowning achievement for the French." He handed Mary the pamphlet and relaxed in his chair, gloating, it seemed, as he puffed on his pipe.

"That and beyond," Mary said with joy. All three of them were in high spirits over the French appearing to have done something miraculous. She had already read the entire document prior to this evening and handed it back to Fuseli. The Marquis de Lafayette Gilbert du Motier had presented the Declaration to the National Constituent Assembly in July, which had adopted it at the end of August. France was marching toward fairer representation and creating civil laws that would unify the French people. "A new constitution will surely follow. But the Declaration, will it work? A king sharing power with commoners seems a far stretch." Much like men sharing power with women. French women had marched to Versailles last month in October to demand equal rights and later had presented a formal petition to the National Assembly, but their calls went unheard.

"Hard to say how far the rebels will go," Fuseli said. "It's too early." He swirled his watered-down port. "Let's hope they develop a more representative approach similar to the United States."

"As compared to a mixed constitutional structure like England?" Mary harrumphed. "Gentlemen, neither would suffice. Even the United States failed. A country that claims to believe that all men are created equal has yet to form a more perfect union. In America, only white men with property can vote. France must do better, or they will accomplish nothing more than shuffle chess pieces on the same time-worn board."

"Women cannot be trusted with the vote," Fuseli said, stating it as if it were a well-known fact closed to dispute. "The French know this."

Mary's jaw dropped. "Surely you don't mean that."

"We've discussed this before. Women's minds are not designed for intellectual pursuits."

Mr. Johnson seemed to fade into the tan fabric of his chair.

Mary pushed to the edge of her seat. "Only because women have not been given the opportunity to develop them." Fuseli couldn't be serious. She had to subdue an urge to laugh at something so senseless coming from someone she held in such high regard.

"Their minds have nothing to do with it." Fuseli did not bat an eye. "Women are too delicate. The rigors of complex problems would cause them to collapse."

"'Tis a sad state when men of your caliber are so willing to dismiss members of my sex," Mary said, fighting to control her urge to erupt into a rant. Fuseli's attitude toward women often was dismissive. She had tried to overlook this tendency. His wife, Sophia, had an active mind, but Mary wondered now if Sophia deferred too much to her husband, letting him dominate in a way that left him unchallenged. As Mary was only interested in intellectual pursuits, it was hard for her to see Sophia as Fuseli's equal, even more difficult now that he had shown such open disregard for a woman's intellect. She glared at him. "Perhaps you consider me incompetent as well?"

"On the contrary, you are a rarity. You've shown yourself quite capable. Yet, I struggle to find someone similar to you."

"Do not seek to patronize me," she snapped. She could feel her face redden. He was being obtuse on purpose. "I'm not rare at all. I had mentors along the way, men who believed women capable." She told him and Mr. Johnson about the academic, John Arden, father to her friend Jane in Beverley, who took an interest in cultivating Mary's mind when she was twelve. About Mr. Clare, the minister when she lived in Hoxton, and his wife, who became Mary's staunch advocates. When Mary was fifteen, they took her in. Mrs. Clare fed her body, while Mr. Clare fed her mind amid the Wollstonecraft's constant instability that made her want to run away. "I should think you an equally enlightened being as these two men, open to seeing women differently from how society pegs us."

"Being enlightened has no bearing on my opinion. I speak what I know to be true: women are best suited to managing home and offspring. It is her vocation to serve the men in her life. Even Rousseau says this. Her strengths are modesty and gentleness. These things are important, are they not?"

Fuseli's arguments were becoming more unreasoned by the moment, though Mary thought she detected a twitch to his lips. Was he toying with her for sport? Or did he really think women were inferior in all ways but one, the ability to attract and serve men? She could not tell.

As Mary was about to chasten such blatant want of intelligence, Mr. Johnson interrupted the tirade forming in her mind. "Might I remind you both that we have gathered here tonight for a different purpose? Back to France, please."

Mary leaned back in her chair and crossed her arms. No matter how much Fuseli claimed to admire her, by virtue of his male upbringing, he was predisposed to dismiss her intellect simply because she was a woman. Just as women had not been educated in the manner they should, nor had men. Society programmed them from infancy to think of women as lesser beings. She stormed inside like a tempest in a bottle. The entire social order needed to be re-ordered, starting with men like Henry Fuseli!

"I want to make sure the ideas coming out of Paris get in front of British readers," Mr. Johnson said, focusing Mary's attention. "If we want to see political reform at home, the most important thing to do right now is to fuel discontent."

"How do you intend to accomplish this?" she asked. In England, anyone expressing support for either the American or the French Revolution was increasingly subject to arrest for sedition. "I don't need to remind you. Your more radical authors are running into trouble with the authorities."

"I'm not saying I want to be the architect of discontent." Mr. Johnson's look was sly, unusual for him. "Only a purveyor."

"Is this wise?" Fuseli asked, lines forming across his brow as he sent puffs of smoke into the air. The more he drank, the more his German accent thickened. "Pitt is turning against Dissenters."

"If the two of you would be willing to translate political pamphlets, I could print them faster," Mr. Johnson said, eyeing them both for a response. "And I'd like each of you to comment on them for the *Analytical Review*." Fuseli also wrote articles for Johnson's and Christie's periodical.

"Of course." Mary was the first to reply. The idea appealed to her desire to help the French cause.

Fuseli clenched his pipe between his teeth and signaled that he, too, would help.

"Batches of news are coming in daily," Mr. Johnson said, reaching for the latest pamphlets to arrive from France and handing them to Fuseli. "We need to act while the public's attention is engaged. Begin tomorrow, if possible."

Fuseli invited Mary to his house, where they could work in his studio uninterrupted.

The plan was perfect. While translating, Mary would also use the time to reform the man's outdated opinions regarding women.

When Mary arrived at Fuseli's home on Queen Anne Street the next day, his house servant led her up a darkened, winding staircase to Fuseli's studio on the third floor. Mrs. Fuseli, the servant explained, regretted not being there to greet her; she was out for the afternoon.

Mary had been to visit the Fuselis numerous times but had never been invited into the artist's creative space. His studio seemed removed from the rest of the house. Upon entering the oversized room, a masculine amalgamation of chemicals, dust, and sweat overpowered Mary. She could almost taste turpentine on her tongue.

At the far end of the room, Fuseli stood in front of an easel, wiping paint from his hands with a stained rag. "You have come."

"You sound surprised."

"Merely pleased." He pushed aside a shock of white hair that had fallen over one eye. He had not tied his hair back as usual. Nor was he wearing his typical formal attire. A large white shirt with ruffles at the end of his sleeves billowed around his torso.

On the walls, an excess of supernatural sketches, some overlapping, all intimate, all harsh, appeared otherworldly. "You seem at home in hell," Mary said, though the room was cold. She shivered without her cloak, which she had handed to the servant, and rubbed her arms to circulate her blood. "I can't help but wonder, am I in the first or the ninth circle?" She wandered along a row of ancient Greek figures levitating in restless anguish alongside tormented figures, many of them demonic, floating with nothing to ground them in a netherworld Fuseli had created. Lifting the corner of a sketch of a street beggar trying to sell a winged cupid to a wary maiden, she inadvertently recoiled at an erotic scene below of a man in bed with two women.

"I admit Dante's imagery has inspired me. Along with Milton's." Fuseli tossed the rag aside and sauntered toward her, his boots scraping across the wooden floor. "The Greeks, of course. And the Romans. Their stories are rich with life's most ... puzzling questions." He motioned his hand toward several canvases of various sizes propped on paint-splattered easels, then turned to Mary. "They give us heroes. My favorite, however, is Shakespeare, the supreme master of passion."

"And the ruler of our hearts." Mary finished the sentence for him with good-natured humor. He had recited the line to her a thousand times.

Alone with Fuseli in his studio, she sensed him as a different person here. She had yet to decipher him. By now she had grown accustomed to his preoccupation with sex; his stories about lurid affairs with women—and men—could fill volumes. His images were no less laden with sexual desire of all proclivities. Here, a story lurked in every shadow. There was something devilish about the artist.

"You're a master at depicting tragedy, but why must you be so dark?" she asked. His paranormal sketches bordered on the occult.

"Art speaks many languages." He padded to an opposite wall besieged with muscular men in bondage and women suffering cruel treatment at the hands of demons. Outsized breasts and male members flashed everywhere.

Fuseli picked up his pipe and tamped down a pinch of tobacco before lighting it. He puffed several times, then spread his hands outward toward his drawings. "The erotica, does it disturb you?"

Behind the screen of smoke he had created with the wave of his pipe, he waited for her reply. The images were upsetting, indeed, but his question was to provoke her. He was like that, testing her, just as his comments the previous evening, she had decided, were to shock her. "Society's rules can turn modesty into a cloak of weakness. I need no such protection."

Fuseli's heavy, half-closed eyes seemed to delight in her daring response. "I did not think you did."

"The *Nightmare*," she said, the studio's images making her insistent on asking, "what inspired it?"

Fuseli shrugged his shoulders. "Artists paint what they like."

"They paint what they obsess over. You alone have taught me this, which leads me to believe *The Nightmare* makes a statement." Mary stepped toward him. "About women. Your feelings toward them? Do you find us unalert? Easy prey?" She meant to chide him. He confused her when he was like this. Before becoming a painter, Fuseli had been an ordained evangelical pastor in Switzerland until he exposed the crime of a prominent man. Was the painting connected to his exile from Zurich?

He shook his head, amused. "You are always asking questions. In this instance, you think too much. The painting is nothing more than an interpretation of dreams, of German legends. It's time you understood my painting technique, which is more important. Come. I shall show you."

Disappointed once again at his dodging her questions about the painting, Mary followed him to a low-lit corner.

"In everything there must be a distortion of scale," he said, "to lure people to the story hidden below the surface. To do so, the artist must cast light against shadows. *Chiaroscuro*, as the Italians say."

She nodded, remembering how in *The Nightmare*, the woman was bathed in light but surrounded by dark images.

"To accomplish this," Fuseli continued, "sometimes I dip dry powder in oil or turpentine. Other times, I use a pencil or a knife and spread the paint across the canvas."

To demonstrate his point, he reached across Mary for a knife. A bolt of electricity shot through her when his arm brushed against her breast.

Fuseli smiled, his manner smug. "My apologies."

Mary swallowed hard, doubting Fuseli was sorry at all. She riveted her gaze on the canvas. She did not like his sudden change in how he was with her; he was acting like a sensualist. But a part of her was curious. Being this near to him, his scent charmed her, like she might like to close her eyes and swim in it, an odd, dizzying feeling.

"In my signature stroke, I move my knife back and forth. Like this."

Mary's hand flew to the small of her neck. His strokes were sharp, almost violent as he left broad streaks of red on the clean, white canvas.

After several thrusts, he set aside the knife and wiped his hands on a rag. Rags were everywhere, like cast-off clothing, stained and dirty. "I have wondered about you."

"I'm hardly one to keep my thoughts secret." Mary's blood chased wildly through her after the swiftness of his strokes, the way he had almost slashed the canvas.

"Your insistence on remaining a spinster. Does it not restrict you from enjoying certain ... pleasures in life?"

Despite a desire to withdraw from him, Mary's feet remained firmly rooted to the floor. "I consider myself enlightened enough not to give in to primal urges, if that's what you mean."

Reaching, he touched her cheek. "Let me draw you."

His finger traced her face, down her neck, alarming and exciting her as his eyes took her in anew, peering below the surface of her skin.

"You would have me sit for you?" she said, holding his gaze, her voice breathless.

"Here. In my studio. No one else would see you but me."

Mary inhaled a sharp breath. He meant to draw her naked. "I think not." She stepped back. Did he lust for her? Mary did not experience a mutual attraction. Not sexually. She understood the allure of charming men who sought to flatter women. They were rakes. Women eventually regretted falling under such a man's spell. Yet, Fuseli captivated Mary. She craved his mind. "You asked about my unmarried status," she said. "It suits me. Just as art speaks many languages, so does love."

"Platonic love, you mean?"

"Rational love. Not of the flesh but of ideas, a merging of consciousness between two minds trading passion through words and ideas."

Fuseli let out an audible sigh. "My dear Miss Wollstonecraft. Mary ... Such considerable intelligence, but so childlike in your views. One day, you will know what it is to yearn, to have no answer for it. One day you, too, will succumb to your passion. Like the rest of us."

"I control my passions," she said, hating that her voice shook. She had succumbed to nothing more than the genius in him.

Mary tapped her pen on the rim of her inkwell and checked the clock. Two p.m. Sun streamed in, casting broad rays of yellow light over open books and papers scattered in front of her. She was immersed in preparing a review of David Williams's *Letters on Education* when her house servant stepped into Mary's parlor, which served as a room for work, dining, and entertaining, and announced, "Mrs. Kendall is here."

Mary welcomed the unexpected break and said to show her in. Flexing her fingers, she stood to smooth her rumpled frock. Besides writing reviews, translating articles and pamphlets into French had consumed the better part of the last year. Along with Fuseli, she supplied Mr. Johnson with enough material to help stir conversation about political reform in London. The work satisfied her. She was forwarding a cause she believed in while cherishing the time spent with her white-haired friend.

"To what do I owe this surprise?" she asked Iris when she entered the dining room. Mary invited her to take a seat.

Iris remained standing and stared at the ceiling, then the floor, her odd behavior producing such disquietude in Mary that she thought someone must have died.

"What is it?" Mary asked on tenterhooks.

Iris shifted her weight from one foot to the other and twice opened her mouth to speak, then clamped it shut.

"Is it Mr. Johnson?" Mary asked, dreading what Iris's answer might be.

"No," Iris said, her eyes telling Mary she was sorry to have worried her that way. "It's not that."

A nervous laugh escaped Mary. Her chest tightened. "Then have I done something wrong?"

"There's gossip," Iris said at last, her words tentative, her gaze turning awkward again.

Assuming Iris meant tittle-tattle about Mary, she waved a hand as if swatting at a fly. "You know I'm not one to pay attention to what people say." She had raised the eyebrows of more than a few staid individuals with her lifestyle. Mary cared not about what she wore, went out with or without a chaperone, and entertained male friends alone at her home.

"This is different."

"Blather about Mr. Johnson and me as lovers, perhaps?" Mary almost laughed. This whisper trickled back to her and Mr. Johnson now and then. He and Mary always made light of it, amused more than anything.

"It's about you ... and Henry Fuseli."

Mary's throat went dry. "Fuseli?" Such shocking news made her insides constrict. She could understand small talk about her and Mr. Johnson being a couple, going about town the way they did. They were a regular fixture at concerts and galleries. But prattle about her and Henry Fuseli baffled her.

Iris twisted her hands together. "Rumor has it ... that you're in love with him."

In love with him? "That's absurd. You've spent time with us. Surely you don't suspect something so unseemly could be true!"

"Fuseli is the primary source of the rumor." Iris pulled up a chair beside Mary, her eyes pleading with her friend to take her alarm to heart. "That's what troubles me. Mr. Kendall says Fuseli carries your letters in his pocket. He's seen them."

"What of it?" Mary laughed again. "People frequently share the contents of letters with others, us included. You of all people know my relationship with Fuseli is one of friendship, not of ardor."

Iris sat back and tipped her head to one side, examining Mary, causing Mary to squirm in her chair. "Are you certain he feels the same way?"

Mary wrestled with herself to stay seated.

"Mr. Kendall says," Iris continued, her eyes not leaving Mary's, "in addition to bragging about your letters, Fuseli has been heard saying you've become his muse."

It was an accusation, a suggestion that Mary had done something wrong. For him to consider her his muse was a compliment, surely, not an insult. "You speak as if it's a crime to inspire one's creativity. You know perfectly well—"

"That he's a philanderer? I fear he's preying on you. You're inexperienced with men."

Iris's voice was gentle, but the suggestion that Mary was naïve was an affront she had not expected from her friend. Mary's unwed status did not diminish her wisdom or judgment as a woman. "Fuseli and I have never been intimate," she insisted.

"Even after the incident in his studio?"

"Yes!" Mary now regretted telling Iris about Fuseli's odd behavior the first day she visited his studio six months prior. The subject of intimacy never came up again between her and Fuseli. To her relief, the exchange had altered nothing between them. They continued their intellectual exploration, she prioritizing her thirst for knowledge over physical desires.

"I'm only watching out for you," Iris said, turning apologetic. "You'd not be the first he's seduced."

Mary exhaled a sharp breath. *Seduced?* "He's done nothing of the sort!"

"I worry you idolize him." Iris narrowed her eyes. "He may be an intriguing individual, but mark me, he's not above deceit. Mr. Kendall says Fuseli thinks only of himself, that you are not to trust him. He thinks—"

"Stop!" Mary held up her hand. The innuendo seemed unfair and was making her distraught. From her best friend, no less. "I don't deny Henry Fuseli has brought new pleasures into my life, but not of the bodily kind. He is and always will be ... peculiarly circumstanced."

Iris looked at her, confused.

"Married to Sophia!" Mary got up and stared out the window where a street peddler passed by. "You mustn't think anything untoward exists between us. If I thought my passion for him immoral, I would conquer it or die in my attempt."

"Are you so sure?" Iris asked, her eyes pinned on Mary.

"Yes, I'm sure!" Stung, Mary turned to her. Iris, nor anyone, had never misunderstood her like this. "Adultery is incompatible with every fiber of my being. My heart is pure, my feelings for Henry Fuseli as innocent as my affection for Mr. Johnson."

Iris looked at her, skeptical. "There's something unsavory about the way he talks about your letters ... about you. Either he is bragging, or he is meaning to expose you in an unflattering manner."

"Utter nonsense." Mary rubbed her forehead. She disliked being cornered, being falsely accused. "Please, let this go. I know the perils of friendship between the sexes." In her advice to mothers and young girls in *Thoughts on the Education of Daughters,* Mary had written that the heart could be treacherous. Women sometimes made poor choices. They were prone to delusions, to imagining the friendship of men they admired would not give way to desiring more from them, or that they might desire more from her.

Iris soon left, convinced, Mary hoped, that she had done nothing dishonorable, but thoughts about Fuseli would not leave her in peace. Restless, she wandered about the room, squeezing and rubbing her hands together as if she had no other way to still them. Her relationship with Fuseli was blameless, was it not? Compared to her feelings for others, her sentiments toward him were unique, to be sure, vaulted by a mix of fascination and admiration, but why should they offend anyone? She stopped to gaze at a sketch of her profile he had drawn from memory and given her. The bond between them was not about physical intimacy. It could not be. Other ways must exist to feel affection for the opposite sex. If relationships were solely confined to the bedroom, where did that leave unmarried women who wished to remain chaste?

Mary, now thirty-one, had been in London for three years. She had not maintained her spinsterhood by being foolish. Hers and Fuseli's was the perfect relationship between a man and a woman. They had no mutual sexual interest, only a meeting of creative minds that came together for the purposes of illuminating conversations. So what if she had become his muse? Had he not become hers as well?

Six

November 1790
Six Months Later

An agitated Henry Fuseli met Mary and Mr. Johnson at the door to his residence. "Have you read Burke's latest piece?" he asked before they even crossed the threshold.

Mary approved of the venom in his voice. "The man's an abomination." She marched in and handed the Fuselis' house servant her cloak. Fuseli was referring to Edmund Burke, a former member of Parliament and long-standing member of the conservative Whig party, who had just published *Reflections on the Revolution in France*. In it, he spoke out against the revolution. As a well-known political writer in London, his words carried weight.

Mr. Johnson, wheezing from the cold, took longer slipping out of his overcoat. "Burke's certainly singing a different tune than twenty years ago." His cheeks were red after he and Mary had trudged through slush under a light falling snow to arrive at five for dinner.

"He's an idiot." Fuseli did not mince words as he led his guests into the dining room where Sophia awaited them with a gracious smile. "He sought to defend Marie Antoinette, of all people. The most hated of royals."

"Miss Wollstonecraft," Sophia said, looking as though she had just stepped out of a French painting in her blue silk floral *robe à la française*. Mary assumed her own colorless linen frock and lank hair must look dingy by comparison as she followed Sophia, whose skirt swished like a dancer's. Sophia seated Mary opposite her in the dining room. Mary tucked her hair behind her ears in a half-hearted attempt to make herself more presentable. The room, adorned with Rococo furniture and gallery-like walls, left her feeling like a misplaced artifact. Ornate plasterwork decorated rose-colored walls featuring Fuseli's paintings, thankfully those without his occult images.

Mary redirected her attention to the men when Burke was mentioned, a subject more fitting for her than attire and hairstyles. "What galls me is that he's made Reverend Price the center of his criticism, making him a caricature in the broadsheets." Not only had Burke referred to the commoners in France as a mob, but he had also attacked her beloved mentor for a sermon he had delivered a year earlier. In *A Discourse on the Love of Country*, Reverend Price had compared the French Revolution to England's Glorious Revolution during the seventeenth century when Parliamentarians overthrew King James II and to the War of Independence in the United States. Either reference alone would have been enough to set off conservatives. Price's words fueled political fires on both ideological sides. Outraged conservatives excoriated Price while radicals expressed pent-up enthusiasm over his words.

"If Burke objected so strongly to Price's views, why did he delay expressing them publicly?" Fuseli asked as a footman poured wine for the table. Mr. Johnson had published Price's sermon in full in the *Analytical Review,* along with Mary's review the following December, nearly a year prior.

"He's insensitive," Mary said. To speak out now, when Reverend Price lay dying in Hackney, was nothing short of unfeeling. Since Reverend Price's sermon had sent shock waves through Great Britain, his health had taken a dramatic turn for the worse, leaving Mary worried.

Mary was but sixteen years of age when Burke jumped into the fray between the British government and the American colonies to argue against using force against the rebels. He urged his fellow Englishmen to work with the colonists to assuage their complaints against the Crown. England could never win a war, he warned, against the kind of determined patriots who had taken up arms on such a distant shore. Now he was criticizing the French for doing the very thing the colonists had done. It made no sense to her.

"I see fear more than anything in Burke's words," Mr. Johnson said, as if he, too, had yet to puzzle out Burke's motives. "I'm not surprised at the way he seeks to protect the British monarchy. It's his conservative stance towards the French king and aristocracy in the face of the commoners' opposition that confuses me."

"The threat of revolution on soil so near England," Fuseli replied, "poses a more serious menace, my friend."

"Indeed," Mr. Johnson said. "Burke is trying to quash any potential resistance in England by exploiting Britain's distrust of France."

Mary agreed. Burke's piece would spread like wildfire. Conservatives would use it to encourage the Crown to take a hard stance against those who disagreed with its policies, which included just about everyone in Johnson's Circle.

"What if I were to write a rebuttal to Burke?" she said, positioning her napkin on her lap. Burke and his pampered sensibilities had tapped a raw nerve in her. "What does Burke know of liberty when he lives his life at the center of the very structure that holds other men, not to mention women, down?"

Fuseli snorted. "Be serious, Mary."

Mary's gaze swiveled to meet his, daring him to spurn her suggestion. If an argument was what he wanted, she was willing. Burke's antics had put her in a foul mood.

"I think she's quite serious." Mr. Johnson pushed aside the bowl of creamy white soup made with chicken broth a footman had placed in front of him. "Say more."

"Burke needs to be challenged." Mary avoided looking at Fuseli by maintaining eye contact with Mr. Johnson. "He defends a social order in which men like him rank themselves above others only because the order has anointed him with an old name and property, a way of governing which denies average citizens the right to choose their own leaders. What personal liberty is there for the rest of us?" She glared again at Fuseli. "Women in particular."

"Burke is a powerful man," Fuseli said, not masking his indignation at Mary's suggestion. "You'd be taking on the entire English establishment."

"To what, may I ask, do you object?" Mary could feel her blood beginning to boil. "Taking on Burke, or *me* taking on Burke?"

"You've never written anything political," Fuseli said, scoffing at her. "Besides, women do not comment on politics in the press. Readers would dismiss you outright."

"I rather like the idea," Mr. Johnson said.

"Do you mean it?" Mary asked. She sat up. The possibility of taking Burke's arguments apart one by one sent a charge through her that made her want to pick up her pen at once.

"Being silent would be tantamount to endorsing his views, would it not?" Mr. Johnson replied.

"Without question." Mary's spoon twitched in her fingers.

"There'll be plenty of people reacting to Burke," Mr. Johnson said. "No one has published a rebuttal yet. Yours could be the first." His eyes glittered at the possibility. "When can you have it done?"

"I'll begin this very evening," Mary said, thrilled at Mr. Johnson's response, in part gloating that he had not allowed himself to be influenced by Fuseli, whose shock had silenced him at the head of the table. The room went quiet. It was then a sudden cloud drifted over her enthusiasm. "Will you attach my name to the rebuttal?" she asked Mr. Johnson.

Fuseli's eyes grew wide, and his mouth dropped open.

Mr. Johnson stared into his soup.

"Anonymous. I see." Mary clenched her jaw. "As you wish. But this will be the last time." She disliked being invisible once more, but now was not the time for arguments. She had to defend Reverend Price by putting Burke in his place.

As well as Henry Fuseli. And all the other men who doubted women. No wonder Fuseli thought women incapable of deep thought. Sophia had not uttered a word during the entire exchange, leaving Mary to wonder if she had understood what they were talking about, let alone what was at stake.

Mary thrust her hands into her hair. Her fireplace mantle clock displayed three a.m. She was two weeks into writing her response to Burke, and nothing sounded right. Voices inside her head parleyed back and forth as she leaned her elbows on her dining table, where papers were strewn about as if a windstorm had struck. She wanted to bury her head and hide. Which license did she, an anonymous reviewer and author of successful educational books and an unnoticed novel, have to oppose traditions many Britons held dear?

She flicked through her pages, smudging ink and losing track of her thoughts. Her reasoning lacked coherence. Nowhere could she detect the substance she so wished to capture. Even her usual attempts at wit fell flat. Plagued with doubt, she pushed the pages away and curled up on her sofa, begging sleep to end the headache that was splitting her head in two.

The next morning Mary tramped across Blackfriars Bridge to see Mr. Johnson, who lay huddled under a blanket on the sofa in his sitting room.

"What brings you out?" he asked. "Come to see an old man die?" His tea was untouched; he looked like a ghost.

"You've just a touch of influenza, that's all," she said, shocked at how pale he looked. She tucked the blanket around his feet. Through their regular exchange of letters, he had relayed to Mary he had not been feeling well, but she had no idea he had taken so ill. She called for Betsy Hunter to warm his tea, then piled wood onto the fire, fright suddenly running roughshod over her. She could not bear to lose Mr. Johnson. Not now. Not ever.

"How comes your response to Burke?" he asked. "Did you bring me any new pages?"

Mary drew a chair close to the sofa and stuffed her hands into the pockets of her cloak. She shook her head.

"What is it?" he asked, rising on one arm. "Why such a remorseful look?"

"I'm stopping. You'll have to find someone else to take on Burke. Fuseli was right. Who do I think I am?"

Mr. Johnson threw off his blanket and sat up. "You're a brilliant writer, that's who you are. Where's this self-doubt coming from?"

Mary's stomach growled. She had not eaten for days. Her hands shook, jittery from having consumed only coffee. Copious amounts of it. "None of what I'm writing makes sense."

Mr. Johnson's eyes narrowed as he surveyed her. "You're aware I've been printing your work page by page as you've been sending it over."

Mary spied her most recent pages on the table next to him. "I'll be happy to throw them one by one into the Thames on my way home." She meant it. Her endeavor had become a farce, one she had created.

"You could dispose of them, I suppose." Mr. Johnson peered at her through bloodshot eyes. He wasn't wearing his wig and looked elfin in his graying, closely cropped hair that maintained few hints of the blond of his youth. "But I find your prose quite eloquent. Very pointed, if I may say. Reason as the basis of one's arguments is an effective way to challenge prevailing sentiments. I'd argue it's your forte."

Did Mary even have a forte? No. She was an imposter. The bottom of whatever lie she had been telling herself about being a political writer was crumbling beneath her before she even started. A groan escaped her. "What if I'm not able to make a compelling argument?"

"Your words are of the soul, a direct contrast to Burke's arrogant platitudes," Mr. Johnson said. "The section on the slave trade alone speaks volumes. 'Such misery demands more than tears.' Who wouldn't be moved by such persuasive entreaties?"

His arguments made Mary feel even more like a fraud. She stood to leave. "I must go."

"Well then." Mr. Johnson sighed. "If you don't have it in you, of course you should quit. I guess you're not up to it after all." He handed her the pages he had gone over. "Do with them what you wish."

Mary sat back down, the pages crackling in her hand. She had not expected him to agree with her so readily. "I didn't mean—"

"I don't want you doing anything too strenuous," he interrupted. "If your lack of formal education hasn't prepared you for this kind of mental confrontation, which requires a different stamina, one that, er, tests your mettle, then who am I to hold you to it?" Mr. Johnson lay back and pulled his blanket over his chest. "You gave it a good go. Don't fret. I'll burn the pages we've already printed and follow your instructions to find someone else to do the job." He closed his eyes. "We needn't discuss it again."

"You would so easily wound my pride, sir?" Mary's lack of education had nothing to do with how she was feeling. And it was not that she lacked mettle.

Mr. Johnson opened one eye. "Don't look so chapfallen. I'm only stating what you've told me yourself. You're the one saying you're exhausted. You're the one insisting you cannot sustain your attempt. To quote you specifically, I believe you said, 'I'm stopping,' no?"

Her words coming back at her sounded like a surrender. What she wanted was to find an avenue forward, a way to meld disparate thoughts into a cohesive rebuttal. She thought of Reverend Price, how she needed to defend him, the righteousness of speaking what was true. "How could I even think about quitting?" she asked, embarrassed by her lack of confidence in herself.

"I was just wondering the same thing," Mr. Johnson replied, his half-smile gracing his face. "My dear Miss Wollstonecraft, go home and pick up your pen."

Mary handed the pages back to him. "Very well then." She looked at her mentor with affection. "You've made me a writer, you know."

"Nonsense." He seemed to blush at her acknowledgment of his influence. "You've made yourself a writer. I don't hold the pen, Miss Wollstonecraft. You do. Your voice is your own, the manifestation of wise and potent thoughts. Embrace your unique thinking and go beyond. Let it soar." He closed his eyes again. "I regret I am tired. You must let me sleep, or I will never get off this sofa, and you will never finish your counterarguments to Burke."

Mary stroked the forehead of the man who had done more for her than her father could ever hope to imagine. She could never let Mr. Johnson down. Not when he once again believed in her more than she believed in herself. More importantly, she could not let herself down. She had forged doubt into resolve more than once in her life. She would do so again.

Mary completed her rebuttal twenty-eight days after Burke's original piece came out. *A Vindication of the Rights of Men* was the first to reach the public. In it, she achieved what she had set out to do. She defended Reverend Price and the French Revolution by attacking the aristocracy in favor of representative governments.

"Your political debut struck a nerve," Mr. Johnson said, looking satisfied behind his desk. He had made a full recovery from his bout of influenza. Outside his office window, snowflakes were collecting on the hats and shoulders of passersby. Christmas was fast approaching. The sun was starting its descent, turning the sky slate blue as bell ringers began their evening rounds.

"It would seem that it has." Her small book had made a big impression. After just three weeks on the market, it had already sold out.

"This calls for a drink." Mr. Johnson pulled a bottle of whiskey from his bottom desk drawer and set out two glasses.

"I thought you'd be more pleased," he said, his face clouding when Mary declined a nip. "Debate is feverish; every major journal and periodical is reviewing it. Even those who disagree with you on political grounds acknowledge the author makes a substantive case for a meritocracy."

It was gratifying to have people agree with her. A warm feeling spread through Mary as she basked in having argued England's constitutional monarchy had outlasted its purpose. More advanced forms of liberty were possible, she had written. Laws and constitutional principles like those Burke characterized as the wisdom of tradition were ignorant, irrational, and oppressive. Great Britain should abandon them and eliminate all forms of privilege. Everyone deserved to enjoy the fruits of their labor and achieve financial independence.

Still, a certain dispiritedness gnawed away at her. "No one knows I wrote it."

"I've been thinking about that." Mr. Johnson poured himself a tipple and joined her on the other side of the desk, where he leaned against the edge. "We need to do another printing soon. What do you say to us bringing you out from behind the curtain of anonymity?"

"You'd put my name on it?" Mary wrapped her fingers around the arms of the chair in which she was sitting and grasped them tightly. She had been waiting for her name to be attached to her writing since signing on with Mr. Johnson. "What's changed your mind?"

"No one can erase the accolades you've received," he said. "Critics have already judged the piece as intelligent and reasoned."

"What did Fuseli say of my rebuttal?" she asked, trying to sound casual. His voice echoed daily in her mind. *Women do not comment on politics in the press.* He had become a sliver lodged below her thumbnail. It had been weeks since she last saw him, and she remained unaware of his opinion on the publication. His endorsement seemed important to her, overshadowing the satisfaction that came from within. She felt certain he would like nothing better than to see her fail as a political writer.

"I believe he thought it quite good."

"He did?" She went still inside, like she dared not breathe. Had she been imagining a renunciation from Fuseli?

"Why do you ask?"

"He's not told me."

"Don't think for a minute he's not paying attention. He is."

Mr. Johnson provided all the confirmation Mary needed that Fuseli thought her work had merit. For now. The truth was, she did not want to wait for Fuseli's approval. She was ready for her name to be on every page she wrote. "Do you think England is prepared for a woman to comment on politics?"

Mr. Johnson smiled, a complete grin this time, rather than his scrimping half-smile. "Probably not, but would that really stop you?"

Mary, too, grinned. "No." Nothing would stop her. "I think I'll take that drink now." After three years in London, Mary was ready to further redefine herself, this time as a political writer.

When Mr. Johnson published the second edition of *A Vindication of the Rights of Men* with Mary listed as the author, an agonizing few weeks followed.

"They're a bunch of hypocrites," she mumbled to Iris. Mary had not expected such a malicious slew of editorials from the same men who had praised the publication when the presumed writer was male. Now they called the rebuttal feeble and labeled Mary as weak-minded. Certain former members of Parliament were the cruelest. Horace Walpole, another Whig and politician, writer, and historian like Edmund Burke, called her a hyena in petticoats.

"You were expecting a parade, were you?" Iris asked. Ahead of them, Mr. Kendall and Mr. Johnson tramped alongside each other in the snow. They were on their way to a play at Covent Garden, where they were to meet the Fuselis. The street was full. Lanterns hanging from carriages floated in the dark. Horses' steaming breath created mini clouds, producing a fog that blurred the path ahead.

"Certainly not," Mary snapped, yanking her beaver hat to just above her brow. Her hair was in disarray. She had been wearing the same frock for days. The critics had bared their fangs when they found out a woman had written the piece. Now the writing was "incoherent." Now the ideas contained within were "trivial." "Why do men, the supposed enlightened sex, refuse to regard women as rational beings capable of having political opinions?"

"Come now," Iris coaxed, "many have praised your work."

The sharp crunch of boots on the snow-packed cobblestones further grated on Mary's already tattered nerves. It was easier to focus on the negative. She had become an outcast overnight. "Even other women have called me immodest."

"While others have spoken up on your behalf, Catharine Macaulay for one. Hers is no minor endorsement."

Macaulay was indeed a respected and accomplished historian who had written to Mary, expressing her admiration for the piece.

"To her I am grateful," Mary replied. "But Mrs. Macaulay is a rare bird." The rest were a flock of starlings flying in perfect formation.

The reaction of the critics was not the only thing agitating Mary. Henry Fuseli must be taking delight in watching each crushing blow that landed on her.

At intermission, Mary had a chance to speak to Fuseli alone. Sophia had excused herself. Mr. Johnson had gone to speak to his friend William Roscoe from

Liverpool, whom he had spotted on the main level, and the Kendalls had stepped away to greet friends in a neighboring box.

"You have commented little about the second edition of *Rights of Men*," she said, making no attempt to mask her dismay over his prolonged silence regarding what she had written.

Fuseli shrugged his shoulders and looked down at the theatergoers. "What of the view? It is quite nice, no?" A friend from the Academy, he explained, had lent them the box they were in on the mezzanine.

Mary had seen little of the play, let alone noticed the view. "I'd hoped you would be more forthcoming in your review of my work. I can't tell if it pleases you or if you agree with those who seek to destroy my reputation."

He faced her at last. "Your work is not subject to my approval."

"Surely you have more to say." Mary hated such coy behavior. She preferred the brash, outspoken Fuseli, the friend who sparred with her, the man who would give her an honest assessment of her work. Something had happened between them, and she knew not what.

"My dear Miss Wollstonecraft," Fuseli replied, his heavily lidded eyes fluttering, "you have captivated many with your words. Their applause should be sufficient."

Mary was about to express that others' praise was not enough so he would understand what his endorsement meant to her, that it was wise men and women whom she'd wanted to reach with her writing. How could she know if she had been successful if her words had not won over the most exceptional man she knew? But Sophia returned, ending Mary's chance. Fuseli turned away from Mary and extended his hand to his wife, leaving Mary on the outside of a glass wall peering in. Sophia's emerald evening gown with a white ruffled neckline and matching green hat, complete with a sweep of white ostrich plumes, complemented Fuseli's perfectly coiffed white spill of curls. Together, they looked exquisite.

Time was like quicksand for the remainder of the evening. When Iris asked Mary if she was ill, Mary insisted she was fine. Later, Mr. Johnson expressed a similar concern and asked her if she would like him to walk her home early. Upon both inquiries, Mary retreated further into the recesses of the darkened theater box. How could she tell either of them that Henry Fuseli no longer valued her as a worthy intellectual partner? All because she had chosen to defy him and write what her mind compelled her to write. Fuseli's attitude presented Mary with another kind of censure, the disregard, perhaps even the disdain, of a treasured friend, an injury worse than the most scathing editorial.

SEVEN

May 1791
Four Months Later

In the looking glass of her spartan bedroom, Mary studied her reflection the way a sculptor might inspect a piece of rough stone before picking up a hammer and chisel. William Roscoe, Mr. Johnson's close friend from Liverpool whom he had seen at the play at Covent Garden, had requested permission to commission a portrait of Mary for his private collection. *Rights of Men*, he said, established her as a woman of high intellect. Fine praise, for Roscoe was a banker, lawyer, and historian. He shared Mary's commitment to justice. Thus, she was happy to oblige him, for he had become her friend, too, through Mr. Johnson. Roscoe hired John Williamson, a well-established portraitist.

The commission raised a question Mary had yet to consider seriously in life. If she was the erudite thinker Roscoe believed she was, what kind of image did she wish to present to the world? She was eager to counter the common depiction of thinking women as unattractive spinsters and instead convey the new genus of women she had set out to become when she moved to London—women as intellectuals, powerful in their own right; women other women would want to emulate.

Unfortunately, the woman looking back at Mary was a frump.

An art student who needed someone on whom to practice had painted Mary once when she was in Dublin. She wondered if the painting still existed and hoped it did not. She had been less than thrilled with the results. Seeing her image through someone else's eyes had disappointed her. She now realized she had not given the fellow much to work with.

This new portrait called for something grand. She straightened her posture. Until now, it had not mattered to her what she wore. She had thumbed her nose at fashion her entire life. However, her persistence in dressing plainly and her reluctance to style her hair were no longer in her best interest. As she turned her reflection from side to side in the looking glass, Mary had to admit it had occurred to her Henry Fuseli also might welcome a fresh look. As of late, he had turned into a mosaic of glass and stone. Gone were their old exchanges. She and Fuseli and Mr. Johnson still spent evenings together in Mr. Johnson's sitting room, but less often. Fuseli's excuse was that the Royal Academy tied up his time. He was an academician there now. When he was at Mr. Johnson's for their evening gatherings, the easy way Mary and Fuseli had once conversed about books and politics and philosophy had turned rushed.

Only when he joined Johnson's Circle for dinner did he seem like the old Fuseli. Was it true what Thomas Holcroft had said, that Fuseli liked to be the most famous among them? Fuseli surely would not resent her for the small bit of attention her writing had given her, would he? She had no way of knowing. He was always arrogant, constantly seeking attention and frequently angry about something. Which kept people focused on him. It also kept them at a distance.

Mary stepped closer to the glass. Fuseli seemed drawn to Sophia's kind of beauty, a woman adorned with ruffles and silks and flounces. Mary frowned; she detested ruffles. Turning each cheek, she searched for blemishes but found none. At least she could forgo face powders or paint. Her propensity to walk miles each day for exercise gave her skin a warm glow.

Her hair was another matter altogether. It lay flat at the crown. She wore it down, and when out, her locks trailed beneath her beaver hat in whatever direction they chose to wander. The furry hat peeked at Mary from beneath the pile of clothing she had been trying on. It would have to go. A hat was a woman's greeting to the world. She'd learned this from Iris, who had an array of hats that she wore just so. Mary needed new hats, possibly two. Something flattering without being garish. She gathered her hair in her hands and piled it on top of her head but found it too ostentatious. A bun next, at the nape of her neck? Also unflattering. She let her hair drop. With a little effort, she could use her natural curls as an asset. She had refused to powder her hair, even in Bath and Ireland despite standing in rooms with ladies of fashion who considered it essential to sprinkle their hair with sifted wheat and ground chalk. However, she must also see powder from a fresh perspective. Mary needed to view everything in a new light.

"Factions are forming in Paris," Iris said to Mary. It was midafternoon in November. They were at a London cafe for the middle class, having coffee. "Why must the wheels of reform turn so slowly?"

"The French are at odds with one another over the pace of reform," Mary said. The Revolution in France had reached its third year. Mary and everyone in Johnson's Circle had hoped for faster progress, but undoing centuries of law and dismantling tradition was proving challenging. The Americans were having a better time of building their republic. They had started with a clean slate, no government at all. The French, however, had yet to settle the matter. Standoffs between men with different notions of who should be in charge in lieu of the king were a daily occurrence.

Despite Mary's ambitious longings for France, today the Revolution was the furthest thing from her mind. Instead of listening to Iris, she was thinking about her upcoming invitation to dine at the Fuselis' home. The fissure between her and Fuseli—whatever it had been—had healed, and they were back to their friendly spars and evenings of deep philosophical reflection with Mr. Johnson. More change for Mary had also been afoot. In September she had moved into a house in Bloomsbury on Store Street, which afforded her a study where she could write, instead of using her tiny dining table for work. Near the British Museum, the area also had a broader array of entertainment than George Street and was still within easy walking distance of Mr. Johnson's bookshop. And it was close to the Fuseli residence. When she moved, she questioned herself whether to ask to board with them instead of renting her own house. In no way would it have been improper. People frequently hosted live-in guests. She could see Fuseli daily, an obvious advantage. He continued to be the most intriguing man she had ever encountered. The most interesting person in the world! Through daily interaction, their relationship could move to the higher level she was seeking, one in which they could exchange an endless flow of ideas. Living with them would also save money. Her family was bleeding her dry.

Listening with half an ear to Iris while she went on about the Revolution, Mary made a mental assessment of her bank account, trying not to worry. She had helped Eliza find a teaching position in Putney, but the school closed, so Mary paid for her to move to Wales, where she was a governess at Upton Castle in Pembrokeshire. While in Wales, Eliza spotted their father and informed Mary of his skeletal appearance. Due to excessive drinking no doubt, Mary thought. He was living in squalor. Likewise, Mary had also helped relocate Everina to Ireland, near Waterford, to look after children for a wealthy family. It was not the lucrative post she or Mary had hoped for after Everina had studied French in Paris. But it was paying work.

As if those two things alone had not helped to deplete her finances, Mary had convinced her brother Charles to leave Ned's employ when she believed her older brother was having too negative an effect on him. Mary set Charles up with a different attorney and paid for his keep. To her great disappointment, Charles had proved himself a laggard and had since skipped town. He was in Ireland, begging Mary to send money. At the same time, without notice, her brother James had returned from the sea. To help him gain a better post and take over his own vessel, she arranged for him to study mathematics from John Bonnycastle. James, too, had squandered the opportunity by sleeping late and missing his classes. She eventually sent him packing on a different boat.

"Hello?" Iris rapped her knuckles on the table. "Is anyone home?"

"I'm sorry," Mary said. "I'm distracted." The French were having difficulty, she agreed. In fact, it was becoming hard to imagine the French would ever turn their government into a democracy.

Yet something else disturbed Mary more. Society's stagnation was another constant on her mind today. "See the women here, their heads bent in conversation?" she said to Iris. "They have not a thing to do." The occasional man shared a table with a woman, but the room was mostly filled with women. The men present had already been to coffeehouses exclusively for them. The time-worn division between the sexes was a scene Mary could have observed a hundred years ago, the only difference being the style of women's dresses and the way they coiffed their hair.

"It is a bit ridiculous," Iris said, "drinking coffee or sipping tea while engaging in yet another round of gossip. Or being ignored." She gestured towards a couple near the wall. The woman seemed on the verge of tears, while her husband was hidden behind a newspaper.

"Meanwhile, men move between the interesting worlds of trade or politics or the arts, while I'm still being criticized, not so much for what I said in *Rights of Men,* but because *I* said it." Mary was still the target of comments intended to humiliate and intimidate her into never writing another political piece.

"Those salvoes will never stop, you know. You've crossed the Rubicon. You can never return to simply being M."

"I don't want to go back to just being M, nor am I entirely frustrated with the criticism I've drawn. I have found usefulness in it. My name is known. I've been pegged as a radical. That means that I have the public's attention." Mary leaned forward. "I've written regarding the rights of *men*, but what of the rights of *women*? My entry into polemical works only touched the surface of what I really believe."

Iris's entire body perked. She wiggled to the edge of her seat, her eyes lighting up. "Another book, perhaps?"

"The women around us are virtuous, to be sure, but someone needs to waken them to what is possible."

"Good luck." Iris emitted a sigh that expressed doubt rather than the encouragement Mary hoped for. "There is the matter of what women *believe* they are capable of. Women are silly creatures trapped in their sensibilities. They accept their lot with docility. We've discussed this a thousand times."

"Imagine if women received a genuine education, discovering their true strengths instead of being groomed for inferiority? With greater knowledge, they'd *demand* more."

"Then you must enlighten them," Iris said. Her excitement was palpable, and she leaned toward Mary. "Women need a voice. No one else has the platform you have at your disposal. It's you, Mary, or no one else."

Mary thought of the portrait of her that John Williamson had just finished. Upon seeing it, concerns over whether her image would represent a new genus of woman had fallen to the wayside. She was grateful for the choices the artist made. The woman on the canvas was the exact person to make a case for her sex to demand a new status. John Williamson had shown Mary as strong and assured. Her gaze met the viewer's as an equal. Her clothing was also just right. She had exchanged her dowdy threads for a smart, educated look: a simple black dress and a white scarf. And she had powdered her wavy hair, which she had cut to shoulder length.

Ready to put her thoughts out to the world, a thrill chased through Mary. For too long, women had been held back by their education and circumstances, preventing them from living a life of true meaning.

"Well, well. I cannot deny that I am pleased. I've been waiting for you to propose something like this for the last year," Mr. Johnson said when Mary stopped by the Churchyard on her way home to tell him of her plans to write about the state of affairs for women. He smiled his half-smile and set aside the manuscript he had been reading and removed his spectacles. "How do you intend to go about it?"

"I want to use my pen for good by arguing for my sex." She paced in front of Mr. Johnson's desk, glancing at the portraits of Rousseau and John Locke, then back at Mr. Johnson. An energy had taken root in her, making it impossible to stand still. Just as she had responded to Edmund Burke, she explained, she pictured writing her treatise in response to Prince Talleyrand of France. Earlier that year, Talleyrand had published a pamphlet proposing a new tier of education for his country. He had argued that a girl's education should remain no more than what was needed to prepare her for domestic pursuits. "Someone needs to counter his message, to seek justice for half the human race."

"Absolutely brilliant. I shall await what you have to say with great anticipation. With all that is happening in France, the timing is perfect." Mr. Johnson leaned back, resting his arms on his chair. "By the way, I'm glad you stopped in. I'm hosting a dinner in a few weeks for Thomas Paine. He specifically requested to meet you."

The invitation honored Mary. Thomas Paine was one of the most famous voices for liberty in Europe. "What interest would he have in me?" After spending years supporting the revolution in America, Paine had returned to England and was now supporting the French commoners.

"He believes the two of you have much in common."

"I suppose we do." The prior March, Paine had published his own response to Burke just months after hers. His *Rights of Man*, a title close to her own *A Vindication of the Rights of Men*, had set off a volley of verbal attacks between him and Burke.

"He's working on part two to *Rights of Man*," Mr. Johnson said.

"And no doubt further irritating the British government."

"To say the least."

"I suppose I'm working on part two as well," Mary said. "I look forward to our encounter. But I haven't said all that I came here to say."

Mr. Johnson tipped his head. "Oh?"

"My name must be on anything I write now and going forward, including my new treatise."

"Are you sure?"

"I've never been more certain. I'm through being anonymous."

Sitting next to Thomas Paine two weeks later at one of Mr. Johnson's weekly dinners, Mary used the corset-maker-turned-journalist's effusive praise for her *A Vindication of the Rights of Men* to avoid fretting over whether Fuseli would show. She had been keeping one eye on the door for him since she had arrived half an hour prior. Mary had not seen him in weeks. Fuseli was always at the Royal Academy. That she longed for his presence bothered her, but it did nothing to lessen her desire to see him.

"Even Mrs. Fuseli complains of my inattention," he had told Mary at dinner at his house the last time she had seen him. "I shall use the same defense I offered to her. My new duties at the Academy leave me less time for friends."

Mary turned to Mr. Johnson's guest. "I must applaud your rebuttal to Burke. I respect anyone who is pro-revolutionary, but your views of the events in France as a new era for enlightened people especially inspire me. I couldn't agree more with you."

"Burke's piece was nothing but theater," Paine said. "It's you who deserves applause. Your rebuttal was the first."

Paine's brown hair was thin and frizzy, tied at the back with a narrow strip of leather, but where his hair made him look like a man in constant disarray, his eyes, imbued with single-minded resolve, made him seem even more formidable than his reputation. His words were spare, but Mary quickly noted how such plain and direct speech could set men and women on fire. *These are the times that try men's souls*, he had written in his pamphlet, *The Crisis*, that spread through the colonies like wildfire shortly after he had written *Common Sense*. She would never think of the words in the same way again after having met the author who helped fan the flame of the American Revolution and traveled with the Continental Army.

Mr. Johnson stood and clinked his knife against his wineglass. By now, guests occupied all the seats. Sans Henry Fuseli.

"To our friend, Thomas Paine." The table turned quiet, and Mr. Johnson raised his glass to the honored guest. "Sir, may you persist in advocating for freedom, inspiring those who yearn for liberty and are ready to battle against their oppressors."

As huzzahs threatened to lift Mr. Johnson's sagging ceiling, Mary spied a man with a dimple on his chin staring at her from across the table. When their eyes met, his face turned a steely red, and he looked away. Restless wisps of brown hair curled down the sides of his face like unruly vines sprouting from his thinning crown. If it were not for his dour face and brooding eyebrows, they would have given him an eager, if not casual, look. Mary had met him somewhere but could not recall. At the Kendalls? She combed her mind for a name, but none came.

"Your opposition to monarchies in *Rights of Man* resonates with a great many at this table," she said, turning her attention back to Paine. "Though I pray Pitt doesn't put you in jail." Just as Paine's confrontation with Burke was heating up, Britain's prime minister was threatening stronger punishments for those expressing anti-government sentiments.

Paine twisted his face upon hearing Pitt's name. "I'll be in France before he makes up his feeble mind."

At this slight against the prime minister, laughter erupted at the table. Neither Paine's outspoken support for the colonists during America's War of Independence, nor calling King George a brute in public, had garnered him any favors with his own government.

Rowland and Betsy Hunter entered with trays of bowls of mutton stew they passed down the table, followed by fresh bread from which men tore off chunks. The men's praise for the bread's tantalizing aroma put a humble smile on Betsy's face. Soon, the clatter of spoons clinking against pewter echoed in the room, all ears tuned to Paine's voice. It was him the men came to hear.

Mary, however, could not stop directing questions at him in rapid succession. Her mind was on France. What was his opinion on the National Assembly? What of Lafayette, who had resigned from the National Guard after the incident at the Champs de Mars, where fifty demonstrators were killed or wounded? Afterward, martial law had been declared in France. What would happen now?

The longer Paine and Mary exchanged views, the less Fuseli occupied Mary's thoughts, and she relaxed into enjoying Paine's enthusiasm for the rights of individuals. He stirred in Mary her own determination to see liberty more widespread in Europe by indulging her, answering with stunning insight the barrage of questions that continued to spring from her.

"I see you have capitulated to Miss Wollstonecraft's irresistible spell," John Bonnycastle said to Paine, after slurping a final spoonful of stew. "She adds a certain flavor to our dinners. Brevity may be the soul of wit, but when it comes to her, we want her to be anything but brief."

Mary chuckled at Bonnycastle's uncanny ability to quote Shakespeare, no matter what the topic, but realized she had been dominating Paine's attention and apologized to Paine and the others.

"I have no objections to your questions," Paine said to her. "I cannot recall having a more pleasant dinner partner. Please, go on."

The surly man across the table released an audible sigh, a clear sign he did not agree that Mary commanding all of Paine's focus was pleasant. Who did he think he was? Gingerbread arrived for dessert, and she shifted her questions to the problem of illiteracy among the masses. Once she did, the man, whose name escaped her, cleared his throat. She ignored him and explained to Paine that she had long been a proponent of education for boys—and girls—in day schools where society would educate them together. All funded by the public.

"In fact," Mary said, raising her voice so all the men at the table could hear, "I am shoulder-deep into a treatise on this very topic as well as other themes regarding women."

"Do tell," Paine said, refilling his and Mary's glasses with canary wine before passing the pitcher down the table.

"I'm ready to throw down my gauntlet." When Mary said this, all conversation at the table halted abruptly. "Truth must be common to all. If natural rights are God given, as asserted by the philosophers we at this table admire, are not all humans entitled to enjoy them? Is it not a sin for one segment of the population to deny them to another?"

Mr. Johnson masked an approving smile with his hand. He alone knew how furiously she had been writing for the past two weeks.

"I suppose you would have women rule men," the sulky man said, his irritation honed after watching Mary command Paine's attention for the entire evening. "Much like a queen rules her subjects."

Some of the men sniggered.

"Not at all," Mary replied to the man. "I do not wish for women to have power over men, only themselves. As for myself, I submit to no man, only reason." Her voice was calm. "Women have for too long been dependent on men. They have yet to know what they are truly capable of or to want more from their existence."

"Can it really that simple?" Dr. Fordyce asked, weighing Mary's words. "Reconsidering the status of women in England is a tall order, one that would require an extraordinary amount of mental elasticity—by both sexes, I might add— neither of which seem willing to depart from what works. Men have their ways, women have theirs, and a good many of both sexes are quite satisfied with things as they are."

"The animal is content because the cage is all it knows," Mary said with patience, for she knew that even among the most progressive, resistance to change was natural. It was easy for men to want more political power because they believed they had little to none already, harder for them to give up the power they had over women, which they enjoyed simply by being male. "What we have is a gap between reason and sentiment. We parcel everything so that men are associated with reason and women with sentimentality. Men should not have to dress up feeling with reason any more than women should have to dress up reason with feeling. No wonder men and women have difficulty understanding each other. I intend to propose a different set of ideals."

The glum man shifted in his seat, staring at the empty bowl in front of him while men at the table who knew Mary well plied her to elaborate. She demurred for the first time that evening, determined to keep the essence of her manifesto to herself until she finished it and would be ready for even the most blaring critics. For it was a declaration of all she believed put into a single book, to be read from beginning to end, to gain the full measure of her intent. "My book is a work in progress; I shan't say more, other than I intend to plead for my sex and others denied full liberty." She glanced at the moody man and resented when he refused to meet her gaze.

"I shall look forward to it with great anticipation," Paine said. "For all their lofty platitudes, America and France still deny women basic rights. Although I will say France has made strides. Women there are beginning to enjoy more liberties. I wish you nothing but success, Miss Wollstonecraft."

"I understand you are working on a second part to *Rights of Man*," someone said to Paine. Mary swung her glance across the table. It was the grim man again. "Can you pleasure us, Mr. Paine, with a preview of what flows from *your* pen these days?" he asked, ignoring her.

"Nothing so interesting as Miss Wollstonecraft's endeavor, Mr. Godwin."

William Godwin. That was his name. A journalist. His dislike for Mary was evident. She did not care for him either, having little time for such narrow thinkers. Men like him had much to learn about women.

At home that night, Mary wrote with searing conviction: *"The mind will ever be unstable that has only prejudices to rest on ... Women are told from their infancy,* *and taught by the example of their mothers, that a little knowledge of human weakness, justly termed cunning, softness of temper and <u>outward</u> obedience, and a scrupulous attention to a puerile kind of propriety, will obtain for them the protection of man; and should they be beautiful, everything else is needless, for at least twenty years of their lives ... How grossly do they insult us who thus advise us only to render ourselves gentle, domestic brutes!"*

EIGHT

1792

In January, Mr. Johnson published Mary's second and most important polemical work, *A Vindication of the Rights of Woman: With Strictures on Political and Moral Subjects*. In months, a second edition in English and translations in French and German were underway. Cartons were being shipped across Europe to places like Paris and Munich and to cities like Boston and Philadelphia in America.

The book's key themes were straightforward. She'd based them on the same principles she had been promoting for more than a decade: Society should educate women in a manner equal to men and give them the freedom to contribute to the betterment of society. As a solution, she called for state-sponsored, coeducational schools. Regarding a host of other commentaries—the rights of the individual, sexual character, the degradation of women, morality and virtue, parenting—she urged society to abolish the unequal nature of the relationship between men and women, most notably marriage, which should, she insisted, be more favorable for her sex. All were daring things to say.

Mary had written the book in just six weeks, a fleeting amount of time. Over eighty-seven thousand words! William Roscoe called her an intellectual Amazon. Even Fuseli conceded that she had written a text of educational and critical value.

After just five years in London, Mary had achieved her dream of being a self-sufficient woman making a living as a writer and living in a home of her own.

Why then was she so sad?

In the spring of 1792, she turned thirty-three and found herself unable to take pleasure in the positive reviews flooding London's periodicals. Endless blackness pressed upon her despite her successes. The streets of London were no longer wide and mysterious avenues ripe for conquering. Something was missing. By summer, Mary's strength of mind had disappeared, replaced with a deepening sorrow. Was it true what Fuseli had once said—that she desired nothing but wanted everything?

Boxed in, even when so much was open to her now, melancholy replaced Mary's days and blanketed her nights. She sought shelter at home, giving in to its darkness the way one gives over to a storm.

A rapid knock at the door woke Mary. Trying to shut the world out, she resented the intrusion. But the rapping was unrelenting. Her house servant must be at market, she thought, leaving only Mary to plod to the door when no visitor was welcome. It was mid-morning in her house on Store Street. She was still in her clothes from yesterday after not having slept. Most nights she laid awake, making it a struggle to get out of bed the next day. Constant fatigue and a persistent sadness, that lonely place she had learned to dread when it neared, continued to prevent her from enjoying any sort of productivity. Melancholy had been a frequent companion since childhood. She was used to how it made her feel, how it robbed her of contentment. Eventually it receded and she could go back to how her life was. This year, however, she had been unable to outrun it.

"Fuseli," she said, wishing she had a hat within reach to hide her uncombed hair. She shielded the sun with her hand, blinking at him. "What brings you out so early?" Her voice cracked.

The sun shone down on his silver hair, making it gleam to a level that sparkled. "On my way to the Academy." He glanced at the sky, then back at her, his eyes kind as though he was concerned about her, the same way Mr. Johnson stared at her as of late. A look of pity that she hated. "It's a lovely day. I thought you might enjoy a walk."

Although she must look a fright, Mary could not refuse him. "Wait here." She scrambled to locate her new bonnet, one she had purchased when trying to adopt a more modern look. Not finding it, she jammed the misshapen, artless straw hat that had replaced her beaver hat on her head and joined him on the stoop.

Neither said anything as they walked toward Bedford Square, the *tic toc* of Fuseli's walking stick on the cobblestone path the lone sound between them. The early days of August had coaxed London's flora into the peak of their bloom. When she and Fuseli reached the gardens, an intoxicating scent of alyssums, phlox, and impatiens enveloped them. Mary had not noticed anything as cheerful as the riot of petunias, verbena, and marigolds in months. They seemed to turn their heads toward her. She breathed, and her shoulders began to release the tension she had been holding tight.

Fuseli lowered himself onto a bench under a sweeping linden tree with branches that seemed to stretch a mile. "Mr. Johnson tells me you've not been yourself."

Mr. Johnson had sent him. Mary's elation at seeing Fuseli wilted like a cut bloom in a vase without water. Everything constricted again inside. "Is that so?" She positioned herself at the edge of the seat. Mr. Johnson had been inquiring about her health, stopping by several times a week to check on her.

"We all thought your recent success would please you," Fuseli said. "Instead, here you are, locking yourself away."

If Fuseli was there to cheer Mary up, he was making her feel worse. "I'm not a complete recluse. I sat for Opie." Another portrait request came to her after publishing *A Vindication of the Rights of Woman*, this time from the artist John Opie. She agreed to it. Mary had become friends with him and his wife. In the portrait, she wore a striped jacket, and he had positioned her reading a book at her desk, a pose usually reserved for male sitters. Beside her on the desk was a pen, the signature tool of a writer. After *Rights of Woman*, she had also received several odd marriage proposals from men she hardly knew, none of which she entertained, of course. The book had made her a minor celebrity.

"The creative process ... it can be fierce," he said, sounding as though he spoke from experience. His eyes roamed the gardens. "Enough to leave one depleted after finishing a major piece of work, an accomplishment such as your most recent book, for example." He turned his freshly shaved face to hers. "The mind was meant to create, to be in constant motion. Have you begun work on your next?"

Mary admitted she had not a single thought about what to write. "It requires all of my energy just to keep up with reviews and pamphlets." She and Fuseli continued to translate what was coming out of France.

The artist planted his cane in front of him and rested his hands on the handle. "You know how much I admire your talent."

Mary broke off a clump of linden flowers and held it to her nose. The creamy yellow star-shaped flowers' scent—honey and lemon peel—penetrated her, making her feel more alert. "If I am so talented, then why do you neglect me so?"

"I don't neglect you. We see each other quite frequently. What more do you want?"

"Your friendship." She sounded petulant, but there was no more honest way to answer his question.

He appeared surprised. "Surely you know you have it."

"And your passion," she said. She hated that seeing him had become like oxygen, a necessary thing for her to breathe in, to breathe out.

Fuseli appeared uncomfortable and looked out again across Bedford Square. "I'm a married man, Miss Wollstonecraft."

"You misunderstand me!" She threw the linden bloom to the ground. Her face felt hot. "I speak not of carnal desires."

He assumed a formal tone with her, one that put him at a distance. "You must take me as I am, my dear. What would you have me do, spend all my time with you?"

She would take him any way she could. "Your companionship is what I seek, to be in constant communication with you. Is it so much to ask?" A growing inferno toward him threatened to burn her to nothing but ashes. What did one do with such feelings? Who else brought out her intellect, her vigor, her enthusiasm for life?

"We shall spend time together in Paris. Possibly that will make things up to you, no?" In a late-night discussion in June, Mary, Mr. Johnson, and Fuseli had formulated plans for a six-week trip to Paris. Fuseli's wife, Sophia, would be joining them. Thomas Paine was a hero there after fleeing London mobs when he published the second part to *Rights of Man*.

"I look forward to nothing more," Mary replied, wishing she did not sound so eager. If only they could leave tomorrow. Instead, their travel party was to leave in a few weeks. It would have to do. Only Henry Fuseli seemed to bring joy to her existence. Time with him in France was sure to lift her from her melancholy.

"It's as if your fame astonishes and disappoints you in equal measure," Iris whispered.

Mary detected vexation in her friend's voice. They were at a concert at Hanover Square in October with Mr. Kendall and Thomas Holcroft, the tickets a gift from William Roscoe, for none of them could have afforded such luxury. The rise and fall of the orchestra's melody reverberated from the arched ceiling in the grand concert hall.

"What if it does?" Mary said, feeling mislaid next to men and women dressed in formal evening wear. She had been out so little it was as if she had forgotten how to act in such a refined setting. She hadn't even changed dresses for the performance.

"I've seen you feeling displaced before, but this time is different. You've written the most consequential text for women in the entire eighteenth century, yet you act as if it matters not."

"Literary satisfaction may be mine," Mary whispered back, sinking further into her seat, "but what reward is there when inside I feel adrift?" *Rights of Woman* continued to receive accolades, but such praise no longer lifted her spirits the way it had after Mary's work had first been published.

Iris leaned closer to Mary. "Talk about town is that you and Mr. Johnson married while in Berkshire."

Mary huffed and rolled her eyes. "Such gossip!" As planned, she and Mr. Johnson and the Fuselis journeyed to Dover on their way to Paris in August. Just before boarding the ferry to Calais, news that revolutionaries had attacked the

Tuileries Palace and were holding the royal family in the Temple prison exploded in the newspapers. France abolished its new Legislative Assembly, replacing it with the National Convention. Mr. Johnson and Fuseli deemed it unsafe to journey on. Nothing could have disappointed Mary more. The Fuselis returned to London. Mr. Johnson agreed to take a detour with Mary to Berkshire as a consolation.

"Of course, I ignored the rumor," Iris said, "but if I may be honest, when you have every reason to relish your success, you seem to prefer self-pity."

To Mary's relief, a woman in the seat ahead turned and glared at them through her lorgnette, a sign they were disturbing others. Mary and Iris silenced themselves.

Mary was glad it was dark so Iris could not see her struggling to avoid bursting into tears. The Bach concerto moved her, making the hall feel thick with mournfulness. Her life was missing something. She could not tell what it was, only that she was lonelier than she had ever been. A foreign restlessness roamed in her. No matter how hard she tried, she could not shake feelings of being lost, searching for but unable to identify what it was for which she longed.

The concert ended, and Mary and Iris stepped out into the brisk autumn air behind Mr. Kendall and Thomas Holcroft. The four began the walk to Mary's home. A raw, fitful wind whipped dead leaves around them, and Mary and Iris moved closer together for warmth.

Mary reached for her friend's hand. "I'm sorry to be so tiresome. I can't seem to shake this mood I'm in."

"I'm afraid we aren't much good to one another," Iris admitted, her own voice listless as they walked. Iris had thought herself with child in July, only for any sign to disappear within a very short time, leaving her bereft.

"I'm considering going to France," Mary said. "To write a series of letters from Paris regarding the Revolution." Still determined to experience the happenings in person, she had been discussing such a trip with Mr. Johnson. And it would take her away from London, where melancholy was keeping her mired in sadness and indecision. "The change would be good for me."

"You cannot be serious." Iris looked aghast. "Unrest has only deepened since August. They're talking about indicting the king, for heaven's sake."

"Which is exactly why I want to go. France is the center of the political universe right now. If they succeed in their quest for liberty, we'll all benefit."

"It's because of Fuseli, isn't it?"

Mary's gait stiffened, and she slowed her step. "Nonsense."

Iris eyed her from the side. "You worship him. I can see it."

"I've told you, it's not that way between us."

Iris stopped walking, her hand still holding Mary's, forcing Mary to halt and face her. "You're pining for a married man. You're the most intelligent woman I know. How can you so reduce yourself?"

Mary wanted to disappear into the shadows. She felt unreliable, unknown even to herself. Henry Fuseli had taken her over. He consumed her thoughts day and night. "I push against it," she said, her lips trembling, "but it presses back; it's become a force that devours me." Even now, Mary writhed inside just thinking of him.

"How deep is this affection?" Iris asked. Her tone shifted from upbraiding Mary to solicitude, not judgment, allowing Mary to let down her protective guard.

"There is a surge in me when he is near." Since Dover she had seen more of him and Sophia, dining even more often with them at their home where their constant welcome put her at ease with the couple. But it had confused her as well regarding her feelings for Henry Fuseli. Time spent with him intensified her affection. She was careening toward something improper and gripped Iris's hand tighter. "I don't know what to do."

"Are you in love with him?"

"In love? What does it feel like to be in love?" Mary did not recognize such emotions. "I only know that I cannot be."

"No, you cannot be in love with Henry Fuseli. But feelings left unchecked will continue to burn inside. You must acknowledge them. If I may say, you have denied any possibility of having feelings for a man beyond simple affection. Pushing them away, avoiding relationships, has kept you from acknowledging natural feelings. You desire more but refuse to acknowledge it."

"Aren't you the expert?" Who was Iris to lecture her?

"I don't pretend to be an expert, but I know love. You, however, are untutored regarding men, which leaves you vulnerable to things that can hurt you."

"Perhaps I'll take a husband in Paris and divorce when I tire of him. The Revolution has cast off rules of old. People do as they please. Even women." Mary was being flippant. She'd never take a husband.

"Perhaps you should. You make light of love, of the bonds of marriage, but I think you are desperate to love."

Mary's gaze dropped to the cobblestones. Romantic love stole from a woman—her identity, her ability to act in her best interest. Though Mary had seen happy couples, the Kendalls primary among them, the costs to a woman seemed too dear if she chose the wrong man. She thought of her sister Eliza, tied for life to Meredith Bishop, but living alone in Wales with no future. She thought of her mother. Better not to choose at all.

Iris lifted Mary's chin with a gloved finger. "Your desires should not embarrass but empower you. Life without love would be a mistake. Love is a bond with the world, as well as the self. It is natural for an enlightened woman like you to desire this inner knowing, even if you are not yet aware that you do. By loving, we become a deeper, more illuminated individual."

"How wise you now sound." Iris had given herself over to love, whereas Mary had not.

"If I may take my boldness in advising you further," Iris said, "I don't think it is love you feel for Henry Fuseli. What you feel is infatuation. Be careful. Strong attraction can imprison a woman in something worse. Infatuation, especially in your case, has nowhere to go."

Iris was right. Mary was falling into the same trap into which countless other women had fallen. She must not succumb to her fondness, this fixation with Fuseli—for that was what it was, a fixation. Her relationship with Fuseli was a meeting of minds, nothing more.

In early December, Mary arrived for tea at the home of the Fuselis at the appointed hour. In their parlor, Mary found Sophia dressed in a cream-colored mantua with tiny blue flowers. "Please, sit." Sophia motioned to a red velvet side chair. The room was lit with candles, as dusk was upon them. Elegant oil lamps with floral designs painted on their chimneys scattered flickers of light on mustard-colored walls. An open book lay on the table next to Sophia. *A Vindication of the Rights of Woman*. Alongside her book Mary recognized Thomas Holcroft's *Anna St. Ives* and *Vancenza* by Mary Robinson, the English Sappho. Sophia seated herself on her settee, across from Mary.

"Will Mr. Fuseli be joining us?" Mary asked, glancing around the room. All day she had been eagerly anticipating time with her friend and mentor.

"He sends his apologies. He's been detained."

Mary asked Sophia if she liked *Rights of Woman*, not relinquishing the hope that Fuseli would show later, but it occurred to her she and Sophia had never discussed Mary's writing in any great detail, and Mary eagerly anticipated doing so. Henry Fuseli was always present when Mary had ever spent time with Sophia, drawing all the attention upon himself. Now, it was just the two of them.

"You've done a great service to our sex," Sophia said. She smiled, and Mary noted how elegant she appeared. Was that what had captivated Fuseli, a woman's ability to be cultured and mannered, refined, versus Mary's tendency to be direct and forceful? Mary had often found reserved women tedious, yet Sophia was not tiresome; she exhibited nothing but grace and poise.

Tea was served, and they talked amiably for over an hour about Mary's book, about its wide distribution, its potential to shift thinking about women, all of which Sophia supported. The easy nature of their exchange reminded Mary how much she enjoyed Sophia's company after spending so much time with her and Fuseli over the past few months. Her frequent interactions with the couple eased her loneliness.

"Conversation with you delights me," Mary said, feeling better, no longer regretting Fuseli's absence. "I've often thought how wonderful it would be if we lived together, the three of us. You, me, and Mr. Fuseli."

Sophia's movements froze, and she stared at Mary, a sudden iciness in her eyes.

A silence deep as the darkest part of night descended upon the room. Mary regretted her foolish words. She had not meant to say them. Or had she? *No!* Her voice betrayed her thoughts. Living with the Fuselis was not something she would have dared to actually suggest. It was a fleeting thought that entered her mind on occasion, nothing more. Now that she had said the words, she was mortified and had no way of taking them back.

"I didn't really mean it. I know us living together would be impossible," Mary rushed to add, an attempt to gloss over what she had done.

Sophia remained silent, glaring at Mary.

"You must forgive me. It's that we get along so well, you see," Mary continued, words spilling from her as if a dam had burst. "The bond we share and our exclusive attachment provoke such foolish thoughts in me." Mary chattered on, the air between them thickening. The more she tried to bury her lack of good judgment, the more ridiculous she sounded. Not even a laugh from her thawed the coldness that had seeped into Sophia. Her eyes bore into Mary until Mary wanted to slink beneath the chair into which she could feel herself burrowing.

Within days, the talk around town was that Mary had proposed a *ménage à trois* with the Fuselis. It was Iris who visited Mary's house to deliver the ugly news.

"I proposed no such thing!" Mary's heart almost bolted from her chest. The thought of a ménage à trois was vile. "Mr. Kendall must defend me!"

"I don't see how he can," Iris said, as agitated as Mary. She paced Mary's parlor. "A lie, once it spreads, is impossible to contain. Especially one like this. The public loves anything salacious. And Fuseli is an influential man, known for his sexual exploits. He's been bragging about your attraction to him for years."

Mary collapsed on her sofa, her face in her hands. "Why would he do such a thing?" Fuseli was her friend, someone who cared about her well-being. Surely he knew what harm such a rumor could do to her reputation. What purpose did such wickedness serve?

For the next hour, Iris tried to console her, but Mary knew once a woman's virtue was questioned, there was no way to counter it. Not when it involved matters pertaining to intimacy. "I must see Mr. Johnson. Only he can make this right."

Iris and Mary trudged to the Churchyard through slush. The day was frigid; the sky could not decide whether to snow or rain as Mary held back tears. At the door to No. 72, Iris signaled her departure. Mr. Kendall was waiting for her, she said. She ran a finger across Mary's forehead and down her cheek, the tender touch between friends. "This shall pass, dear friend. Do not lose hope. You are loved and known by many who will readily attest to your virtue."

"A thousand people could speak in my favor, but one lie cancels all testimony to the contrary. You were right. I've been naïve and foolish about Henry Fuseli." Mary was raging inside at him, angrier at herself for giving him the tools to discredit her.

She found Mr. Johnson in his dining room. He, too, had heard the claim. From Fuseli himself. The conversation with Mr. Johnson was awkward at best. He did not see how he could stop Fuseli from saying whatever he wished to whomever he wished. Nor did he seem willing to get involved.

"I don't doubt your side of things, nor your sincerity," he said, looking troubled, his face reddening. He seemed unsure who to protect—his friend of twenty years or Mary. "What is it you want? I do not question your virtue, but it is not my place to meddle in affairs between others."

Mary could see she was getting nowhere with him. Ever the diplomat. Always the man behind the scenes. She wandered to the fireplace, where a fire crackled. In her haste, she had forgotten to bring her reticule and had no handkerchief in her pocket. No longer conscious of or caring about decorum, she wiped her dripping nose with her sleeve. "Is the offer for me to go to Paris to write about the Revolution still open?"

"If it is your wish," he said. He got up, his chair scraping across the wooden floor, and offered her a worn but clean and pressed handkerchief. Standing together, they stared at the fire in the room where Mary's writing began. The stack of logs collapsed, sending sparks flying. He clasped his hands behind his back. "If you go, you must promise me you will be careful. It's dangerous there. Especially for a woman traveling alone."

Did Mr. Johnson not see how equally dangerous it was for Mary to stay in London, where her reputation was on the line?

Two days later, Mary placed a clean sheet of foolscap in front of her. Nothing was left for her in London except whispers and suspicious looks that made her feel under subtle but constant attack. She was living in a glass house, her intentions to be close friends with the Fuselis mutilated by Henry Fuseli's debauched notions. For all Mary's lofty ideals, England was still a world controlled by mores and conventions that held her sex hostage. In France, where revolution was underway, Mary would be free.

Dear Mr. Johnson,

My wayward heart creates its own misery. Why I am made thus I cannot tell. We must each of us wear a fool's cap; but mine, alas, has lost its bells and has grown heavy. I find it intolerably troublesome.

But I have made a decision. I intend to leave for Paris at once, where I will, as we discussed, write my observations and send them to you to publish in the Analytical Review. I shall not now halt at Dover, I promise you. For as I go alone, neck or nothing is the word.

—M.W.

PART II

Revolution

1792–1795

*"My blood runs cold, and I sicken at thoughts of a
Revolution, which costs so much blood and bitter tears."*

Mary Wollstonecraft
Letter to a friend (1795)

NINE

December 1792
Paris, France

At nine o'clock in the morning on December 26, the slow beat of a lone drum pierced the eerie silence. Mary watched from her second-story room as the coach carrying King Louis XVI passed below her window on the way to his trial. The hotel she had arranged as her residence in Paris was located on rue Meslée in the prestigious Marais district and was in proximity to Le Temple, where the royal family had been imprisoned since August.

Along the street, people flocked to their windows to observe the spectacle from the thin security of their homes. The strained look on their faces and the solemn expressions of the national guards surrounding the coach made her shiver. For the past eleven days, the king had been on trial at the National Convention. Today marked the beginning of his defense. If found guilty, he most assuredly would be executed. Anarchy would likely follow. If set free, those opposing the monarchy would revolt against their fellow Frenchmen.

Now that Mary was in Paris where she would act as a sort of reporter, writing a series of letters she and Mr. Johnson had agreed to for the *Analytical Review*, objectivity seemed harder to muster. The sight of a man being taken to a trial which everyone expected would lead to his death made her uneasy despite her relief over the French monarchy's end. Following intense debate, the National Convention abolished the monarchy the previous autumn, coinciding with the previous visit she had attempted with Mr. Johnson and the Fuselis.

Mary sneezed into her handkerchief. She had been in France for two weeks, bedridden the entire time by a debilitating head cold. Up close, the reality of the sacrifices necessary to form a democratic republic was unsettling. Disturbed by what she had just witnessed and unable to stop circling the room, she draped her coverlet around her shoulders before cleaning a space on the small desk in her room. After sharpening her quill pen, she began a letter for the *Analytical Review*. Her fingers, numb from the cold, paused her pen from scraping across the page only long enough to replenish her ink.

... The nascent French government was trying to exercise a new order, a new way of operating as a country of self-ruled men ...

... It had yet to find its way ...

... The movement was far from victorious ...

... The Ancien Régime had been in place since the Middle Ages. Discarding it wiped away centuries of law and tradition ...

Mary's pen stopped mid-sentence. Depending on the outcome of the king's trial, what happened when the old laws no longer ruled a nation? Who would govern France until a new body was established to enforce laws? Would pursuing the common good prevail, or would power corrupt the few in charge? These were the questions that burned in France.

And what of the king and his family?

The doomed monarch's face haunted Mary all day, forcing her to halt her writing. That evening, twice, she saw eyes glaring at her through a glass door to her balcony. Later, when Mary turned in for the evening, she imagined bloody hands outside her window. She dared not snuff out her candle.

"Now that your health has improved, you must explore the city," Madame Aline Filliettaz said the next day at breakfast, going out of her way to extend Mary a belated welcome. Madame Filliettaz and her husband owned the hotel and had only returned the prior evening after spending Christmas with his family in Marseilles. Madame Filliettaz's mother was headmistress at the school where

Mary's sister Eliza had taught in Putney, making Aline Filliettaz a fellow expatriate. She was similar in age to Mary. Around them, a brazen sun streamed through windows framed by colorful red and white floral chintz curtains. The room boasted an ample use of gilt filigree on every wall and cornice. Overhead, a polished, dark-beamed, coffered ceiling enriched the atmosphere, as did gleaming white tablecloths. Most of the tables in the hotel's dining room were empty, however. With all the uncertainty swirling about, few foreigners were visiting Paris. Most had already fled.

"One of my servants will drive you," Madame Filliettaz insisted when Mary told her she planned to visit Thomas Christie, who had left for France at the beginning of the Revolution and stayed. "What time shall I arrange for your departure?"

Mary helped herself to an omelet stuffed with herbs and vegetables, available only because the hotel had its own chickens and kitchen garden. Food otherwise was scarce. "That won't be necessary. I prefer to find my own way."

Madame Filliettaz's hand flew to her neck, and she let out a gasp. "You must not go alone. The streets are not safe!" She patted multiple layers of ivory lace cascading down the front of her peach-colored pouter-pigeon dress, tapping her fingers rapidly.

"Trust that I will be fine." Mary was used to roaming about London on her own. Traveling on foot would help her capture the essence of what was unfolding in the city. She could not unearth such details from a cab.

"As you wish," Madame Filliettaz said, her worry unresolved. She patted her lace with more force. "Refrain from speaking English in public, especially when without companions. Those sans-culottes are malevolent! They will accuse you of being a noble. Or a spy. Ignore them." She narrowed her eyes. "They are nothing but commoners. If they shake a pike at you, steer clear. They are itching for a fight."

Mary's fork stopped halfway to her mouth. "I shall pay heed." Her attempt to enjoy a rejuvenating morning after being limited to her hotel room for weeks was off to a poor start. She tried to push aside the inkling of dread that Madame Filliettaz had unleashed by asking what route she might recommend.

Within the hour, a new red cloak she had purchased for the trip clasped over her shoulders, Mary trod along rue Meslée with directions tucked into her pocket.

The winter in France had been harsh thus far, and a rush of frigid air spiraled beneath her skirt. Stepping with care to avoid patches of ice, she craned her neck, taking in the lovely French architecture. For the first few blocks, Paris was as she had imagined, quaint and sophisticated. Snow-topped roofs pitched at sharper angles than those in England, and tall second-story windows arched, compared to the squared-off windows she was accustomed to seeing. To her surprise, however, familiar Baroque influences like those in England were visible.

She looked forward to seeing Thomas Christie. And his new wife. When he first moved to Paris, he had taken a married French woman as a mistress and fathered a child with her. Sexual taboos no longer applied to free, revolutionary France. He was doing what everyone else was doing, he had told Mary. Instead of waiting for his mistress to divorce, however, he had up and married Rebecca Thomson, an English expatriate living in Paris, and joined her family's lucrative carpet business while still keeping a hand in the *Analytical Review*.

Closer to the city center, Mary slowed her step. A foreboding permeated the thick wool of her cloak. She placed her handkerchief over her nose to stave off the penetrating odor of garbage and dung littering the streets as vandalized buildings with deep gashes in their walls replaced residential houses. Graffiti oozed like bleeding wounds on defaced signs. Sans-culottes indeed strutted about, standing out like peacocks in their blue *carmagnoles* and striped pantaloons or plain trousers, protests against the silk knee-breeches preferred by the nobles and the bourgeoisie. Blue and red liberty cockades pinned to the sans-culottes *bonnets rouges* were yet another indication of the new freedoms the commoners had claimed. Further on in a public square, statues of the Bourbon monarchy lay scattered like dead criminals.

A feeling of wanting to turn back pressed at Mary. Determined to travel on, she avoided eye contact with anyone and kept her head down, scanning the area and keeping a proper distance from the sans-culottes. But as the streets narrowed, there was little room to maneuver. She slipped in behind a family to make herself less conspicuous in her red cloak.

Despite her efforts to blend in, fishmongers and fruit sellers shoved goods at her, desperate to make a sale. She shook her head at each of them. When one woman dressed in brown homespun lunged at her, Mary hastened away and left the family behind, her hands shaking, her breath coming in shallow gasps.

Men's shouts erupted from behind, and she pulled into an alcove where she pressed her back against a wall to hide herself. A band of sans-culottes ran past her in pursuit of a shabbily dressed man, their wooden shoes clacking like gunfire against the cobblestone. The wind carried their words away, making it impossible to make out what they said, but she could tell they were taunting him. About to step out and defend the man, Mary froze. Her stomach capsized when the sans-culottes caught the man and began clubbing him.

The commoners' fight for freedom looked glorious from London, but the sans-culottes' revolutionary justice Mrs. Filliettaz had warned her about produced a different, haunting picture that would forever remain imprinted on Mary's mind. Parisians' drained and dirty faces warned of a hunger for something more than food. Their desire for revenge against a class of people who had oppressed them for centuries lingered like smoke on a scorched landscape. The sans-culottes left the man crumpled and bloodied on the street.

Mary ran to help him. "Are you all right?" she asked in French.

His eyes were wild with fright. "Non!" He covered his head with his arms and kept shouting, "Non!"

When she tried again to address him, the man fled. She stared after him, her heart beating like a hunted rabbit's. She quickly went on her way.

"You walked all the way here by yourself?" an incredulous Mr. Christie asked upon her reaching his charming rococo-style house made of stucco on the other side of the city center. "Why didn't you hire a cabriolet?"

Mary handed her cloak to the butler, her heart still threatening to break out of her chest. "I needed the exercise." She would hire one on the way home, she said, relieved to have arrived without being accosted. "What had the man done wrong?" she asked when she recounted what had just occurred on the street.

"Probably nothing. Welcome to revolutionary Paris."

His tone was wry, nothing like the young man who had packed his bags for Paris nearly four years prior to marvel at the spectacle of a nation determined to redefine and redistribute political power. A new reality appeared to have taken root in him. He was businesslike and led her through light, airy rooms that intimated a carefree aristocratic lifestyle she would not have expected of the egalitarian Mr. Christie. The click of her boots on the tiled floor sounded invasive in the quiet, serene atmosphere surrounding her. When they reached a spacious library with fine paintings and fashionable furniture arranged against a palette of pastel colors, she noted to Mr. Christie how the house reflected modern, secular tastes. As if apologizing for the splendor, he explained that the home belonged to his wife's parents.

"You remember Rebecca?" he said.

An exuberant, tawny-haired woman rose from the sofa. Mary had met Rebecca the previous summer in London prior to the Christies' nuptials.

Bustles had replaced French panniers and hoops, slenderizing Rebecca's tall figure. "Your reputation precedes your arrival. All of Paris is eager to meet the English intellectual." She reached for Mary's hands and kissed the air alongside her cheeks.

Mary would have liked to probe deeper into what Rebecca meant by calling her the English intellectual, but Mr. Christie wasted no time and led her to a table flanked by ferns and arching palms in ornate cache pots next to a window.

"I'm glad you're here," he said, pausing as a maid poured steaming coffee. "Your task is to chronicle the unfolding Revolution in real time. You'll have to work quickly. New developments are occurring at a rapid rate."

Mary wrapped her hands around her cup to warm them. Sunlight sank into her down to her bones, thawing her, as she listened to Mr. Christie describe in detail the current situation regarding the Jacobin Club, members of the bourgeoisie. There was growing friction between its two leading factions: the Girondins and the Montagnards. Mary knew the Girondins represented the moderate wing; the Montagnards were radicals demanding speedier reforms.

"The Montagnards want a complete end to the monarchy. Now," he said. "They've aligned themselves with the sans-culottes, giving them power in sheer numbers."

"And the outcome of the king's trial?" Mary asked, thinking back to the expressionless king reduced to riding in a tumbrel.

"All but determined."

Sorrow for the king rose again in Mary. She was no monarchist, but she loathed violence, even when it was against a king, and she wondered if any society could engineer a peaceful revolution. She had to believe it could. What hope remained for democracy if nations could only attain it through violence?

"The Girondins still hold the upper hand," Mr. Christie said, "but it remains anyone's guess how long they will be able to sustain their position if the king is executed. They wish to negotiate a peaceful, democratic solution with the Montagnards, but the possibility is growing more doubtful by the day. The Montagnards would have killed the king outright by now."

He sounded ominous. The sense of dread that had planted itself at breakfast with Mrs. Filliettaz wended deeper within. It was one thing to support a movement; it was another to find oneself in the thick of it. Mary wondered whether she had given her decision to come to France proper consideration. The rule of law seemed especially important right now, and by all accounts, a sense of order was evaporating. Despite being a hated monarch, the king remained a human being. Would he be tried fairly? Or was the trial a sham?

"Have you seen the guillotine?" Rebecca asked from the sofa where she was reading a book while Mary and Mr. Christie conducted their meeting. She had strawberry-colored cheeks and faint, bewitching freckles. In her fetching green, low-necked gown, her earnest expression reminded Mary how young Rebecca was, not over twenty by her recollection. "They say it is a more humane way to execute a person, but I see nothing humane about it."

"I've not seen it," Mary said, her shoulders shuddering, "only illustrations." The image of an angled blade slicing off people's heads had a way of making a lasting impression.

"I'm afraid you've come to Paris just as things are reaching a fever pitch," Mr. Christie said, as if sensing Mary's trepidation over being in France. "No one can predict where this is going. The commoners still have no relief. Numerous men are vying for power. We must report to the outside world as much as possible. Things are likely to escalate any minute." He handed her a sheet of paper. "Here is a list of contacts, people you should affiliate with if you can. They are close to what is going on behind the scenes at the National Convention. I'm hoping your reputation as an author will allow you to earn their trust."

Mary scanned the list and recognized a handful of names, influential people she had read about. It would not be easy to break into their exclusive ranks.

"Helen Maria Williams is hosting a party at her home this weekend for you to meet some of the people on the list," he said. "She's a fellow countrywoman from England. Johnson says you know her."

Mary nodded. She had read Williams' book *Letters from France* last year. The *Analytical Review* had found it favorable. She was planning to call on her. The possibility of seeing a friendly face lifted her dampened spirits.

"Come to the party with us," Christie said. "And I must warn you, no more wandering the streets alone. I want you safe when you're here."

Mary did not argue when, at the close of their visit, he called for a cabriolet for her. While he did, Mary wondered how she was going to stomach daily demonstrations of violence.

Mary steadied herself on Christie's arm while Rebecca graced his other when they arrived at Helen Maria Williams's party the following week. In Dublin Mary had often attended politically charged gatherings hosted by Lord and Lady Kingsborough, who regularly held parties with dignitaries and citizens on the leading edge of Irish politics. But in Ireland, they spoke English, even if it was marked by brogues with pronunciations sometimes hard to render. Here Mary hoped her French would be passable. Her academic mastery did not match the nuanced expressions of native speakers. In conversations with the maids at the Filliettaz's, she struggled to grasp their complete message.

Helen Maria Williams could command a room with the bat of an eyelash. She held her guests under a spell as, with the sleekness of a lioness, she approached Mary and the Christies. The attractive writer, poet, and expatriate had a reputation for using her pen with blunt force to get her way. She was also an outspoken proponent of the French Revolution.

"We shared a mentor in Reverend Price," Helen said to Mary when she and Helen's acquaintance was reestablished through the exchange of pleasantries. Her voice was deep and sultry, a match for her dark eyes. "His death almost destroyed me. I can't believe it's been two years."

Mary agreed their loss was acute. The sublime melody of a string quintet in the far corner of the room added a note of nostalgia. Reverend Price had died just months after the second edition of Mary's *Rights of Men*.

Helen clasped Mary's hand. "He would be proud you traveled all this way when most people are too afraid to risk life and limb. Come, let me introduce you to men and women he would approve of."

In her honey-colored taffeta gown, Helen's curvaceous figure glistened in the contemporary apartment she shared with fellow Englishman John Hurford Stone. Helen and Stone were not married. Stone already had a wife stowed away in England. Helen did not seem to mind. She appeared to have adopted the French way of life—using wit and cynicism to great advantage. She pointed out to Mary one person of influence after another, whispering in Mary's ear their roles in French politics or the arts.

"So, you are to write while you are here?" Helen did not miss a step as she sashayed between glasses of champagne brimming from crystal stemware and edged past guests sampling food from a buffet of vegetables and roast meats and gravies. The tangy smell of cheeses and the tempting aroma of pastries whetted Mary's own appetite.

"My letters are to mark the Revolution's progress," Mary replied. "After several years, what changes have occurred? What's next in store? I'll also comment on happenings. If they execute the king—"

"If?" Helen faced her. "Think of it as when." She lowered her voice. "There are two important women for you to meet tonight." With an imperceptible nod, she motioned toward two couples behind her. "Do you see the man with a beaklike nose on the left? The Marquis Nicolas de Condorcet. Next to him, his wife, Sophie. The marquis is an advocate for women's suffrage, Sophie an accomplished salonnière."

Salons had evolved in France as a woman's sphere of influence and served as centers of intellectual and cultural conversation for men and women. As the person responsible for entertaining her guests, the woman of the house set the agenda and facilitated the conversation, affording her unusual leverage.

"And the second couple?" Mary asked.

"Madame Roland and her husband Jean-Marie Roland de la Platière." Helen shielded her mouth with her fan. "Madame Roland is also a distinguished salonnière. Both women are writers. Both husbands are influential Girondins who support Jacques Pierre Brissot."

Brissot. Based on Mary's reading, she knew Brissot was, perhaps, the most prominent Girondin leader.

"Madame Roland is her husband's most trusted advisor," Helen said, "making her a target of criticism for being an outspoken woman even though she says little in public. She believes women should play only a modest role in politics. However, when the men are meeting at her home, she sits nearby, pretending to read or do needlework. Do not be fooled. She is listening all the while. Her husband—and Brissot—seek her advice. She regularly contributes to their letters, bills, and speeches. No one, however, is to know she is helping them."

"What of Sophie?" Mary asked. She found the de Condorcets an odd-looking couple. Sophie had a mass of blonde hair and a handsome, petite face that rivaled Marie Antoinette's, whereas her husband was rotund and balding.

"Equally influential over her husband. Unlike Madame Roland, she *is* an advocate for the political rights of women and *does* invite women to her salons. You will want to secure an invitation as quickly as possible."

"You must call me Sophie," Madame de Condorcet said when Helen introduced Mary to her. She wrapped her small-boned hands around Mary's in a firm grip. "*A Vindication of the Rights of Woman*, oui?"

Her warm welcome took Mary by pleasant surprise. "You are familiar with my work?"

"When a woman writes such bold ideas, the world takes notice. I welcome you to my salon so we may explore your words together. I will be sure to invite Olympe de Gouges. She is my friend and frequent guest."

Mary tried not to gush. She had long admired de Gouges, the French playwright, activist, and author of the *Declaration of the Rights of Woman and the Female Citizen*. "An honor, certainly." De Gouges' visceral response to France's National Constituent Assembly's 1789 *Declaration of the Rights of Man and of the*

Citizen, which ignored the rights of women, had, like Mary's *A Vindication of the Rights of Woman,* gained international attention.

Sophie asked Mary what she planned to do while in Paris.

Mary informed her that she had been assigned to write about the Revolution for a London journal.

"Make sure this is wise," Madame Roland interjected, her white fichu gleaming against her black dress. She surveyed the room, searching for spies, it seemed, before locking her sober gaze with Mary's. "Take care what comes from your pen. Danger lurks when a woman speaks her mind. Especially in Paris, where there are many sides." Contempt crept into her voice. "It wasn't always this way. Now anyone's words can—and will, I fear—be held against them."

Mary's cheeks turned warm with embarrassment. How inexperienced she must appear to Madame Roland, waltzing into a foreign country to write about its war against itself.

Sophie de Condorcet pulled Mary to the side and whispered in her ear. "Pay heed to what Madame Roland says. Helen and I shall advise you on what to say. And what to avoid." It was as though Sophie and Helen had already discussed how to assist Mary in her mission.

"Will the Montagnards eventually take over the National Convention?" Mary asked. The question had plagued her since her first conversation with Mr. Christie. Their leadership appeared devoid of any potential benefits.

Sophie peered behind her before answering and kept her voice private between them. "Their hostility grows. They are shutting down salons, resorting to violence for their demands. They've taken their message to the lower classes, the poor and less educated, who are easy to manipulate, allowing the Montagnards to fuel animosity towards the middle class and intellectuals, claiming they are the people's true enemies."

"And if the Montagnards succeed in gaining power?"

Sophie's pained expression told Mary all she needed to know. France would turn on itself, jeopardizing everything people like the Condorcets and the Rolands had been working so hard to achieve in the name of liberty. "Listen for the names Maximilien Robespierre and Georges Danton. You must be careful. They are increasingly suspicious of British liberals who support the Girondins; we don't want you becoming their target."

Nor did Mary want to get caught in French crossfire. Robespierre was a French lawyer doing his best to emerge as the Jacobin leader. He pretended to represent the people, but many saw him as too radical. A near-religious fury emanated from his speeches.

"Birds of a feather already flocking together," said a voice Mary recognized. She spun on her heel to find Thomas Paine grinning at her. "I wondered how long it would take before you joined us."

The radical was a welcome sight. "Were it not for you," Mary laughed, "I'm not sure I would have had the courage to come to Paris!" They spoke as though they had seen one another the day before. She caught him up on the news from London, while he filled her in on Paris and what she could expect, given the current state of affairs.

Nothing could have made her evening more complete. Mary's arrival in a foreign land had not started out easily. But seeing the face of someone she admired, reuniting with Helen Maria Williams, and meeting two very important women suggested things were finally pointing in the right direction. That night, she wrote to Iris, who had sent her a letter to say that she missed Mary.

Mary's pen danced across the page.

My dear Iris,

I was much gratified by your kind letter. It was good of you to write. Though I would wish rather to talk with you than write. All the affection I have for the French is for the whole nation, and it seems to be a little honey spread over the bread I eat in their land. I am almost overwhelmed with civility here ...

TEN

April 1793
Four months later

France proved to be the fresh start Mary needed. Her faux pas with the Fuselis became a distant memory when she found herself a celebrity all over again in Paris for her writing. A new set of people considered her a revolutionist for both her *Vindications*. Her status as their author gained her entry into distinguished political gatherings and salons. Sophie de Condorcet even asked her to propose an education plan to submit to the National Convention.

The fight for power shifted daily between the Girondins and the Montagnards, like moves in a chess game where the pawns were the French citizens. Even Mary, a reporter with keen perception and a quick grasp of nuances in discussions and policy statements, struggled to keep pace with the changes. Mary's prior writing also marked her. How long would she be safe in Paris? The Convention had formed a Committee of Public Safety to act as a war council, its primary goal to defeat the new Republic's enemies, both foreign and domestic. The Committee of Public Safety was the child of Danton, a powerful Montagnard pushing for a Revolutionary Tribunal to stamp out counter revolutionaries.

Reacquainting herself with Thomas Paine, who was now a rebellious leader in France, further directed attention on Mary as a foreign national. Paine was doing what he did best—stirring men's passions. He, too, had aligned with the Girondins, putting him in opposition with the Montagnards.

"I no longer want you using the regular mail delivery to send information to Mr. Johnson," Thomas Christie said, as the coach carrying him, his wife, and Mary arrived at rue du Faubourg-Saint-Denys to attend a salon Thomas Paine was hosting for Girondin sympathizers. Paine was renting a mansion once owned by Madame Pompadour. "There's talk of mail being censored. If the Montagnards muscle their way into taking over the National Convention, anyone opposed to them will be accused of plotting against the Revolution."

Before getting out, Christie scanned the darkened street lit only by lamps with pools of light extending to their bases, then the grounds of the mansion where more lamps blazed in the night, searching, it seemed, for nefarious activity. He had been silent the entire way, as if danger lurked at every turn.

"How shall I communicate with him if I cannot use the mail?" Mary asked, her body straining with attentiveness as she followed his example and surveyed the area for anything that might seem out of place. Sophie de Condorcet had warned them of an approaching shift in winds. Whose side one took in Paris was all anyone talked about these days. Were you a moderate or a radical? The other obvious question was whether one was a royalist.

"We'll have to rely on private couriers," Christie said. "There are enough people traveling between Paris and London for us to send information through them." His eyebrows drew together. "I cannot stress to you the importance of keeping your guard firm."

Trepidation nibbled at Mary. Out of concern for her safety, Mr. Johnson was urging her to return to London, and she wondered if she should. She had unwittingly taken a side in the factions dividing France. However, going home was not her desire. Not yet, she told herself as a coachman handed her out of the carriage. Danger was building, but Paris was just getting interesting. A stream of potential suitors had been vying for her attention ever since Helen's party, and Mary, the avowed spinster, admitted to liking it. Perhaps Iris had been right; perhaps Mary wanted romance in her life after all. Gustav von Schlabrendorf, a Count from Prussia and an Enlightenment thinker, had already professed his love to her.

In London Mary would have chased such men away, but in Paris, she found herself accepting their overtures. She had made the mistake of thinking her friendship with Henry Fuseli protected her from ever having to face romantic feelings. However, her affection for him woke something inside her she previously had refused to acknowledge. She now found herself yearning for affection in a way that would allow her to maintain her singlehood yet more fully enjoy the pleasures of male company. Her French counterparts were teaching her how. In Paris, love could be had without the usual strings attached. The notion thrilled and terrified her.

Inside the mansion, Mary took delight in watching Thomas Paine work the room in his dark blue waistcoat beneath a double-breasted red and white striped cotton tailcoat. Even clothes were playing a part in fostering a more egalitarian lifestyle in France. New fashions represented the watershed nature of the moment underway. Now anyone could buy fancy attire, not just royals and nobles. French men had also ousted wigs with the nobles and wore their hair closely cropped.

Approximately thirty guests had assembled in their silks and hats. Chairs for guests lined the perimeter, but almost everyone milled about. A table covered with a green velvet cloth holding a bronze candelabra—a leftover from Madame Pompadour, for it was not in keeping with Paine's populist tastes—held an array of meats and sweets. Dogs hoping for a stray morsel wedged their way between guests filling their plates. In one corner, men played a game of chess with others looking on.

Politicking in action.

As Paine had neither a wife nor a love interest, Helen had assumed the role as hostess and looked like an imperial topaz in her gold dress. Her skirt swished as she circled the room, making sure guests had refreshments. Passing Mary, she handed her a glass of champagne.

"Do you see that man behind me staring at you?" she whispered in Mary's ear.

Mary spotted a well-groomed man dressed in gentleman's clothing near a table replete with spirits. The crystal glass he held caught the flicker of a nearby candle. His eyes locked with hers. Gooseflesh prickled her arms and neck as her glance traveled to the dress Rebecca had talked her into borrowing from her for the evening, a burgundy cotton featuring a slim-fitting bodice trimmed with delicate lace, cut much lower than Mary would have selected for herself. The men gathered around Mr. Johnson's weekly dinner table would not recognize her. Along with her borrowed silk stockings and a pair of Rebecca's brocade shoes, the clothing made Mary feel elegant in a way she could not have dreamed would feel quite as good as it did with a handsome man gazing at her. She fingered an earbob dangling from her ear and wondered if the matching satin ribbons Rebecca's lady's maid had wound like vines through her upswept hair were still in place.

A moment later, the man was standing next to Mary and Helen.

"Mademoiselle Williams, might you be willing to introduce me to this lovely creature?" he asked Helen.

"Mademoiselle Wollstonecraft, I present Captain Gilbert Imlay."

Imlay bowed. "The famed author."

He had heard of Mary, then, or perhaps he had asked someone about her upon his arrival this evening. Either way, his knowledge of her as a writer flattered her, and she presented her hand. His accent marked him as being from the States. "An American, I presume?"

"Kentucky," he said, kissing her hand. "Have you heard of it?"

His voice had an unusually lustrous quality to it as if crafted by a master violin maker. "The frontier," Mary replied, tingling where his lips had grazed her skin.

Captain Imlay flashed a smile. "America's West. Where men's fortunes lie."

"Then I should think you are traveling in the wrong direction." Refined as he was, the way he looked at her décolletage made her wish she had worn a fichu. Never again would Mary allow Rebecca to dress her. She had to resist tugging up her bodice.

"Excuse me," Helen said, leaving Mary alone with the stranger.

"Your first salon?" Mary asked, searching for something other than her breasts to occupy his attention. She had her own difficult time not staring at his wavy chestnut hair, unbound and hanging to his shoulders, but ordered, showing at least part of him could behave itself.

"Not my first. *A Vindication of the Rights of Woman*, correct?"

"Indeed."

"I also read *A Vindication of the Rights of Men*. I'm a writer. Like you."

Mary had not met many Americans who had read both of her political works, a male no less, and an energy passed through her, a hope that he was a man of substance who surpassed others. On the surface he was handsome and articulate.

There were many handsome, articulate men in Paris, however. Captain Imlay struck her as a man of ideas.

"Last year I published my first book," he said, which he described as a topographical description of the Western Territory of North America based on his own explorations. Mary recognized the title. Several London periodicals had reviewed it. At the time, she had pictured the author as some rugged, lone man wandering the wilderness killing bears for food and subsisting on berries. The individual next to her was anything but rustic.

"You're an adventurer," she said, seeing him as someone who could feel equally comfortable in the wild and in a Parisian drawing room. "Or are you still a soldier, Captain Imlay?"

"Neither. I'm a businessman now. And I still write. I'm working on my second book, about an English family that emigrates to America and travels west to settle in Ohio Territory. If you read my draft, I think you would see that I share your sentiments regarding slavery. It's abominable. America needs to rethink who is free among men—and women." He swirled the liquid in his glass, peering into it as it revolved, then looked at Mary and added, "They should enjoy the same freedoms as men."

How quickly he had surprised her again. Most men did not think or express such sentiments, and she could feel her esteem for him rising. "Then you must hope the French are more judicious when it comes to women."

"You'll hear no argument from me."

"But why are you in Paris? You can write a book anywhere, and I doubt you're here to evangelize about women's equality."

He grinned. "I'm here to talk about America."

"At a time like this?" His mission seemed ill-timed. The French struggled without a functional government while its people faced dire food shortages. Bread lines ran for blocks.

"I must admit, things have taken a disturbing turn since the king's demise." Imlay glanced about the room. As expected, in January, the National Convention had found the king guilty of high treason and had executed him by guillotine.

"Will you try to be an influence?"

Captain Imlay harrumphed. "Hardly. I'm a businessman, remember? Though I'm here on a diplomatic mission. Will you return to London now that France is at odds with Great Britain?"

"When aren't they at odds?" The prior February, France had declared war on Great Britain, making British subjects enemies of the French overnight. Mary was in the middle of a war. A number of British expats were going home; those wanting to remain on the Continent were departing for places like Switzerland and Italy. "Though it certainly complicates things."

"Brave of you to stay."

The unbridled respect in his voice made Mary flush. His dark brown eyes took her in, and he listened with complete concentration as she spoke, making her feel he heard her as his equal. "I've considered leaving," she said, her voice catching. His attention made her conscious of each part of herself, aspects she never usually thought of—how she must look to him, what meaning he took from her words. Thus she chose what to say with care, lest she expressed a sentiment that might change the opinion of her that he had formed based on her writing. "I'm writing a book about the Revolution." Given the evolving tensions, Mary had abandoned the idea of a series of letters. It would not be safe to publish them. After spending time with Madame Roland and Sophie de Condorcet, it became clear that writing accounts of happenings in Paris could bring wrath upon Mary.

"You can write a book anywhere," he said, echoing her own words to him.

Mary smiled. "Touché." She decided against informing Captain Imlay of London's unsafe conditions for her. England was taking a hard line against anyone seen as a radical. Moving to France had lumped her together with people viewed as dangerous to the British Crown. Conservatives at home had branded her a dangerous revolutionary in two countries.

"Robespierre seems to be getting his way with more frequency. I'd be careful if I were you."

"The authorities here aren't paying attention to me," Mary said, trying to make light of Captain Imlay's warnings, which reminded her of the peril she was placing herself in by staying in Paris. With the recent change in mood, Mary's education plan had fallen by the wayside, and Sophie de Condorcet, Madame Roland, and Helen all had discontinued their salons in their homes out of fear of reprisal.

"That's not what I hear."

He intended caution, not flattery, and he was not wrong.

"I see Brissot is here," he said. "If you'll excuse me."

Captain Imlay left Mary standing alone, relieved to have a moment to herself. Helen came up behind her. "Well?"

"Well, what?" Mary had difficulty tearing her gaze from Captain Imlay.

Helen gave her a knowing look. "Someone finally has your attention."

"There'll be no conjecture from you." Mary stood on tiptoe to see Captain Imlay greet Brissot, who was surrounded by people.

"We'll see." Helen drifted to the door to greet the Rolands, who had just arrived on the heels of Brissot.

Under Helen's expert hand, Thomas Paine's salon soon was underway. Mary took the spectacle in like the newcomer she was to the French way of doing business, but her focus was on Captain Imlay. He listened well to others, his sharp inspection seeming to take in every word, his eyes tracking every movement. When Helen asked him to speak about the newly formed States, a savviness emerged as he relayed the lure of expansions West in North America. Mary, who prized intelligence more than anything in an individual, swam in his words, experiencing something delectable while listening to his tales of pristine wildernesses. She and the audience sat forward in their seats, rapt, as he described fish that ran in swollen streams, the blue and purple panoramic view of tree-covered hills that rolled on for an eternity. When he finished, there remained something unsaid, an intangible aspect of him that left her wanting to hear more.

"He's a naughty one," Helen said to Mary when the evening was done and Captain Imlay had departed into the night. "But isn't that what women ultimately adore in men?"

Mary had never claimed to know what drew women toward certain men. As for herself, in Paris, where rules regarding behavior were more relaxed than in London, she was open to a little mischief. When she and the Christies made their own exit and drove away in their coach, her thoughts were consumed by Captain Gilbert Imlay. Thomas Christie, however, kept looking out the rear window as though worried someone might be following them.

Mary peered out the curtain of Helen Maria Williams's apartment, careful not to attract attention. Outside, revolutionaries in their red liberty hats roamed, their pantaloons billowing in the breeze. Paris was no longer safe for anyone, including the Girondins, who had recently lost their majority in the National Convention. Just days prior, eighty thousand Parisians had taken to the streets demanding the Girondins expulsion, accusing them of being anti-revolutionaries. Making matters worse, the Montagnards had arrested Madame Roland and were holding her prisoner in the abbey of Saint-Germain-des-Prés.

"She should never have gone to the Convention," Helen said, fury emanating from her. She paced her apartment like a caged panther.

"Madame Roland did what she thought was best." Mary tried to calm Helen, even as she acknowledged her own lament over Madame Roland's foolish decision. After Madame Roland's husband, Jean-Marie, fled the city under threat of arrest, she went to the Convention to defend his name, shifting their wrath to her.

"She won't be the last," Helen warned. "It's only a matter of time." Her voice quivered as she rattled off the names of people she and Mary knew who had fled Paris or had already been arrested. She could just as well have been reading the guest list for her next party.

Mary's own hands trembled. Anarchy loomed. Maximilien Robespierre was in complete charge. He and other radicals had placed numerous moderate deputies of the Convention under house arrest. The Montagnards had also passed a new law limiting revolutionary tribunals to three days. No witnesses. No defense of any kind.

Mary entreated Helen to stop pacing.

"How can you be so calm?" Helen said, admonishing Mary. "Have you heard nothing I've said? They've moved the guillotine to the Place de la Révolution. You must go home to England. At once."

"You should be the one contemplating leaving. Your salons, along with your poems and translations, have marked you as a moderate—"

"But I am not alone here. I have John and my children. Unless ...."

Unable to meet Helen's suspicious gaze, Mary stifled a smile and reached for a book on Helen's table, where she pretended to scan the table of contents.

"Have you and Captain Imlay become lovers?" Helen asked, her voice turning eager.

Mary glanced at her, sheepish at being discovered. For a woman who had fought to be independent her entire life, her existence now centered on a single individual, Gilbert Imlay. For the past month, the two had become inseparable. The Revolution no longer pressed upon Mary in the same way; she was a changed woman, giddy, even a bit reckless, but everyone in Paris was reckless. The winds of change had swept in a devil-may-care attitude among men and women alike.

"It happened so fast," she tried to explain, setting aside the book. "At first, I wasn't sure if I should accept his advances, but something sprang open in me." For the first time in her life, Mary was in love. For real, not some infatuation, but a veritable romance. Uttering her feelings aloud made her sound like a lovesick adolescent, yet she cared not. Her openness to Gilbert was driven by a curiosity that had been lurking. She gave in at last to urges she once thought unspeakable based on memories of her father's abuse of her mother behind the closed door of her mother's bedroom. Her heart floated the way a kite soared against a headwind, high and glorious.

"I can't blame you," Helen said. "Who could resist looks like his? A bit of a flirt, mind you, but charming. Very gallant. Especially for an American."

It was true. Gilbert had a magnetic quality. "I fell into his arms so freely," Mary said, still shocked at how easily he had captured her affections. After just six weeks, Gilbert professed his love to her. In the space of a breath, she lost herself to him. That night, he took her to his bed in his apartment in Saint-Germain-des-Prés. Since then, every day was a mile long until she saw him again, until she could hold him and press her face close to his. After years of denying any form of sexual pleasure, Mary no longer associated chastity with virginity; being chaste was being true to her beloved. She ran her hand lazily across the silk surface of the back of Helen's sofa. Just thinking about Gilbert transported her. When she understood he had no more interest in the institution of marriage than she, she decided he was perfect for her exploration into love. Mary could enjoy physical intimacy and still maintain her independence.

"Your own revolution from within," Helen said, smiling and shaking her head, pleased and happy for Mary by the looks of it.

"Captain Imlay has asked me to go to America with him," Mary said to Helen. The same thrill as when he first put forward the idea revisited her, and she let out a small cry of glee that rang through the room.

Helen clasped her hands together, glittering with anticipation. "And?"

"I agreed!"

"I shall regret it when you go." Helen laid an arm across Mary's shoulder. "When is it the two of you plan to sail?"

Mary's elation plummeted. "Not for some time, I'm afraid." America was of great interest to European powers. Countries, Great Britain primary among them, were seeking to gain a foothold in America. An ex-spy with connections to several key Americans, including Thomas Jefferson, Brissot was determined for the French also to gain more territory in North America. Called upon by Brissot, a specialist in foreign policy within the Legislative Assembly, Gilbert, based on his knowledge of America's Southwest Territory before it became the state of Kentucky, was really in Paris to advise on how the French could wrest Louisiana from Spain. Spain ruled part of Louisiana, England, the other. If the French launched a rebellion against the Spaniards, the lower Mississippi could be theirs.

Of course, Mary could not share any of this with Helen. Gilbert had sworn her to secrecy.

Despite Mary's internal intrigue, Helen's agitation resurfaced. "I don't like the idea of you staying here. Swear to me you will act with care. Our homeland is at war with France; you must exercise caution in all you say and do."

Mary promised. If it was up to her, she and Gilbert would leave tomorrow. Helen was right. Paris was dangerous, growing more so by the day.

That night in Gilbert's arms, Mary asked, "Are we in harm's way?" Moonlight cast a swath of light over the bed, sealing them within the walls of his bedroom. He was a shield around her at a time when she felt less safe in Paris, especially after the scene outside Helen's apartment earlier that day.

"Why would you ask such a thing?" he said, his voice fading into sleep.

Mary turned on her side to face him and explained that on the way home from Helen's, a sans-culotte stopped her and questioned her loyalty. She spoke to him in French, hoping she could pass as a local. He saw through her and questioned why a British citizen was in Paris.

"What did you tell him?"

"I gave him a false name and said that I was soon to leave Paris." She had not liked lying, but had she not, she feared he would have arrested her. "We should leave Paris. Now." Mary could not believe what she was saying after she had worked so hard, had waited years to get to Paris. But that was prior to Great Britain being drawn into a war with France.

"We aren't activists."

"But surely they know my sentiments based on my books alone. And if the radicals find out you're secretly working for Brissot, they'll arrest you."

Gilbert propped himself on one arm, his look sober. "This is France's fight, not ours."

"Are we not part of it by being here and openly siding with the moderates?" Any fear she might have experienced two months ago was different now. There was more to lose. She had Gilbert.

He lay back down and draped one arm over his forehead and stared at the ceiling. "I'm not here to fight. I'm as passionate a defender of liberty as you, but America is neutral in the war between France and England. I've paid my dues for liberty."

Mary fingered a six-inch scar that ran from his collarbone to his shoulder. "Is that where you got this?"

"Yes."

"Where?"

"In a battle."

"Is that all you are going to say?" Gilbert's family had been well established in the States for almost a century. His ancestors, he had explained on one of their first outings together, had emigrated from Scotland in the late 1600s, settling in what eventually became New Jersey. Gilbert was five years older than Mary.

"At Monmouth."

"When?"

Gilbert yawned. "1778. Why all these questions?"

"It's my nature," she said, wide awake, wondering how he could want to sleep with all that was happening around them. "What of the others in your battalion?"

"I haven't much to say, really." Gilbert rubbed his eyes. "I was shot. My active military service ended."

"Then what?"

Gilbert let out a soft chuckle. "My dear girl. Does it matter?"

My dear girl. Mary nestled close to him. Who knew another human being could smell this good? She kissed his scar, the lightest touch of salt making its way to her lips, to her tongue. "Of course it matters. I want to know everything about you."

Gilbert twisted and untwisted a length of her hair around his fingers. "Some things I cannot say. I ask that you trust me and leave things at that."

"You act like you were a spy or something," Mary said to tease him into revealing a bigger part of himself than he seemed to be willing to allow. On certain things, he was tight-lipped, adding to her curiosity about his past. When he offered no response, she shot up in bed, covering her breasts with the sheet. "Were you a spy?"

"No, I wasn't a spy." Gilbert chuckled as he pulled her to him and tucked her body against his like two spoons before wrapping his arms around her in a firm embrace.

Mary let herself settle against him. "Tell me more."

"Well ... after being wounded, I explored some of America's vast wilderness areas, beyond where anyone had yet settled. Initially for the government. Then for myself. After a few years, I became infected with a disease like no other. I fell in love with land." A dreamlike tone weaved its way into Gilbert's description. Mountains, buffalo, insects, raging rivers ... riches waiting for people brave enough to claim them.

The America he described seemed ideal, a land where anything was possible, unlike in Europe where land was handed down through generations.

"How long were you in the wilderness?" she asked.

"For a while. Then I met a man named Daniel Boone." Gilbert released her and sat up and rested his arms on bent knees. "The man's a legend, I swear. A true frontiersman. I bought ten thousand acres from him on the west side of the Cumberland Gap, an area that cuts through the Allegheny Mountains. The land was like a paradise."

"Was?"

Gilbert threw up his hands. "I lost it all. I overextended myself and couldn't pay the banknotes. Before that, I owned other land in Virginia. That fell through, too."

Mary sat up alongside him, finding it impossible to sit still while listening to such a remarkable tale. "Is that why you're here?"

Gilbert extinguished a sigh. "You could say that." He turned his gaze to hers. "Look, I've been straight with you, Mary. In truth, I'm here for purely economic reasons. After I lost the acreage in the Alleghenies, I bought and sold many more tracts. That's the thing with land. It gets under your skin. Buying and selling starts to own you, takes over everything you do."

Gilbert sounded like Edward Wollstonecraft, and for a moment, Mary stilled inside, unable to find the words to respond to him. She wanted to see him through her own eyes, not the sins of a father who had uprooted his family in search of a dream, only to end up broke and disgruntled.

"You're a land speculator," she said, praying to herself he would deny it.

"I used to be."

Mary released the anxiety mounting in her. Then he was not like her father.

"Once I make enough money to buy land in Kentucky, I'm going back," he said, pulling her down beside him and stroking her hair. "And you're going with me. Don't you see? By making my fortune here, we won't need to depend on the banks."

An uneasiness persisted in Mary beneath her skin, looking for a place to nest. "Where do you intend to find riches here in Europe?" Amassing a fortune was hard enough, let alone during immense upheaval. Money was as scarce as bread in France.

"My dear girl. It's not for you to worry about. I should think you'd be willing to trust me after all the time we've spent together."

Gilbert Imlay was laying bare before her the essence of who he was—ambition, an earnest desire to explore and acquire land. Inside she knew that he would never stop searching. The next mountain, the next river, would always call to him. Perhaps it was his wayfaring ways that made him so alluring. He was a voyager. A risk taker, as mysterious as the mountains he so fantastically described—the only kind of man Mary could envision by her side.

"Of course I trust you," she said. Wasn't that what it meant to love someone?

"Can we rest now?" he asked, already half asleep.

Mary closed her eyes. Because of him—and only because of him—she would stay in Paris. For now. All she could think about was boarding a ship west as soon as possible.

ELEVEN

June 1793
Two Months Later

Affairs in Paris took yet another ominous turn, deepening Mary's agitation at being in a place where fights and riots could erupt at any moment.

"My wife and I urge you to move at once," Monsieur Filliettaz said to her in early June. He whispered, though Mary and Madame Filliettaz were the only people with him in the couple's private kitchen. Tocsin bells rang in the distance as clouds slid across the sun, robbing the morning of its early glow and each of them in the room their sense of security. "We have arranged a cottage for you in Neuilly-sur-Seine. You will be safe there. Our former gardener oversees the grounds."

His meaning was clear. Mary's swift departure would prevent the authorities from arresting the Filliettazes.

Or Mary. The National Convention had decreed that any French citizen housing a foreigner must write the person's name in chalk on their front door. Mary's British citizenship branded her a possible spy.

She reached across the table and clasped Madame Filliettaz's outstretched hand. "I understand. I'll leave as soon as I can arrange transportation. But what of you?" Madame Filliettaz was as British as Mary.

Madame Filliettaz let out a soft cry that sounded like a wounded bird. She covered her mouth with her embroidered pink handkerchief to silence herself.

"She is married to a Frenchman," Monsieur said. "We will, however, go to my family in Marseille. No one is safe in Paris under Robespierre, not even those of us who are French." His words revealed his disgust. Robespierre was turning into a dictator determined to eliminate anyone considered a counterrevolutionary.

"You must go back to London," Mrs. Filliettaz managed to say, withdrawing her hand and blowing her nose.

Mary could no more return to London than she could stop the bloodshed in Paris. "I've met someone."

Madame Filliettaz's expression shifted to one of sympathy, as if Mary's late nights made sense to her now. She looked at her through bloodshot eyes, which showed deep bags beneath from shedding tears. "If he is not French, warn him as well. If Robespierre gets his way, neither of you will escape harm."

"America is France's ally," Gilbert said, shaking his head later that evening when Mary tried to convince him to join her at the cottage. "Besides, I must conduct business somehow. Neuilly is but four miles northwest of Paris, an easy journey. The main thing is that you'll be outside the city gates. I'll visit as often as possible."

"What if you're unable to pass through the tolls?" Mary asked. Traveling in and out of Paris was becoming more difficult. Tensions were mounting. Stories about people arrested for no apparent reason flooded the broadsheets.

"Leave that to me," he said, trying to inject confidence in her decision to leave Paris, though his face was grim.

Mary slept little that night. In Neuilly, she might be outside Paris's gates, but she would not be immune from arrest. If taken into custody, it would be the end of her. No one walked out of Robespierre's prisons unless it was to the guillotine.

Edmund Burke had predicted the Revolution in France would end in disaster. It was too disordered from the start, its ideals too lofty, too abstract. He had prophesied further that the revolutionaries would fail because they were not paying proper attention to the pitfalls of human nature and were discarding the centuries-old structures on which they had built their entire society.

A sick realization wormed its way into Mary's thoughts. She remained convinced the Revolution was the natural consequence of intellectual improvement, but she wondered now, had Edmund Burke been right? Was the Revolution heading for disaster? How much longer could she and Gilbert risk staying in France?

Mary moved the next day, one of the Filliettazes' grooms driving her in their cabriolet with Gilbert riding alongside on horseback.

To her relief, outside the gates was nothing like what raged inside Paris. Far from the city strife, a cottage with gleaming white plaster walls and trim the color of lemons and a matching yellow door met her when the cabriolet turned off a dusty road into a secluded wood. Flowers tended with meticulous care circled the tiny cottage's foundation. She felt like a small slice of Eden had been handed to her when the Filliettazes' former gardener presented her with a key and a basket of bread and soft, melty cheese, along with ripe, fresh-picked strawberries still warm from the sun.

He and the groom left Mary and Gilbert alone to settle Mary in the cottage. Inside, a vase with fresh roses and lupines emitted a sweet, floral scent, softening the cottage's otherwise earthy, fecund dampness. More fruit overflowed from a wooden bowl on a table for two. The cottage's few other furnishings were sparse, the exact kind of appointments Mary would have chosen herself.

She and Gilbert had lunch, and before he left, they agreed to meet on Saturday at the barrier at Longchamps. As Mary watched him ride away, her heart galloping after him, she began counting the days until she would see him again.

While in Neuilly, Mary intended to spend time on her book about the Revolution. The cottages and woods proved to be the perfect setting, allowing her uninterrupted time. The gardener stopped in daily with a fresh basket of food and requested to do whatever chores needed to be done, even offering to make Mary's bed. Mornings, she worked on her book. Afternoons, she penned letters to Gilbert, and to Iris and her sisters, along with Mr. Johnson, whom she kept abreast of her writing assignment. Communication with England was difficult in the face of war between the two countries, and she was not receiving word from any of them, leaving her to worry. She did not want to tell her sisters about Gilbert. Not yet. They would disapprove of her consorting with a man, surely not one she had taken on as a lover. But she wanted them to know that she was safe.

June 13, 1793

My dear Eliza!

    I can scarcely tell you how very uneasy I have been on your account ever since the communication with England has been stopped. I write with reserve because all letters between France and England are opened. I am now at a house of an old gardener writing a great book and in better health and spirits than I have ever enjoyed since I came to France ...

The following Saturday Mary arrived at Longchamps Gate well in advance of the time she and Gilbert had arranged to meet. More traffic seemed to be flowing out of the city than in. Most of those entering were farmers with wagons of meat and produce, guarding their loads as if hauling gold. The haggard appearance of those leaving told her life inside the gates was worsening. Bedraggled children stumbled barefooted behind their parents. Even more appeared unescorted by an adult, and to them she gave away the coins in her pocket until the last *sou* was gone.

Gilbert rode through the gate and spotted her, his grin unmistakable despite clouds that warned of rain forming in the distance. When he reached her side, he slid from his saddle and wrapped her in his arms.

"I missed you," she said, her voice breaking.

"My dear girl." He pulled back from her. "You're not sad, are you?"

"Not now." His shirt muffled her voice. The familiar smell of him calmed her, and she leaned in, not wanting an inch to separate them.

Gilbert slung his horse's reins over his shoulder, and they ambled towards the cottage. "How are you filling your days?" he asked.

"Writing." Prior to Mary leaving Paris, she had been helping Gilbert with his novel, encouraging him to be deliberate in including the concerns of women. But helping him had left her with less time for her own writing. Her forced exile was a blessing. "The cottage and the countryside energize me. I can pen my thoughts for hours without stopping. But I must admit, as I try to capture history in the making, Paris's elegant gates no longer appear as magnificent porticoes."

"It's worse on the other side," he said, motioning his thumb back at the wall surrounding Paris. "It's becoming a slaughterhouse. Violence has erupted everywhere. Those who've seized power are lawless; they're terrorizing people." Gilbert recited stories of people being attacked in the streets or guillotined with no evidence to indict them.

"Why not go to America now?" she asked, stopping mid-stride. "Why stay here?"

Gilbert stopped and turned to face her. "We can't leave. Not yet. The change in power may have thrown things into disarray, but it has also created unexpected opportunities."

"What do you mean?"

"I've gotten into shipping."

"Shipping?" The idea seemed preposterous. Mary found it difficult to keep to herself her opinion that it was a poor time to open a fleet in Paris. Starting a shipping enterprise with countries at war showed a lack of good judgment. "You're being reckless. France is not only at war with Britain; it's also at war with Holland and Spain and is still at odds with Austria and Prussia. Blockades surround every major port in and out of France."

"You needn't concern yourself."

Gilbert's tone was brusque. He walked on, leaving Mary open-mouthed and staring at him, her concerns festering. Gilbert did not like discussing his business affairs with her. In truth, Mary did not care to know the finer details. His desire to own land, to amass wealth, were part of a man's inner self that made no sense to her.

A drop of rain fell. Mary glanced at the sky. More rain was sure to come. Feeling angry at Gilbert put her off balance. She did not want to fight with him. She had yearned for him all week and sought only the enchanting rhythm of his voice. In time, perhaps his rationale would become apparent to her. She would put aside her concerns over his new business venture. For now. She caught up to him, and they walked in silence until a thunderstorm cracked the sky open, bombarding them with rain. They burst into laughter and ran to the cottage, where they cocooned themselves, not talking of shipping and blockades, but discussing writing and books and the promises America held. As rain gave sustenance to the crops in the surrounding meadows and orchards, the Revolution seemed a million miles away.

The initial expression Mary saw on Gilbert's face was one of joy the moment their eyes met each Saturday when he rode through the Longchamps gate. His barrier face, she called it, became an image she carried with her until their next meeting.

"What is it?" she asked one Saturday. It had been over two months since Mary arrived at the cottage. This week Gilbert had pulled his hat low. His brow was barely visible, and his lips were locked in a thin line.

Gilbert dismounted in a flurry of dust and reached for her arm. "There's been an insurrection," he said under his breath as he led her away from the throng of travelers exiting the gate. His eyes darted around them, watching for anyone who might be listening. "Royalists in the south of France have taken control of the seaport city of Toulon."

Royalists, a conservative faction that had remained staunch supporters of the king, even after his death, were intent on restoring the Bourbon monarchy. Their activity centered in France's southern provinces. Toulon was miles away. "What does that have to do with us?" Mary asked. Skirmishes happened every day.

"The National Convention just passed the Law of Subjects, effectively detaining all British citizens in France."

Mary's skin prickled. The authorities could take her into custody any minute—inside the gates of Paris or not.

"I want you to move into the city." Gilbert's voice was urgent in a way she had never heard him speak, heightening her anxiety at the news.

"Paris seems like the last place I should be," she said. Apprehension crawled up her spine. "Where would I live?"

"With me."

Mary's throat went dry. "I couldn't." She would not even consider it. To flout a sexual liaison by living with a man went against her better judgment, even in Paris, where such bold behavior would be within acceptable boundaries. Besides, living with Gilbert still would not protect her from being arrested.

Gilbert pulled her close. "We could pretend we're married. By acting as my wife and taking my name, you'd be an American in the eyes of the French authorities." He had already been to the American Embassy, he explained, and spoke to Gouverneur Morris. Morris had agreed to forge a certificate of marriage. "It's all the proof we'd need."

Blood throbbed in Mary's ears, drowning all other sounds, making them no more than a thrum. She would follow Gilbert anywhere, just to be with him. But to pretend to live as man and wife ... what would her sisters say? What kind of example would she be setting for them? They would lambaste her, as would any anyone in England. Her reputation as a virtuous woman would be dragged through the streets.

"Look, neither of us wants to get married." He held her by the shoulders. "That doesn't need to change. Your continued freedom, however, is under threat. As is your life. I'll not leave you stranded here outside the gates."

"Surely now would be the time to go to America, would it not?" Under this new threat, she wanted out of France, to leave behind the constant bloodshed.

Gilbert wrapped her in his arms. "We can't, not yet. I'm up to my neck negotiating new shipping deals. If I'm successful, it will give us all the money we need to go to the States." He stepped back and held her again by the shoulders. "Don't you see? We'll be able to buy the land we've been dreaming of and more. We just have to be patient."

Patience. That state of mind so foreign to Mary. Owning land was his dream, not hers. That he spoke of them as "we," however, meant that his future included her. The small gesture touched her. Why worry about her reputation in London? She would never return there; she would be going to America. "I'll move in with you," she said, breathless at uttering the words. God was answering her prayers, though not in the way she had intended. When had he ever?

Gilbert pulled her close, his breath warm in her ear. "Good. I've already registered you as my wife."

Mary laughed and let her body release into him fully. "You knew I'd say yes."

"Hoped is more like it. I have to return to the city. Things are unraveling dangerously fast. I'll be back in a few days to pick you up. Remember, when you get to Paris, you'll be Madame Imlay."

Madame Imlay. How volatile the Revolution was becoming in France! The title meant nothing more than the promise of protection during troubling times, Mary said to herself. She would still be Mary Wollstonecraft.

Before leaving the crowd, she caught the name of the soldier who led the Jacobins to victory at Toulon. A Corsican by the name of Napoleone di Buonaparte.

TWELVE

September 1793
Paris

When Mary and Gilbert neared his apartment later that week, she saw how Paris was a city under great strain. Saint-Germain-des-Prés had been and still was a center of revolutionary activity.

"Carry your papers, evidence that you are my wife, everywhere, even on a walk," Gilbert warned her. "Especially when you visit friends."

If they had not already fled, Mary thought. How many of her friends remained in Paris? Maximilien Robespierre's radical regime was imprisoning expatriates who had at any time supported the moderate wing of the Jacobins; the rest of the expatriates in Mary's circle were leaving France. Even Thomas and Rebecca Christie had been taken into custody. To Mary's relief, Thomas Christie had successfully negotiated the couple's release. They were now in Switzerland.

Gilbert was saving her life by pretending to marry her. As the cabriolet rumbled along on the cobblestones, Mary was sure of it as she observed him keeping watch, riding his horse alongside the cab. Their subterfuge nettled her, and she picked at the cuff of her sleeve as she listened to the creak of his saddle's leather, which had become as familiar a sound to her as his voice. She must accept their scheme as a necessary lie to escape arrest, she told herself. It also meant that he loved her as she did him, making them partners in a world that had turned treacherous. She trusted him with her life. She relaxed in her seat at having someone with whom to share the burden of uncertainty. Madness seemed to have erupted in Paris.

So it was that Mary began navigating Paris by masquerading as an American. She reunited with Helen Maria Williams and Thomas Paine, and she wrote, taking care to hide her notes and manuscript on the Revolution when not working on it. Should the authorities raid her and Gilbert's apartment, she did not want her words indicting her. She walked daily, the need for fresh air too powerful to sequester her, but she did not wander beyond their small neighborhood except to visit friends in prison, to whom she brought food and listened to their stories of survival, her only way of helping them.

"I live on bread and plums," said Count Gustav von Schlabrendorf from Prussia, one of Mary's early suitors when she first arrived in Paris. His eyes lit up when she visited him at the Conciergerie, a prison for those awaiting execution. Schlabrendorf could have been assigned to a cell with a bed, he explained, but he was content to sleep on straw amid the filth and rats, where even there, bribes were a way of life. "There are two kinds of inmates in prison: men of rank and foreigners," he told her. "I make sure to request little. Asking for more luxurious supplies would mark me as a man of means, a crime against Robespierre, who confiscates peoples' wealth."

When Mary asked if he feared what might come next, he shrugged his shoulders. His graying hair had grown wild, and his beard extended to his midsection. He was older and richer than most of the revolutionaries, and wiser, and though he remained vigilant, he had managed to maintain his sense of humor. "Two mornings in a row, I was scheduled to be executed. On the first, I pretended that I had mislaid my boots."

"On the second?" Mary asked, a penetrating chill ripping through her. The smell of slop and vomit, of bodies that had not been washed, of rotting straw and the excrement of vermin and rodents, burned in her nostrils in the gray, almost black light of his dank cell.

Schlabrendorf threw up his dirty hands. "They forgot to call my name." His hands landed with a thump in his grimy lap, and he leaned closer to her. "The guards are idiots. Still, my dear, you will take care when you visit prison, no? Being from anywhere besides France marks you as an enemy of Robespierre, but especially so if you are a citizen of Great Britain."

His warning was not lost on Mary. Her visits to Schlabrendorf continued, however, as did visits to other prisoners she knew. The weekly excursions became a part of her routine.

In October a swift knock rapped at her door.

"Mr. Paine," she said, surprised to see her rebel friend standing outside her door.

"The authorities have seized Helen Maria Williams and her family." His glance darted to the sides as if looking to see if anyone had followed him. "Robespierre's henchmen took them from their beds in the middle of the night and are holding them in the Luxembourg prison. I urge you to leave Paris at once!"

"But Mr. Imlay and I—"

"I know about you and Mr. Imlay. Your ruse will keep you safe." He paused. "For a time."

Mary fidgeted about him knowing her and Gilbert's secret. They had been keeping their sham union a secret out of caution. "You speak as if I should not trust him," she said, gooseflesh running up her arms.

"Be wise, my dear, in how long you let this charade go on, whether it is in your best interest to stay here in Paris ... whether Mr. Imlay is being frank with you."

Paine was being cryptic, which put Mary on edge. What was he talking about? He spoke as if Gilbert was up to something villainous. "Mr. Paine, please. If there is something you know, you must tell me."

He paused as if weighing his words. "I did not intend to alarm you. Business is rife with uncertainty was all I meant." He gave her what she assumed was a smile to assure her. "Come, I will take you to Helen," he said, changing the subject, "if it is your wish to see her."

Mary grabbed her red cloak and followed him out the door, forgetting Paine's words about Gilbert and thinking only of Helen.

They walked to the Luxembourg, Mary having to take two steps for every one of Paine's. He was like Mr. Johnson in that he had grown protective of her. His enigmatic words about Gilbert's business came back to her now, and she decided they were nothing more than paternal in meaning. Perhaps he was referring to her own activities. Days earlier, Helen had begged Mary to destroy the book she was writing about the Revolution. "You are putting yourself in danger," Helen had warned. "Any criticism of the radicals will be met with harsh repercussions." Helen's words at the time had seemed overly cautious. Now they wrought havoc on Mary's already thin sense of security.

On the outside, the Luxembourg, a former palace, appeared the grand house it had been when it served as a residence for the Royal Family for centuries. In 1610, Marie de Médicis had commissioned the three-story cream-colored stone building on rue de Vaugirard after the death of her husband, Henry IV. The complex formed a square, its matching wings were French with their classical mansard roofs, but de Médicis' Tuscan influence was still evident.

"I shall take my leave here." Paine stepped into the shadow of a tree. "Please give Helen my regards."

"You're not coming in?"

"It would not be wise."

Paine, too, was seeking to avoid arrest.

"Godspeed," she said to him, and he disappeared before she could say more.

Mary took a deep breath and strode with false confidence toward the Luxembourg. Its massive doors reminded her that French court had never been without intrigue and espionage. What courtiers had traveled this very path in hopes of an audience with the king or his queen? What lies did they tell to achieve their desires? The necessity of deception seemed clearer to her now. It meant life or death for some. Guilty of her own trickery, she patted her papers with Gouverneur Morris's signature in her pocket, then hurried up the walk, her head low and covered with the hood of her red cloak.

"I knew you'd come," Helen said, crossing the room to embrace her.

"Are you comfortable?" Mary asked, glancing about the room, uncertain she could remain as cool as Helen appeared to be in light of her imprisonment. "May I bring you something? Anything?"

"We're comfortable." Helen offered Mary a seat. Under her breath, she added, "If you don't mind a guillotine hanging by a thread over your head."

Unlike the miserable cells French citizens occupied in various locations around Paris, the Luxembourg was used for genteel expatriates like Helen and thus was not a conventional prison. Helen's family had been assigned large rooms with windows and comfortable furniture, and two of their servants from home accompanied them. Doors were locked at night, but not during the day, she explained, though they could not leave. They were, however, able to cater their meals from the outside, which did not make the fact that they were kept against their will any easier. But it helped that she could continue to write and was working on translations of French-language works into English and writing sonnets. "To distract me," she said in her driest of tones.

"Then you have something to sustain you."

When Helen held a finger to her lips, which Mary took as a signal that someone could be listening to their conversation, Mary ceased questions about writing or telling Helen of news from outside the prison.

"Don't come to see me again," Helen whispered in Mary's ear before she left hours later. "Stay away for your own good; being my friend will implicate you. John has connections. We will go to Switzerland as soon as they can arrange a release for us."

October 1793 / Vendémiaire, Year II

French radicals were not satisfied with toppling a monarchy. Those now in power were determined to construct an entirely new social order, one that would result in freedom and equality for all citizens. In October 1793, the National Convention replaced the Gregorian calendar with a new French republican calendar, dating its inception to the year prior when they declared France a republic. October became Vendémiaire.

Mary found the changes a false attempt at equality, and in her mind, she rebelled against them. Day after day, broadsheets circulating Paris with news regarding actions taken by the Revolutionary Tribunal demonstrated in plain sight all the makings of an authoritarian regime at work. Not long after Helen's arrest, they executed Marie Antoinette by guillotine at the Place de la Révolution, heightening everyone's fears, Mary's included. Two weeks later, they carted Jacques Pierre Brissot and over two dozen other moderates to the guillotine, all on the same day. The hair on Mary's neck rose when she read that as tumbrels carried them to their horrible fate, the condemned men sang *"La Marseillaise."*

France's national anthem echoed in Mary's mind until four days later when the Tribunal executed Olympe de Gouges.

"A crowd was there," Gilbert reported to Mary that evening in their sitting room. He had a hard time hiding his frustration against Robespierre and the sham the National Convention had become. He spoke with both fists clenched.

"Tell me. Tell me all of it," she said. She resisted being party to France's gruesome display of bloodshed by refusing to attend executions. But this execution was personal. She wanted every detail this time, even when Gilbert warned they were grisly.

"After leading her onto the platform, the radicals stripped her naked."

Mary fought against a wave of nausea. *Those animals!* "Why?"

"To prove she was a woman after she had written such 'manly' things."

"It was to humiliate her!" The walls closed in around Mary.

Gilbert lowered himself onto the sofa, his weight causing Mary to fall into him as he wrapped his arms around her.

"Then what?" she whispered, barely able to breathe.

Gilbert described the scene on the platform holding the guillotine. As he did, Mary pictured the French playwright's graying hair. Her round face. The high but sturdy pitch of her voice. Her words had inspired Mary. Olympe had advocated for free speech, had spoken in favor of better conditions for women and children, especially orphaned children. She had condemned slavery and had campaigned against violence and oppression of all kinds.

"You'd have been proud of her," Mary heard Gilbert say. "She was brave to the last moment. Just before her head fell, she proclaimed loudly so all could hear, 'My sentiments have not changed.'"

As Gilbert said these last words, everything went black for Mary.

Memories of Olympe de Gouges remained with Mary as the week wore on, Olympe's voice and spirit present in Mary's mind from the moment she placed her head on her pillow, imagining it was a chopping block beneath the guillotine, until she woke the next day to the same litany of horrors in the papers.

The very next week, when the Tribunal executed Madame Roland, who had been imprisoned since June when Mary left for the cottage, the senselessness of killing, of snuffing out voices, shook Mary to her core. Madame Roland's defiance to the end brought Mary some comfort. 'O Liberty! What crimes are committed in thy name!' were the last words she had spoken before her head fell.

At least Sophie de Condorcet was safe. Mary knew this through Thomas Paine, who still visited her and sent notes. But Sophie's husband, the marquis—the man who supported free and equal public education, equal rights for women and people of all races, the man who advocated for a constitutional government—had gone into hiding after the Committee of Public Safety issued a warrant for his arrest. How long before they arrested Sophie?

Or Mary.

At dinner three evenings later, she pushed her food around on her plate.

"I need to go to Le Havre for business," Gilbert said, disrupting the silence precipitated by Mary's depressed mood.

Mary dropped her fork onto her plate, sending a sharp clatter through the room. "Le Havre is over a hundred miles northwest of Paris. You'd leave me here alone?"

They each used the shortened name for Le Havre-de-Grâce, the second largest port city in France, which had just renamed itself Le Havre-de-Marat in honor of Jean-Paul Marat, the influential Montagnard sympathizer, whom a young woman by the name of Charlotte Corday had murdered in his bath the previous summer. In Mary's opinion, Charlotte Corday was a heroine who did France a favor by killing Marat. "I have killed one man to save a hundred thousand," someone heard Corday say at her trial. Mary had read it in the broadsheets, admiration for the woman spilling through her. Later, she read that Corday was executed by guillotine.

"I'll only be gone a few days," Gilbert said, the look on his face suggesting surprise at Mary's reaction to him announcing so sudden a departure.

"Then I'll go with you to Le Havre." It was not a request but a declaration that she would not be left behind, not now.

Gilbert still seemed perplexed at Mary's reaction to him leaving. "It's a long way, and I'll be traveling by horseback. It wouldn't be safe for you."

Nor would it be safe here without him! How could he not know how each death, each report in the broadsheets, had robbed her of any peace or feeling of security? "Have the events of the past weeks not affected you at all?" Her voice was porcelain, as though it might break.

"I haven't completely forgotten about you." He placed his hand on hers and smiled sympathetically as if all would be well. "I've arranged to have Colonel Norris look in on you. He's assured me he'll be more than happy to provide you whatever you need."

Mary yanked her hand from Gilbert's. "Colonel Norris." She hated Norris, one of Gilbert's American associates. The man was drunk half the time and moved about in silence, a leer twisting his lips.

"I can't very well manage my ships from here," Gilbert said, resentment building in his voice.

Mary almost leaped from her chair. Was there no end to his lust for wealth? "What about America?"

"I can't let this opportunity pass. Shipping between France and America has been lucrative. But Sweden and Norway are ripe for investment."

Talk of shipping animated Gilbert, injecting him with renewed energy. Mary's resentment, however, also turned spirited. When so many around them suffered, he remained preoccupied with filling his own pockets. He was being greedy *and* irresponsible. Shipping was not even safe. "What about the blockades? And what about currency? French silver remains an illegal currency in Britain. Austria, and Prussia as well."

"That's because France is at war with all of them." Gilbert's response was tart, unusual for him. "Scandinavian countries are not and are more than happy to accept French silver as payment. You might as well know I've arranged a contact in Sweden. A man by the name of Elias Backman. He's willing to convert French silver into currency I can use with England *and* the Americans."

The explorer in Gilbert, the part of him Mary hated, was on full display. She had no influence over it; he was as out of reach as America when he talked so. "You're being reckless," she warned. She could forgive the most important part of his shipping enterprise: delivering goods from America to France. It had become his principal source of income, and it was for a just cause. The goods he delivered were sustaining the French commoners. But this was pure greed talking.

"You must trust me. If my plan works, we'll be richer than either of us could imagine."

He effortlessly spoke the word "trust," detached from its obligations. "Your fixation on wealth is unbecoming," Mary said, boiling inside at his self-interest when all around them friends were waiting for the executioner, dying for their convictions. Those were the people she admired. "There's more to life than having fine things."

Gilbert's jaw tightened as though reading Mary's dislike of him having a commercial enterprise. "You need to put aside your shame at me being a tradesman. I'm not a member of the landed gentry, nor do I wish to be. My family prides themselves on making money." He stood up and threw his napkin onto his plate. "That's how we do things in America, Mary. Ambition. Drive."

Gilbert stomped to their bedroom, leaving tracks across Mary's heart. She stared at his empty chair across from her, her frustration with Gilbert a quickening within. It was true. She *was* starting to be ashamed of him. Did she truly desire to be linked with a man whose only goal was wealth? He was chasing wealth like a money-grubber. Memories of Edward Wollstonecraft's avarice came back to her in waves, buried emotions she had sought to put behind her.

Mary threw her own napkin onto the table and trailed after Gilbert. "But why Le Havre?" she asked from the doorway to their bedroom.

Gilbert pulled his travel bag from under their bed and snapped it open. "Le Havre is the best place for breaking through the blockades."

Blockades. Tumbrels. Guillotines. They were all Mary could think of as Gilbert jammed clothing into his bag. Did he even have a heart? Or was greed all that flowed through his veins?

"You seem unaware of how difficult the last few weeks have been for me," she said. "First Olympe, then Madame Roland ... What if I'm next?"

Gilbert held the shirt he had been examining in midair, not looking her way. "You can't possibly think that."

"Why not?" He knew that her sister Eliza had written that British newspapers were reporting Mary as having been arrested in France. In England, her writing had been as bold as that of Olympe de Gouges. Bolder. What if her writings had come to the attention of The Committee of Public Safety? "What if I'm on a watch list in Paris?" Her voice choked on tears pooling behind her eyes.

Gilbert stopped packing, the concern Mary had been waiting to see finally registering in his eyes. He walked to where she stood and enveloped her in his arms. The walls swirled around her. Mary felt as though she might faint. He could not leave. Not now!

"America is France's primary ally. You're protected as long as you have your papers with you stating that you're married to me."

Mary buried her head in his shoulder. He was the only person—the only thing—she could count on anymore in Paris. "It won't be the same without you here." It was not just fear that preyed on her nerves. She would miss waking up with him, miss the time in the evening when they discussed their respective days. He had become a part of her, an embodiment of everything that was Paris.

"I won't be long, I promise."

They stood for some time in each other's arms, all the while Mary wondering if she should go back to London, before it was too late, before she found herself confined to a prison cell. But London was not any safer. Eliza had also reported mobs threatening to burn Mary in effigy if she were on British soil for what they perceived as her association with the rebels in France.

Later, however, when the day was done, they made love, Mary shedding her fears by giving herself to him so that everything could return to the way it was between them. Steering through life-threatening terrain linked her to Gilbert beyond mere affection. Her tie to him was stronger than love—the human instinct to survive joined them. He had become rooted in her, and she surrendered to him, and in doing so, she yielded to his ways.

Gilbert's week in Le Havre turned into two, then three. Mary's anxiety mounted with each extension as news of terror on the streets of Paris chipped away at any remaining sense of well-being. Thousands were meeting their death under the blade of the guillotine. She ruminated over whether to return to England. But travel would be perilous; she had waited too long to leave. Mary had no choice but to embrace a self-imposed house arrest for her safety. She only left her apartment for exercise, walking up and down the street daily. Colonel Norris looked in on her, delivering a steady stream of newspapers and broadsheets. Printed in black and white for all to see was a bloodbath underway in Paris. Mary's one house servant went to market and supplied Mary with a meager set of meals. Food was scarce, so there was little to eat. What did it matter? Mary could not keep food down in the mornings.

One evening she pattered to a corner she had claimed for herself in the sitting room of their gleaming white apartment to write to Gilbert. The rooms featured newer styles of architecture and had lofty ceilings and tall, narrow windows. During the day, sunshine flooded them with luxurious warmth and light. Tonight, looking out the windows into the blackness of night put Mary in a pensive mood. If she and Gilbert were never together, all the money in the world did not matter. He had yet to understand what she knew all too well: money purchased nothing worth having. But she was bound to him now.

Dearest,

I have just received your letter, and I feel as if I could not go to bed tranquilly without saying a few words in reply to tell you that my mind is serene and my heart affectionate. Ever since you last saw me and I was inclined to faint, I have felt some gentle twitches, which make me begin to think I am nourishing a creature who will soon be in my care. The thought has not only produced an overflowing of tenderness toward you but has

made me very determined to calm my mind and take exercise, lest I should
destroy the child in whom we are about to have a mutual interest.

Leaning back in her chair, Mary looked upon her reflection in the window. She was thirty-four and single. Wherever she might travel in Great Britain or on the Continent, penalties for an unmarried lady with a child were harsh. Even Paris. Robespierre was returning his nation to its pre-Revolution rules regarding women, eliminating the advances they had temporarily enjoyed. Shame tried to crush Mary, but she refused to let it. Once again, she resolved to find a path through the rules that burdened women's lives.

Still, she had never envisioned becoming a mother, and she wondered if she would be good at it so she could safeguard her child from suffering the ills of parents like hers who stole from their children more than they gave. Mary wanted her child to grow up strong with a mind all its own. She had no intention of marrying Gilbert. She did not want a real marriage; her independence still mattered. She had worked too hard—for herself, for all women—to relinquish it. It occurred to her, however, that the little twitcher growing inside of her was sure to want a real father, and she ran her hand across her middle, which had yet to show any sign of life growing within. How quickly life was changing. When Mary came to Paris, all she wanted was her freedom. Now what she wanted most was for her, Gilbert, and their child to be a family.

THIRTEEN

May 1794 / Floréal Year II
Six Months Later
Le Havre-de-Marat, France

On the day of her birth, Françoise Imlay peered at her mother through bluish-gray eyes. May 14, two weeks after Mary's thirty-fifth birthday. Despite Fanny's skin being mottled and the temporary distortion of her ears from traveling through the birth canal, she was to Mary the most beautiful baby in the world.

"My little Fanny," Mary said, watching with fascination the rise and fall of her baby's chest, feeling with her fingers the beat of a tiny heart. Mary named her after Fanny Blood, whom she thought of now. Had Fanny lived, she would be with her husband in Lisbon. Mary would have moved to Lisbon to care for her. And Fanny Imlay would never have been born, something Mary could not comprehend. Her life would never be the same going forward, nor did she want it to be.

Fanny opened her tiny mouth and yawned before fussing. In January Mary had joined Gilbert in Le Havre, living with him in a house on rue de Coderie that was close to the wharf on the River Seine. She had been eager to leave Paris. Thomas Paine finally had been taken into custody along with an ever-growing list of Mary's acquaintances. While she worried about each of them, however, Le Havre was a respite from the terror. She and Gilbert had returned without difficulty to the easy way they had lived together in Paris. While Gilbert tended his growing shipping enterprise, Mary used the time to finish her book on the Revolution. And to prepare for this day.

"The wet nurse will arrive soon," the midwife said, glancing at Mary with fondness after having helped usher a new life into the world. "There is a shortage." She began to gather soiled sheets and cloths.

"No need." Mary fished inside her nightshirt for her breast. "You may cancel your request. I intend to suckle my baby."

The midwife rushed to Mary's side. "But Madame, a wet nurse is best. And less burden for you. You will ruin your lovely breasts."

Mary ignored the appalled expression on the midwife's face. She would raise her daughter following the advice of medical books that claimed the benefits of a mother's milk.

After feeding Fanny, Mary refused to let the midwife place the baby in the cradle, and she held Fanny tight, marveling at her tiny hands, the intricate nails the size of a pebble on toes smaller than the tip of Mary's little finger. If she had to describe at that moment the way love pulsated through her veins, she would not have found the words. It was clear now why mothers sacrificed as they did, why they went to extreme lengths to protect their children. They had no choice; they would die for their child. As would she.

Would Gilbert feel the same way? He was gone on business, a frequent occurrence. When Mary asked him what took him away so often, all he offered was that he was busy, nothing more, not telling her where he went or why. She had been too busy preparing for Fanny's birth to mind. Now his absences weighed on her. Outside her window, ships went out and came in from the sea. Masts of various sizes bobbed at the quay as men loaded and unloaded cargo. Like ants going up and down planks. Le Havre was a welcome change from streets flowing with blood in Paris. The tang of the water. The smell of fish and of salt in the air. Here, Gilbert was in his element. Instead of becoming more attuned to the demands of domesticity, however, he seemed to be moving further away from Mary. Her stomach hardened as if a stone had been growing there and she only now noticed.

Gilbert returned within the week. When he first looked upon Fanny, he displayed the very kind of rapture Mary had hoped, and her frustration with him melted at seeing him with their daughter. She prayed their relationship would be filled with affection, not the kind of blusterous relationship she had had with her father.

"She's beautiful," he said in a hushed voice, tucking Fanny in his arms, cooing as Mary had, equally transfixed.

Mary forgave Gilbert for being gone, for being inattentive. They finally were a family. Wanting to savor what precious time they had together, she let go of the reprimand she had been rehearsing in her mind.

If only the euphoria would have lasted.

"What is it?" she asked Gilbert that night when their attempt to resume relations had fallen flat. "Is it the milk? I'm sorry. I can't control it." She was soaked and handed him a towel she kept nearby after wiping herself dry.

"It's fine," Gilbert said, rising and slipping into his trousers.

"It won't flow like this forever." Mary was referring to her milk. "It's just that I want to give Fanny every advantage to be healthy. A wet nurse would deny her the most important advantage of all, a closeness with her mother."

"Yes, your progressive principles," Gilbert said, regarding her insistence at nursing. He had objected to it. "So you've mentioned."

His voice had a double edge to it. In the darkness, she could not discern if he was being flippant or hurtful on purpose. When he added that Fanny sucked so manfully and so often, he suspected she would grow up to write the second part to *Rights of Woman*, Mary became defensive. "You needn't be gruff. You want her to be strong, don't you?"

"Of course, I do." His look was sharp.

"Then why are you so distant?"

Gilbert ran his hand through his hair. "I'm sorry." He wandered to the window overlooking the harbor. The moon illuminated his profile, showing him preoccupied with something other than Mary. When she pressed him further, he removed himself to the parlor that night to sleep on the sofa, leaving her alone to wonder what had become of her lover?

In June Gilbert departed for Paris saying he would be gone for two weeks this time, leaving Mary with growing consternation over the sudden shift in his affections. He was aloof, and his temper had grown short. Had Mary known what was soon to occur, she would never have let him go. Fanny fell ill with a fever the day after he departed. Days later, she was vomiting. Inside her mouth, small red spots were forming on the surface of her tongue and on the walls.

"Smallpox," Mary whispered, finally voicing her deepest fear.

"You must call a physician," her maid urged, appearing ready to bolt from the room.

"I'll handle this," Mary snapped. "Her body will heal itself." Mary sounded certain, but inside, she was not. "Bring cool water and towels."

The maid froze, her mouth agape.

"Now!" Mary barked, praying to herself that what she had read in her medical books proved right. "We'll keep Fanny as clean as possible. Order all our goods delivered to the house so we don't expose anyone else."

Within hours, a rash broke out on Fanny's face and spread to her arms and legs. Even her hands and feet were affected. In time, pustules covered her from head to toe.

Word of the terrifying disease spread. The maid told Mary that neighbors accused her of being reckless for not contacting a physician.

"I care not," Mary said. A physician would only purge and bleed Fanny, which would weaken her.

By the fourth day of Fanny's fluctuating fever, sores started filling with a thick fluid. Her fever stayed high. For the next ten days, Mary and her maid took turns washing Fanny's pustules with warm water twice a day.

"The treatment seems to be working," her maid said. She smiled a hopeful smile at Mary.

The tension in Mary's shoulders eased, and the frantic racing of her mind slowed. The worst appeared to be over.

Two days later during Mary's turn at vigil, however, Fanny turned as white as a death shroud. Mary's own heart stopped as she held her cheek close to Fanny's lips. Fanny's breath was almost indiscernible. Mary checked her fever. It had gone sky high again.

With haste Mary dragged her rocking chair close to the window and cradled Fanny in her arms, wiping her with a wet cloth, letting the harbor's cool breezes wash over her. An anvil pressed upon Mary's chest. Her mother, weak though she was at standing up to the heavy hand of a heartless spouse, had not lost a single child when mothers were likely to lose her children to disease or an accident. Mary, who had tried to do everything right, was about to lose her first. What had she done wrong?

Hours passed, Mary anguishing over whether she had done the right thing by not calling a doctor. By the time a yellow-orange line cast a haunting glow on the horizon, signaling a rising sun, her arms had grown numb. Fanny felt still in them, a weight that had grown heavier. Certain she was dead, a tear slid from Mary onto Fanny's forehead. When it did, a small cry erupted from Fanny, startling Mary. She quickly pressed her cheek to Fanny's. The fever was breaking! Mary checked Fanny's stomach. Scabs were forming on her pale but perfect skin.

"My little Hercules," Mary whispered, clutching the child to her. Fanny would live.

"I've been clear about why I need to go to Paris," Gilbert said the following month, tucking his white shirt into his trousers as he dressed for the day. A gust of wind sent their bedroom curtains billowing. "I won't go over it again." His tone was unrelenting.

"And I won't stand for it!" Mary flung off the bedcovers. The bustle of the harbor was already underway. The groan of ships and clang of steel were close, as if Mary stood on the quay in their way. Gilbert had only been home a few weeks, and they had argued the entire time. "Fanny isn't even two months old! We almost lost her."

Gilbert tugged his boots on, refusing to look at Mary. "I'm sorry. It can't be helped."

"Of course, it can. You're in charge."

Gilbert selected a clean cravat from a drawer, then strode to the window of their second-story bedroom, where he stood and tied a knot, craning his neck in both directions, taking in the sky, a bloodshot red. "A storm's brewing."

Mary studied him from behind, the rise and fall of her shoulders growing more rapid with each second he ignored her demands to stay. Gilbert's growing tendency to remove himself even when present was leaving a disturbing wake. He was two distinct people. One stayed close; the other hovered at a distance. The sudden duality of his nature was exhausting Mary. She glared at him; her jaw clenched. "You should be more vigilant regarding your obligations at home."

Outside, a ship's bell warned vessels in its path. "Making money should be as important to you as it is to me."

A tremor passed through Mary. She clutched the collar of her nightdress and pulled it close about her neck. Her pen, her one true path to being an independent woman had slipped through her fingers. Like one of Robespierre's prisoners, she could almost hear the door to the Conciergerie closing behind her. She was completely dependent on Gilbert. Fanny consumed all her time, making it difficult to write anything sellable.

"There's something I need to tell you," Gilbert said.

A different tension bundled beneath Mary's skin. "What is it?"

Glistening beads of perspiration trickled down the sides of his face. "Do you recall when Robespierre flung open the doors at Versailles and auctioned off everything he could get his hands on?"

Mary nodded. Robespierre had condemned the ownership of luxury items and confiscated the country estates of scores of aristocrats, then sold off their belongings. Precious artwork, gold, silver, furniture. Even China and French porcelain. Anything of substantial worth.

"All of it sold well below its value," Gilbert said. "Now the items are worth a veritable fortune."

"You've been trading in them," Mary said, gasping as the true nature of his shipping enterprise became apparent to her.

"You had to have known. You filed some of the paperwork."

"How dare you make me an accomplice!" For a brief time, when Mary had first arrived in Le Havre, she had offered to help Gilbert with some of his business transactions, filing and writing memos for him. "I wasn't aware I was dealing with contraband! Had I known, I would have refused. Why are you telling me this now?"

Gilbert crossed the room and reached for her hands. "Because I've arranged transportation for some of the French Bourbon monarchy's silver to be sold in Sweden. If I'm successful in offloading it, we'll finally make our fortune."

Mary jerked her hands from his. "You're talking about the black market." Who was this person standing before her? What had he become? He must be up to his neck in illegal trade. And she had been party to it! One lie was turning into another with Gilbert. How many others were there between them? "Have you no sense of what's right or wrong? If the French and British governments, both of whom consider me a dangerous radical for my writings, knew of my involvement in your sordid affairs, they'd imprison me, leaving Fanny without a mother. Why would you take such a risk?"

"Because it pays. Be honest, Mary, you know I've been smuggling for some time."

"Yes. Soap and other goods from America the French need to survive. You're contributing to the Revolution effort."

"While shipping to Denmark, Hamburg, and Sweden—also on behalf of the French government. I took the opportunity to slip in some cargo of my own. Not so much the authorities would notice."

Gilbert was playing both sides! France was at war with almost all of Europe; they could execute him in multiple countries. "How do you get away with it?" she asked, incredulous over his audacity. "The authorities can't be that easy to fool."

"Oh, but they are. Remember Brissot's plan to take Louisiana from Spain? My affiliation with him allowed me to go undercover and enjoy certain ... privileges in France. Working for the United States at the same time allowed me certain ... *other* privileges." Gilbert dropped his chin, peering at Mary from beneath raised brows. "Do you understand what I'm saying?"

The events of the past year returned to Mary with astonishing clarity. Their falsified certificate of marriage from Gouverneur Morris. How Gilbert and she had lived free of harassment when everyone else they knew lived in constant fear. The way the authorities allowed her to visit friends in prison without consequence. It all made sense now. She was the only British citizen she knew to escape arrest in Paris. Gilbert had his own set of connections. It also must have been why she had been able to arrange a passport without incident when she wanted to come to Le Havre.

Mary's hand flew to her mouth. "You're a spy after all." Her legs gave out, and she collapsed onto a chair. All the while she had been worrying about the French authorities accusing her of being a spy, she had been living with one.

"Not anymore." Gilbert rushed to her side. "I was a spy once, for General Washington. After being wounded. For several years, actually. But after the Louisiana plot fell through last autumn, I no longer work for either side." He jammed his thumb to his chest. "Now I work for me. For us. Because I get much-needed supplies into France, the French authorities look the other way."

"I don't know you anymore," she said, rubbing a hand across her brow. She got up and paced their bedroom. Had she ever really known him? Prior to meeting Gilbert, she would never have been taken in so easily by a charlatan, would never have even stood in the same room as a thief.

"Don't you understand? If we want to go to America, if we intend to live out the dream we've talked of for more than a year, shipping is our only hope."

"I no longer want to go anywhere with you. What truth is left between us?"

"I won't always need to take such risks," he said, trying to ease her consternation. "I just need to smuggle the silver out of France by getting the ship safely past the British blockade that circles Le Havre's harbor. After that, I can take more prudent runs."

"You're doomed if you're caught," she warned.

"I won't get caught. Not if you help. I have thirty-six platters bearing the French monarchy's crest. All solid silver. I've another thirty-two bars of pure silver. Together they're worth a king's ransom."

Gilbert led Mary to the edge of their bed, where they sat while he explained he had hired a man named Peder Ellefsen, a Norwegian, to captain the *Liberté,* a ship he had purchased, which Ellefsen agreed to sail to Gothenburg, Sweden. With Norway under Danish rule, Ellefsen would sail under the Danish flag. The authorities would ignore him. Sweden, Denmark, and Norway were neutral in the war between France and Britain.

"However," Gilbert added, "I've been summoned to meet with the French authorities precisely when the *Liberté* is scheduled to sail. Some shipments they want to arrange with me. While I'm gone, I need you to ensure the silver is loaded."

"What?" The thought horrified Mary. "Why me?"

"You're the only one I can trust. As you've so accurately pointed out, Norris is a drunk."

"You can't win. The French will arrest you for selling national treasures. The British will arrest you for trying to run the blockades." It wasn't just the blockades that terrified her. Algerian pirates roamed the northern coasts of Denmark and Germany. The looming threat of them was legendary.

"If stopped by the authorities, Ellefsen has agreed to say the ship belongs to him, making it impossible to trace its cargo back to me."

Mary crossed her arms and turned her gaze away. He disgusted her. She wanted to run from the room, to wake Fanny and take her away as far as possible.

"You owe me, Mary."

He was right. She owed him her life for pretending to make her his wife in Paris. Had he not, the French authorities would have arrested her, she was certain of it now. She would have met Madame Guillotine. Dread spun in her like a silk web, his growing deception leaving her feeling trapped when a far more important matter pressed at her.

"You owe me as well," she said, facing him. "We've a child together. I'll help. Though I warn you, this must be the only time."

In the waning days of July, Gilbert left for Paris, leaving Mary alone with Fanny. After Gilbert's departure, news reached Le Havre: a coup in Paris had overthrown Maximilien Robespierre. Behind that, a letter arrived from Gilbert.

Relieved to hear that he was safe, Mary rocked Fanny by the window overlooking the harbor. Robespierre's own allies within the National Assembly had turned on him. They seized power and sent him to the Luxembourg. The jailers there, however, were too afraid to imprison him and took him to the Hotel de Ville, where Robespierre tried to shoot himself in the head but only wounded his jaw. The next day, the National Assembly executed him and twenty-one others by guillotine.

Mary shook her head at the naked irony of justice. She never imagined the Revolution would evolve into such a bloody affair. In the end, the people turned on Robespierre. But one more death, one more slice of the guillotine, even if severing the head of a tyrant, offered Mary little cause for celebration. She had joined the misadventures of the French Revolution by agreeing to load Gilbert's stolen silver.

Not long after Robespierre's death, Mary watched as the *Liberté* drifted away from the quay under the command of Peder Ellefsen. She seethed inside. Around her, the sea was at work. Ships sailing. Men hauling. Shouts swallowed by the wind. She had grown used to the rhythm of the harbor life she had adopted. Today, however, the waters looked murky instead of clear. She had done everything Gilbert had asked. She had witnessed the Bourbon platters being stowed in secret. Afterward, she had given Ellefsen his last instructions. How she hated Gilbert's crooked business affairs, which sucked people in like the slick muck along the water's edges!

Mary lingered, her gaze fastened on the silvery-blue horizon until long after the *Liberté* was out of sight. She should have refused to help Gilbert. The entire time on board the *Liberté*, she had felt party to something sinister and had been eager to disembark, to wash her hands of it. A sixth sense rose, one that as of late refused to leave her in peace. Gilbert, she was learning, was good at weaving webs of secrets. What others might he be keeping from her?

Cicadas seeded the night with a buzz that would have otherwise been a welcome, placid sound through the open windows were Mary not reeling inside. She and Gilbert were in their sitting room in late August. Mere weeks after returning from Paris, he had just announced his intention to leave again the following week, this time for London. With Robespierre no longer in power, Gilbert expected legal trade to resume with England.

From the sofa, Mary closed William Blake's *Visions of the Daughters of Albion* she had been reading. "How little you must regard me." Her words seethed with the kind of bitterness she detested in a woman's voice.

"I don't disregard you. Shoring up contacts, that's all," Gilbert said as he hunched over his desk, dipping his pen into his inkwell, filling in the lines of his ledger as he spoke. "You're welcome to join me if you like."

"You know I cannot go!" Now was the worst time for her to return to England, and Gilbert knew it. Prime Minister Pitt was arresting people on suspicion of treason and libel, among them Thomas Holcroft. Even Mr. Johnson had been summoned by the government to defend publishing the works of radicals. The Treason Trials, as they were called, were part of England's backlash against the French Revolution. More arrests, Mr. Johnson had warned in his letters to Mary that were finally getting through censors, were imminent, his own a distinct possibility.

"Then I think it best you wait for me here in France," he said in the matter-of-fact way he had adopted with her. Everything had changed between them.

"And what of Fanny and me?" She could not hide how she resented his unexpected announcement, and she glared at him, furor pulsating in her. He seemed oblivious to what a prolonged separation might mean to her and his baby.

Gilbert turned in his chair, facing her at last. "I've already thought of that. I suggest you move back to Paris. I still have the apartment in Saint-Germain-des-Prés. I can arrange for Norris to provide you with money as needed."

How easy it was for Gilbert to shuffle her and Fanny about like they were cargo. "So I am to become a kept woman?" Wasn't that what being shunted off to Paris meant? He was abandoning them.

"Just because I am away does not mean you or Fanny are not constant in my mind." Gilbert said, putting down his pen. "I thought Paris would be best for you. I'll be back soon, I promise. Two months at the most."

He looked hopeful. The Gilbert of possibility. Mary could not argue with the wisdom of her staying in France. Here at least she was Madame Imlay and Fanny a child perceived as born in wedlock. Society's rules had not once mattered so much, but they did now. How long was Gilbert willing to go along with their fabrication of being wed? In London, where more people knew Mary, their ruse was especially important to maintain. She was a mother now. The pretense of marriage was all that kept society from casting her out along with her child. If Mary's secret was revealed, her life as a writer would be over. She would never publish again. Most damning of all, Fanny would be deemed a bastard.

"I shall await your return in Paris," she said, feeling trapped like she had when he asked her to help load the silver on the *Liberté*. What other choice did she have but to go back to the city where they had met? Every choice she made reflected on Fanny. She would do anything to protect her from harm, even if it meant swallowing her pride. With Robespierre dead, Paris was said to be returning to normal. The added possibility of reuniting with friends was further cause to go back. Those arrested as counterrevolutionaries were gradually being released from prison. Expatriates who had fled to other countries were returning to their homes and apartments. And Gilbert said he would come back to her. He had promised.

Mary quietly retreated to the bedroom they shared less often these days and closed the door, where she leaned against the wood as if to hold herself upright. Her fear of exposure was eroding the ground between her and Gilbert, ground that was slipping away like the edge of a worn cliff crumbling beneath the weight of their continued guile. When she and Gilbert started their lie, they never talked about how to end it.

PART III

Seeing Clearly

1795-1796

"St. Paul says that we see through a glass darkly,
but he does not assert that we are blind."

Mary Wollstonecraft
Letter to a friend (1787)

FOURTEEN

April 1795
Eight months later
London

Two different pasts greeted Mary when she crossed the threshold of the house Gilbert had rented for them on Charlotte Street in London. Her arrival should have felt like a homecoming; the house was in Soho, a block from her old house on Store Street. But her long-awaited reunion with Gilbert was hardly what she had envisioned. He brushed his hand along the edge of a table behind the sofa as if Mary and Fanny were forgotten relatives he did not know what to do with now that they were here.

Charlotte Street, named after Great Britain's queen, was home to artists and architects, a set Mary could imagine herself liking. Instead, she wondered if leaving Paris had been the right decision. *Business alone is what keeps me from you*, Gilbert had assured her in March. *Come to any port and I will meet my two dear girls with a heart all theirs.* Come to any port she did. When Mary feared Gilbert was never coming back to Paris, she decided she must go to London or risk losing him forever. She and Fanny traveled by ferry across the Channel, then took a coach from Brighton to London.

"I taught her to say Papa," Mary said, relieved to be holding Fanny in her arms so Gilbert could not see how her hands shook. She tried to coax Fanny into saying hello, but Fanny buried her face in Mary's neck. "She's feeling shy. She needs to get used to you again."

Fanny was almost a year old now, almost twice the size as when Gilbert had last seen her. He stared at the scars smallpox had left on her face, then looked away as if he found them painful to see.

"And this must be Marguerite," he said, focusing his attention on a young woman with a bag in each hand standing in the doorway.

Fanny's nursemaid curtsied. "Bonsoir, monsieur." When Mary had moved to Paris the prior autumn, she hired Marguerite Fournier, a young woman from Paris who hailed from a large family and was looking to earn her own living. When Mary asked her to accompany them to London, Marguerite accepted with joy. "What is there for me here? You are my family now, oui?"

"First time in London?" Gilbert asked Marguerite in French.

"Oui, monsieur." Marguerite's dark hair was tucked neatly under her white cap, making her round cheeks, which were always red from a persistent skin condition, stand out like ripe apples.

Gilbert. Ever the affable gentleman, Mary thought, as she listened to him inquire about Marguerite's past, how she liked England, whether he could get her anything. How easily he could address the nursemaid, but not her.

"You'll no doubt want to get settled," he said to Marguerite. He turned to Cook, a kitchen servant he had hired, who had just entered the parlor with tea. "Please take the baby and her maid to the discussed nursery room."

When they left, Mary willed Gilbert to look at her. Despite finally being in the same room with him again, she still felt like a cast-off. This was not the man who had flooded her entire being with his seductive, alluring presence, the man who had tantalized her with stories of adventure and promises of America. Even his silk-lined voice sounded different. She had waited the entire journey to see his eyes, for them to tell her if he loved her still. Now that she was here, neither his voice nor his eyes told her what she longed to know. Her spirits, which had been high in anticipation of seeing him, were felled as if an ax had been taken to them.

"You look well," he said after a miserable silence.

A fire sputtering in the hearth had done little to take the edge off the chill in the room. But when Gilbert said her name, Mary moved toward him, the ache for him to touch her making her want to run into his arms. "I stopped nursing Fanny." She did her best to sound cheerful. "To regain my strength." The real reason was to make herself more attractive to Gilbert. She hoped he did not notice the dark circles under her eyes or that she had lost weight in Paris, where her spirits had become depressed waiting for him, wondering all the while if he loved her, or if someone new had stolen his affections. His present detachment left her with new questions. Had he invited her to London out of obligation? Did he want her here at all? Mary touched the plain white cap, the one married women wore in England to signify their marital status. She hated the way it marked her, but she wore it out of caution—and hope. Her marital status on this side of the Channel remained unknown to her. They had never discussed it in their letters. Was she to be Gilbert's mistress in London, or was she to present herself as Mrs. Imlay?

Rather than remain steeped in awkward silence, she took in the room. The furnishings reflected Gilbert's taste for fine things. Walls painted saddle brown. A beige sofa and a scattering of wood-framed side chairs with padded backs and seats the color of tangerines. In the corner, a desk for writing next to shelves for her books. At least he had considered that much.

"I should leave you to unpack," he said. "I'm sure you've much to do."

Panic leaped inside Mary's chest when he reached for his coat. "You're leaving?" They were navigating shoals at the water's edge, and she was drowning. In Paris, melancholy had descended on her with a vengeance. The strain of their separation, the uncertainty between them, had thrown her into an abyss like no other she had experienced in her life. At one point her despair ran so deep she wanted to die. It had frightened her at the time to feel so hopeless. The same wretchedness stabbed at her again now, an echo of her desire to be done with this life, which, without Gilbert, had turned cruel and empty.

"Mary, I —" He shifted his stance, refusing to look her in the eye.

"Yes?"

"I mean no injury to you or to Fanny, but I must be honest. I intend to maintain my freedom. I've been living in London as a single man and plan to continue to do so, coming and going as I please."

Gilbert could just as easily have punched Mary in the gut. The feeling inside her would have been the same. Dizzied by his unexpected, cool response to her arrival, she reached for the back of a chair to hold herself upright. "Are we not to live together after all?"

"I shall try. But I offer no promises."

He spoke gently, but all Mary heard was callousness. A sudden reaction of wanting to lash out at him stole through her, the bitterness of anger spreading with it. Didn't he know? Without him, she was an unwed mother. She needed the protection of his name. Mary mustered the last bit of energy she had left and stood straight. "Do as you must. But know that I intend to present myself as Mrs. Imlay." She, too, could make demands.

"As you wish."

What Mary wished was that she had stayed in Paris where she could at least pretend they had a future together! That he could be so indifferent left her knotted inside. He was acting as though their life in Paris or Le Havre had never happened. She felt invisible, forgotten.

Gilbert apologized for having to leave so soon, but with no hint of remorse, he abandoned Mary in her new parlor.

How could things have gone so awry?

If Mary thought Gilbert distant when she first returned to London, his lack of attention diminished further by the day. He was polite, diplomatic as was his usual self, but below the surface, he was as taut as a stretched rope. Her own confusion over where they stood as a couple made it difficult to shoulder the ambiguity alone. In time, her own mood soured.

"Must you go?" she asked again one evening when Gilbert signaled his intention to leave after one of the few dinners they had shared since she had been in London. Marguerite had taken Fanny to bed, leaving them alone in the dining room. "I thought you might read to me in the parlor."

"I'm afraid it can't be helped. Something's come up." He rose and checked his watch, then stuffed it into his fob pocket.

"Is this how things are going to be, you hardly acknowledging us?" Mary asked, no longer able to suppress her despair at Gilbert's indifference toward her and

Fanny. "Why did you invite us to London if all you plan to do is act as if we're not here?"

Gilbert frowned, a lover's glare saying she had gone too far. "You're harassing me again."

Mary softened her tone, reminding herself she was on shaky ground with him. "Before, I didn't need to harp at you to spend time with me." Perhaps it would be better if he cast off her and Fanny. She would not have to try so hard to matter again to him. She picked at a loose thread on the sofa "Everything was once so agreeable between us ..."

He tipped his head to the side, surprised, it seemed. "Is it not still?"

"It is *not*. You're never here. When you are, your mind is elsewhere. I don't know who or what Fanny and I are to you anymore. I'm not sure I ever did."

Gilbert rested an elbow on the mantel of the fireplace in the dining room and stood in silence, rubbing a forefinger across his lips.

"We can't go on like this," Mary said. "I won't. I must know where things stand between us."

Gilbert returned to his chair at the table. In the past, he would have taken her hand in his to allay her fears, would have taken pains to tell her all was well, that she was overwrought, that she had nothing to worry about. Instead, he made no move to touch her. He leaned forward and steepled his fingers like an arrow to the ceiling, refusing to look at her. "I'm divided." Gilbert paused. "Torn between a zest for life and you and Fanny. I need ... variety."

"What does that mean?" Mary asked, her heart thrashing in her chest. "Nothing surpasses the importance of our child. You're her father!"

Gilbert looked at Mary at last, his eyes offering a blend of sorrow and appreciation, igniting hope in her that something between them remained in his heart. "I admire you, Mary. From the day I met you. And I've loved you. I gave that love without expectation. You, however, expect too much in return."

"That's unfair. I only asked for what any woman would expect. Love and affection. Undivided attention. The assurance of there being no one else with whom you'd rather spend your time. You give me care and consideration, not devotion. Not desire. We've not shared a bed since my return, and you've hardly spoken to Fanny. Why did you insist on us coming to London?"

"Because you were lonely." Candles lighting the table had burned nearly to their stubs. What little light remained flickered on Gilbert's face. "You said you missed me. Our being in the same city seemed paramount to you."

"Is it not to you? Have we really such different feelings for one another?"

Gilbert let out a sigh. A sudden weariness, a feeling of failure Mary seldom saw registered in his eyes. "I'm afraid there are bigger things than our relationship about which to worry."

"What is it?" she asked. "I want to help. I want to be part of your life, Gilbert, including helping you with what is not going well."

"The *Liberté*. It's been sold out from under me."

Mary swallowed hard, knowing what the *Liberté* meant to Gilbert, the extent of his investment. "What about the silver?"

"Nowhere to be found. The French authorities have called me to Paris to account for the portion of the shipment belonging to them."

For the rest of that night and into the next day, the story of the *Liberté* spilled from Gilbert one ugly layer at a time. When the ship first arrived in Norway the prior autumn, Peder Ellefsen claimed it as his, then sold it—after making off with the silver. Ellefsen, however, denied any knowledge of where the silver was. Gilbert had theories of his own, but no one knew for sure. As for the *Liberté*, Elias Backman, Gilbert's contact in Sweden, had purchased it back for Gilbert. The vessel suffered damage in a storm and was somewhere in drydock in Sweden.

"Surely, there must be some way to persuade Ellefsen to pay you for the ship's damages at least," Mary said, incensed over the way Ellefsen had manipulated them both. "He can deny he knows anything about the silver, but you had documents proving the *Liberté* was yours. I saw them. I saw him load the silver."

They were walking in the Soho neighborhood, the midday sun bearing down upon them after Mary demanded fresh air in order to make sense of the predicament they were in. To passersby, she and Gilbert must have looked like a normal couple on a leisurely stroll, not two people embroiled in a case involving international theft. If Mary had learned anything about Gilbert's affairs, it was that shipping was a treacherous business. The seas were trackless, lawful only so far as nations could exercise control in expanses both vast and turbulent.

Like love. Mary was finding it to be as turbulent. Talking about the *Liberté* shielded them from addressing their own falling out. She hid behind the story of the silver ship like a child behind her mother's skirt. Time with Gilbert kept alive the hope that he still loved her, that his inattentiveness was due to his preoccupation with the *Liberté* and the missing silver.

"Officially, I was to sell the silver," Gilbert said, drawing her attention back to the cargo. "The proceeds were to be used to purchase a cargo of grain in Hamburg for the French government."

"Officially? The French government knew about the silver?"

Gilbert nodded.

Another detail he had failed to disclose last summer. Her hand tucked into the crook of his elbow, Mary's nails dug into the sleeve of his frock coat. His ability to be secretive and get away with it, even with her, was maddening. "Then why were you so worried about getting through the French embargo? Ellefsen simply needed to get past the British blockade, which you said turned a blind eye to Norwegian vessels."

"Because I had more silver than I'd registered with the French authorities."

Mary should have guessed. Gilbert was swindling the French government.

"I brought charges against Ellefsen through Elias Backman," he said, "but I lost the case in a Norwegian court."

"So, Backman knew about the silver?"

"No. I kept Backman out of it. I didn't tell him anything about the silver, intending to alert him when it arrived to avoid him being implicated should something go wrong." Gilbert swiped his walking stick at nothing, making a whipping sound. "It's a royal mess."

Everything seemed a mess. The loss of Gilbert's investment in the silver. The *Liberté*. Their own lie about themselves. It gnawed at Mary the way a worm burrowed through rotting wood.

"Could you go there for me?" he asked, squinting at the sun.

Mary halted her steps. "To Scandinavia?"

"To settle this business about the *Liberté*. We're in this together, are we not?"

Together indeed, even if Mary had unwittingly been party to it, had been too trusting. But he was right. She was culpable as well for assisting him.

"No one could state my case better than you," he said as she weighed whether to go. "As an internationally acclaimed author, you'd be above suspicion. Your writings give you moral ground. I have no such credibility."

His praise elevated Mary in a strange way. At least there was still something he valued about her. Perhaps she could help. In *Rights of Woman,* she had railed against women who put their trust in romantic hopes, had mocked women who believed it was the female's job to gain and keep the affections of her man. Now that she understood the power of love, she better understood a woman's choices. Love was not a simple equation of giving and receiving; love was staying when one wanted to run. It was accepting what was ugly alongside what was good. If she could help solve the mystery, she could prove herself to him. Perhaps it would reignite his feelings for her.

"I could leave by June," she said, the opportunity to win back Gilbert's affection too tempting to resist.

"You're sure?" Gilbert asked, eyeing her with pride. "It will be the summer season in Scandinavia, but travel could still be dangerous."

He could ask anything of her right now, and she would do it. "I'll take Fanny and Marguerite with me. No one would molest a mother and her child."

"You're a courageous woman." Gilbert brushed a strand of hair from her eye, the most tender thing he had done since she had returned. "I'll draw up a letter giving you power of attorney to act on my behalf."

Mary reached for his hand and held it to her cheek. His fingers were soft and warm, giving hope that he could love her again.

"Your health has declined, my friend," Mary said to Mr. Johnson when she visited him several days later. "I hope you are taking better care of yourself than looks suggest."

Mr. Johnson managed a weak smile and sighed. "Indeed. My asthma tortures me. How I've missed your face. I feel better just seeing you."

Of all Mary's friends, Mr. Johnson had remained the most constant. Iris was in Manchester nursing her father, who had taken ill, so it was Mr. Johnson on whom she leaned. Fanny had accompanied her on the visit. The reserved bachelor fawned over her like a besotted grandpapa. Rowland Hunter led Fanny and Marguerite to the kitchen, promising Fanny sweetmeats from Betsy, leaving Mary and Mr. Johnson alone to reminisce at his dining table.

"You've been a great comfort to me these past years," she said. Being in his dining room offered her a much-needed lull amid the swirling talk around the *Liberté*. She could almost see members of Johnson's Circle filing in. "Without your letters, I surely would have despaired in France."

"Motherhood hasn't changed you. Fanny is a most amusing child."

"She brightens even the darkest of days. I only wish her father thought so."

"Imlay's not thrilled you've returned to London, I take it?" Mr. Johnson stirred cream into his tea before tapping his spoon against the rim of his cup, sending a resounding ping through the room. He did not like Gilbert. Mary could tell by the way his jaw firmed when they talked of him. Only Mr. Johnson knew their union was not real; Mary had confided in him while she was still in Paris. "Were you hoping you would actually marry when you returned to London?"

"That was never my intention. I don't need marriage to be happy. I don't expect to be loved like a goddess. I want to be valued for who I am, to be able to trust Gilbert, to count on him through a commitment marked by sincere actions and sentiments, not a piece of paper binding us together."

"I see."

Behind Mr. Johnson, *The Nightmare* hung in full view. "I'm going to Scandinavia," she said, staring blankly at the sleeping woman. For the first time, she felt an affinity with her. Was it a lover that had left the woman bereft, or had life broken her in some other way, leaving sleep her only escape? Without listing the finer details, she explained to Mr. Johnson the situation surrounding the *Liberté*.

"The nerve of him," he muttered under his breath. With undue force, Mr. Johnson set his cup in his saucer. "After all he's put you through, I should think he would have enough pride to fix his own mess. I don't trust him, Mary. I simply don't."

"I need to start earning money again." Especially now if things fell through with Gilbert. "What do think of me writing about my time in Scandinavia?"

"A travel book?" Mr. Johnson had already published her book on the French Revolution, which was receiving middling attention.

"It would give me something else to think about besides rogue captains and blackguards."

Mr. Johnson's eyes grew round with concern.

"I jest," she said, smiling to ease his fears. Writing, she insisted, would give her something useful to do while she trekked through foreign lands among people she did not know.

"Don't let him be a riptide that pulls you under," Mr. Johnson warned of Gilbert. "You cannot coerce love."

Was it so obvious why she was going to Scandinavia?

When Mary returned home late that afternoon, Gilbert met her at the door.

"I was just about to depart," he said. "I stopped to leave you this. It's the letter of attorney we discussed, giving you complete authority to act on my behalf in Scandinavia."

> *Know all men by these presents that I Gilbert Imlay citizen of the United States of America residing at present in London do nominate institute and appoint Mary Imlay my best friend and wife to take the sole management and direction of all my affairs and business ...*

His best friend and wife! She clung to his words as a swell of love filled the empty spaces his indifference had created. She was doing the right thing. Love resided in him still.

"Then it's set," she said, cheery that her mood since arriving in London was finally taking a turn for the better. She, Fanny, and Marguerite would travel two hundred miles north to Hull. From there they would book passage across the North Sea to Scandinavia. "I've just been to see Mr. Johnson. He gave me an advance to write a travel book," she added, hoping it would please Gilbert.

"Splendid. With both of us going separate directions, little cash will be left in reserve." Gilbert checked his watch. "I have to go."

It was not the watch he had been carrying, and Mary scrutinized it. When he saw her staring at it, he quickly slipped it back into his fob pocket.

"A new timepiece?" she asked. Certain she did not recognize it, her brow crinkled. She had seen his other watch, a silver piece, a thousand times. The timepiece he had shoved into his pocket just now was gold with blue trim and featured elaborate scrollwork on the cover. "May I see it?"

"It's just a watch, Mary."

His tone was condescending, setting off an alarm inside of her. "If it's nothing, why won't you show it to me?"

His eyelids flickered, an imperceptible twitch. "I'm not your ward."

He was hiding something. Mary could not allow herself to be blind to his ways. He was a new and different Gilbert than the one she had known in France. She held out her hand, dreading what he might place in it. "We've enough lies between us."

Mary trembled when he placed the timepiece in her hand. It felt cold against her skin. The back of it was smooth and bore an inscription. Blood thundered in her ears when she read Gilbert's name, the current year, and the name of a woman.

Mary thrust it back to him. Gilbert's possible infidelity had crossed her mind, but she chose not to dwell on it. A gift exchange like this, however, signaled something beyond a casual dalliance. "Who is she?"

Gilbert remained silent and averted her gaze as a pain as real as a dagger stabbing through Mary's heart squeezed the breath from her. She turned his chin with her finger so that he faced her.

"An actress," he said at last. "I met her last fall when I first arrived in London. We've been together since January."

January. The remoteness between her and Gilbert did not stem from the *Liberté.* He had found someone else, a substitute, while she waited for him in Paris, an insult worse than cutting Mary and Fanny from him altogether.

Mary's pain turned to anger. Sharp words flew between them, Mary accusing Gilbert of lying to her, of keeping her captive. Gilbert defended himself, saying nothing should prevent him from seeing other women.

"Go," Mary said to him, her body trembling, her words flat, useless in expressing the rage she felt at being deceived by him in yet another unscrupulous way. She did not wish to look upon him any longer.

"You're being irrational."

"Leave!" she shouted, pointing at the door.

Gilbert did as Mary demanded, taking the air out of the room with him.

Alone, Mary stumbled to her bedroom, where she locked the door.

A knock startled her from her slumber. "Madame Mary, you must wake up," she heard Marguerite say.

Mary stumbled to her bedroom door and opened it. "What day is it?" she asked, holding her hand to her head, her hair in disarray. A searing headache threatened to split her head in two.

"You have been sleeping for two days," Marguerite said, her usually red cheeks drained. Anxious, she wrung her hands. "Shall I call for a doctor?"

After Gilbert's confession, Mary had sequestered herself in her room, refusing even to see Fanny. At first she denied the reality of him having another love, telling herself that his affair meant nothing to him. For what other reason would he bring her to London? But she had convinced herself he had lied. He did not mean anything he had said about wanting her to be happy.

"I need air," she said, brushing past Marguerite.

"You do not look well. Would you like Fanny and me to accompany you?"

"I shall be back soon."

Mary roamed Charlotte Street without aim. She felt herself unraveling, unmoored in what was newly real to her. The premise of lasting love had always been suspect in her mind. Gilbert was proof that it was indeed a false proposition. With nothing left to hold on to, her life was devoid of hope, a feeling so black she could not see in front of her. Within minutes she found herself at the British Museum, where she was glad for the thicket of people gathered so she could lose herself in the sea of colorful ladies' parasols against the contrast of men's dark hats. She was ruined. Mary Wollstonecraft, the high-minded intellectual touting her love of virtue and freedom for women, soon would be outed as an unwed mother, Fanny known henceforward as a bastard. And it was all Mary's fault.

A statue of Aphrodite with eyes cold as stone stood next to her in a reflecting pond. Mary ran from it. Tears blurred her path, and she stumbled. A man caught her by the elbow. "Are you not well, mistress? May I assist you?"

Mary broke from him and ran until out of breath. She bent over and rested her hands on her knees to catch air. She may not have married Gilbert, but she had done something much worse, something much more dangerous than walking down the aisle. She had given him her *soul!*

They would have to divorce. A pathetic laugh erupted from Mary They weren't even married! Had they been, a couple could only divorce for reasons of infidelity or cruelty in England. Even if she was willing to accuse Gilbert of either offense, they would have to petition Parliament to grant them a dissolution. Another ruse, another deception. She would have been better off leaving her head in France, a victim of the guillotine instead of the folly she was in now.

Mary straightened her back and looked around, her shoulders still heaving. A woman exited an apothecary, the customary sign with the horn of a unicorn swinging in the wind over the door of the shop. She carried a bottle in her hands, one that to Mary was unmistakable. The bottle reminded her of someone she once knew well and pitied.

That night, Mary checked on Fanny as the child slept, stroking her hair, and running a finger along the contour of her tiny face. Her cheeks were soft, as though made of fine silk that could not be of this earth. Touching them produced an ethereal sensation in Mary. They, along with the sound of Fanny's breathing, put Mary closer to heaven, a place that would be easier than being in London. An hour passed until she tore herself away.

In her room, Mary balanced herself at the edge of her bed, where she stared at the laudanum she had purchased at the apothecary. A small, clear vial. She lifted it, a strange weight in her hands as she tried to remember a time when Elizabeth Wollstonecraft did not have one like it at her bedside. She had taken it to the very end. Which of her mother's pains had been the greatest, Mary wondered. Being married to a cruel man like Edward Wollstonecraft? Or the list of ailments that plagued a deteriorating body in which a broken spirit dwelled? Elizabeth Wollstonecraft was forty-one when she died, five years older than Mary was now.

The apothecary had spiced the laudanum with cinnamon, telling her to take only a small bit at a time. Mary tasted it. Bitter. Like Mary's life had become. She poured it into a glass and added wine, then took a drink. Then another, followed by another, each swallow forced, until the vial was empty. She wanted to deaden the pain of Gilbert's revelation. He was replacing her. She could not bear it.

Mary was floating suddenly, as though she had climbed onto a cloud. She reclined on her bed, where the cloud floated in circles. Faster and faster. A hum rang in her ears as she hovered toward a pending void, dark and inviting....

A shadowy outline moved toward Mary. A familiar voice called to her.

Gilbert.

Mary struggled against his arms. She wanted to stay in the void.

The sun blinded Mary. It was morning. She shielded it with her hand, grasping for a marker. Where was she?

Gilbert sat in a chair by her side, his eyes closed. His gentle face, reminiscent of their time in Paris. He had grown a mustache while living in London. She thought how well it became him, as did his hair, which had grown to his shoulders. Waves of chestnut curls rimmed his face like a picture frame. She stirred, and his eyes opened.

"You frightened us," he said, his gaze turning anxious when he saw she was awake. His eyes watered. "Had Marguerite not found you in time ...." He dropped his face into his hands, then quickly raised it and his eyes met hers. "I can't even say it. You must consider Fanny, Mary. You must consider yourself. What were you thinking?"

Feelings Mary had been holding inside for months burst from her. She did not try to hide her tears; she let them flow, releasing with them her humiliation. Her regret. He had ignored her and Fanny, she tried to say between sobs, had left them in Paris to languish. "I'm just so tired," she said, the lingering taste of laudanum acrid on her tongue. Her mouth was dry, as if stuffed with paper. Her head throbbed.

Gilbert stroked her cheek and wiped her brow with a cool cloth.

"Come home to me." She reached for him. "To Fanny. We were happy, were we not?"

Gilbert looked away, no words coming from him.

"It's done then." Mary dropped her hand and turned to a blank wall.

Gilbert laid down behind her and pulled her close, tucking her body against his like he did in Paris. "Don't think about us right now," he whispered.

What else was there to think about? Mary relaxed against him, like paper curling against a flame.

FIFTEEN

June 1795
Five Weeks Later
Sweden

Mary searched the horizon of the Kattegat Sea as if hope alone could make the *Liberté* appear. But the sea held her secrets close and offered a picturesque view instead, a silent, peaceful scene that, after staring at it, produced in Mary the sort of rapture derived from sudden pleasure, a feeling she had not met with in more than a year. Sweden was cold, a forlorn place. Breezes sent needles of ice through her woolen frock. Cut off from everyone she knew, she briefly escaped the horrors of her embittered life. She forgot the pain Gilbert had caused her. She forgot about her brush with death. After eleven fretful days of being tossed about in raging winds on the North Sea, she and Fanny and Marguerite would sleep tonight on solid ground.

They picked their way over jagged rocks piled on the shore, taking in fresh air before turning in for the night. Mary and Gilbert had agreed she should still go to Scandinavia after she drank too much laudanum. To get away from London, away from prying eyes. Her tiny entourage had started their journey to Scandinavia in Hull as planned, where the captain of the cargo ship promised to take them to Arendal, Norway or Gothenburg, Sweden, depending on which way the winds blew. To Mary, either would suffice. Peder Ellefsen had deserted the *Liberté* in Arendal; Elias Backman lived in Gothenburg. Her mission was clear: find the missing silver or collect restitution and arrange for repairs to the *Liberté*. She would go to the Prime Minister of Denmark if she must to hunt down the thieves. When she returned to London victorious, Gilbert would see her and Fanny as his real treasure. He would leave his mistress and come back to them. They had even discussed the possibility of meeting in Switzerland when her voyage ended.

She was lucky to have made it out of England. The cargo ship was cheaper, but after boarding in Hull, the sails went slack, locking them in a windless harbor for six days. When the ship finally sailed, halfway through crossing, the skies turned angry. Gale winds and violent waves blew it off course. At one point, the storm was so severe Mary was certain the ship was to become her tomb, her final resting place the bottom of the sea.

But the storm eventually subsided, as they always do, and two sailors had rowed her and the girls from the cargo ship to an island from which she hoped to seek passage to Gothenburg. There they met a sea pilot, who had ferried them to the Onsala Peninsula, where she now stood, and insisted they stay with him and his wife. Mary had readily accepted the offer. He spoke English, and her bones bore the overwhelming fatigue of a long journey. They all needed rest. Fanny was teething, and Marguerite had been seasick the entire time on the ship. Mary, for once, appreciated the cloak of anonymity. The sea pilot had no idea who she was, nor did he ask why she was traveling alone with a child and nursemaid. They would leave first thing in the morning when the sea pilot would take them to a station where a coach would transport them the remaining two and twenty miles east to Gothenburg.

A fishing boat rowed into the harbor, oars batting against its wooden sides, sending ripples in its wake. The smell of fish and the work of the sea reminded Mary of happier times in Le Havre.

"Mamma," Fanny said, calling to Mary from a cluster of rocks.

Mary crouched beside her. "What is it, darling?"

Fanny pointed at heartsease peeping through crevices of gray boulders brindled with lichen.

"Shakespeare's flower tinged by love's dart," Mary said, her voice quiet. *Love in idleness.*

"*Pensée*," quipped Marguerite, coming up from behind. Her cheeks were turning ripe again after being sick at sea. "A harsh environment for such a small flower, oui?"

"Oui." A pansy. Small but tenacious. Mary wished she had such enduring grit. The look of curiosity on Fanny's face as she picked the flowers further kindled

Mary's resolve to find the missing silver. Mary was not just there to reclaim Gilbert for herself; she was there to claim him for Fanny, too.

"In *A Midsummer Night's Dream*, a play by a very famous writer," Mary explained to Fanny, "this flower was white until Cupid shot it with his arrow." She pointed to the dark purple center. "Here is its wound."

A breeze lifted Fanny's chestnut curls into sweet disarray that matched her gaiety as she giggled at Mary, the edges of her lips still red from the lingonberry jam the pilot's wife had fed her for supper.

"The flower of love. A good omen," Marguerite said.

A chill sweeping ashore from the water signaled it was time to retire for the evening. Mary slipped a heartsease into her pocket.

Inside the cottage, the pilot's wife led them to a room with beds covered with dazzling white muslin. Sprigs of juniper strewn about the floor emitted a piney scent throughout the room. An earthenware stove the same cobalt blue as the sea sat nestled in the corner, where it radiated blessed heat. Marguerite flopped onto one of the beds and disappeared into the folds of goose down.

When she and Fanny were finally asleep, Mary moved a chair next to the window to write to Gilbert. Her body was tired, but her mind was wide awake. Each day of the journey, she had written to him, saving the letters to post on land. The letters were a lifeline, a means of keeping her afloat.

Though it was almost midnight, no candle was necessary as she began her missive. An amber glow where the sky met the sea was still visible. They were too far below the Arctic Circle to experience the midnight sun, her hosts had explained. Mary was seeing a white night, the space in the day which was neither light nor dark but in between.

Dear Gilbert,

I labor in vain to calm my mind—I am overwhelmed by sorrow and disappointment. Everything fatigues me—this is a life that cannot last long. It is you who must determine our future. We must either resolve to live together, or part forever. I cannot bear these continued struggles ...

Mary paused her pen and looked out her window at the village maypole near the shore, its ribbons floating in the breeze. Besides missing the summer solstice, they had arrived a day too late to experience Midsommer, Sweden's national holiday that marks the end of winter on the longest day of the year. She imagined Fanny and Marguerite dancing around the maypole, laughing amid other children's cries of glee. As the legend goes, Midsommer is a time of magic when plants acquire healing powers, when flowers can predict the future. On that night, young women pick seven kinds of flowers and place them under their pillow, hoping to dream of their future husband.

How Mary wished she could predict her own future! Her life was like a North Atlantic iceberg, the largest, deepest part of her submerged below the surface of the sea. What meaning her existence held seemed to grow more elusive with time, not less. While waiting for the cargo ship in Hull, a kind doctor she had met and his wife had taken her and Fanny and Marguerite the ten miles to Beverley, a place Mary had lived for a time as a child. She realized what as a child she thought was a cultured town was actually just a small village. Walking with Fanny's hand in hers in Westwood Common had reminded her of happier days when she had escaped her mother's detached state and her father's violent nature by spending time with friends she had made, talking of books they had read, writing silly poems to each other, and going to her first dance. People she knew still lived in Beverley in the houses that seemed not to have changed, whereas Mary had changed a great deal, so much that she was no longer sure of who she was, or who she would become. She was now a sojourner, like Rousseau, who had felt dejected and alienated when writing *The Reveries of a Solitary Walker* before his death. Like him, Mary was at present a keeper of regret and sadness. Geography was the easy part. What she longed for most was a map to her soul.

But she had a letter to finish.

My friend, I have dearly paid for one conviction. Love is a want of my heart. Love, in some minds, is an affair of sentiment, arising from the same delicacy of perception for the beauties of nature and poetry. They must be felt. They cannot be described.

*I endeavor to recover myself. The desire for regaining peace in the pure
atmosphere of Sweden lifts me, and I hope to hear from you soon. I cannot
tear my affections from you. Though every remembrance stings the soul, I
think of you constantly. Ah, why do you not love us with more sentiment? ...*

Mary folded the letter to Gilbert and retired. She did not have seven flowers,
but before she laid her head on her pillow, she slipped beneath it the pansy she had
picked.

Elias Backman had done well for himself. His bright red house, trimmed in white,
as were most of the houses Mary had seen thus far in Sweden, sat tucked on the
shore of a small lake in a forest of beech, pine, and spruce trees just outside the city
limits of Gothenburg. He had all the essentials: wife, children, a warm hearth, and
laughter. Mary needed no coaxing when he invited them to stay the night. She and
her tiny entourage had arrived on June 27, three weeks after leaving London.

At home, Backman presented himself as every bit the devoted family man
Mary remembered from when he had stayed with her and Gilbert the prior summer
in Le Havre. His straight, flaxen-colored hair, tucked behind his ears, brushed the
tops of his shoulders as he spoke, his movements animated. When not traveling the
seas managing his commercial shipping affairs, his family was his priority. His four
boys, all under the age of six, had been vying for Fanny's attention from the
moment they met her. Dressed in red-and-white-checkered flannel, they chased
Fanny around the table in the Backmans' kitchen after Mrs. Backman had served
everyone a hearty breakfast of crisp *knäckebröd*, hard cheese, and *filmjölk*, a
fermented buttermilk, served over *gröt*, a porridge made of oatmeal. The tastes did
not suit Mary, but she was grateful Mrs. Backman did not serve foul-smelling
herring for breakfast. The sea pilot had warned Mary that Swedes ate it at almost
every meal.

"I suppose you'll be wanting to discuss the missing silver and the ship, then,"
Elias Backman said, stroking the morning stubble on his chin with his thumb and
forefinger while he and Mary nursed cups of steaming *kaffi*. Coffee was revered in
Sweden. Backman winked while explaining his consistent possession of this

contraband. Sweden's king had banned it, fearing coffee would make Swedes too much like the French.

Mary arranged her pen and notebook. "Tell me everything you know." They spoke in French, the only common language between them.

"Aye. It's a bit mysterious, that be the devil of it. The ship landed in Norway in late August. A port called Goos, where it dropped off Peder Ellefsen. From there the cocky lad directed his first mate, Thomas Coleman, to wait a few days before sailing on to Sandviga. You remember the rascal Coleman, no doubt."

"The American from New England. Go on." She had met Coleman when he and Ellefsen loaded the ship in Le Havre.

"From Goos, Ellefsen rode to Arendal on horseback. So goes the story. According to Coleman, he waited in Goos as instructed. Ellefsen does not dispute either of these points. From there, however, the men's stories diverge like two meandering rivers. The silver disappears, and no one's been able to locate it since. When Ellefsen was accused, folks would nay believe the son of one of the city's leading citizens could commit such a crime." Ellefsen, he explained, was one of fifteen children from a family of substantial wealth.

Mary, too, found it hard to fathom that a young man so gallant could be such a lout. Her own recollection of Ellefsen the previous summer was of a pleasant man about her age, not a spoiled, arrogant sneak predisposed to stealing things that did not belong to him. She apparently had mistaken manners for scruples.

"Go back to when the *Liberté* reached Scandinavia," she said, trying to align the facts in her head. "What happened from the time it left France to when it landed in your hands?"

For the next hour, she listened as Backman relayed the string of events as he knew them.

"I reported the missing silver to the authorities," he said when he had gone through most of the pertinent details, "and the damage to the ship."

"Damage?"

"Someone had taken an ax to the side of it. After that, ice locked the ship in at Kristiansand until March. Without the proper papers proving it belonged to Gilbert, technically Coleman owned it. 'Tis when things got heated."

"At the trial, you mean?"

"Oh, aye. Sixty-nine witnesses in all. In the end, it boiled down to Coleman's word against Ellefsen's regarding both the silver and the ship. The authorities found a document in the captain's quarters verifying the ship belonged to Gilbert Imlay, but by then Coleman had doctored his own set of papers. That's also when one of the judges in the case was removed. Judge Wulfsberg had done prior work for me. For this reason alone, Ellefsen's lawyers argued that he was biased. Things weren't looking so good for Gilbert, so I bought the ship back for him. The ship is not an entire loss. Once it's repaired, Gilbert can use it again for cargo."

He seemed relieved about this, though all Mary wanted was for Gilbert to leave the shipping business altogether. "And the silver?"

"Ellefsen and Coleman continue to point their lying fingers at each other."

Fanny crawled onto Mary's lap, prompting Backman's youngest son to climb onto his. Mary and Backman pushed coffee cups and papers out of the children's reach.

"Where's the ship now?" she asked.

"In Strömstad. Waiting for you to authorize repairs." Backman's son slid off his father's lap. Backman leaned forward and pulled his coffee cup toward him. "If you want to solve the mystery of the silver, Mary, I suggest you start your inquiries there. I can accompany you and act as a translator."

If Mary could examine the ship, perhaps she could uncover some clues. But the thought of trekking through Sweden's back country with a baby in tow seemed almost as formidable as finding the silver. "I'm not sure Fanny is ready for another trip just yet." Fanny pulled at her ears, and a rash had developed around her mouth.

Backman grinned as he motioned his head to where his wife and Marguerite chit-chatted like tree pipits. "Leave Fanny and her nursery maid here. As you can see, my wife is lonesome for her home country."

Over the top of her spectacles, Mary glanced at Marguerite and his wife washing and drying the dishes. Backman's wife, a vigorous Frenchwoman, had taken a liking to Marguerite, making such a fuss over her that Mary worried if she left Marguerite and Fanny behind, Mrs. Backman might try to find a husband for Marguerite just to keep the dear girl in Sweden.

"Truthfully," Backman said, lowering his voice while Mary contemplated his offer, "'tis not Fanny I worry about. You aren't your merry self. Stay here a few weeks and recuperate before going to Strömstad. 'Tis nay bother to us."

His kind words reminded Mary how worn out she was. She avoided sharing details about her melancholy or her attempted suicide or Gilbert's mistress.

Backman believed Mary was Gilbert's wife; she wanted to keep it that way. "We shall delay," she said. "Your offer is most generous."

The minute she closed her notebook, the consequence of her decision to go to Strömstad began to sink in. The journey would take them a hundred miles north of Gothenburg. In the Land of the Midnight Sun, she feared her darkest nights were yet to come.

In the weeks that followed, with Marguerite available to tend to Fanny, Mary took advantage of the peaceful surroundings at the Backmans' homestead. The pristine summer air of the north acted as medicine for her fractured soul. At Backman's urging, she slept outdoors at night on a porch attached to the house. "To cleanse the lungs," he had said, looking at her like someone in need of convalescence. He kept watching her, observing her from behind his round spectacles. What did he really know about the silver? Mary had no reason to question his honesty, but if Peder Ellefsen could fool her, why not Elias Backman? When it came to health, however, his advice proved well-founded. The Swedes were a culture at one with nature and understood its ability to nourish the body as well as the soul. The sound of water lapping against the lake's shore lulled her to sleep each night after the last cowbell sounded.

In time, Mary's head cleared, and a stamina she had forgotten she possessed, trickled into her bones. Elias Backman and she also spent time wandering Gothenburg's streets, Mary marveling at rows of trees and stone bridges built by the Dutch. Gothenburg was a burgeoning world trade center, she learned, with a massive port, a city on the rise as an important economic center in Europe. Rich merchants and government officials were more than happy to meet with her when they found out she was writing a book about her Scandinavian sojourn.

"Your color is returning," Backman said to Mary while she helped weed his vegetable garden one afternoon. Fanny pottered up and down the rows, stooping now and then to investigate things appealing to a toddler's eye, colorful bugs among them.

"I feel better." Mary swooped to prevent Fanny from putting one in her mouth. They had been staying with the Backmans for three weeks. She had gained weight, which she attributed to the Swedes' long morning and afternoon *kaffi* breaks during which they served pastries and enjoyed conversation for hours, many of hers spent with Gothenburg's merchants. Talking with them made her feel connected again to a larger world, one she realized she had almost forgotten existed outside of the one she had created around Gilbert Imlay. She was even seeing Fanny in a new way, as a glowing, curious toddler; she had never felt closer to her little girl and wrapped her in her arms until Fanny squirmed free.

"Are you ready to go to Strömstad, then?" Backman asked, leaning back on his heels.

"I am." Being outdoors for days had stirred something in Mary. Living in a city for years, she had been missing a connection to the earth. Its natural rhythms was finding its way back to her, and she let it roam freely. She was feeling sturdy again, capable of achieving her mission.

Backman smiled, looking pleased. "I suggest we leave the day after the morrow."

Mary dug her hands into the dirt. "I'm ready."

The steep, rocky slopes of Sweden's verdant taiga continued to draw Mary from her melancholy. There were the lush moss-carpeted surfaces beneath towering canopies of trees that, had she been alone, she would have liked to lie under and rest. Magnificent trees—aspen, pine, spruce, larch, ash, beech—they were all there, too, soothing her like strong hands massaging the wounds she carried inside her. The surrounding beauty became the very air she breathed.

Her entourage had grown to four, with Backman joining Mary, Fanny, and Marguerite. Mary had insisted the girls accompany them. They all rode together in a rented open wagon, the most economical way to journey in Sweden. The sharp, piney scent and utter pageantry of millions of acres running from the southern tip of Sweden north to the tundra made up for the shake and rattle of their rustic mode of transportation. To Mary's disappointment, however, the sun stayed hidden behind clouds in an endless sky that fell into a distant sea. It was summer in Sweden.

And though the snow had disappeared, frigid air held a lingering grip on the wild, backcountry landscape. Wind cut like a knife through layers of wool down to her linen. She wrapped Fanny in extra blankets and held her close, wondering if she had taken them all on an endless chase that had no beginning and no end.

An abundance of wildflowers offered a banquet for the senses to ease her uncertainty, as did scenic valleys dotted with grain and dairy farms. Lakes with nothing but log huts on their shores and the occasional red cottage charmed her the most. The rustic dwellings seemed to shiver naked on the rocks. With no clear pathways to a door, they reminded her of druid's haunts.

At day's end, they rested in small villages and stretched their legs. Mary walked among the inhabitants, inquiring about lives lived in such a forest, recording notes for her travel book. At night, streams outside the inns murmured, easing her into slumber until the next morning, when she performed her daily ablutions in icy waters, the refreshing sting waking her.

After three days, they arrived in Strömstad, which offered little more than a blustery welcome. Rocky ground sloped to the water, making the frontier town seem barren other than clusters of fir growing between red houses trimmed in white. An empty feeling seized Mary when she looked out across a windy, desolate land. How could an answer for her possibly lie here?

"I can sell the ship," Backman said, leaning into a gaping hole in the side of the *Liberté*. His doubtful words echoed inside the cavern as a fierce gust of wind blew in off the water. "But it will cost three times its worth to repair it."

Mary slapped a hand against the ship's weathered, salt-crusted boards. The gash was the size of the wagon they had ridden to Strömstad. "I have to get to Ellefsen. He must confess about the silver and cover the cost of the repairs." Her anger was not solely at Ellefsen; she was put out at Gilbert as well. Before leaving Gothenburg, she had arranged to have her letters forwarded. With each mail rider that passed them on the road to Strömstad, she had hoped at least one carried a message from him. But no letter awaited her at the post, leaving her feeling even more alone in her mission.

"Give me a few days to shore up a crew to fix the ship," Backman said. "If you insist on confronting Ellefsen, I suggest you travel on to Tønsberg first. Judge

Wulfsberg lives there. It's possible he still can arrange for an out-of-court settlement. He has a reputation for solving these kinds of cases."

Even one that had languished in Norwegian courts for a year? It was a gamble. Prior to coming to Strömstad, Mary knew having to journey on to Norway was a distinct possibility. But Tønsberg was not only northwest of Strömstad; the town was all the way across the Kattegat on the Norwegian coast. And she would not have Backman to act as an interpreter in Tønsberg. He had been clear in saying he could only go as far as Strömstad. She glanced at Fanny and Marguerite playing a game of tag on the shore, the shrill sound of Fanny's cries of glee tugging at Mary's battered heart. The trip would be too much for Fanny.

"Leave the babe and go on by yourself," Backman said, as though reading Mary's hesitation. "I can take Fanny and Marguerite home with me."

Behind him, Marguerite caught Mary's gaze, intuitively aware, it seemed, that they were talking about her and Fanny. Marguerite was not as comfortable as Mary over them traveling alone through a foreign countryside. She had trembled the entire journey through the taiga, constantly reminding Mary she had not a pistol or a knife for protection should someone accost them. Mary ached at the thought of leaving Fanny, but Backman was right. From here, Mary must travel alone. They agreed to rest a week before either of them departed. Perhaps, Mary hoped, by then a letter from Gilbert would arrive.

Time seemed to have ignored Strömstad. Surrounded by a field of boulders, with more rocks piled along the shore to support its inlets, it seemed cut off from the rest of civilization. While Backman arranged for repairs to the *Liberté*, Mary collected notes for her travel book. The people of Sweden possessed striking features that captivated her. To Gilbert she wrote: *The complexion of many, even of the young women, seem to be bleached on the bosom of snow ... I wondered from whence the fire was stolen which sparked in their fine blue eyes ...*

Other small things intrigued her as she rambled about town with Fanny and Marguerite. Trees shrinking from the wind. Clergymen reciting prayers in the small Lutheran church. The hospitality of a family. The humanity she found in the social and political customs of these Northern peoples and their beliefs warmed her, making it easy for her to fill her notebooks with interesting observations.

On July sixteenth, with still no word from Gilbert, Mary stuffed her disappointment into her old travel bag and planted kisses on Fanny, then waved goodbye as Backman and the girls headed south. She, in turn, walked the few miles to the ferry that would take her to Larvick, Norway by way of the Oslofjord in the Skagerrak, the strait between Sweden, Norway, and Denmark. From Larvick, she would book a coach to transport her an additional thirty miles north to Tønsberg. With any luck, she'd arrive by nightfall.

Hours later on the ferry, Mary lay down on the floor and let herself dissolve into the rhythm of the waves. For the first time since Fanny had been born, she was truly alone. She slept as if she had not closed her eyes in years.

SIXTEEN

Tønsberg, Norway
One Month Later

Mary brushed her fingertips across the rough surface of the ruins of a castle outside of Tønsberg. The remnants of *Castrum Tunsbergis*, a once vast fortress, had become a touchstone for her. Its thousand-year-old stones were scabbed with green and brown and yellow lichen, their edges worn by the elements, a testament of endurance against the wear of time, imparting hope that she could withstand the collapse of her own stronghold, the home she had been trying to create with Gilbert. In her pocket were letters she had finally received from him. Two were dated late June, forwarded by Marguerite. Two days later, five more letters had arrived, all dated from July.

Upon a moss-covered rock, she read each letter again. Her missives tortured him, he said. When in one letter he wrote that he had broken off with his mistress, the possibility of Mary and Gilbert reuniting bubbled to the surface. But in the pages that followed, he became aloof again through words that neither embraced nor released her.

Mary folded the letters and stuffed them into her pocket, then picked her way through the long grass until she stood at the edge of the small cliff on which the castle perched. She wanted to be done with Gilbert and considered throwing his letters into the sea. He deserved to be abandoned, just as he had abandoned her and Fanny. But for all Mary's faults, giving up was not one of them. Having been in

Norway for a month, she could not stop now. She never intended to stay so long, but Judge Wulfsberg needed her to help build the case against Ellefsen.

Fortunately, Tønsberg was a tolerable place in which to be stranded. She gazed upon boats rising and falling in rhythm with silver-tipped waves glittering across shimmering water as fishermen let out their nets. Seagulls hovered overhead in anticipation of a free meal. Mary let her mind rest on the stark harmony between land and water until the view transfixed her, leaving her feeling as if she had been dropped from the clouds into a strange land, one that felt paradoxically like home. As a child, Mary's refuge from her family's constant tumult was nature. As in Gothenburg, she embraced the peace of the outdoor world, taking in the unique and quiet beauty a place like Tønsberg offered. When not visiting the ruins, she rode horseback, exploring the countryside at leisure. Tønsberg's Lutheran church steeple served as a compass that always led her safely back to town.

Tønsberg was the oldest town in Norway. The inn had no English speakers, but the mayor, who spoke English, arranged for a woman to visit Mary twice daily as an interpreter with the inn staff. She also taught Mary several practiced phrases in Norwegian and Danish. Danish was the official language of Norway, which was under Danish rule.

Today Mary was on foot, and she turned her thoughts to a cove a mile away whose mineral waters the woman at the inn claimed had healing powers. All Mary usually saw there were seals cavorting in the water, but because the cove was secluded, she could swim unnoticed.

She set out on a path along the shore and within a short time came upon a fisherman's wife slitting open fish and cutting off their heads before sending them down a makeshift table—a plank between rocks—to girls who were small, not even ten. Daughters likely. The girls removed the insides, cut the fish into strips, and hung them to dry on twine stretched between sticks. Their long flaxen braids swished in time to an invisible clock. The quickness of their hands and the nimbleness of their feet impressed Mary, and she stopped to watch. An older woman worked alongside them at a slower pace as if time was no longer her master; a grandmother, Mary guessed, her weathered skin a darkened brown from too many summers and wrinkled by winters that were harsh. Generations of women working together. Doing what must be done to survive.

"*Goddog*," the fisherman's wife said to Mary. She smiled and went back to severing fish heads in single, clean strokes. The heads landed in a bucket, making a wet, slopping sound. The pungent odor of harvested fish was strong, but Mary was used to it now and found it an almost pleasant smell, fishy and salty, yet another part of Tønsberg.

Mary returned the greeting for a good day. The woman looked tired, and her hands were red from blood, as was her apron from cutting the fish. The family's clothing looked otherwise clean, but ragged. One of the girls glanced at Mary through the corner of her eye and smiled like her mother as she pulled entrails from the fish and threw them into the bucket with practiced aim, her hands red, too, up to her elbows. "*Goddog,*" she said.

They talked for a short while, Mary and the women and the girls, the barrier of language keeping them from entering an easy exchange, but there were smiles and words and gestures that led to expressions they could understand between them. The day was warm. The fish had been plentiful. *Ja*, they were tired. But not so much.

"*Hav det godt*," Mary said when it was time for her to go. *Be well.*

In Norway, the people were kind. Merchant or upper class, they enjoyed one another's company without regard to social rank. Coming from England, Mary found the relaxed boundaries between classes to be as refreshing as a cool glass of buttermilk stored in a farmer's well. But the lower classes of servants and farmers and peasants were a poor people overall who worked hard for little pay, and it was this, perhaps, that produced a low feeling in Mary as she walked away. Here, like most places, society was uneven. Through no fault of their own, the poor were left with little more than enough to provide themselves with shelter and food. When trade was driven by greed rather than justice and a desire for fairness, it was they who suffered. Mary had seen this repeated everywhere she had traveled in life. Industries and vocations should create independence but also benevolence, she believed. She would write about this in her travel book.

To reach the cove, Mary rowed across a small, shallow section of water. Using a boat left by a farmer for anyone to use, she guided the small watercraft between rocks. She had become good at rowing and found it an agreeable way to pass the time. When she reached even ground good for a landing, she pulled the boat out of the water, then stripped down, removing even her shift, before wading into the cold water.

She swam for a time before floating. Ripples of water played against her arms and legs, making her feel like a child again until a deep loneliness for Fanny settled in her breast. Until arriving in Tønsberg, Mary had not had time to herself since Fanny had been born, and she realized how exhausted she had been from the constant demands of motherhood. She missed her child, but it was her mother she thought of at present after seeing the fisherman's wife and her daughters. Women did what their mothers did, and their mothers before them. Elizabeth Wollstonecraft had raised seven children with no help or support from Mary's father, who offered only violence and poverty. Was that why nothing rejuvenated her mother, why with each passing year she turned colder and more hostile, forcing Mary and her siblings to seek succor elsewhere? When a woman has been depleted, what was left of her to nurture others? Had her mother simply been worn out by all that was required of her, beaten down, crushed under the weight of disappointment?

Shifting clouds prompted Mary to consider the way her own spirit had diminished, not because of being a mother, but because of Gilbert. Her parents had abandoned her as a child; now Gilbert Imlay was deserting her. Alone and floating under a clear, blue sky, she pieced together the last few years, reconstructing events, plotting each moment in a line, from when she fell in love with Gilbert, to when she tried to escape into a stupor brought on by laudanum. Their downward spiral had started before Mary learned of his mistress. It had begun in Le Havre. But Mary had refused to see it.

The clouds held no answers. Mary swam to shore where she dried herself in the sun before dressing, wondering if life as it had become for her was still worth the air she breathed. She did not like to think of being no more, of losing herself to death. Her existence had become painful. But it seemed impossible that her active, restless spirit should cease to exist, for that same spirit was equally open to joy, as Tønsberg and all of Scandinavia were reminding her.

A young starfish below the surface of the water caught her eye. She poked at it. The starfish turned cloudy and flipped on itself. Its shell was soft, like thickened water, not like those with hardened edges she had seen on shore. This starfish, because it was not fully formed, had a white edge and four small, purple circles in the center that floated over fibers that looked like white lines. She picked it up. Out of the water, the starfish turned into a colorless jelly. Her mother came to mind again. Did Elizabeth Wollstonecraft stay with a brute, fearing she would become nothing if plucked from the only world she had known?

Was Mary doing the same by clinging to Gilbert?

For years Mary had rejected her mother by rejecting her own body. By rejecting sexual desire. In doing so she had inadvertently separated herself from who she was, dulling her instincts with men. When she made the plunge into love, she had no intuition to guide her ....

Despite her parents' failings, Mary somehow had grown into a determined person, had found her place in the world as a writer, which gave her agency, even if she, the sworn spinster, had become a handmaiden to love. *A handmaiden to love!* Of all the ways to disappoint herself! It was this trap she must escape. Mary had seen the different ways a man could hurt a woman; now she saw how easy it was for a woman to be party to her own demise. She had been angry at her mother for letting Edward Wollstonecraft erase her as a person and injure her children; now Mary realized she had taken her mother for granted. It was hard being a mother, harder still when the father did not do his part.

Mary wanted to leave a different set of footprints for Fanny, a path to womanhood that would protect her heart the way a thorn protects a rose. She let the starfish go. Wounds divided families. They could also bind them together.

Rowing away from the cove, the harshness she had felt for decades toward her mother receded like the tide. She forgave Elizabeth Wollstonecraft for being indifferent. When she did, Mary's own stricken heart lifted. Her oars glided more freely through the water. She would take herself back from Gilbert. If he would not have her when she returned, she would find a way to free her heart from him.

First, however, in one last effort, Mary must unravel the mystery that brought her here. When she returned to Tønsberg, she would tell Judge Wolfsburg she must leave for Risør. It was time to confront Peder Ellefsen in person so she could finally go home to London.

The boat on which Mary arranged passage to Risør coursed up a lengthy, narrow waterway, pushing against a forceful current. A foul smell intruded upon the otherwise fresh salty air, and she covered her nose with her sleeve. The water, a dark, glassy veneer, hid a labyrinth of rocks lurking just below the surface. An expert sea pilot tacked left, then right, to avoid their jagged edges while Mary's gaze darted along the shore. She imagined pirates skulking at every turn.

At the end of the waterway, Risør, Norway's third largest shipping center, appeared to have no more than two hundred houses. Instead of the red and ochre charm of buildings in Sweden, starched white dwellings with roofs the color of blood, sat perched on rocky ledges, reminding Mary of bird nests, each house with hundreds of steps leading to the front door. Planks hung between them for walking.

"The rise into town is steep, but it's not so bad further up," the pilot said, pointing toward millions of acres of boreal wilderness. He was from the United States and had served in America's War of Independence. When he found out Mary was married to an American, he took extra care to ensure her safe passage.

The forest was indeed a breathtaking backdrop to the shanty-looking timber town. They had passed thousands of logs floating out to ships waiting at sea to transport them around the world. "What are the people like?" she asked, wondering what to expect when she met face-to-face with Ellefsen.

"As nice as any you'll find in Norway. Inland, it's pretty countryside. There's a lot of shipbuilding here. Risør is an old Norse name that means island of thickets."

"Fitting," she grumbled.

"What's that?" the pilot asked, holding a hand to his ear.

"Nothing," Mary replied. "Can you take me directly to the British Consulate?"

"Not quite, but I can get you close. We'll dock at the pier ahead. From there, it's only a short walk."

"Confront the man yourself? Are you mad?" the English vice-counsel said to Mary at the British Consulate, his tone scolding. He tapped his fingers on his desk.

"If you know of an alternative, I should like to hear it," she said, feeling tart toward him when she had only met the man. "Ellefsen is a conniving thief."

The vice-counsel was not very encouraging, leaving Mary to wonder why she had bothered to seek him out. Ensconced in his office, surrounded by rolled up maps and books encased behind glass doors, he struck her as a man who did not like to make waves. She should have known better than to expect the British government to help an American. Who was Gilbert Imlay to them? She gathered her things and stood to leave.

The vice-consul sniffed through his nose, then released his breath with a huff. "That's the pity of it. I don't have a single word of advice to offer."

Mary sat back down.

"When you have money, you can buy just about anything," he continued, not noticing she had almost left, "including the law. The Ellefsens have bought every lawyer between here and Kristiansand." He went on to describe the measures he had taken to bring Ellefsen to justice.

He had been quite thorough, it seemed, and Mary began to lose faith. If the British government had not been able to prosecute Ellefsen, what chance did she have?

"Come now, don't feel too discouraged," the vice-consul said, a smile finding its way into his otherwise grim expression. "Allow me some time to give your situation proper cosideration. You've come all this way. I hate to see you leave disappointed. We don't get many visitors from home. Dine with me and my wife tonight at our home. The view opens to the sea and is magnificent. I'll arrange for some of our fellow countrymen to join us. It will do you good to see them."

Mary doubted that seeing anyone other than Peder Ellefsen would help allay her feelings of frustration. Nonetheless, she accepted his invitation.

After three separate conversations over the next several days, the vice-counsel concluded he had already done all he could to intervene on Gilbert's behalf. Mary's only remaining option was to request a meeting with Peder Ellefsen.

She sent him a note by courier that very same day. To her surprise, Ellefsen responded within the hour, leaving her to suspect he knew she was in town and why. The following day, at three o'clock in the afternoon, Mary met him at a tavern specified by Ellefsen. Inside, she claimed a table in a darkened corner, her back toward the wall.

"Water, please," she said in a phrase of practiced Danish to the buxom tavern maid.

The maid rolled her eyes at Mary's paltry request, spraying sour breath at her before turning away, no doubt expecting something more remunerative. She would have to pry skillings from someone else's pocket, thought Mary. The tavern sent crawls up her spine. She was counting the hours until she could leave Risør. From its rocks and brackish water to its steep topography where she had to climb two hundred steps to walk a hundred yards, the town closed in on her from all sides.

Mary jumped in her seat when the maid returned and slammed a glass on the rough, wooden table, water splashing over its rim. She half expected to see fins floating in it. She longed to return to her room. Fusty-smelling men covered in dirt and grime stared at her like ticks emerging from deep cracks in rotting wood. Acrid smoke from their pipes plumed over pewter tankards of ale. Shots of *akevitt* were lined up at the ready.

The maid clomped away just as Ellefsen, prompt and well-dressed, sauntered into the room. Instead of the sea captain's clothing he had sported when Mary had first met him in Le Havre, he was dressed like a dandy in a tailored dark blue frock coat with silver clasps. Ornate white embroidery decorated his cuffs; matching white embroidery extended down the front of the coat. The heels of his brocade shoes the same blue color as his coat clicked on the wooden floor. He joked with the men, a prince among his looters. Every one of them must be in his pocket.

When he finally acknowledged her from across the room, his demeanor changed to one of staged delight. He tucked his hat under his arm with more ceremony than was needed in such a backwater establishment and straightened his embroidered lapels with hands that looked to have never touched a rope or a sail, let alone handled cargo, and strode to her table.

Ellefsen bowed like a diplomat. "Mrs. Imlay."

Mary folded her hands in her lap, her nails cutting into her palms. "Mr. Ellefsen." By the looks of him, she doubted he had ever been a sea captain.

Ellefsen lifted his elegant coattails with a snap and glided onto the chair across from her. "I trust your stay in our humble corner of the world has been agreeable. You picked a splendid part of the year. I always tell people our summers offer the best in the way of hospitality. I hope your lodgings are ... congenial." Fortunately, Ellefsen spoke French. He was not much older than Mary. His blond hair lacked distinction in Scandinavia, but his glasslike, heron-blue eyes pierced his cod-white skin, making him appear as if he had just surfaced from the deep.

"I cannot and do not wish to complain," Mary said. Her words were as stiff as her back. His triangular face and pointed chin were more pronounced by a trimmed, devilish beard he had grown.

"I understand a book is underway describing your travels. It would delight me to serve you with particulars. My family of ironmasters and shipowners has a long history in the area. Longer than any other resident." He smirked. "We have many tales to tell."

Now Mary was sure he had spies. How else would Ellefsen know she was writing a travel book? "I suspect you know why I am here." She astonished herself at how cool she sounded.

"*Au contraire*. I don't care to speculate. It can lead to ... misunderstandings."

Ellefsen tended to pause before as he spoke and tip his chin down and to the side.

"As you wish," Mary replied, choosing her words with care. "You're the only person who knows what happened to my husband's shipment of silver. He demands you return it. If you've already sold it, you are to reimburse him for its total value."

Ellefsen picked at an imaginary speck on his cuff and flicked it on the floor. "And your other demands?"

"Full restitution. Captain Imlay insists you pay him for the value of the ship in addition to the silver. You had no authority to sign the *Liberté* over to Thomas Coleman. The ship was your responsibility until it was in Elias Backman's hands."

"I see." His smile, pleasant but bland, did not spread to the rest of his face. "What price have you attached to this ... restitution?"

Mary handed him the figure she and Judge Wulfsberg had arrived at for the silver and the ship, taking into consideration currency exchange values and interest.

Ellefsen glanced at the document, then slid it back at her. He smiled again, with sympathy this time, his look of solicitude taking Mary aback. "I'm sorry for this whole affair. I truly am. I can understand your desire to recover your investment. I would do the same in your ... position. I am a benevolent man. You must believe me when I say I would like to help, even though I had nothing to do with the loss of your silver."

Mary prepared to counter his claim of innocence, but Ellefsen held up a hand, stopping her.

"As for the ship," he continued, "my mother and I have discussed this issue." His look hardened. He leaned across the table and lowered his voice. "We cannot meet your terms."

Mary gripped the edge of the table. Judge Wulfsberg had warned that Ellefsen's mother was the power behind the family enterprise. "Cannot, or will not? Your family has immeasurable wealth."

Ellefsen sat back, looking satisfied with himself. "Wealth is one thing. This ... is business."

"I watched you load the silver," Mary hissed. "I was there when you signed for its receipt. How dare you steal from us?"

"The authorities found no evidence of wrongdoing on my part. I owe Captain Imlay nothing."

Mary's shoulders rose and fell, her breath quickening. "You self-righteous double-dealer. You paid off witnesses to give false testimonies, then arranged for a high court appeal before the lower court even issued a judgment."

Ellefsen snickered, then shook his head. "Why should I feel compelled to pay off a smuggler captured in his own snare?"

Mary cringed. It was true. Gilbert was a smuggler, making it harder for her to defend him. "Elias Backman said—"

"Elias Backman." Ellefsen swatted one hand off to his side. "Backman is a gnat. A pest. Swedes are always accusing us Norwegians of some kind of knavery. You mustn't listen to them. They will fill your head with rubbish. Plenty on either side of the Kattegat will swindle you at the first opportunity."

The meeting was not going as planned. Ellefsen was not taking Mary seriously. She fisted her hands under the table. "Pay me, or I shall go to Copenhagen and speak directly to the prime minister of Denmark on Captain Imlay's behalf."

"Ah! Bernstorff? When you see Andreas Peter, tell him that Margrethe Ellefsen sends her regards. I believe my mother dined with him and his lovely wife, Augusta Louise, not long ago when she visited them in Copenhagen."

The Ellefsens were on first-name terms with the prime minister. Mary held her gaze. She should have suspected as much.

Ellefsen crossed his arms. "May I tell you something else of possible interest?"

Mary stood. "We're done." She jammed a finger at his chest. "But this is not the end."

"If you are looking for the silver," he said, folding her hand into his clammy grip, "you are looking in the wrong place. Perhaps you should ask ... Captain Imlay."

Before Mary could jerk her hand from his, he kissed it, his lips cold, then stood, rising to two full heads taller than she.

"You must visit Risør Church during your stay." He let go of Mary's hand and smoothed his jacket. "Our ancestors built it in 1647. The church is of no grand size, but its Baroque style will appeal to your ... distinguished taste. It deserves mention in your book. You are a fine writer, Miss Wollstonecraft. Good day to you."

Had Mary had a fish in her hands, she would have thrown it at Ellefsen as he meandered toward the door. He had called her Miss Wollstonecraft. Did he know she and Gilbert weren't really married? Most of all, what did he mean when he told her to ask Captain Imlay about the silver?

SEVENTEEN

October 1795
Two Months Later
London

Back in London, the house on Charlotte Street closed in around Mary, turning her fretful. During the day, she slept. At night, she ruminated, her mind fixed on regrets. Her sojourn to Scandinavia turned out to be an utter failure. It was not as if she had not tried, she told herself again, a spinning repeat of what she had told herself the day prior, and the day before that as she revisited each step of her journey, trying to figure out what she had done wrong. After going to Risør to confront Ellefsen, she had returned to Gothenburg to pick up Fanny and Marguerite. Not yet willing to give up, she journeyed on to Copenhagen, where she met with the Danish prime minister. Andreas Peter Bernstorff showed no willingness to intervene. In one last valiant effort, she booked passage to Hamburg to sift out reports that the silver might have ended up in the hands of pirates. All for naught. Hamburg was a den of locusts, a hiding place for thieves. During the final leg home, the further Mary sailed from Sweden and Norway, the more her hopes that she and Gilbert would ever reunite sank. The melancholy she had battled against by going to Scandinavia seeped back into her, retaliation, she thought grimly, for trying to outrun it.

In London, matters were even worse. Already in a mental fog from lack of sleep and not eating, her mind carried the additional weight of gnawing unrest. In the volley of letters Mary and Gilbert had exchanged while she was in Scandinavia, he had insisted he maintained an affection for her. Though his words kept her close, they also kept her at arm's length. Gilbert had written when Mary was in Tønsberg to say that he had broken off his relationship with the actress. But now that she had returned, Mary sensed he had formed a new attachment. She could not live this way. She had to know: what was next for her and Gilbert? To her it meant the difference between a life where she could hold her head up in public and the death of her reputation as a lady.

Mary lumbered to the kitchen, her hair in disarray, her dress rumpled beneath the woolen rug wrapped around her for warmth. "May I speak with you?" she asked Cook, her voice shaking.

Cook glanced up from her preparation table in the kitchen. Flour speckled her apron. A dish of meat pie sat half-finished between them. "What can I do for you, mistress? Supper'll be ready in an hour. You look like you could use the nourishment. You've got thin as a rail."

"It's not that," Mary stammered. "I need to ask a rather difficult question."

"Ma'am?"

"I've noticed Mr. Imlay acting strangely since my return," Mary said, her movements rationed as she approached Cook. A blast of heat from the oven made the room feel like the underworld. She swooned and reached for a nearby counter.

Cook dashed to Mary's side and held her elbow. "Steady there. Are ye alright, dear? Yer white as a ghost."

Cook's look of genuine concern emboldened Mary, and she composed herself. "Have you any knowledge whether Captain Imlay is keeping another woman?"

Cook dropped her gaze to her hands and rubbed the dough still clinging to her fingers. Crumbles fell to the floor.

She knows.

The faint sound of Fanny waking from a nap came through the walls.

"Please," Mary said. "I'm the mother of his child."

Cook's eyes blazed as they met Mary's, and she jammed a fist on her hip. "There's a house where Cap'n Imlay sometimes tells me to send two meals." She looked away then, as if even she could not stomach the truth of some men.

"Can you tell me the address?"

"Aye. He'll fire me. But 'tisn't right of him, what he's doing."

Mary recognized the address, a house not far from where she stood. A double insult. Gilbert was seeing someone right under her nose. Her cheeks burned. Mary had probably passed the woman on the street. She pictured the two of them poking fun at her, laughing over how they were outwitting her.

She stepped outside, letting the autumn air slice through her. Goosebumps formed on her skin and neck. She walked in a daze, as though heading toward the guillotine in Paris for her own execution.

At the address Cook gave her, Mary pushed the door open without knocking. On a sofa, Gilbert nuzzled a woman's neck. He sprang to his feet. "Mary, I —"

"I thought we might still live together," Mary said, her body heavy as though weighed down with stones. "How wrong I was."

Gilbert stepped toward her. "I can explain—"

"Stop!" He was so clear to her now. She had known what she would find before opening that door. Seeing him with another, however, made it impossible to deny what she should have been willing to acknowledge all along. The answers she had traveled north to find in Scandinavia had been in London all the time.

In love, Mary had leaned on a spear, and it had pierced her heart. All the strength she had resurrected in Scandinavia dissolved like the starfish she had held in her hand at the cove. She made sure the latch closed behind her.

The morning after, like a broken limb lying on the ground with nothing left to do but molder, Mary gave in and began what would be her last letter to Gilbert, her last letter to anyone. Drinking laudanum the prior spring had been a means to numb herself from Gilbert's deceitfulness. This time she had but one thing in mind. Rousseau had once posited that when one's life had turned too ill and was no longer good to anyone, it was permissible to deliver oneself from it. Rational suicides, as they were called, were common in Paris. French politicians with their backs against the wall chose to kill themselves rather than face Madame Guillotine. Mary better understood why now. Like them, she could not bear what was ahead.

October 10, 1795

Dear Gilbert,

I would encounter a thousand deaths, rather than a night like the last. Nothing but my extreme stupidity could have rendered me blind so long. You had assured me while I was still in Scandinavia that you had no attachment. You have lied, again. It will always be so with you. I shall make no further comment on your conduct. Soon, very soon, shall I be at peace. Let my wrongs sleep with me. When you receive this, my burning head will be cold.

Your treatment has thrown my mind into a state of chaos; yet I am serene. I go to find comfort. I shall plunge into the Thames where there is the least chance of my being snatched from the death I seek. My only fear is that someone will try to prevent me from ending my hated existence.

Send Fanny to Paris with Marguerite to live with a German family that I befriended there while waiting last year for you; Marguerite knows where to find them. I do not want Fanny living with you. You love her not, and she deserves a home with those who are good and kind. Give all my possessions to Marguerite.

God bless you! May you never know by experience what you have made me endure. Should your sensibility ever awaken, I pray that remorse will find its way to your heart and that I, the victim of your deviation from moral conduct, will appear in your mind and fill you with regret.

Before Mary propped the letter on the bureau in her room where it would be easy to find, she took one last look at herself in her looking glass, staring at her sunken eyes. Her life had become a nightmare ....

Mary slipped out of the house, taking care not to make a sound.

The air was cold as ice beneath a roiling black and gray sky. Rain bit at Mary, stinging her eyes, distorting the path ahead. She had been happy in London. Still, no protest came from within. The Thames drew her like a magnet, and she followed, letting it seduce her to a landing she knew.

"Can you take me to Battersea Bridge in Chelsea?" she asked a waterman, a silhouette in the hazy glow of a lantern on his boat hanging from a rod shaped like a staff. The Thames smelled foul.

"Aye, miss. In ye go."

The wind muffled thoughts that, like vengeful selkies, tried to rise to the surface as the waterman rowed Mary away from the shore. Her mind felt as though she was already underwater, her thoughts drifting to the rhythmic push and pull of the waterman's oars.

Fanny.

Only she was hard to leave. Mary wrapped her arms around her torso and rocked, tears mixing with rain and blinding her. Fanny would not find her in the morning. A sorrow worse than death turned into suppressed sobs that wracked her shoulders as she tried to imagine the woman Fanny would become. Vibrant. Intelligent. Independent. She hid deeper under the hood of her red cloak and covered her hands with her face. She was no longer fit to raise Fanny. A child so innocent did not deserve the persecution of being her daughter, not now that Mary had sacrificed all sense of propriety, had lost all virtue.

The boat neared Battersea Bridge. A tower clock showed it not yet ten p.m. Mary wiped her eyes, the wool of her cloak rough across her face. "I'll give you six shillings if you row me to Putney Bridge," she said to the waterman. Far too many people were still crossing. Someone would try to rescue her. She would not allow it. By the time they reached the Putney several miles upriver, an hour would have passed. Fewer people would be milling about.

The waterman glanced at the sky, then examined Mary from under his black hat. Rain slicked down its brim, obfuscating his face, but she could see that he peered closer at her, his eyes gray, clouded with doubt. He had probably seen a hundred women like her, lost and running.

"On such a gloomy night," he said, "I should think ye'd be lookin' fer a bit drier a place."

She dropped her hand into the water and let her fingers play as though she had endless time.

The waterman sighed. "Aye, then."

Rain pelted Mary's hood. The vibrating sound lulled her into a trance, and she gave in to the motion of the boat. Had she known how illogical she would become loving Gilbert, she would have loved him less. *I would not have loved him at all.*

At Putney Bridge, the walkway was clear of people.

"Are ye sure ye want to go up there, miss?" The waterman swung his glance at the bridge, then back at Mary.

"I'm sure."

"Let me take ye someplace else," he urged, concern for her pressing in his voice. "I wouldn't charge ye none."

She looked away. If she met his eyes again, she would lose her resolve to the kindness of a stranger. She handed him the fare and hastened out of the boat.

"God be with ye!" he shouted.

The wind swept his words under the bridge.

On land, Mary gathered stones and stuffed them into her pockets, then walked to the middle of the bridge, where she took in the Thames, absorbing one last magnificent view. Late at night on walks home from Mr. Johnson's dinners, she loved standing on Blackfriars Bridge, watching the water on its way to the North Sea. Or welcoming it on its winding path all the way from the Cotswolds. The river had always made her feel alive, a part of London that mattered. She was a writer then. A philosopher. Now she would use the river to carry her away.

She stared at the water foaming below in its fury. "You must take me. I have nowhere else to go." It was a lot to ask of a river, even one as mighty as the Thames. But Mary's journey was over. She flung herself into the water, keeping her hands stiff at her sides.

The Thames squeezed her in its fist and pulled her down.

EIGHTEEN

"To take your mind off things as you recover," Mr. Johnson said, handing Mary a trio of books wrapped in brown paper and tied with a string. He looked at her with the same awkward, distressed expression everyone did now, adding to the self-conscious way she thought about herself. They were in the sitting room of Thomas and Rebecca Christie's house in Finsbury Square. The couple had returned from Paris while Mary was in Scandinavia and were living indefinitely in London. A servant of theirs swept the hall, her broom a steady swish, swish, swish, like waves against the banks of the river.

Mary rubbed her arms to quell the thrumming inside. Two weeks had passed since she jumped off the bridge. A pair of boatmen had rescued her two hundred yards downstream. Some days she felt like she was below the surface of the Thames again, the smell of rotting fish and sewage an overwhelming stench. The bitter taste of algae lingered on her tongue, and her lungs still burned from swallowing gallons of river water.

"I didn't really want to die," she said. She set the books aside. "I've a stubborn will to live. But I despise who I've become. I should have known well before I came back from Paris that Gilbert never intended to live with me again."

"Come now," Mr. Johnson said. "How could you have known? You trusted him."

"No, it's my fault. I was too set on making him love me." Mary was furious at herself. She was a smart woman, wise enough to never have put her faith in someone who had shown he would lie at any turn to get what he wanted. How could she have been so witless to his ways? He showed even more of his true colors at the end in the most unforgiving of ways. The boatmen had taken Mary to Duke's Head

Tavern in Fulham. When they asked for her next of kin, she gave them Gilbert's name and address. Gilbert never showed. He sent a physician with dry clothes and instructions to take her to the Christies' home.

"Perhaps now you can let the past go," Mr. Johnson said.

Mary reached for his hand. "Thank you for being here."

Mr. Johnson blushed at her outward display of affection. "Will you stay with the Christies much longer?"

"Mr. Christie has found me a place a few doors down. I move next week."

"'Tis a good plan."

Mary let out a sigh. "Is it? Even with my reputation being called into question?"

She was referring to a piece printed in the *London Times*. The paper did not name her. Mary was nothing more than the *elegantly dressed lady in her second attempt on her life in desperation at the brutal behavior of her husband ... resuscitated by a member of the Royal Humane Society.* But everyone in London's literary circles knew it was her. If the *Times* had not published anything, she and Gilbert might have been able to keep the matter private. She would never know who knew of the incident. The downside of fame. Everyone thought your business was theirs.

"You mustn't think about that now. The clipping will be forgotten. The main thing is that you are alive, and Fanny has a mother. What of money? Will Imlay support you?"

"He's balking at it."

Anger flared in Mr. Johnson's eyes. "Surely, the man owes you! After all the trouble you went through, chasing after his silver." He stood up and thrust his hands in his pockets, jingling the coins in them with his fingers and pacing.

Mary had left Scandinavia not knowing what to believe and told Mr. Johnson what she thought really happened to the silver, theories she had formed, from it sitting in Ellefsen's warehouse until the shadow of suspicion passed, to it lying at the bottom of some restless sea.

"It's just as well," Mr. Johnson muttered. "Good riddance to Imlay and his gross misdeeds. He'd swindle his own mother if it profited him."

"But where does that leave me and Fanny?"

"You can never go back to who you were before you left for France," he said as if he, too, missed the Mary he used to know. "But you can embrace the woman you've become, find another man to love, one who will cherish you."

"How can you possibly say such a thing?" The mere thought of loving another man reviled her. She had hardened, even if on the outside she must look to others like a jilted woman, desperate for someone to take her in.

Mr. Johnson looked shifted to one of concern. "Fanny will need a father, will she not?"

"No. Who she needs is me. I'll not love again." It was the only thing Mary was sure of anymore. "I shall raise Fanny alone. It will be her choice if she loves one day. I, however, will seek to ensure that if or when she does, she will have the strength to preserve her inner being in a way that I did not."

In *A Vindication of the Rights of Woman*, Mary had written that the woman who could govern herself had nothing to fear in life, a truth she believed now more than ever. She wanted independence for Fanny. And she wanted it for herself.

From the box of books in her new sitting room, Mary's head popped up. A sudden knock startled her. She had moved in this very day to her own house in Finsbury Square. Only the Christies and Mr. Johnson were aware that she was here.

Except Gilbert.

Mary brushed the dust from her hands. The possibility of seeing him deprived her of her brief moment of productivity, and she resented him stopping by without notice. But she had been seeking to negotiate maintenance for her and Fanny, and he was being obstinate. Perhaps he had changed his mind.

"It's you," she said, stunned.

"Have I interrupted anything?" Iris Kendall asked, holding a box decorated with a floral pattern and tied with a ribbon.

"Not at all! How good of you to come." Mary pulled Iris into a warm embrace. Her mood leaped at seeing her friend.

"It looks like Mr. Johnson's bookshop in here," Iris said merrily.

Almost four years had passed since Mary had left for France, yet Iris had changed little. The cold had made her cheeks red. Free spirit that she was, on her head she wore an old, green felt hat, and around her neck, a red and green and black plaid wool muffler. She looked like a gypsy. Iris could have passed for a young man were she not wearing a black and white thin-striped skirt.

"So it does," Mary said, pushing away a strand of hair with her forearm. The house was bare except for crates of books and other items Gilbert had sent over from the house on Charlotte Street. A few pieces of furniture stacked at the perimeter waited for someone to put them in some type of order.

"The Christies said I'd find you here." Iris set aside the package and removed her gloves. "I'm sorry for all that's happened."

Mary forced a smile, wondering if Iris noticed the way her left eye drooped slightly, a malady, according to the doctor, brought on from continued anxiety. "I'd love to offer you tea, but I have none. I've sent Fanny's nursemaid to pick up food and other items for our pantry."

"Fanny. Your daughter?" Iris's voice ballooned with excitement. "Is she here?"

"I'm sorry, no. She's with her nursemaid."

Iris beamed at Mary. "I've been picturing her. I want to see her as soon as you will allow me. Does she look like you? Do you like being a mother?"

Mary was eager to answer all her questions, but with Iris she needed to be honest. "Finsbury Square is just a temporary stop, I'm afraid." Mary did not even plan to retrieve her belongings she had stored prior to going to Paris.

Iris's smile faded. "So London isn't permanent?"

"I'm considering Switzerland. Or Italy." Paris would have been her first choice, but Gilbert planned to move there with his doxy. "I'm surprised you're still willing to be seen with me." According to Rebecca, rumors finally were circulating that Mary and Gilbert weren't married. It was only a matter of time before the truth came out, even though Mary still called herself Mrs. Imlay. Gilbert had agreed to it for Fanny's sake. Or, knowing the real Gilbert, Mary assumed he consented because he did not want those in their circle to view him as heartless.

"You know I don't subscribe to gossip," Iris said. "You and I will always be friends. Perhaps you will change your mind about moving. I, for one, hope you will stay here for a very long time." Iris retrieved the package she had brought and presented it to Mary. "Something to welcome you."

Mary noticed how Iris bubbled. Something in her seemed to vibrate. She had never seen her so animated. "Slippers!" she said when she untied the ribbon and opened the box. "How thoughtful." She held them up to admire them. "How did you know I needed new ones?"

"I didn't. I just want you to be warm."

Iris's gift blanketed Mary with affection. Despite not seeing Mary in years, Iris knew exactly what she needed—a new home where she could find comfort. "And what of you, dear friend? What news do you bring of you and Mr. Kendall? Are you both well?"

"Better than well. I am finally with child!"

Mary saw it now, the way Iris's eyes sparkled, the way her skin glowed.

"Congratulations! I thought you had given up —"

"The doctors insisted there was no reason I shouldn't be able to conceive, so I kept praying and hoping until one day I noticed my monthly courses had not visited me in some time." Iris almost danced on her tiptoes as she told Mary she was expecting in the spring. "Now that you're a mother," she said with uncharacteristic shyness, "I was hoping you'd show me how it's done." Iris had never known her mother, had never been around small children.

"Of course," Mary said, self-reproach seeping into the crevices of her confidence as a mother. Who was she to give advice? Twice she had been willing to leave Fanny motherless. "You'll be a wonderful mother, Iris. I'm not going to tell you that it's not challenging." Iris had an idealized vision of motherhood. She did not know yet of nights when sleep did not come until dawn, of worrying every time her child was out of sight. The constant doubt. *Am I doing this right?* Yet being a mother had brought Mary deep happiness, and she relayed this to Iris with enough conviction that she began to believe that she could be of help, and Iris to her as well. Parenting alone was hard. To have someone to talk to about cleaning soiled baby clouts or how to arrest croup appealed to her as much as receiving a new medical book on parenting from Mr. Johnson, a gift she always welcomed.

"But are you too busy?" Iris asked. "Are you writing?"

Iris's question dampened the temporary lift in Mary's mood that her visit had prompted. "Presumably a travel book about my trip to Scandinavia. I'm quite unmotivated." In fact, Mary had not an ounce of inspiration and would have given up on the idea had she not spent Mr. Johnson's advance prior to going to Scandinavia.

They talked for the better part of an hour, sitting on boxes in an empty room, Mary telling Iris of Scandinavia, saying nothing more about Gilbert.

"You could fill volumes!" Iris said. "I shall await your travel book with great anticipation. Don't be idle for long; you must get started. There are a great many who would delight in reading about such an unusual journey. There isn't another one like it. Certainly not one written by a woman."

Iris left then, promising to visit again the next day when she would demand an audience with little Fanny.

Alone again, Mary faced the empty shelves in her sitting room, and for a moment, loneliness pressed on her. But invigorated by seeing Iris, she opened crates and began to arrange her books. A rhythm from doing useful work emerged, reviving her. *Thoughts on the Education of Daughters,* the book she would always cherish for birthing her career as an author, stared at her from the bottom of the first box. Her pulse quickened. Mary picked it up in earnest, caressing it as she would Fanny. More than a decade had passed since writing it. She dug for the rest of her titles. One by one, they surfaced. *Mary: A Fiction. Original Stories.* Both *Vindications.* Her recent book about the history of the French Revolution. Like a collector reminded of forgotten treasures, she exclaimed her good fortune to an empty room, and with reverence, she placed them together in a prominent place on her shelves so they would remind her of her accomplishments.

She worked now at a steady pace to unpack the remaining crates, her mood improved, until none but one remained. The letters she had written Gilbert from Scandinavia. Mary had asked him to return them to her. Her hands moved as if without command to remove the lid. In typical Gilbert fashion, the letters were arranged in chronological order. They were all there, pages showing the shape of her words—a forward slant that revealed that she wrote quickly. Long lines across her *t*'s that stretched across the entire word. Em dashes—her signature mark—the only form of punctuation that kept pace with the rapidity with which she thought.

She read the letters one by one. When she reached her time in Tønsberg, her words reminded her of naps under the rock ledge at the ruins, the contentment she had found in vistas of the sea, the peace of trekking through the woods. Of riding horseback or rowing to the cove. Tønsberg had replenished her vigor. Mary grimaced, too, at the way she despaired in her letters throughout her journey, prostrating herself at Gilbert's feet, begging him to come back to her. Her letters did not record her journey as she remembered it. Not all of it, anyway ...

Mary paged through the journals in which she had recorded her travel notes, stopping when words caught her eye to read descriptions of people, of the places she had been, of all that she had seen. Leaping out at her was the other Mary, the woman who was curious about the world, the woman who reveled in making connections with new people and cultures. On those pages, she was a particle broken off from the grand mass of society, alone, but still part of a mighty whole. How astounding to realize she had never been afraid during her wanderings, except for losing Gilbert. The rest she took in stride.

Mary had been on two journeys, a melancholic sojourn that took place within, the other a tour of foreign lands in which the outer Mary was strong and overcame her doubts, enabling her to achieve new heights of self-discovery. During a time of utter aloneness in Scandinavia, she still could see how full the world was. What began as a search for lost cargo had turned into a search for her former self. She had found that self. For a time, she had been a sturdy sunflower bending toward the sun, capable of anything she set her mind to doing. Oh, to be that woman bending toward the sun again! *I cannot live on dreams lost to me forever.* Tired of self-pity, a vision for her travel book came at last—part memoir, part descriptive observations, part philosophy, like Rousseau and so many other travelogs she had read for the *Analytical Review*. Imbued with new energy, Mary riffled through her letters, possibilities flying from the pages. She would write the book in the form of letters, not the exact letters she wrote to Gilbert, but based on them. Notes from her journals would round out the narrative.

And what of Gilbert? Here was the easiest fix of all. He would serve as her unnamed recipient to make her travels seem personal, intimate, to make readers feel as if she was writing to them. Only those closest to her would know it was Gilbert to whom she was speaking. And Gilbert would know. She would have the last word. And she would not hold back.

PART IV

Vindicated

1796–1797

"If there be any part of me that will survive the sense
of my misfortunes, it is the purity of my affections."

Mary Wollstonecraft
Letter to Gilbert Imlay (1796)

NINETEEN

January 1796
Three Months Later
London

The wind howled outside, cold air seeping through the seams of Mary's window, causing the flame of her candle to flicker as she huddled under her bedcovers to stay warm. She read again the strange letter she had received addressed to Mrs. Imlay. The words took her by surprise. *It haunted him to know another possessed her affection*, a man wrote, He was taking a chance, he said, in expressing his feelings ...

> *I have discovered the very being for whom my soul has for years been languishing: The woman of reason by day, the philosopher that compares and combines facts for the benefit of present and future times, who in the evening becomes the playful and passionate child of love ...*

The mysterious letter was unsigned. The boyish simplicity of his affection when thinking of her, the letter said, reminded him of his days as a fanciful and ardent youth. In the last paragraphs, his words became more urgent, more desirous:

> *One in whose arms I should encounter all that playful luxuriance, those warm balmy kisses, and that soft yet eager and ecstatic assaulting and yielding known only to beings that seem purely ethereal; beings that breathe and imbibe nothing but the soul. Yes, you are this being ... I never touched*

your lips, yet I have felt them, sleeping and waking, present and absent. I feel them now ...

Playful luxuriance. Balmy kisses. Ecstatic assaulting and yielding ... Who had summoned such ardor toward her, and when? Not even Gilbert had used such amorous utterances in his many letters.

Mary's pulse quickened as her shadow stared at her from the wall, reminding her she was no longer a virgin. The words of one so besotted dangled the thrill of affection, reviving memories of France where she had tasted love in all its forms, had been privy to the private joys of deep intimacy between a woman and a man. A longing to be the object of someone's tender devotion still burned inside, haunting her like a dead spirit, an emptiness not even Fanny could fill. On nights like this she would welcome the skin of another to warm her, a man's arms wrapped around her in protection.

But the treasure of human closeness could no longer be hers. She had given in to passion once; she would not do so a second time, only to be left again, empty as a turned-over cup.

Mary had asked Mr. Johnson the day prior if he knew who had sent the letter. He had vacillated in his typical polite fashion. "Surely it would be best if you married. For real," he had said. "Think of what's best for you and Fanny."

Mary crossed her arms and glared at him. "You would prostitute me so easily?"

"Now, Mary, don't be so harsh." Unable to refer to her as Mrs. Imlay, he had resorted to calling her by her first name. "I can assure you, the letter is from an honorable man who would be a good husband. And a good father."

So he knew who had written it.

He refused to say more, and Mary huffed at him and left. It was like Mr. Johnson to busy himself with Mary's well-being, and now Fanny's. He had turned sixty that year and was the only "family" Fanny knew. Mary recognized she should be grateful for his loyalty. Her sisters had turned cold. When she had written to say she was back in London, they had again asked to live with her. Everina was working for a family in Dublin; Eliza was still in Wales. When Mary said no, they asked for money. When she said no to this as well, for she had none to give, she heard little more from them.

Mary blew out her candle. She would find out who wrote the letter. The expressed affection of this would-be suitor, no matter how well intended, was ill-timed. She was still healing inside from her tumultuous breakup with Gilbert. She would never be the same again. Her heart now resided in a locked box. When she found out this man's name, she would put an end to his deliriums.

Whoever he was, he certainly had a way with words.

The following day, Mary perused the titles of a small collection of books on a table in the Kendalls' apartment in Somers Town, wondering why she had come. The expressed purpose of the tea was for them to reintroduce Mary to William Godwin. Godwin had published his own political treatise in early 1793 when Mary was in France. *Enquiry Concerning Political Justice and Its Influence on Morals and Happiness* had thrust him onto the stage alongside her and other so-called radical philosophers. What his fame had to do with her and why she should meet him escaped Mary. Her last encounter with William Godwin was at Mr. Johnson's dinner for Thomas Paine four years prior, when Mary and Godwin had ended up trading fire across the table. But Godwin was good friends with Iris and Mr. Kendall, both of whom insisted Godwin and Mary had much in common. Mary doubted she and William Godwin shared anything other than that they were two authors. Iris had been persistent about Mary meeting him, however, and Mary had not the will to deny her.

"It's good to see you out," Thomas Holcroft said, coming up alongside her. "I was afraid you'd turned into a recluse."

Mary had run into Holcroft several times while visiting Mr. Johnson. They had picked up as if she had never been away, a true mark of their comfort with one another. His rust-colored sweep of curls, clipped short in a nod to French revolutionaries, framed his face, making him seem much younger than his one-and-fifty years. By contrast, she had found her first gray hair earlier that week. Women aged, while men became more striking, Mary thought. Even nature was against her sex.

"Mr. Johnson insists I can't avoid society forever," Mary said, setting aside the book she had been pretending to read. She remained melancholy in the aftermath of her second attempt at suicide, and, hiding, spent as little time away from Finsbury Place as possible. Mary was unsure who in the room was aware of her secret. Each sideways glance made her feel like she was walking into nettles. Was she Mary Wollstonecraft, or was she Mrs. Imlay? She doubted even she could answer them.

"I expected to find you basking in your success," Holcroft said. "You've risen from the flames. Yet here you are at a party, keeping to yourself. 'Tis so unlike you."

"Only fools tempt fate." Success, Mary knew, could be all too fleeting. Holcroft was referring to Mary's travel book *Letters Written During a Short Residence in Sweden, Norway, and Denmark*, which she had found the fortitude to write in November and December. Mr. Johnson had published it as part of a new edition of *A Vindication of the Rights of Woman* at the beginning of January—under the name of Mary Wollstonecraft. "To reintroduce you to the public," he had explained as his rationale for combining texts and using the name readers were familiar with. Mary did not care how Mr. Johnson managed the publication; she was counting on revenue from sales to rescue her from mounting debts. Gilbert still had not come through with a stipend for her or Fanny.

"Allow me to get you some tea," Holcroft said, and disappeared into the small ensemble gathered, leaving Mary alone again just as Mr. Kendall came up from behind.

"You remember William Godwin?" he said.

Mary turned to see Godwin, who had arrived fashionably late, looking not all that fashionable. His white shirt was crisp for a change, and his cravat well-tied, but his dull gray coat was too large. The seams sagged below his shoulders.

"Mr. Godwin," she said.

"Mrs. Imlay." Godwin offered the same perfunctory nod Mary had afforded him.

He, too, had exchanged his thinning, shoulder-length hair for a short, smart-looking cut and parted his hair down the middle. His hairline had receded further, otherwise, little seemed to have altered the man's demeanor. He still had a dour way about him, which she found irksome.

Godwin seemed to feel similarly toward her. They stood, a coldness between them, neither having anything to say to the other. To Mary's relief, Holcroft returned with her tea and he and Godwin struck up a conversation, leaving her to observe the two. How a churlish man like Godwin could write anything of public interest puzzled her. She had not read any of his work, but he seemed backward, ill at ease, as if being in the company of others was beneath him.

He surprised her when he turned to address her a second time. "Are you enjoying your return to London?"

His face and neck turned scarlet when he spoke to her. Perhaps his standoffishness might have more to do with being shy, and her hardness toward him eased. She said, "I seem to be making my way."

"When we last met, you were adamant that the resistance in France would unleash freedom across Europe," he said. "What do you think now, six years in?"

The Kendalls had no doubt made the same claim to him regarding what in common she and Godwin had, and she assumed his question came out of a forced obligation. Still, Mary appreciated him asking about France and not her. Though how could she explain that living through the middle of a revolution seemed easy compared to her life now? In the flames of the fire in the hearth behind Godwin, she could see the faces of Sophie Condorcet, Madame Roland, and Olympe de Gouges. How insignificant her life seemed, considering what they had done in the face of real danger. Compared to them, Mary was a coward. She thought of Helen Maria Williams and imagined what she would say about Mary's attempts to end her life: *Are you serious, darling? For a man?*

"Mrs. Imlay?" Godwin said, the dimple in his chin softening his stern face.

"Perhaps you don't wish to talk of it," Holcroft said, looking worried about her.

"It's not that." Mary had not attended a social gathering in months. Exchanging pleasantries when nothing about her life was pleasant except Fanny seemed trite. She was barely making ends meet and had yet to return to being her old self. But she was here, and Godwin and Holcroft waited with expectant gazes. "The heat of the fire made me lightheaded for a moment. I'm no less devoted to liberty for men and women. Though I admit to seeing governments differently now."

"How so?" Godwin crossed one arm and rested his chin on his other hand, allowing his ink-stained index finger to settle on his lips. The role of government, Iris had informed her, was his signature topic. He leaned toward her as though his interest was genuine.

At that moment, a woman walked up to Godwin and placed a proprietary arm through his. "I do hope Mr. Godwin isn't sermonizing," she said to Mary.

Holcroft cleared his throat and covered a slight smile with one hand.

"Mrs. Imlay," Godwin said, "I present to you Mrs. Elizabeth Inchbald."

Mrs. Inchbald raised her eyebrows and tipped her chin to one side. "*Mrs. Imlay?*"

Mrs. Inchbald's voice carried a mocking tone, making Mary's spine turn rigid. She recognized Inchbald as the author of several decent plays and a novel which she had reviewed some seven years ago.

"I don't believe I've had the pleasure," Mary said, alarmed that Mrs. Inchbald might know the truth about her and Gilbert. Her teacup rattled against its saucer until she pulled her elbows close. "But I'm familiar with your writing." Mary's review of Inchbald's novel had been uncomplimentary and hoped she did not remember, though writers remembered that sort of thing forever. Now Mary tried not to confuse her literary judgment of the woman's writing with her impression of the rouged person standing next to her. A flood of auburn hair dwarfed the woman's tiny face, and heady rose water perfume permeated the surrounding air, enlarging her already overgrown presence.

"Is *Mr.* Imlay here?" Mrs. Inchbald asked. Her flutter of lashes implied censure along with her wan smile.

Besides being an author, Mrs. Inchbald was a stage actress, older than Mary as far as she could tell, and attractive. Her beauty, however, would not be enough for the stage. A slight speech impediment must keep her from major roles, Mary thought. She seemed to be playing a role now, that of being a mischief-maker, a scene Mary wished not to see.

"Mrs. Imlay and I go back years," Holcroft said, stepping closer to Mary. "I'm delighted she has returned to our midst."

"Aren't we all," Mrs. Inchbald said. Another wan smile.

"Mr. Imlay has business that will take him to Paris soon," Mary hastily added, working to keep her voice steady. For now, the line would suffice, but later she must find something more convincing to sever herself from Gilbert.

"You'll be alone then. I myself am a widow." Mrs. Inchbald tilted her pointer-like nose in the air, then smoothed her skirt. "One adjusts to being alone. Eventually. Especially with someone as dependable as Godwin to escort you about town." She smiled at Godwin, who blushed an even deeper shade this time. "Though it is important to guard one's reputation. London is a small town. Will we be seeing more of you, *Mrs.* Imlay?"

"I believe you will," Iris said, coming to Mary's rescue. "You must allow me to introduce you to my other guests, Mary."

"She's beastly," Mary whispered as Iris led her away. Her previous review of Mrs. Inchbald's play had included phrases like "insipid dialogue," "uninteresting caricatures," and "childish tricks." Little did she know at the time how accurately her review described Mrs. Inchbald in person.

"Men flock to her," Iris said, sounding a warning. "I can't stand her piety, but Mr. Kendall seems taken with her acting. One would think she's a duchess by the way she holds court. Watch yourself. She doesn't like competition."

Mary looked askance at Iris. "She needn't worry about me." Mary had no intention of competing with Mrs. Inchbald, or any woman. "I'm done with men."

Iris arched a brow and smiled. "We'll see." Before Mary could respond, Iris introduced her to Amelia Alderson, an aspiring writer visiting from Norwich.

"Mrs. Inchbald is my chaperone," Miss Alderson explained, leaving Mary to take immediate pity on the young woman, who was vibrant and pretty. A painter would find her an ideal model for producing the most alluring of portraits. Her auburn hair was swept back with a Grecian braid below the crown. She had dark, heavy brows, eyes of brown that saw through others, and a small mouth with a protruding lower lip that made her look tempting. Her light blue dress with corresponding lace was fine without being showy. Mary liked her immediately. Amelia Alderson was self-assured and spoke well, leaving Mary to presume her a woman of intellect.

"I just finished reading *Letters from Sweden*," Miss Alderson said. "The book excited the philosopher in me, but I was most taken by the woman in you, a true creature of feeling and imagination. A woman traveling alone with her child. How remarkable a story."

Miss Alderson's effusive praise was unexpected, and pride seeped into a space in Mary where no other feeling seemed possible. Early reviews for *Letters* had been favorable, but hearing the reaction of a reader, a woman whom Mary's words had so obviously touched, produced true satisfaction. For the next hour, Mary and Miss Alderson talked of books and travel as if they were old friends.

By the time Mary left that afternoon she felt like a normal human being, a sentiment she had not been able to claim in months.

"Citizens should trust no government institution," William Godwin insisted. He spoke with conviction, making everyone sit up in their chair, Mary included. "The law sided with a man guilty of murder simply and only because the man was rich."

To herself, Mary wondered, was that the fault of government as an institution, or was it because the too few in power tended to elect corrupt men?

Several days after tea at the Kendalls' apartment, Rebecca Christie was hosting a small dinner party at which guests were discussing Godwin's novel, *Caleb Williams*. Mary had not been following the conversation that closely. But despite what she had observed in France, she still believed representative government was best for its citizens, unlike Godwin, who denounced any form of government. Raise people to be educated, to be moral citizens, he said, and no set of rules governing their actions will be necessary.

Was such a thing possible?

Mary experienced a twinge of envy when Iris goaded Godwin into a friendly debate. Iris was quick on her feet.

Like Mary used to be.

The Mary of old had yet to show up at anyone's table. It was a small gathering, and those present seemed entertained by Godwin and Iris's exchange of witty repartee, allowing Mary's thoughts to disappear into the dark gravy of a beef stew footmen ladled onto the plates. She had not wanted to come; she was here to keep

Rebecca company. Her family's business had dispatched Thomas Christie to Surinam to oversee affairs there, leaving Rebecca by herself.

Godwin certainly had the room's attention. Without meaning to, Mary compared him to Gilbert, who was always at the rim of her thoughts. At times like this, the pain of missing him was acute. Both men had a sort of magnetism that made people stop and listen for the same reasons—they had a brilliance about them. But their similarities ended there. Gilbert was smooth, debonair even, whereas Godwin was abrupt, sharp. He could run roughshod over a less capable conversation partner. And whereas Gilbert would have seduced the entire table by now with his wit, leading everyone to believe him clever and refined, Godwin seemed incapable of disguising his true feelings. He used words to provoke others into meaningful debate, to share ideas and imagine a better political future, rather than manipulate them like she had seen Gilbert do.

Shame at her own ability to fool others poked at Mary. Trotting herself into society as a married woman ate away at her ability to relax. She picked at her food, pushing it around on her plate like Fanny did. Who was she anymore? Had she been pretending to be a writer as well? Whatever propensity for words she might have had at one time, like that which Godwin now displayed with admirable finesse, she no longer possessed. Concentration eluded her. She could not think straight, not even now when she should have been engaged in the spirited dialogue at the table. The miles she had traveled and the scandal she brought upon herself had wrung all talent from her. In the present conversation, it did not help that she had not read the book.

"My exact point in *Caleb Williams*," she heard Godwin say to Thomas Holcroft, also in attendance. "I wrote it as a call to *stop* governments' tyranny."

By now, Mary had lost complete track of the discussion. She must abandon all thought of Gilbert, she scolded to herself, lest she suffocate from the desolation she carried around inside. Politics still roused her, and she renewed her effort to listen and picked up threads of meaning. Godwin lacked tact, but he used literature to forward his political ideals, much as she had attempted to do through the principal character in *Mary: A Fiction*.

"Your hero, Caleb Williams," she said, warming up to the topic, "is meant to illustrate life's harsh realities and draw sympathy for the poor, is he not?"

Godwin leaned back, hooking his arm on the corner of the back of his chair. "Precisely. Caleb has no chance of rising in life because of the lowly circumstances of his birth."

"Between you there is a shared a compassion for the poor," Iris said, looking at Mary, then at Godwin. "Have you read Mary's recent *Letters*?" she asked him.

"I regret I have not," he said, looking at Mary with curiosity.

"Your descriptions of a wild, harsh land mesmerized me," Iris said to Mary. "Reading, I felt as if I was walking alongside you, breathing the same crisp, clear air, taking in nature's sublime beauty."

Mary demurred. She did not deserve such accolades, and Iris was making her comments for Godwin's benefit; she had already expressed to Mary her sentiments about *Letters*.

"It is far more than a travelog," Rebecca interjected, conspiring with Iris, it seemed, to focus conversation on Mary. "Such candid personal introspection makes it far more. The lens into your soul at a time of great uncertainty reflected a spiritedness many of us wish we possessed. Brava."

"Your compliments, both of you, are most kind," Mary said. Her friends were matchmaking, and she wanted them to stop. Mr. Johnson was doing enough damage in that category. But she appreciated her friends' sentiments about her book. "I've always viewed solitude and reflection as central to my well-being. Writing *Letters,* I was able to look back on my time in Scandinavia, which proved to be restorative while there and in the months that followed." A younger Mary would have thought such a book mawkish. Not so anymore. Her bare expressions of the heart drew readers in, and this pleased her.

"I found your commentary on social issues equally compelling," Mr. Kendall said. "You must read it, Godwin."

Mary thought of the fisherman's wife and her children working a day's labor for little pay. "I am delighted you found it so," she said to Mr. Kendall. She did not just focus on nature in *Letters*. Critical social issues like commerce, prison reform, land rights, and divorce laws, as well as lighter, less controversial topics like gardening and salt works, had made their way onto the pages.

Footmen arrived with a rich cherry clafoutis for dessert, the sweetness of the delectable French dish wafting through the dining room as another footman filled the ladies' glasses with sherry and the men's with cognac from Mr. Christie's private collection. While Mary and Mr. Kendall discussed the importance of a society's benevolence, Godwin listened with undivided attention, leaning forward on his arms, his eyes never wavering from Mary.

It was quite possible, Mary decided, that her compassion for the poor really did align with Godwin's, and this gratified her for reasons she could not fathom.

Several days later, as Mary was reading to Fanny in her sitting room, Marguerite entered with a note. Her look was one of concern. "The courier said it's urgent, Madame."

As Marguerite bit her lip, Mary tore the message open, her glance flying to the signature before reading through the contents. Mr. Kendall. Her lips trembled as she raced through the words, reading them aloud. There was an emergency. Could she come to their house right away?

Having no money for a cab, Mary sped on foot through a thin layer of crusted snow. Memories of Fanny Blood dying after childbirth attacked her senses. *I must remain calm.* Iris was at least five months away from delivering her baby and was healthy, not weakened with consumption like Fanny Blood had been. Still, Mary knew how quickly things could turn. The agony of losing her friend all those years ago swooped down on her as she realized she was running, her red cloak flying.

Mr. Kendall hung his head when she arrived. Tears had left streaks down his cheeks.

"Where's Iris?" she asked, frantic.

"In our bedroom."

Mary uttered a silent prayer of thanks. Iris was not dead. "Is it the baby?"

The same kind of sorrow she had seen in Fanny Blood's husband flickered in Mr. Kendall's eyes. A miscarriage. He pressed his thumb and index finger to the bridge of his nose to staunch his tears.

Mary put her hand on his arm to comfort him. "Take me to her."

"I warn you, she's inconsolable."

In the bedroom, Iris lay on her side, facing a wall papered with white lilies of the valley and green stems. Mary was confused. No signs of a miscarriage were anywhere. No stripping of beds. No leftover wash basins. No sickening smell of blood that had pervaded her sense of smell for months after Fanny Blood died.

Mary laid a hand on Iris's shoulder. "My darling friend."

With coaxing, Iris turned her splotched face to Mary, her eyes rimmed in red. "There never was a baby," she whispered.

"How is that possible?" Iris showed all the signs. Her courses had stopped. In the morning, she was queasy. Her breasts were tender. Even her abdomen had begun to enlarge. Mary had seen it with her own eyes.

Iris sat up and wiped her eyes. "My monthly courses started last night. This morning the doctor called it a false pregnancy."

"My sweet Iris," Mary said, caressing Iris's brow, trying to imagine what pain Iris must be feeling.

"I wanted a baby so badly I willed myself into thinking I was pregnant until my body believed it."

Iris leaned against her and cried as Mary cradled her friend in her arms. Mary knew from the medical books she had accumulated how the mind could trick the body. The mysterious pregnancy of Queen Mary of England. Soldiers who lost an arm or leg and insisted they could still feel its pain years after their amputation. People who thought they were blind who woke up to find their sight had miraculously returned.

A woman's will was strong; it made her powerful. But it could also misguide her. Mary had learned that lesson well, making it easy to see how Iris could have fooled herself.

Together, the two friends wept.

TWENTY

Two Months Later
April 1796

"I hear a new determination in you," Rebecca said to Mary, squeezing her hand. Her eyes were bright with hope. One of her maids had just taken Fanny to the kitchen for a biscuit, leaving the two of them alone. "Do you mean it this time?"

"I am resolved to move on," Mary replied, knowing how many hours Rebecca had listened to her complain about Gilbert. "A heart can be easily fooled, and now I must reap the consequences. But first, I must bury the past."

She had just returned from Sonning in Berkshire, where she and Fanny and Marguerite spent time with an old friend Mary had met in Newington Green. When the friend had learned that Mary's husband had abandoned her, she invited her to recuperate in the country. Following an unpleasant encounter with Gilbert at the Christies in February, Mary had seized the chance to get away. The trip resulted in what she had hoped. Healing. Tired of living in the margins, Mary finally saw the futility of her emotions. It was nothing but stubborn folly to hold on to Gilbert. It was time to regain her sense of independence. To reclaim her ability to live according to reason, rather than let sentiment heave her along in life.

"Relinquish the past you must. I think it a capital plan, as would Mr. Christie if he were here," Rebecca said, patting Mary's hand. Mr. Christie was still in Surinam. "But what of our friend, Iris? It's her letters that worry me now that you will be settled."

"As they do me," Mary said. After Iris's false pregnancy, she had removed herself to Manchester and the comfort of her childhood home. Alone. Without Mr. Kendall. She was still there, refusing to come home. "Between the lines of her letters, I sense her mental state is still fragile. I know too well what havoc melancholy can bear on a person. Time away will do her good."

"Or it can deepen one's pain." Rebecca looked forlorn. "My Mr. Christie is still away. I can only imagine how Mr. Kendall would be a comfort to Iris, were he at her side. They are so very much in love. Would you not agree?"

As were the Christies, and Mary could not ignore the great sadness she felt for both of her friends who had made love matches. Perhaps that was the key to marriage, to wed someone whom you loved not just because he swept you off your feet, but because the initial bond had been formed on the basis of trust and respect. She should have known that a relationship founded under the veil of falsehood could never rise to one of truth and honor. It was a simple fact of human intercourse: lies beget more lies.

"I believe my own way became clear to me while I was gone," Mary said. "I've decided to move."

"To the Continent? Please tell me you are not leaving London. I should be much too lonely here with both you and Mr. Christie away."

"I intend to move within the city. For now. To an apartment on Cummings Street. Mr. Johnson has offered me my old position as a reviewer at the *Analytical Review* and the added role of editorial assistant. I start immediately." It was just what Mary needed to get back on her feet.

"Has Gilbert come through with his promise of a stipend?" Rebecca asked.

"Sadly, no." Gilbert had finally moved to Paris, leaving Mary poorer than she had been in some time. *Letters* was selling so well that it was being translated into Swedish, Danish, and German, and Mary's other books still generated some revenue. But her combined royalties were not, as Mr. Johnson had warned her when she first started out as a writer, adequate to support a household. Had she just herself, she might have had sufficient funds to live the austere life she had once sought. But she had a child now, and two servants. To enable Mary to devote more time to writing, she had hired a housemaid to cook and clean.

"Here to stay, at least for the foreseeable future, you'll want to start getting out again." Rebecca paused, her smile cunning while she gauged Mary's reaction. "William Godwin came looking for you while you were in Sonning. I believe he admires you."

"And pigs fly, to borrow a favorite phrase of your Scottish husband's. When did this occur?"

"Right after you left. He'd read *Letters* and wanted to discuss it with you. He's asked about you often since. I told him your broken heart still suffers. Godwin's an empathetic man. Underneath his detached exterior, he displays great sensitivity to your situation."

"I doubt my situation occupies his mind at all," Mary said, intrigued that Godwin liked *Letters*. While in Sonning, she had read his *Enquiry Concerning Political Justice* and *Caleb Williams*. Though she did not say so to Rebecca, she admired his work as well.

A horse cantered toward Mary as she walked. The way the rider wore his hat low and leaned forward in his saddle was reminiscent of another place, a different time. Refusing to allow memories to cast a shadow over her improved spirits, she stepped with care to avoid deep ruts snaking the entire width of New Road. Her move to Cummings Street was helping to fulfill her goal of moving forward. The apartment was located in a new part of London that still maintained its rural charm, and she took in the refreshing appeal of the countryside, noticing how rapidly spring advanced day by day this time of year. Cowslip and bluebells had sprung up overnight following fierce rain the previous day. To her left, a brickworks factory butted up against market gardens and farmers' fields. Yards away, cows grazed on lush grass a hopeful color of green, while ewes and newborn lambs sipped at a creek that wended its way down the hillside where bramble grew at the edges.

The rider reined in his horse next to her.

"Hello, Mary."

"Hello, Gilbert."

His saddle protested under his weight as he dismounted, the squeak of leather a sound she had heard so often.

"May I join you?" he asked as he slung the reins over his shoulder.

"We seem to be going different directions." She had not seen him for months. "I don't mind."

Mary resumed walking. "I didn't expect to see you back in London."

"Tying up loose ends," he said with characteristic nonchalance.

"I see." When he flashed his smile, Mary did not go weak at the knees. Instead, a feeling of victory passed through her.

"You're looking well," he said.

Mary's shoulders tightened. Empty compliments would find no purchase with her. She realized she hated him. Another small conquest within. "I should think you would be asking how your daughter is."

Gilbert stared ahead. The steady clop of hooves padding along in the dirt was the only sound until a lamb on the side of the road bleated, breaking the silence between them. "How is the little one?"

"Her name is *Fanny*. She's almost two now. Perhaps you've forgotten that as well."

They passed St. Pancras Church. Tombstones with moss and lichen creeping up their sides stood like small watchmen, keepers of the grounds. Several leaned to the side. Further up, a pile of soil marked a fresh grave waiting for someone to assume their final resting place.

"I see you still go by Mrs. Imlay."

Mary stopped in her tracks. "We had agreed—"

"Yes. Yes, of course. Fine."

"Does Fanny also have permission to carry your name? Or have you changed your mind about that as well?" By now, Mary was ready to breathe fire at him. She no longer expected Gilbert to arrange financial support for her; repeated requests had fallen on deaf ears. But he owed their daughter a name, and he had a responsibility to hold up his end of parenthood. "You may refuse to provide her with love and affection, but you have an obligation to ensure her physical well-being."

"Now, Mary. Under the circumstances, I believe I've been more than generous."

Mary jammed her hands on her hips. "Your conduct may satisfy you, but it does not me. You're not the person I once believed you to be. You're a miserable human being, one without scruples or a soul. Regarding me, do as you please. Whatever passed between us no longer exists. I have survived the misfortune of loving you. But I implore you one last time: take care of your little girl." She stomped toward home, leaving Gilbert standing by the roadside.

To Mary's surprise, several weeks later, Gilbert sent a bond for Fanny. One would have expected satisfaction to alight after having won at least one battle with him. Instead, disgust filled her after having had to work so hard to secure something that should never have been in question. Honor alone should have prompted his actions. She shoved the bond in the top drawer of her desk and walked out the door for her daily constitutional. She needed to clear her mind, or there would be no writing today.

Mary walked without direction. She had dived into writing and editing, her job reassuring her she could still think after more than a year of depressed spirits. She could still write and review books and articles with a keen eye. The work energized her. And she had re-entered society by accepting dinner invitations, among them a weekly dinner with Mr. Johnson and occasionally dining with Henry and Sophia Fuseli, with whom she had rekindled her friendship. She also dined regularly with Holcroft or the portraitist John Opie, along with a growing number of other new acquaintants. Mary was starting to feel like herself again. But she would never forget Gilbert's ruthless abandonment of her and Fanny, thus she maintained a wall around herself.

Upon crossing Chalton Street, Mary recalled that William Godwin lived at No. 25. A few weeks prior, she and Rebecca had been his guests at the theater for the opening night of the stage version of *Caleb Williams*. He had been amiable that evening, likable even, and she began to see why the Kendalls enjoyed his company.

Mary smiled to herself. The man could be charming when he put his mind to it. Also attending the play was the annoying Mrs. Inchbald along with Amelia Alderson, whom rumors said had caught Godwin's bachelor eye. Mary had congratulated him on the play, though she was sorry to see that it had received horrible reviews the following day. Since she had not had a chance to ask him about his reaction to *Letters*, on a whim, she knocked at his door.

"Mrs. Imlay?" Godwin said when he answered. He looked astonished to see her.

She had shocked herself as well, unsure why she had stopped. "Out for my daily stroll." It was forward to visit a man's home unchaperoned. While she had long discarded most of society's conventions, perhaps she had been mistaken in assuming he had. A coyness passed between them, and she was suddenly embarrassed to be standing at his door. "I took the liberty to say hello," she said, to fill the awkward space between them. "My new apartment is mere blocks from here."

Godwin's eyes did not leave hers, his expression marked with confusion.

"My apologies." Mary had to resist the urge to laugh at seeing a confident man like him addled. She had only ever seen him fully composed. Feeling like she had overstepped, however, she motioned to leave. "I see I've interrupted you —"

"No. Forgive me. Please come in." His cheeks turned a flustered crimson.

"Are you sure?"

"I eschew formal etiquette. You are welcome anytime. You surprised me, that's all."

His invitation seemed sincere, and she stepped inside. Godwin's apartment was as she might have envisioned it. Impecunious, like Godwin, but functional.

"Have you lived here long?" she asked, glancing around.

"Only a short time."

Godwin's words echoed in the almost empty space where blank walls stood at stark attention. A sofa was there, but chairs were few and carpets and curtains were absent. A lone coat rack by the door shouldered a small collection of men's dark hats and frock coats, while several pairs of shoes lined the baseboard below, among them a pair of red Moroccan slippers that looked out of place in the room's gray palette of colors.

A strand of hair had escaped Mary's annoying cap and tickled her cheek. One could defy the rules in most things, but touting herself as Mrs. Imlay, she was obliged to wear the cap society demanded of her. She shoved the strand behind her ear.

"I heard you came in search of me," she said. The baffled expression on Godwin's face prompted her to add, "At the Christies? In February?"

His brow relaxed, showing he remembered. "I had just read your book about Scandinavia. Your genius commands my admiration. I count it as one of the most moving pieces I've read in a long while." His dark eyes peered into hers, and he took a step toward her as if to examine her. "You've suffered. You spoke of your sorrows in a way that dissolved me in tenderness."

Mary flushed at his compliment. Up close, he smelled of hard work, of persistence, a scent that made him seem like a good and honest man. His eyes no longer seemed brooding, but trustworthy. "Such delicate disclosure pleases me beyond expression," she said, her voice hitching as she clasped her hands at her breast. "I read *Caleb Williams*. Your book brought forth a similar sentiment in me as well."

Godwin, as if conscious of their sudden closeness, stuffed his palms beneath his armpits and stepped away, reinstating distance between them.

"We must discuss both. When time allows," she added, also taking a step back, "not now, when I've sprung in on you." She cleared her throat and looked about the room. A blanket folded beside a pillow on the sofa caught her attention. Someone had recently slept there.

"My friend, James Marshall," Godwin said. "He works for me and stays here sometimes. Research, help with publishers, that sort of thing."

"I see." She crossed the room to the door of a small study. "Is this where you write?"

"Every morning, eight to one."

Like clockwork. "May I peek?"

"Er, be my guest."

Floor to ceiling bookshelves took up two of the four walls. Mary's finger ran across a row of spines. All of her favorites were there. Locke. Rousseau. Swift. Shakespeare. "We share a great many titles. Your copy of *Pilgrim's Progress* looks as if it came from Bunyan's cell," she teased, pulling it from the shelf and paging through the worn volume, careful not to let pages that had come loose drift to the floor. "Your favorite?"

"My aunt's. A Bunyan devotee. We read it together when I was five."

Mary stifled a smile. "An indelible impression, I suspect, on so young a mind."

Godwin's stoical face relaxed. "Let's just say I learned how to sit for long periods of time. My aunt practically raised me."

"But now you are an atheist." He had made this clear in his writings.

Godwin shrugged his shoulders.

"And your penchant for order? From your aunt as well?" Mary asked with humor as she slipped a nod at the neat, single stack of papers on his desk. Lined up in a straight row like tiny footmen waiting to do his intellectual bidding were his writing tools, a supply of sharpened quill pens and inkwells. "Your handwriting is exquisite," Mary said, referring to perfectly shaped lettering in the address of a piece that looked ready for the post. One could barely read her own writing, and her desk was always a terror. She could see they were opposites. A week was the longest she could recall her desk being kempt, well before Fanny was born. Stacks of papers and discarded inkwells buried themselves under stained blotting paper and open books were always turned facedown.

"One of my schoolmasters was a former penman," he said. "He demanded a certain ... strictness of form."

"I ran a school once."

"I know."

She clasped her hands behind her back and dropped her gaze to the floor so he would not see her burning cheeks.

"One need not search far to find out more about the celebrated Mary Wollstonecraft," he said.

Wollstonecraft. He had said it without judgment, but hearing her maiden name caught Mary off guard. Godwin must know she and Gilbert weren't married, or he would not call her by her maiden name. He and Holcroft were the closest of friends, and Mr. Johnson had revealed her secret to Holcroft. What must Godwin think of her having a child out of wedlock?

"I had no other option," she said, not sure if she was apologizing for losing her school or for having an illegitimate child.

"I tried to open a school once. I couldn't get enough pupils. I suppose I'm not handsome enough."

It was as close to being humorous as she had ever seen him, and she let out a laugh. Alone, without others, he did not seem as brooding or as impatient.

"I should go," she said, her senses growing keen from being alone with him. Their conversation having steered so close to her personal life, she became aware of her being here, of his presence, of him looking at her. She walked to the door.

Godwin followed and held it open for her. "I've enjoyed our visit."

Mary stepped outside, then turned to face him. "I'm relieved to have not scandalized you."

"Not at all." He smiled. "I was wondering..."

"Yes?"

"Would you be available to take tea with me tomorrow?"

A feeling long dormant stirred inside of Mary. A desire to have conversation. To get to know someone new. "Perhaps you would like to come to my apartment?"

"That could be arranged," he said, blushing again, only this time he did not look away.

James Marshall, Mary learned, was not only Godwin's occasional secretary but one of his closest friends. A few weeks later, he ferried meat pies, brown bread, and muffins from a local coffeehouse to two large tables pushed end to end that took up half of the main room in Godwin's apartment. Godwin was hosting a dinner party, a rare occasion, guests said. So rare, Godwin reminded them, that it had never happened before.

Godwin looked out of his element in a crimson under-waistcoat and the red Moroccan slippers Mary had spied during her first visit. The mood in the room was festive despite the host's apparent discomfort; William Hogarth could not have painted a finer scene of colorful ladies' dresses and men's waistcoats worn by the guests. Present were Thomas Holcroft and the insufferable Mrs. Inchbald, Amelia Alderson, and several out-of-town acquaintances.

The Kendalls were also there, sitting next to Mary. Iris had finally returned from Manchester. She had become thin in her absence, and her skin had taken on a sallow tone. Time away had not produced the intended effect of healing. She remained bereft.

"I think it sweet of you to host a dinner party at your apartment," Mary heard Miss Alderson say to Godwin while waiting for him to seat her next to him at the head of the table.

Mary leaned over to Iris. "What of those two?" She had grown to enjoy Godwin's company. They had taken tea several times and encountered each other at Holcroft's for dinner twice. "Are the rumors true about him and Miss Alderson being in love?"

Iris looked perplexed as to what Mary could be talking about. Mary tipped her head toward Godwin and Miss Alderson. Only then did Iris eye them over the rim of her third glass of wine. "It's obvious, isn't it?"

Was it? Mary had probed one evening to see if he and Miss Alderson were romantically involved, but Godwin looked at her in a bewildered sort of way and denied any attraction, saying that her father was a good friend of his. Why, then, had he seated Miss Alderson next to him?

Godwin had grown up in a Dissenting home, had attended Hoxton's Dissenting Academy at the same time Mary had lived in Hoxton when she was fifteen, and had gone on to become a Unitarian minister. He eventually left the clergy to become a writer. He had never been in a romantic relationship, or so he claimed. Was this his first?

Iris took a large gulp of wine, finishing off her glass, ignoring Godwin and Miss Alderson and directing a scathing glance at Mrs. Inchbald sitting between Samuel Parr, a Whig and a reformer visiting from Northamptonshire, and his protégé, James Mackintosh. Mackintosh glittered among the bookish types at Godwin's table.

"Look at her," Iris said. "Throwing herself at Mackintosh. Is she not aware his wife died recently?"

"You never said, are Godwin and Miss Alderson in love?" Mary asked again.

Iris seemed disinterested. "Who knows? I hear she is to return to her home in Norwich soon. If she is set on matrimony with Godwin, she's in for a surprise."

"What do you mean?"

Iris poured herself more wine. "You've read his works."

Mary and Mr. Kendall exchanged worried glances. Since her false pregnancy, Iris had taken to drinking more. "That's enough, my love," he said gently, reaching for the bottle.

Iris looked crossly at him. Not wanting to be privy to what he said to Iris next, Mary turned her gaze away and examined Miss Alderson, feeling unsettled in the oddest of ways. Mary had no claim on Godwin. He was nothing but a friend. The more time they spent together, the easier it was to see why he was popular with women, however. His mind nourished her own intellectual cravings, cultivating them like a field in spring, a diversion from work and motherhood that made her feel alive after her senses had been fallow for so long.

Just then, Mary caught Godwin looking at her while Miss Alderson spoke to Holcroft about the last play he had written. If Godwin was in love with her, his lack of attention could have fooled Mary.

"May I sit next to you?" Holcroft asked Mary, after dinner when guests had moved to softer seating. Others milled about, sipping port. Mr. Kendall had taken Iris, who had drunk too much wine, home.

Mary patted the sofa. "You may." The question about Godwin and Miss Alderson had been carping at her all night. Holcroft would know what was brewing between them.

"You fit nicely into Godwin's circle of friends," he said. "You and he seem to get on well."

Mary spotted Godwin across the room talking to James Marshall. Godwin did not seem to know how to entertain after dinner and was asking Marshall something about how to proceed now that his friends had no food to distract them. "Please, not charades," she heard him say, and hid a smile with her hand as she returned her attention to Holcroft. "He's different. Clearly not so disagreeable as when we first encountered one another."

"In case you hadn't noticed, a small swarm of handsome women fawn over him since he became famous. Fairs, he calls them. All wanting to shape him." Holcroft harrumphed in a jovial kind of way. "They had a blank canvas on which to paint their image of the man behind the words. That awkwardness you mentioned. They've convinced him to pay attention to his dress without him knowing it and have improved his social interactions considerably." He leaned his head toward Mary and lowered his voice. "Especially with members of the opposite sex."

Holcroft had offered Mary the perfect segue. "Are he and Miss Alderson a couple? I'm told he favors her."

Holcroft chuckled. "Would you care if they were?"

"Aren't you the daft one." She glanced about the room at how others were occupying themselves as proof of her indifference. Mrs. Inchbald still had her hooks in Mackintosh. Someone was asking Samuel Parr if he really had a portrait of Edmund Burke hanging upside down in his study. "It's just that Godwin seems to enjoy Miss Alderson's attention."

Holcroft took a sip of port. "What man wouldn't?"

Mary reluctantly agreed. Miss Alderson lit up a room. She was young and spirited and could engage in sprightly conversations with the most educated men.

"Romance is not in the cards, however, to answer your question about Miss Alderson and Godwin," Holcroft said. "You must keep in mind, to Godwin, freedom is everything. In love as much as anything else in life." He turned and gazed at Mary. "Much like you used to argue. Marriage was also once against your philosophy. I had so hoped you had formed a new perspective."

"I can't say that my philosophy has changed." As much as Mary had envisioned spending the rest of her life with Gilbert, not once did she consider marrying him. Had Gilbert asked her, however, toward the end, upon reflection, she was not certain she would have said no.

"There are good reasons to marry despite what you and Godwin say," Holcroft said. "Genuine affection. Mutual admiration. Security."

Under his prolonged gaze, Mary's neck turned warm, and she fingered the cuff of her sleeve. *What is he saying?* "I wish for nothing but Fanny's love."

"Someone with your passion is not destined to be alone. You are the very soul for which men languish."

Holcroft's eyes were filled with desire, suddenly confirming what Mary must have known all along but had been too unaffected to consider. "Did you write the letter?" she asked. *Please say that you did not.* While Mary held Holcroft in highest regard, she had no feelings for him beyond what siblings held in their hearts for one another.

"Of course, I did." He paused, assessing her reaction. "Do you really mind so much that it was me?"

He flattered her, but that did not change her feelings. "Above all else, you alone must know how much I treasure our friendship. But I am not cut out for affairs of the heart. My deepest affections are mine alone and shall remain so forever." Love comes, she wanted to say, then dies, only to leave a woman stranded.

Holcroft let out a wistful sigh. "You've changed, you know."

Mary tipped her head.

"Oh, you're still the revolutionary, but you have a maturity I did not see before. Whatever life has dealt you these last few years has underscored your beauty. Inside and out. I dare say you're more lovely than ever."

Holcroft, too, seemed to have changed. Being held in Newgate Prison during the Treason Trials had given him time to think, perhaps as Mary's own tribulations had forced her to reexamine her own life. "Promise me we shall always remain the closest of confidantes?" she said, eager to preserve what was between them—a friendship, a shared history that allowed them deep conversation and the ability to confess essential truths to one another.

A rueful smile crossed his face. "Indeed, we shall always be friends. But mark my words, you will love again, and I, for one, shall be happy to watch as it blossoms."

They both stood. "You will see no such thing." Mary returned his smile, touching him on the shoulder with a heartfelt appreciation for their ability to remain friends. "It is I who will feel great joy watching as *you* find love again."

"I believe someone wishes for your attention." Holcroft's glance shifted to behind her.

William Godwin had crossed the room and stood waiting to speak with her.

William Godwin abhorred the institution of marriage. While Mary had pointed out in *Rights of Woman* how marriage could be construed as a form of legal prostitution, Godwin in his own writing had called it the worst of all laws, an affair of property.

In the weeks ahead, their disdain toward men and women walking down the aisle gave them an odd piece of ground on which to form a friendship. It was not the only thing they found in common. Their staunch views regarding the shortcomings of government and the strictness of society made them allies in a world they objected to for its patriarchy and its refusal to see things through a modern lens. Before they knew it, they were on a first-name basis, spending several afternoons and evenings in each other's company on a weekly basis. Each feeling as they did toward marriage, Mary believed they were safe from forming an attachment beyond friendship, and she welcomed his attention.

"You don't strike me as someone often at a loss for words," William said one evening when he asked Mary about her relationship with Gilbert Imlay. While enjoying tea at her house the day after she had made her impromptu visit to his apartment, he had confessed that Holcroft had told him she and Gilbert were not married.

Damp night air washed over them, a half-moon their only other companion. They had just spent the evening at Holcroft's, where a lively game of charades had sent guests into fits of laughter. William hated charades and had fallen asleep but woke in time to insist he walk Mary to her door.

The occasional voice from inside the houses they passed interrupted the sound of carriage wheels in the distance and the crunch of their steps, a reminder of hidden lives around them, fictions behind closed doors no one knew other than those who lived behind the curtains. How could a man like William Godwin, who claimed to have never been in love, understand affairs of the heart?

"Being at a loss for words does not explain the reason for my reticence to be forthright with you," she said. "Call it a reluctance to reveal my true self." Mary knew William Godwin would eventually ask about Gilbert Imlay. On the surface, she had an apartment, was working, and found great comfort in mothering Fanny. Deep within, however, she remained mired in a lie. She was posing as Gilbert's wife. Her deception pricked at her, punishment for dishonesty.

William remained silent, prompting Mary to risk his judgment. "I wasn't intending to fall in love. When I first arrived in Paris, nothing mattered more than experiencing the Revolution, writing about it as events unfolded. But when I met Gilbert, I let my heart be free. For once I didn't have to please anyone but me. Tired of constantly trying to control my emotions, I decided to taste what everyone was talking about—love, *romance*. Paris was so permissive, so indulgent. A delicious feeling strikes when you find the door to your cage open, no matter who's been holding the key. When I stepped into the world of intimacy, my priorities, how I viewed the world—even how I pictured myself—changed. I became a different person, and I liked it. But there was a price to pay. A man's burning imprint on my soul was unexpected. I'd let my protective guard down, and when my relationship with Captain Imlay ended, I lost myself. Alone now, I find I am without direction." For all the times Mary had warned women of the dangers of being overly sentimental, in the end, she had fallen prey to sentiment, one of her greatest disappointments.

"You mustn't be so hard on yourself. You are a brilliant woman," William said. "But you have your flaws. We all do."

He was honest, a quality of his she valued. She would have liked to know what her flaws were through his eyes, but she did not ask. She could guess at them. Her passion had not left her, but her confidence had. Mary was still impatient, still demanding in oh, so many ways. Were life easier now, her sorrows would have been worth it. But life was not easier. Her daily existence was as hard as it had ever been. Despite being older and more knowledgeable, she was still poor, still searching for answers to life's questions. Though now they were questions she could not have thought to ask twenty years prior.

"I do not presume to be without shortcomings," she said. "I am a woman of contradictions. Though I no longer know what is good, or what is truth."

"'The mind is its own place, and in itself can make a heaven of hell, a hell of heaven.'"

William's quote from Milton sparked resentment in Mary. "That was Satan speaking in Milton's poem. He was trying to pretend that it was as good to live in hell as it would heaven."

"I only mean to suggest the depth of your despair lies at your own feet." William said, glancing at her from the side as they walked. "It is your view of things that keeps you from seeing what is right in front of you."

Mary bristled, and she inched away from him as they walked. William could not know what it was like to be loved, then discarded and replaced by another.

"A woman like you can and must shake off this state you're in," he said, not waiting for Mary to say more.

"I have made mistakes, done things that are unforgivable. What virtue have I left?"

William stopped mid-stride. "All of what you have ever had and more." He took her hand and in his. "You judge yourself too harshly."

His insight pierced through her façade of being in control. Mary wanted to pull her hand away. But his fingers were warm as he threaded them in hers, and she let her hand rest in his. She wanted to tell him everything.

"Your heart is wounded," he said gently. "Your virtue always has and will continue to rise above all others. People saw you before and still see you now for your intellect, for your passion. But you must allow the very qualities that define you the freedom to thrive again. If I may be so bold, only you stand in the way of your happiness."

Mary pulled her hand away and walked on. "Everything I do is to retrieve what I have lost." She sounded sharp, but not at him. She was angry at herself. At times like this, she wanted to fly away, to blot out all of what had happened in the last year.

"Stop waiting for your purpose," William called from behind. He caught up and resumed his place alongside her. "Go find it."

He seemed earnest, his ministerial tendencies on display. Why he cared about Mary or her purpose at all annoyed her. William had quit God to become an atheist because he objected to the way religion tormented people with guilt. Wasn't that what he was doing now? Making her feel responsible for her suffering? "You wish to save me, perhaps?" she said.

"Only you can save yourself. Through forgiveness."

Mary wanted to laugh. "You would have me forgive Gilbert?" William was being absurd.

"Not Imlay. Yourself." He reached for her hand again and kissed it this time, holding it firm. "Learn from your mistakes instead of reliving them."

Mary's thoughts swirled. If she only knew what to do with her enduring sorrow .... Sometimes she was certain she was fine; other times she found herself plunging headlong back into her despair. "Are you always so full of advice?"

"Not usually. Only when I care about the person whom I wish to advise."

He must care deeply, then, about Mary, further confusing her as they strolled in silence, their fingers still twined.

"Imagine if we had met all those years ago in Hoxton," she said when they reached her stoop.

"What might each of us have thought of the other?"

"It makes me wonder if we've lost precious time."

"We're different people now. Did you ever think you would become a famous author and philosopher?" he asked. "A solitary traveler?"

"I hardly recognize myself sometimes." Mary was, by definition, all those things. But that she no longer considered herself any of them left her longing for the life she had once lived. In that woman's wake was a ghost of who she had been.

"I'll be going away soon," he said.

His sudden announcement reminded Mary of all the times Gilbert had made a similar declaration, how each time they had caught her off guard. The same dread came over her now, along with questions of whether William would come back or what might change between now and his return. "Where will you go?"

"To Norfolk. To see my mother." He fingered a button on his waistcoat, twisting it between his thumb and forefinger. "Did I tell you she's good at repartee? Not as accomplished as you in that category," he teased, "but an able conversationalist."

Mary already missed him. "She will be delighted to see you."

"Is it true what is said, that absence makes the heart grow fonder?" He turned shy again, like they were words he had never used before and did not trust.

"Indeed." Would he think of her? Would he miss their afternoon walks around Somers Town? Standing alongside each other, their shoulders touching lightly as they bent over his dining table, poring over the draft of a play she had been working on? Would he miss Fanny, who called him "the man" when he visited? "When do you depart?"

"The first of July."

Two weeks away. Mary had no right to want him not to leave, but she did.

"Perhaps ..." he said, then paused, "perhaps you will think of me while I am gone?"

Mary's cheeks flushed, warm against the cool night air. "I shall think of you daily. How long will you be gone?"

"Three weeks."

"I will miss our conversations." Though she wished he would not go, his departure would give her time to examine her sentiments. With Gilbert her feelings had been on fire the moment she met him, a charge of electricity that trampled all reason. Conversely, her growing affection for William was driven by curiosity, the slow burn of mutual friendship, rather than the fury of a revolution.

"May I write?" he asked.

"I should be disappointed if you did not." William had written her a poem a few weeks earlier, a man's faint declaration of affection. At the time, she had teased him for being lackadaisical. His words were absent of feeling, she had told him, hoping to needle him into expressing his sentiments more clearly. "Of course, I'll expect real letters."

William looked confused. "Real letters?"

"Ones in which you express your true affections."

He smiled then and turned to depart, looking back once to wave at her as he walked away.

Did Mary see a buoyancy in his step, or did she just imagine it?

TWENTY-ONE

June 1796

When William left for Norfolk, Mary set aside the play she had been writing. Prior to his departure, he had helped her see the disjointedness of her scenes and the lifeless nature of her characters. Inspired by his writing, she began a novel that would represent the themes she had put forth in *Rights of Woman,* much like *Caleb Williams* had characterized William's political views in fiction.

Mary also moved to a house at Judd Place West in Somers Town and took out the things that had been in storage since she left for France, including the desk on which she had penned both *Vindications.* She and Fanny also added to their family a sheltie puppy they named Gulliver. Money was tight, as usual. Mary's pride kept her from using the bond Gilbert sent for Fanny's care. The money felt tainted, ill-gotten by a man without a conscience.

"What do you think of my new house?" she asked Iris, who had dropped by with a vase of flowers. Mary walked her through the rooms. It was not a fancy dwelling. The wood throughout was the color of ripened stalks of wheat, most of it bruised and dull from prior wear. Wainscoting the same color lined the perimeters.

They ended their tour in the parlor, where the walls were covered with floral paper—blue and yellow flowers on a soothing, cream-colored backdrop—and found Marguerite entertaining Fanny and Gulliver with a ball of yarn on a brown carpet with bits of tan and red and burgundy that Mary had scavenged from a secondhand shop. Iris dropped to the floor and scooped Fanny in her arms. "Hello, my darling." She hugged Fanny tightly until the two-year-old wriggled free and went back to chasing yarn.

Mary's new house servant entered. "Tea, ma'am?"

"Yes, please," Mary said, noting the clock, which showed four p.m.

"Could I bother you for wine instead, please?" Iris asked, removing her hat and gloves, tossing them on a side chair.

Mary looked sideways at her. "At this hour?"

Iris gave the impression of being irritated that Mary would question her and plopped on the sofa. "I should be entitled to drink wine when I choose, should I not? Or are you going to turn into Mr. Kendall, monitoring my every move?"

"Of course not." Though perhaps Mary should. Iris imbibed more frequently and consumed greater amounts of wine than she had prior to her false pregnancy, giving Mary cause for concern. Against her better judgment, "Wine for Mrs. Kendall," she instructed the servant. Mary wanted to caution Iris against turning to spirits to soothe her broken heart, but she knew that Iris's feelings were tender yet, that she continued to agonize over not having become a mother. Only recently had Iris begun getting out more, showing up at Mary's, often unannounced, usually requesting to spend time with Fanny or to take her for a walk outdoors. Mary worried that chastising Iris about her wine consumption would deter her from coming and Mary would lose her influence.

"Might your move have anything to do with William Godwin?" Iris asked when the servant left the room.

It was Mary's turn to sound defensive. "Whatever could you possibly mean?"

"Your new apartment is nearer his home on Chalton Street."

"A mere coincidence, I assure you." Mary and William had been keeping their relationship under wraps, even from Mary's best friend.

Iris eyed her as though trying to detect if Mary was keeping a secret from her, causing Mary to shift uncomfortably in her chair. "It seems to me," Iris said, "you and Godwin were spending a great deal of time together before he left for Norfolk."

Mary glanced at Fanny, who giggled at Gulliver's attempt to untangle a paw wrapped in yarn. "I do like Mr. Godwin, as you well know, but you mustn't imagine anything more than a friendship between us."

The ball of yarn landed at Mary's feet, and she tossed it across the room, the yarn unraveling by yards as Gulliver and Fanny dashed for it. Iris was discreet, but if word of the growing affection between Mary and William got out, William would have to account for being the regular visitor of a married woman, and Mary would have to defend herself against accusations of being loose. She cared little about what people said about her, but William despised being the topic of speculation.

"Godwin may have no ability to flirt," Iris said, continuing to survey Mary for a reaction, "but I've seen the way his gaze follows you."

Mary bit her lip, longing to tell Iris of her feelings for him. "Godwin would be well advised to look elsewhere." Even though late at night, all she could think of was what William might be doing, where he was, or when he might next write. He had been generous in his correspondence, penning letters to her often, giving her the impression of his own deepening feelings.

"Don't misread an inability to express emotions as his having none," Iris said as the servant returned with a tray. After taking a sip of wine, Iris crossed her legs and leaned forward, resting an elbow on her knee and dangling in her hand her glass of wine. As she spoke, she swirled the liquid about, bobbing an ankle. "I can't quite figure out what's going on. Mrs. Inchbald says that William is in love with Miss Alderson, Thomas Holcroft is in love with you, but that you are in love with William. Miss Alderson, however, apparently is in love with Holcroft. What do you say to that?"

Iris took another sip, this time to avoid grinning, though her gaze remained locked on Mary.

"What I'd say is that Mrs. Inchbald should mind her own business!" Mary made no effort to hide her exasperation. "Who does she think she is?"

"Don't blame Mrs. Inchbald. According to her, Miss Alderson was the source of the information." She paused, then added, "If you've no feelings for Godwin, then I suppose you don't mind that he plans to see Miss Alderson in Norwich. Just yesterday Mrs. Inchbald revealed that Godwin plans to propose marriage to our fair maiden. Such was the reason for his trip."

A proposal? "If ardor exists between Miss Alderson and Godwin," Mary said, "who am I to object?" Her whole body sank. *How was such a thing possible?* William had just sent her a poem last week, much improved over the first. In it, he had clearly expressed his admiration for her. To add to her confusion, in a letter that had arrived the day prior, he sounded nothing like a suitor about to ask for the hand of another.

"Though I doubt he will propose. I believe his eye has shifted to you." Iris grinned at last, seeming to take delight in seeing Mary vexed. She chuckled. "You have caught William Godwin's attention, and he has likewise caught yours! There will be no proposal. Not in Norwich, anyway." She sat back in her seat, looking satisfied.

Mary picked up Fanny and held her close, stroking her chestnut curls. "Would it be unwise," she asked Iris, "to entertain love again?"

"No! You are holding proof of its beauty."

"But I'm afraid." Only moments ago Mary felt as though a trapdoor had gone out from under her. "Of being hurt again." Of being abandoned, she wanted to say, but Mary could not bring herself to utter the words lest she invite the very thing that terrified her most. She had crawled her way up from the bottom of an abyss and never wanted to visit such sorrow again.

"We all hurt inside over something," Iris said, resigned, it seemed, to her own ongoing sorrow. She set aside the wine and slid to the carpet. "Come to me," she said to Fanny.

While Iris occupied herself with Fanny, Mary contemplated what Iris had said about William. For all his lofty ideals, beneath his progressive exterior, William Godwin was old-fashioned regarding certain things, which included beliefs about the way women should comport themselves. Mary saw it as a bias he and all men held, whether they would admit it or not. Miss Alderson was handsome and fine and had a sharp mind. Being young, she was malleable compared to Mary, who was older and led an unconventional lifestyle. Why would he choose Mary over Miss Alderson?

Mary retrieved his last letter from her desk and handed it to Iris. "What am I to make of this?"

Iris read the letter aloud, having to hold it high to keep Fanny from ripping it from her hands.

June 13, 1796

Dear Mary,

Now, I take all my gods to witness that your company infinitely delights me, that I love your imagination, your delicate epicurism, the malicious leer of your eye, in short everything that constitutes the bewitching ensemble of the celebrated Mary.

Shall I write a love letter? May Lucifer fly away with me if I do! No, when I make love, it shall be with the eloquent tones of my voice, with dying accents, with speaking glances (through the glass of my spectacles), with all the witching of that irresistible, universal passion. When I make love, it shall be in a storm, as Jupiter made love to Semele, and turned her at once to a cinder. Do not the menaces terrify you? Shall I send you a eulogium of your beauty, your talents, and your virtues? Ah! That is an old subject; besides, if I were to begin, instead of a sheet of paper, I would want a ream.

Please ask Marguerite to drop a line into my letter box, signifying to the janitor, or jailor, Mr. Marshall, that I expect to arrive in one week at seven o'clock in the morning, to depart no more.

Your admirer,
William Godwin

"It is the truest of love letters!" Iris said when finished, beaming from the floor. "I declare myself completely vindicated of having made any false accusations. The man is completely in love with you. And he will be home soon to prove it."

Mary could not suppress her own smile. Before her was a second chance for love.

William had not stated what time he planned to arrive at Mary's house. On the day he was to return to London, she rose early, taking special care to make sure her appearance was in order, putting on her best dress.

"*Tu es belle,*" Marguerite said to her when she saw her.

Mary grinned, so jittery over seeing William, she found it hard to keep her hands still. "Will you keep Fanny occupied when he arrives?"

Marguerite clapped her hands and nodded, and they giggled together like schoolgirls. The anticipation caused by the newness of love, of seeing William again in person, filled Mary with irrepressible hope that her life would once again have joy in it. Such was the transcendent way of romantic love, a love different from all others in its ability to spark happiness.

But when an hour passed with no sign of William, Mary tried not to let her disappointment show and moved away from the window where she had been waiting and busied herself in her study.

Another hour passed. And another, until the afternoon faded into twilight. Mary's hopes of seeing William retreated with the setting sun. Twilight turned into dusk, and she retired early, overcome with a deepening sadness. Memories of Gilbert's lies came back, snaking through her like a viper looking to bite.

That night Mary slept fitfully. William had lied to her as well, she feared. When she woke up the next morning, she strode to her study, refusing to look out her window. She would write, if nothing else, to keep her from dwelling on William breaking his promise, to keep from perseverating over when he would arrive. She retrieved the manuscript of the novel on which she had been working. He had agreed to comment upon it when he returned. Since he did not call, she would send the draft to his apartment.

After binding her pages with string, she attached a note:

William,

> *I send you, as requested, the altered manuscript. Had you called upon me yesterday I should have thanked you for your letter—and—perhaps, have told you that the sentence I liked best was the concluding one, where you tell me, that you were coming home, to depart no more—But now I am out of humor. I mean to bottle up my kindness, unless something in your countenance, when I do see you, should make the cork fly out—*

> *Mary–*

The next day passed with still no word from William. No one seemed to know where he was, not even James Marshall. By now, Mary's disappointment was turning into fear. A list of all that could go wrong raced through her mind. He had been in a terrible accident. He had been accosted by highwaymen.

He had changed his mind after all and proposed to Miss Alderson ....

It was the last of these thoughts that seemed most probable. Sometimes reason splits the heart in two. A decision is made at the last minute that alters things forever. Spent from worrying, Mary retired early for the third night in a row.

It was to her favor that he had chosen Miss Alderson, she told herself on the way to her bedroom. It was better, she reasoned as she climbed into bed, to lose William now rather than throw her life back into chaos by falling in love. Happiness was independence, raising Fanny, writing books and reviews. Her friendship with William would be enough, she whispered to herself as she blew out the lamp. Though she would see less of him now, with Miss Alderson as his wife, for she would occupy his attention.

"Madame Mary?" Marguerite called through the closed door.

Mary flew to a sitting position. Perhaps William had arrived at last. "Come in."

Marguerite entered, balancing a small tray with a flickering candle lighting up her youthful face. She set it down and handed Mary a steaming cup of tea.

"Merci," Mary said, resigned that Marguerite had not brought word of William after all. "How kind of you." The tea smelled spicy and herbaceous, but not sweet enough to lift Mary's spirits. She leaned back against her pillow.

"He will come." Marguerite's round cheeks glowed in the candlelight.

Mary turned her head away. "I'm a fool, Marguerite."

"No, madame. You mustn't give up. Something detained him unexpectedly. We know from our travels these things happen, oui?"

"Oui."

"You must believe. The eyes. They always tell. I am witness to how Mr. Godwin adores you."

Mary sighed. A lovely sentiment for a lady's novel, but it was not real life. She must let her feelings for William die before they destroyed any peace of mind she had left.

Had William come four days prior instead of the next day, Mary would have rushed into his arms. Instead, she observed him with an indifferent eye across the threshold of her house, wondering if she should let him in.

"I came as soon as I could," he said, hat in hand. The sun was dipping low into the afternoon sky. When Mary did not respond, his smile faded, and his cheeks turned red like the feathers of a cardinal. "Shall I come back another time?"

Mary stepped aside and motioned for him to come in.

"I've made you worry." He swiped a hand through his hair, studying her.

"I make no claims on your time." She straightened a pillow on the sofa.

"Are you upset with me?" he asked, turning his hat in his hands, his fingers crushing the brim.

Seeing that he was okay, Mary felt relieved. But the last four days had exhausted her. "William, I—"

"I know I'm late. You must be unhappy indeed. I spent a few extra days with my family."

"Your family?"

"I have twelve siblings," he said, blinking over her surprise. "It takes time to see them all."

"What about Miss Alderson?"

William's brow furrowed. "Miss Alderson?"

"Did you propose to her?" Mary quaked like a sapling, desperate to know but afraid of the answer. A look of guilt seeped into his expression, as though he had been found out, and justification for prying into his private affairs emboldened her as he occupied his gaze with the hat in his hand. "You must be honest with me."

"Her father wished for it." He raised his eyes to Mary and stepped toward her. "But I did not. You cannot imagine you have long been out of my thoughts. You're all I've thought about this last month."

Mary did not believe him and stepped back, her anguish like a cloth twisting between her hands, her feelings wrung dry.

He looked confused. "My letters ... they were quite clear in expressing my sentiments. Were they not?"

His letters had meant everything to her, but they had led her down a dangerous path as well, one that was sure to lead to heartache. "I cannot do this, William. I've been lied to, cheated on, abandoned—"

"But not by me."

"When you didn't arrive when you said you would, it reminded me of how painful having affection for another can be."

"I'm sorry. I didn't know it would mean so much to you. Can you forgive me?"

Mary knew that if she did, there would be no turning back.

"Tell me you've been as miserable apart as I," he said, his eyes revealing what Mary could not deny was true affection.

Fanny burst into the room. "Mamma!" She wrapped her arms around Mary's legs and pointed at William. "The man is here."

William kneeled beside Fanny. "Hello, little miss." He fished in his pocket for a sweet.

Fanny held out her hand expectantly. When William placed a sorghum drop in the palm of her hand and closed his fingers over hers, Mary pardoned him for being late, for seeding doubt in her mind, for she knew then, with great certainty, where her own sentiments lay.

TWENTY-TWO

Mary basked in what was turning into a verifiable romance with the unlikely William Godwin. Letting herself feel again after hiding from the threat of heartache freed her to further return to her true self. They resumed dining together, doing so with more frequency, and letters passed between them multiple times a day, with James Marshall and Marguerite serving as messengers. After dining as one, however, Mary and William still went their separate ways. She maintained the freedom to do as she pleased; he as well chose what he wanted to do, continuing to escort other women to the theater or galleries or concerts. The arrangement seemed the most prudent path and suited Mary. She could enjoy his company without having to explain it to others. But while her own feelings for William soared inside like a bird taking flight in spring after surviving a deadly winter, she had yet to fully gauge the degree of his attachment to her. When William invited her to meet at his apartment after lunch to discuss the draft of her manuscript, her stomach flitted about. She was eager to hear his review. The manuscript was far from finished, but William was a better writer than she was; his advice would be valuable. And they would be spending time alone.

"The feelings expressed by your characters are of the truest and most exquisite kind," William said. "What will you title it?"

"I'm not sure." His assessment thrilled her, and she wanted to bask in the glow of his compliment. "The narrative is more disposed toward passion than manners."

William set the manuscript aside and settled next to her on the sofa. "And you?"

Mary laughed at his lopsided grin. "Me?"

"Have I done you wrong as of late, flogging me as you have in your letters?"

The corners of his mouth turned up in a playful way, giving him a boyish look, and Mary wanted to trace her fingers over his lips, but kept her hands still as her pulse quickened. So near she could feel the heat of him through his white muslin shirt and black waistcoat. "If you mean chastising you for spending more time with Mrs. Inchbald than me, then you deserve it." Her light-hearted response did not match her resentment. Mary wondered how William truly felt about her. Mrs. Inchbald was possessive of him, making Mary dislike the woman all the more.

"You sound envious."

"Maybe I am." Perhaps her and William's decision to act so freely did not sit so well with her after all. Mary knew how love and jealousy could be twins. A fear of being less important to him than the overbearing widow lurked in her. Not that he had been inattentive since returning from Norfolk. But she found it hard to trust him when the inferences of affection so discernable in his letters were absent when they were together. "What I mean is, do I matter to you more than all the others, or am I just another fair?"

"Don't you see?" he said, pressing their palms together, twining his fingers with hers. "You've set my imagination on fire. I can think of nothing and no one else."

His intimacy igniting Mary's own desires, she leaned against him to absorb the warmth emanating from beneath his waistcoat. "Not even Mrs. Perfection?" Mary giggled at his nickname for the horrid widow.

"Especially not Mrs. Perfection. Isn't it obvious?" He gazed at Mary with newfound wonder. "I wish to woo you, but I don't know how it's done. Or have I deceived myself as to your feelings?"

"It is I who worries you are deceiving me." Mary paused, her pulse speeding now. "Have you ever kissed a woman?" Last week, Mary, Iris, and Rebecca had tea with Miss Alderson, who had returned to town. The three who had known William the longest insisted he had not done so once.

William cleared his throat. "I'm afraid I have little experience." His face turned a rusty red, but he kept his gaze fixed on her.

It was true then. He had never kissed anyone. "Experience matters little in the affairs of the heart." Mary's more recent observation of him was also correct. All these years, he had guarded his affection. The philosopher who stayed clear of matters beyond logic and reason avoided getting close to women. "What matters is acknowledging what one feels."

"Feel? I don't know how to feel. My quiet, sensible lifestyle is empty without you," he groaned, leaning his forehead against hers. "You've destroyed my ability to act rationally."

"Do you love me?" Knowing what awaited them if she and William dared to embrace their sentiments, she laid the question bare between them.

"How could you not know?" William buried his head in her neck. "Your words in *Letters from Sweden* were enough to make any man fall in love with you."

Mary wrapped her arms around him. If William Godwin had never kissed a woman, then he was going to need a tutor. She pressed her lips to his. To her enchantment, he responded without reserve.

Below William's second-story apartment window overlooking Chalton Street, people milled about as the day grew dark. Three days had passed since Mary and William had professed their love to one another. Since then, their kisses had grown longer, more ardent.

Mary billowed her skirt to cool herself. She should have walked home by now. Enough humidity had pooled in the air to assume a downpour was imminent. The bodice of her thin, gauzy dress clung to her damp skin. If she left now, she could avoid getting drenched.

But desire made her stay the way a seed in the ground roots itself in one place after having been planted. She tossed aside her hated cap and unpinned her hair, then loosened her curls with her fingers as William watched from his sofa, a lamp illuminating one side of him, a shadow eclipsing the other.

"I'm a virgin," he said as she moved toward him.

Mary nestled alongside him, close enough for their bodies to touch. "I cherish that about you." She kissed him long, not just with her lips, but with her entire body.

His hands explored her, finding her breasts, her hips. But when their kisses became too heated, he pulled away. "I do not wish to dishonor you."

"You do me no dishonor if it is my choice, when our actions are born of love and mutual consent."

"Society sees it differently." He rose from the sofa and crossed the room, as far away from her as one could be while occupying the same space.

"Are we society, or are we free beings?" she asked, heat rising in her over his sudden reversal toward being intimate.

"If it were only that simple." William ran his hands through his hair. "We may be free, but propriety demands—"

"That women be less sexual than men?" Since when did he care so much about society?

William strode to the window, his back to Mary as he glanced up to a darkening sky. Clouds were closing in overhead. "Men suffer not when they act upon their urges."

Mary stiffened, withdrawing the part of her she had freed—her sexuality, her naked desire for another. "What you mean is women aren't allowed to have wants or needs, let alone urges and desires. *Society* takes sexual behaviors for granted in men. *Society* accepts it as a male prerogative. Apparently, you believe it, too." William was just like all men after all. Despite his progressive stances about personal liberties, he remained trapped behind a set of outdated rules. And he was judging her for wanting to dispense with them.

Thunder rumbled. Moments later, rain slicked down the window. In William's reflection, Mary could not ascertain whether she saw guilt or torment. He had turned opaque to her.

Regretting that she had come, that she had exposed her yearning only to be refused like she was strumpet, she grabbed her cap. "I'm leaving. I'll not allow you to shame me for being a woman."

William wrote the next day to say he was not feeling well, that Mary had not considered him the way she ought to have the night before. She had mortified him, he said, by disregarding his feelings.

Had he not upset her? He was making too much of what had transpired—or did not transpire—something Mary could only attribute to his inexperience with women. Men's egos were tender, and he was, for all his fine qualities, still a man. She penned a response, hoping to put him at ease. In her note, she chose to say nothing about the matter other than to ask if he had felt lonely after she left and enclosed a newspaper to show him she harbored no hard feelings, hoping her gesture would soothe any anxiety he may be feeling.

But she heard no more from William the entire day. That night, as each hour passed, a queasy uncertainty began to dismantle the happiness she had allowed herself to enjoy since his return from Norfolk. In bed, she stared at the ceiling, suspended between two worlds and two sets of rules, one for men, another for women. How frustrating that men could have sexual partners outside of marriage, but women were not allowed such freedom. Even when a woman found relations within a marriage enjoyable, a husband was likely to consider her a harlot. Such double standards galled Mary. Why should women be denied sexual pleasure, married or not? It was natural to want to experience bodily ecstasy with another. But the situation begged a question. William's reaction to her sexual overtures made her doubt herself. Should she go through with this affair? Or should she end it now before disappointment—before melancholy—seized her should William suddenly walk away?

After a sleepless night, Mary had only her pen to which she could turn.

Dear William,

> *I am thoroughly out of humor with myself. Mortified and humbled, I scarcely know why—I fear that I have lost sight of what is true. Could a wish have transported me to France or Italy, I should have caught up my Fanny and been off in a twinkle, though I am convinced that it is my mind, not the place, which requires changing.*

My imagination is forever betraying me into fresh misery, and I perceive that I shall be a child to the end of the chapter. You talk of the roses which grow profusely in every path of life—I catch at them; but only encounter the thorns.

I would not be unjust for the world—I can only say that you appear to me to have acted injudiciously; and that full of your own feelings, little as I comprehend them, you forgot mine—or you do not understand my character. I am hurt. But I meant not to hurt you.

I should become again a <u>solitary walker</u>. Adieu!

Mary–

When finished, Mary handed the letter to Marguerite, a growing pit in Mary's turbulent stomach.

Hours later, a letter from William arrived at the hands of James Marshall. Instead of tearing the letter open, Mary stared at William's perfect script. His perfect folds. Inside, his words likely marked the end of their relationship. A goodbye before they had even begun.

Dear Mary,

How shall I answer you? In one point we sympathize. I had rather at this moment talk to you on paper than in any other mode. I should feel ashamed in seeing you.

You do not know how honest I am. I swear to you that I told you nothing but the strict and literal truth, when I described to you the manner in which you set my imagination on fire on Saturday. For thirty-six hours I could think of nothing else. I longed inexpressibly to have you in my arms.

Why did I not come to you? I am a fool. I feared still that I might be deceiving myself as to your feelings, and that I was feeding my mind with groundless presumptions.

Like any other man, I can speak only of what I know. But this I can boldly affirm, that nothing that I have seen in you would in the slightest degree authorize the opinion that <u>you have lost sight of the true</u>. I see nothing in you but what I respect and adore.

Mary pressed her lips together and closed her eyes, allowing his words to sink in. To know that she had not lost his esteem, that he had created a resting place for her in his heart, allowed her distress to melt into the folds of her dress. She opened her eyes, joyous, and read on at a faster pace.

I know the acuteness of your feelings, and there is perhaps nothing upon earth that would give me so pungent a remorse, as to add to your unhappiness.

Do not hate me. Indeed, I do not deserve it. Do not cast me off. Do not become again a <u>solitary walker</u>. Be just to me ... you will discover in me much that is foolish and censurable, yet I pray a woman of your understanding will still regard me with some partiality.

Hate him? Never! His words were like sweet jam on her lips. How could he not know that she would always be partial toward him?

Upon consideration I find in you one fault and but one. You have the feelings of nature and the honesty to avow them. In all this you do well. I am sure you do. But do not let them tyrannize over you. Estimate everything at its just value. It is best that we should be friends in every sense of the word; but in the meantime, let us be friends.

Suffer me to see you. Let us leave everything else to its own course. My imagination is not dead, though I suppose, it sleeps. Be that as it will. I will torment you no more. I will be your friend, the friend of your mind, the admirer of your excellencies. All else I commit to what the future brings.

Be happy. Resolve to be happy. You deserve to be so.

Send me word that I may call on you in a day or two. Do you not see, while I exhort you to be a philosopher, how painfully acute are my own feelings?

Wm. Godwin

Mary clutched the letter to her breast. William was telling her to embrace her fears; he was really telling himself. He was afraid. Was it always so with a man of forty when he faced his first love? But she wondered still, did he truly love her, or did he just want to be her friend? It remained unclear to her. The philosopher in him had once written that the act of choosing someone to love was a matter of reasoning, an intellectual exercise. He was wrong. *The heart has its reasons which reason knows nothing of… We know the truth not only by the reason, but by the heart.* So said the French philosopher Blaise Pascal a century earlier. When it came to her heart, even if reason had left her, Mary knew truth now, for in William, she saw it. She had been so sure she would never love again, yet she loved him as surely as she loved Fanny.

Mary wrote William a response. Instead of calling on Marguerite to deliver it, Mary hastened to Charlton Street.

When William answered the door, he stared at the floor.

"I wanted to deliver this to you in person," Mary said, handing him the letter. She touched his cheek. "You may call on me now. You may call on me always—"

William pulled her inside and wrapped her in a fervent embrace. "I was stupid to deny your passion. I never imagined our friendship would evolve into love the way it has."

Nor had Mary, yet it was as if her life depended on him loving her.

They dined together that night at her house.

And the next. When they finished eating, they strolled all the way into London and back. When they returned to Mary's home on Judd Street, Fanny was in bed. Marguerite, too, had retired.

Mary led William to her bedroom, where he willingly followed. She closed the door, sealing the two of them inside.

Afterward, Mary curled into William and stroked his hair, which was growing long again. "What really made you afraid?" she asked, referring to the way he acted three days prior. "It wasn't what I expected."

William looked serene by her side. He had not held back, had not hesitated the slightest. Nor did Mary. Being together came naturally to them as she knew it would.

He ran his fingers along the contours of her shoulder, down to her waist. "I suppose I was apprehensive. Of hurting you. Of losing my independence. I'm a private man, Mary. Seeing you every day. Sharing a bed. I'm not used to it."

Mary snuggled closer. "I understand." It was she who once had said the two sexes mutually corrupted each other. She also said, however, that they could improve each other under the right circumstances. She and William held equally strong opinions about love—about everything. Yet they were as human as any man and woman, subject to the same breathtaking passions, the same intoxicating urges that even reason could not explain.

"I'm afraid of you at times," he said. "Ingrained in men from an early age is to think a certain way about women, to view them as objects to be adored. But you're fearless. Delicate yet strong. I become a different person when I'm with you. Helpless without you; invincible in your presence, like I can win in this world." William struggled as Mary did to earn enough money to pay his bills. A writer's life was a beggar's life.

"Men to me were villains," Mary said, thinking of her own hesitation to embrace love, how for many years, she had tried to resist it. She knew now that she feared her sexuality because she associated it with being dominated by a man, an apprehension precipitated by the tragic fate of her mother. "When I was twelve, I used to stand guard at night outside my mother's bedroom, waiting for my drunken father to come home, for I knew that he would beat her." She had not shared this with William, and she wondered if he would think differently of her knowing what violence she witnessed as a child.

"You were trying to protect her?"

"I was trying to save her. I wanted her approval. For her to see that I would not let her down, even though she had let me down by giving in to his savagery instead of having the strength to fight back, to walk away."

William pulled her closer. "Was she ever forthcoming in praising you?" His voice turned soft, as though he already knew the answer.

"No. She kept her approval from me. My mother was the victim of continued violence, and it destroyed her, including her capacity to love her children the way they deserved to be loved. It took me a long time, but I eventually discovered that intimacy is not violence, which I believed as a child. Intimacy does not make a woman subordinate; it empowers her to be in charge of her body. Using force to hurt someone, to dominate them, to damage their spirit, that is violence."

"I'm not a villain then?"

His gaze teased her, a lightness Mary needed at present after revealing her mother's plight. She was thirty-eight but could feel like she was twelve again, the memory of such acts of abuse still having the ability to make her shudder. "As you can see," she said, letting his arms shield her from her past, "I've changed my mind considerably in that regard. Though I am curious. How is it you've never been with a woman before me? Having seen the attention you receive from beautiful women, I find it inconceivable." And he was a passionate man. At least he had been with her moments ago.

"I have never loved anyone. Not as I love you."

His answer was simple, but honest, showing Mary what she meant to him. To know she was truly loved, fully accepted for who she was, filled her with a new euphoria. She did not want their first night together to end, and she wrapped herself around him.

"There is one small matter that troubles me," he said.

Mary anticipated his forthcoming words. Her rapture was to be short-lived, after all. "My presumed husband is in Paris."

"We have to be careful."

Mary flopped back on her pillow. She had been thinking the same thing. If she became pregnant, the complications would be fierce. "There are powders. Or condoms. Shall I arrange something? I could send Marguerite." Mary despised the thought of doing so, but ladies did not request such things, whereas servants made those kinds of purchases all the time for their employers. Helen Maria Williams had told her this, too late, of course.

"Leave it to me. I'll talk to my friend Dr. Carlisle."

"Shall we inform people we are a couple?" She would have to tell Marguerite, whom she could count on to be discreet. But she was thinking of Iris. Mary disliked withholding anything from her best friend, especially when she wanted to share her joy of being in love again. And she was worried about Iris's excessive drinking, which had continued.

William stroked her hair. "I think not. The London press would pounce on a love affair between two radicals and skewer us both. Given our stated views regarding love and marriage, we'd have no peace."

"Are we to lie, then, about what we mean to each other?" Mary asked, dread at adding another lie to her life enveloping her. Lies destroyed relationships; they destroyed people as well.

"Not a lie. Think of it as a veil. A curtain over our privacy. Certainly, we are entitled to that. You are a married woman. Or so the public thinks."

Mary and William agreed to continue to attend parties alone and entertain guests separately, seeing each other when and how often they chose.

Mary could not argue with William's pragmatism. As he placed his body onto hers again, she let go of her worries. She had grown to live with the lie about Gilbert the way trees in Scandinavia found ways to grow on rocky hills and along craggy shorelines. She could not change society, but she could live as she chose. What choice did a woman in her position have other than to be chaste, a choice Mary did not desire? Intimacy offered affection impossible under any other means, sensational pleasures she wanted to enjoy. She moved with William, giving in to the fluttering inside until earth surrendered to heaven, a sacred place she wanted to stay, a place that would harbor her as a woman, as a lover, and as a friend to a man she respected and cherished, her heart proving an enduring ability not only to open up again but to heal.

William left at midnight, and she hugged his pillow, warm, still bearing the earthy smell she would forever attach only to him. In her mind, she followed him home and pictured him opening his black calfskin journal in which he recorded all his daily actions, each page with straight lines ruled in black ink with a pen by his own hand. In it she could see him writing: *August 18. Chez elle.* At her home.

TWENTY-THREE

Autumn 1796

Throughout the fall and into the winter, Mary and William settled into a relationship that ran contrary to society's established rules for couples—the prejudices of mankind, as William called them. She lived her life as a single mother, raising her daughter alone, while William played the role of a single man about town. For Mary it was a happy time after years of sorrow and insecurity. She had become accustomed to it being just her and Fanny. By now, Fanny was two and a half years of age.

Sadness struck, however, when the boundless Thomas Christie died of a tropical disease in Surinam, reminding Mary how fleeting life could be.

"We shall no doubt miss him," Mr. Johnson said to Mary as they walked home together from Mr. Christie's memorial service.

Mary noticed the impact of losing his protégé on Mr. Johnson and slipped her arm in his. "Rebecca is bereft. I wish I knew how to comfort her. Had they a child, it would console her."

"As our Fanny consoles you?"

"Indeed." Mary never expected to become a mother; now she could not imagine being childless.

"As she does me. What of our little Fanny? A father for her, I mean. Every little girl needs one, does she not?" Mr. Johnson remained intent on finding Fanny a father.

Mary would have liked to tell Mr. Johnson she had found love again. Especially now. His health was declining. Did Fanny make him think of his own mortality, of what he would leave behind when he passed? But she could not break her promise to William.

"May I see Fanny?" Mr. Johnson asked, releasing Mary from having to respond to his question about Fanny needing a father. "I believe a visit with her will lift my spirits."

A light snow began to fall. They walked to Mary's house, her hand nestled in his elbow. *God bless Mr. Johnson.* As usual, he was right. How nice it would be for Fanny to have someone to call Papa. And the child, Mary thought, that she suspected was growing inside her.

In early February a stray, weather-beaten calico followed Mary and Fanny home.

"What shall we name him?" Mary asked Fanny when it became clear the cat had no intention of ever leaving them.

"Puss." Having returned home from a brisk walk outdoors, they were hanging up their wraps.

"A fine name for a cat," Marguerite said, who met them at the door. "You can be its mother," she said to Fanny.

"I can't. We already have Mamma. The Man can be its Papa."

Mary hung up Fanny's cloak. "Is that so? What an imagination you have." She sent Fanny off with Marguerite to eat their supper and slipped into her study, where she closed the door and leaned her head against the coolness of the wood. She did not know whether to be happy or alarmed, only that she could deny it no longer. She was with child, she was certain. Her courses had failed to visit her three months in a row. Morning nausea was constant, and on any given day, her mood shifted without warning. William's solution to avoiding a pregnancy had been to implement the chance-medley system that included avoiding sex on the three days after the completion of her courses. It was, he had insisted, a sure way to avoid pregnancy.

It was not. At her desk, Mary penned a note to her friend and physician, Dr. Fordyce, to expect her.

Two days later, she lifted her petticoat to keep it from dragging in the slush following days of snow and trudged to St. Thomas's Hospital in Southwark to see him.

"You can expect to deliver in late August or early September, I'd say," Dr. Fordyce said while Mary finished dressing behind the screen in his examination room. "Hearty congratulations to you both. Does Captain Imlay know?"

Fully clothed, Mary stepped out into the open. "It's not Imlay's child."

Dr. Fordyce looked up from the note he had been writing.

Mary's palms were moist with perspiration. "We must keep this to ourselves."

On the way back to Somers Town, thoughts swept through her mind as vehicles clipped past. She encountered men and women going to and fro but hardly saw them. Hot, she opened the buttons of her cloak to let in air. At the start of the new year, Mary hinted to William about a possible pregnancy. He had convinced her it was a false alarm.

Mary held her hand to her abdomen as if to protect the child growing within from the harshness of a world that did not accept all forms of love. Having another baby did not bring fear; the new life she carried was already part of her. And she had proved she could manage on her own. Having reinvented herself before in London, then in Paris, and again after finding her way after Gilbert Imlay, Mary would start anew once more. She would survive. If life had taught her anything, it was her ability to resurrect herself. A woman of strength found a way no matter what obstacles she encountered. She would raise her illegitimate children alone, for she knew, William Godwin would never marry.

How unfortunate. She had changed since declaring she would live life singly. After years of fighting the threat of matrimony, she would very much like to be William Godwin's wife. Gilbert had proven to be nothing but a lover, someone who was as disposable to her as she had been to him. With William, however, Mary was a woman in love, a far different sentiment that would last because it was real. But not only would he never marry, to the world she was Mary Imlay, wife to Captain Gilbert Imlay.

A horse-drawn wagon sped by and splashed slush on her skirt. *C'est la vie.* Such is life. In her mind, Mary started to make plans to leave London.

Instead of parting that night after a supper of cold meat and bread along with a bit of cheese and shared bites of an apple, Mary and William stayed in together at her home. Fanny was in bed, and Marguerite had gone out for the night. Mary had fretted through the meal, hardly touching a bite.

"How is that possible?" William said when she announced they were going to have a baby.

"Do you really need to ask?"

William swallowed hard, his Adam's apple rising and falling several times. "Are you sure?"

"I'm sure." Mary chewed the inside of her cheek. When he said nothing more, she left the table and flopped onto her sofa, where she called Gulliver, who was sleeping on a tattered blanket next to the hearth. The dog crawled into her lap, where she petted him, a space in her chest turning hollow. William's face told her what she needed to know. He did not want a child. Mary was not surprised, only low-spirited. She had held on to a fleck of hope that she could let go of now and move on. Such resignation often spurred her into action, but tonight it made her want time to stand still so they could enjoy their last moments together, for tomorrow William would surely be gone.

"I suppose we should marry," he said, joining her on the sofa.

"You needn't feel sorry for me," she said, looking squarely at him. She did not want his pity. "Fanny and I shall go to Switzerland. No one would be the wiser. The children and I will begin a new life. You can go on as if we'd never met."

William's mouth fell open. "What?" He looked at her in horror.

"You despise marriage."

"As do you!"

"Not anymore. I see things differently now."

"Perhaps I do as well."

"You can't."

"Why not?"

Mary bit her lower lip. "Because you've said nothing that would ever lead me to believe you hold anything but contempt for marriage."

"For the institution, but not for you! And certainly not when it involves a child. Our child. Do you really think I haven't thought about the possibility that you'd conceived? I'm not an imbecile, Mary. You told me you suspected you were with child in December. I've thought of nothing since."

"But you've kept it to yourself."

"Then I shall no longer keep you in suspense. I believe we should marry."

Mary tensed inside. He could not mean what he was saying. "A repudiation of marriage is one of your signature philosophies." She looked at him, confused. "Your readers will castigate you as a masquerader."

With delicate poise, Puss climbed onto William's lap, one eye surrounded by orange fur, the other black. A white streak running down his forehead to the tip of his nose made him look as if he was wearing a mask.

"I am an enquirer," William said as Puss curled into a ball and he stroked the cat's fur, "not a dogmatic deliverer of principles. Just because we've written a few books, the public doesn't own us. We are free to make our own decisions." He slid an arm around Mary's shoulder and drew her close enough to rest his chin on the top of her head. "In this case, we must be practical."

What did being practical mean? Mary wondered. She had lived as a second thought in a man's heart once and wanted no part of it. If she and William married, it needed to be for the right reasons. "I don't want to marry because I'm with child. I would only wed because we can't stand the thought of not spending the rest of our lives together." She held her breath. If he did not feel the same way, she would not marry him, even as the possibility of being his wife produced a thrill inside that reinforced the depth of her affection for him.

"I wouldn't marry just anyone. Nor would you. The fact is, the public will rule against us either way, even our friends. If we marry, it will cast Fanny as illegitimate. If we don't, they will label our baby a bastard. We must do as we see fit, what we believe is right for us and for our baby. And because we love one another. These are not mutually exclusive ideas. Fanny will benefit as well from having a real father."

Mr. Johnson's words rang in Mary's ears. "But marriage was never what you had planned for yourself." She did not want William to feel snared into proposing any more than she wanted to feel cornered into saying yes.

"Ah. The best laid philosophies. How I wish they were as easy to live out as they are to construct with pen in hand." William shifted to the floor on one knee, dumping Puss without ceremony, and took Mary's hand in his. "I am a recluse half the time. My home is my workplace and lacks any form of creature comfort. I make barely enough money to live on. If I have a little left over at month's end, I send it to my mother and siblings. But I love you, Mary, which is the only reason to wed. Beyond that, how can we deny our child a proper family? How can we not love and protect him with everything we have?"

"Him?" Mary smiled.

His eyes twinkled. "Master William, of course."

"Do you mean it? You truly want to wed?"

"I do. Or do I wait to say that?"

He was being humorous. Mary smiled. "You don't worry that marriage will change us, that it will take away from who each of us is?"

"Why must it? We are just a fraction of what we will be. What I know is this: I am at my best when I am with you. You've made me rethink my entire existence." He kissed her hands and laid his head on her lap. "I want to take care of you, to wake up next to you every day of what is left of my simple life, and at night, take you in my arms, not worrying about who knows we are a couple. I want us to grow old together."

"I'll marry you, William Godwin," Mary said, her voice filled with resounding joy. "On one condition."

William raised his head. "Which is?"

"That you will love me—and only me. I must have first place or none."

"You know my fealty lies with you."

"Make sure you tell Mrs. Perfection." Mary said it in jest, but she meant it.

"You mustn't worry about Inchbald. She's just a friend. As are any of the women I escort. It is a social construct, me accompanying them to social events, nothing more."

"And will that change when we are wed? I'm growing tired of sharing you." Mary envisioned them a modern couple but worried he might find another woman more interesting, more attractive. After Gilbert, the fear of losing him to someone else lurked in her like a thief hiding under the bed. "I won't be subservient to you," she added, her words expressing firmness. "More than anything, I'll not be under a man's rule. We must live as equals, not as the baron and the feme. And you must stay true to me."

"Why can't we continue as we are, each of us maintaining our independence? Our love has grown because we have allowed each other to act and be who we are, not what society dictates. If we are to commit to the convention of marriage, no one says we cannot do it our way."

"My thoughts as well. We shall shape marriage to suit us instead of wearing the yoke we have fought to avoid." She smiled at the thought of such a revolutionary idea. They could enjoy the best of both worlds. It would also be practical to design a marriage to fit them. William had plodded through life for years as a single man working in solitude. She foresaw how the bustle of even a small household with two servants, a puppy and a homeless cat, let alone a toddler and a new baby, would exasperate a man held together by dependable routines and predictable schedules. William needed quiet time to contemplate the shortcomings of humanity that he wrote about, the things that only properly applied reason could fix. And just as William went about town as he pleased, so did she. She liked running her household without having to ask a husband's permission regarding what to buy or how to spend her time. Mary also took pleasure in choosing when she had dinner and with whom, or selecting which concerts or plays she attended. "We shall reinvent the institution of marriage itself," she said, her excitement growing. "If the public objects, we shall simply think of them as too dull. Those bold enough to advance before the age they live in must learn to brave censure."

"We just have one problem."

"I'm presumed to be wed already." This problem was harder to fix, and defeat loomed in Mary. "What are we to do?"

"Leave it to me."

Mary prayed his solution worked better than his chance-medley system of birth control. Regardless of their actions, condemnation was inevitable. She would at least have William at her side, and this alone calmed her.

Something else ate away at Mary. That night, lying by William's side before he left to go home, Mary thought of Iris, who still struggled with her inability to conceive. How would she feel when she found out Mary was pregnant a second time? It did not seem fair that Mary was twice blessed when Iris could find no comfort in remaining barren. Mary had received a note from her that day in which Iris sounded more forlorn than ever.

Mary went to see her friend the very next day to deliver fresh bread and a nourishing broth, put together by Mary's kitchen servant, only to find Iris had been crying.

"I'm not a mother," she groaned. Iris was reclined on her sofa and had not even dressed. The fire in her sitting room had gone cold, and the curtains were still drawn. Not even a lamp was lit. "What have I done to be punished so? I want a baby growing in me! No one but you will even talk to me about my false pregnancy. The subject is taboo; everyone thinks I lied."

"No one believes that for a minute," Mary said, smelling wine on Iris's breath. Her teeth and lips also were red. Mary spotted an empty decanter on a side table. Iris was numbing her pain with spirits.

Mary opened the curtains and lit a lamp, then stoked the fire. "I'm going to warm this broth, and when I come back, we're going to come up with a plan. We must get you out of the doldrums. And off wine."

Iris raised a guilty look at Mary.

Mary strode to the kitchen.

"Having spent as much time as I have under the suffocating cloud of melancholy, I do not want to give advice," Mary announced upon her return, carrying a tray and a steaming bowl of broth. "But I know some of what you're experiencing, how sorrow skews one's thinking. Nothing may seem right with the world, Iris, but you have choices to make."

"At times I can't breathe. Mr. Kendall doesn't understand. I've become so angry with him I don't even want him in my bed." Iris wiped her eyes with a handkerchief. "He won't even talk about having a baby anymore. He accuses me of letting it consume me."

"Has it?" Mary handed Iris the bowl of broth.

"Papa says I mustn't think about it so much." She swallowed some broth but refused the bread.

"A long time ago, a friend of mine died in childbirth," Mary said, taking up a chair alongside the sofa. "I told you about her once."

"Fanny Blood. The woman you named Fanny after. Her child died a few weeks after she died."

Mary nodded. "You remind me of her. I loved her with every breath I took. To this day I can still hear her voice." Mary cleared her throat, the memory of Fanny still able to produce fresh pain. "When Fanny Blood left this world, I was certain I had died, too. Or so I thought. It wasn't until my friend Reverend Hewlett in Newington Green encouraged me to write that I began to think of anything besides my lost friend. He said writing would help me get past my pain. To this day, I am thankful for his advice, even more grateful to myself for heeding it. His encouragement prompted me to write my first book. I believe the act of writing, of having a way to express myself other than through the despairing lens of grief, saved me."

"Please don't tell me to write a poem," Iris moaned.

Mary tipped her head. "Why not?"

"Because that's what Mr. Kendall also says."

"What if he is right? Your pain must go somewhere, Iris, otherwise it will come out sideways, or at you from within, and you become a prisoner to it. In time, pain becomes destructive." Mary was proof of that. "More than a year has passed since your disappointment."

Iris blew her nose and wiped her red-rimmed eyes. "Every night, Mr. Kendall leaves my writing box on the table beside my bed."

"And?" Mary said, raising her brows in hope.

"I can't bear to open it."

"You must find the courage. Listen to me, Iris, I know how hard it is to do something for which you have no energy, no desire—no will." She stroked Iris's hand. "Whether writing would help release your sorrows and put them to rest is hard to say. But it's worth trying. You have a gift in how you put words together; they become illuminated on the page. I can say with great sincerity, my own pen saved me more than once."

"It did?" Iris sat up.

"I swear it. First when Fanny Blood died, then a second time, when my love for Gilbert Imlay threatened to destroy me. When I returned from Scandinavia, I wanted to die. Writing *Letters* helped me see that I was still alive, that nothing could destroy me but *me*. Only my mind could save me. I wish now that I had busied myself sooner, that I had reunited with friends like you long before I did. Sentiment must not outweigh reason; a woman needs both to secure lasting happiness.

"You have a radiant mind. And you have the gift of time. Use them both, and they will serve you well. The light will come in again, Iris. It did for me. And it will for you as well. When it does, your passion will burn again." She held up the empty decanter. "And you must stop this."

Much to Mary's dismay, two weeks after she and William decided to wed, her sister Everina showed up at her doorstep unannounced. During the prior year, she and Everina had begun corresponding again through letters. Everina, who had been living still in Dublin, was en route to assume a temporary position in Etruria, near Stoke-on-Trent, with the family of Josiah Wedgwood. The Wedgwoods were close friends with William. Mary had helped arrange the job for Everina. She had not expected her to come to London before going to Etruria.

In truth, Mary thought little of her family these days, and Everina's arrival, though not unwelcome, produced added stress going into a new future that was sure to be rife with criticism. When people found out Mary and Gilbert had never been married, there would be hell to pay. Her good name would be in ruins. And the fact was, the distance between her and her siblings had widened over the last two years. Eliza had not written at all after she had asked to move in with her when Mary returned to London from Paris. When Mary told her no, saying she and Gilbert shared an intimacy that would make Eliza living with them uncomfortable, Eliza became fully estranged from her.

Everina, however, had stayed in contact but wrote sparingly. Laced throughout her letters was stern disapproval over Mary's suicide attempts and unbridled criticism of her book of letters from Scandinavia as being far too personal. To her sisters, Mary's life had become a string of scandals.

Not scandalous enough, however, to keep her from asking Mary for money. When she arrived, Everina complained of her clothes being old and frayed. "I can't very well go to work in rags," she said. "Not working for a family like the Wedgwoods." The Wedgwoods were founders of the Wedgwood Pottery Company.

"You must believe me when I say I have no money to give you," Mary said. They were at the weekly outdoor market in Somers Town, buying meat and vegetables. A light drizzle made it an especially miserable day. The hems of their skirts were dirty from walking through the accumulating mud, and Mary was tired. She wanted to help Everina; Mary would help anyone in need. She knew what it was to have insufficient funds. But there was never enough money. One bill after another arrived. She was months, in some cases, years behind in payments. She had not been this poor since arriving in London a decade ago.

"What about Fanny's father? Does he offer no support?"

Everina's accusatory tone did not sit well with Mary. She regretted admitting that she and Gilbert had never been husband and wife. From then on, Everina had taken a superior attitude toward her. "He came through with a small bond to be used strictly for Fanny's care, that's all," she said with uncharacteristic sternness. They stopped at the butcher, where Mary ordered a rooster and shifted her basket from one arm to the other. "The bond helps me maintain Marguerite's services. Beyond that, he's disappeared altogether. His creditors show up every month looking to be paid. He left town without settling his bills. Perhaps now you will understand the straits I find myself in."

Everina's pout was like that of a spoiled child. "But you're working again for Mr. Johnson and have published all those books. Surely you can spare me something. You managed to arrange for James to go to France."

Another thing Mary wished she had not told Everina. Their brother James had recently visited. Having abandoned the sea, he aspired to join the Revolution in France. "I provided James with travel funds and contact information. That is all. He left the next day." Mary had suggested he go to Philadelphia, where their brother Charles had invested in a calico mill. But James declined her suggestion, like he had so many others. When he left, she happily bid him farewell.

Everina refused to be deterred. "If you were able to help James, then you must have something for me. We are your family, Mary. You have surpassed all of us with you success."

Mary opened her mouth to remind Everina of the money she owed her from the last time she had visited Mary four years earlier, but she clamped it shut. Digging up old resentments would deepen the animosity growing with each passing conversation.

They walked in thick silence back to Mary's house, weaving between carts and wagons, not looking at each other. Mary longed to confide in Everina about the baby and her engagement to William. But she and William were keeping their plans to marry secret, at least for now. Besides, Everina had already shown she would never be able to comprehend how complicated Mary's life had become.

"You didn't have to take it upon yourself to pay for your maid's son's education," Everina said all of a sudden.

"How do you know about that?" Everina was referring to Mary's house servant who cooked and cleaned for her.

"Marguerite told me."

"She's a widow with a young son. I cannot stand by and watch a poor child denied an education. I could scarcely take on tutoring him myself. Perhaps you could tutor him during your stay."

"I'm only here for a month," Everina said. "Then what would you do? You'd be back to paying for a tutor."

The little tart. "You could save me a month's worth of tuition!"

"If you're so poor, why not ask Joseph Johnson to help? He's come to your rescue more times than I can remember."

"Joseph Johnson," Mary explained, working viciously to respond to Everina's saucy comment without blowing up, "has, in fact, tried to help. He reached out to Charles in America, asking him to repay me for the help I gave him as well as repay the money Mr. Johnson lent him." Charles refused to reimburse either Mary or Mr. Johnson.

"You both wrote to Charles?"

"He was flippant, as usual," Mary replied. Charles even had the audacity to tell Mr. Johnson that as Mary's publisher, he had made more money from her books than anyone, therefore he should be the one to support her. Mary's siblings were turning out to be disappointments, all of them. Just like their father. "I've not only all of you begging me for help, but I'm also still sending money to Papa. It wouldn't hurt you and Bess to take a turn in supporting him."

"That's Ned's responsibility. It seems to me someone ought to be able to help you out." Everina was uninterested, it appeared, in being that person. "What about William Godwin? You two seem to get on. Fanny surely is very taken with him."

Mary had introduced William to Everina, but every time he visited, Everina mewled about like an elderly aunt who had lost both manners and a sense of humor. William was unimpressed with Everina and wondered out loud to Mary how two such different people could come from the same family.

"He's a good friend, nothing more." In her head, Mary started counting the days until Everina departed. Mary and William were both coming into their marriage broke. She questioned her ability to contribute to their financial well-being. It was proving difficult to find time to write without interruption, thus work on her novel was progressing at a snail's pace. Being a mother and managing a household consumed all her time. Carrying a child made her doubly exhausted by the day's end.

They passed a millinery. "I shall meet you at home," Everina announced, her eyes lighting up when hats displayed in a store window caught her eye. "After that I'm going to the dress shop. I should tell you I also plan to dine tomorrow evening with Miss Cristall."

Thank heaven. Mary would write to William and invite him to dine with her. He never had to worry about finding time to write.

"My sister is wearisome and embarrassing," Mary said to him the next evening. "Even Puss doesn't like her. He attacked her with his claws this morning, then tried to escape through the chimney. Everina insists I get rid of him."

"I wish you could get rid of her. I find her to be a crank and regret us recommending her to Josiah Wedgwood. After all you've done for your sisters, they should be grateful to you."

Her family's continued dependence on her troubled Mary, and she rested her head on one hand. "When our mother died, I inherited the responsibility of caring for my younger siblings, especially my sisters. I don't resent the burden that was placed on me, but I feel guilty that I wasn't more successful in shaping their characters. They've all grown up to be self-centered and inconsiderate. Even Ned has nearly bankrupted himself. Everina tells me he hasn't been sending our father his monthly allowance."

"Your siblings can't expect you to fill in where your father failed to execute his responsibilities." William reached across the table and placed his hand over hers. "Not with a child to raise and another on the way. You must stop sending your father money. You must stop sending money to any of them."

"You are right, as always. It will be easy this month to refuse Papa. I don't have any money to send. I'll write to him tomorrow and explain my situation."

William reached inside his frock coat and produced an envelope. "For you," he said, handing it to Mary. "I've been watching how much you struggle. I don't want you in need of anything if I can help it."

Her eyes grew wide. Inside was fifty pounds. "Where did you get this?"

"It doesn't matter. When we marry, both our financial situations will improve. But until then, no more funds to your family."

Mary willingly agreed, only to find in the weeks following Everina's departure that her sister had left a bill at the dressmaker's and at the milliners. To be paid by Mary.

TWENTY-FOUR

March 1797
Two months later

March 29 began like any other day. Mary wrote until lunch. When William arrived at one p.m., she kissed Fanny goodbye and handed her to Marguerite for a nap. Mary and William headed on foot to New Road.

The two walked in silence, each absorbed in their own thoughts. A rabbit darted across their path, startling them both. Its light brown fur with bits of black and white camouflaged it for now as it bounced across the meadow and disappeared over the hill. Before long, however, the meadow would be green, and the rabbit's ability to hide would disappear.

The sun was still high by the time they reached St. Pancras, the old Saxon church resting unperturbed next to the River Fleet. Being an atheist, William would have preferred a different venue, but contrary to what many believed about Mary, she maintained her Christian beliefs and insisted on a church ceremony. St. Pancras was close by and known for administering quick weddings, no questions asked.

The church was simple inside, a long, narrow space with dark wooden pews and white plaster walls. Pictures of saints and stained-glass windows underscored the sacred nature of the space, helping to settle qualms ticking about inside Mary. James Marshall was there to greet them and led them up the aisle. The church was otherwise empty. Their footsteps echoed in the cavernous space, the sound evaporating into a high ceiling, where wooden beams ran from side to side. On the stone steps of the altar, a priest waited with his clerk ready to serve as a witness along with James Marshall.

Mary Wollstonecraft and William Godwin were not as youthful as most of the brides and grooms to stand in front of God at the altar at St. Pancras. In a month Mary would be thirty-eight. William had turned forty-one a few weeks earlier. She hoped the priest did not notice the round bump at her middle. If he did, he gave no sign. Without fanfare, he began as if preaching a Sunday sermon, his high-pitched voice echoing through the nave.

His words sounded far away. Mary was doing the one thing she swore she would never do—she was pledging herself to a man. For the rest of her life, she would be Mrs. Godwin. She stuttered over her vows twice, and she could not stop blinking at the priest. But William steadied her on his arm, his hand warm over hers, his eyes assuring her that his love had no conditions even as he, too, kept running a finger between his neck and collar as if he had tied his cravat too tight. At the close of the service, however, after they had professed to love one another for an eternity, Mary was strangely content. Life had taken the proper turn.

Afterward, they walked home at a slow pace, bright yellow daffodils displaying their showy colors next to the road. Mary turned her face to them, letting their sunny dispositions caress her. No more reservations. No more fears about her children's parentage. No more questions about her status. She was married now. To her relief, she did not feel any different, though her entire universe had changed.

Happy as newlyweds, Mary and William had just one more gauntlet to cross. When they reached the crossroad where the paths to their respective homes diverged, Mary asked, "Have we been wise to be so secretive?" Other than Marguerite and Marshall, no one knew they were getting married. No one even knew they were a couple. William had preferred to keep their union quiet.

"They shall know soon enough." A brooding expression passed over his face like a cloud. "We will give them but one chance to drag our reputations through the coals. After that, the veil will be lifted. You'll have no more secrets."

With the softest of kisses, they parted ways and walked alone to their separate homes.

The following week, Mary and William moved to an apartment at the Polygon in Clarendon Square in Somers Town, just steps away from where each of them had been living. The new Georgian-style three-story complex was a semi-circular building with fifteen sides and thirty-two houses, each with a small, wrought-iron balcony on the two first-floor windows facing the street. On the inside perimeter, renters shared an outdoor courtyard.

The couple's decor was minimal, a melding of their modest tastes. A vast expanse of windows allowed in fresh air and bathed the rooms in warmth. From their bedroom on the top floor, Mary and William looked out over the very meadows she wandered daily, an Elysian field, her own pastoral place of rest and comfort. Here, life would be easier.

The move also served as the public announcement of their marriage. Within their immediate circle, Thomas Holcroft thought them the most perfect of couples but told William in private that their secrecy pained him. Why had they not trusted him? Others were less charitable. One couple with whom Mary had dined every third Sunday for the past year wrote to say they no longer welcomed her in their home. Mary excused them as they were of the old order, a society not open to progress. Sarah Siddons, an actress friend of hers, was another who withdrew from her completely but did so out of extreme caution, she assured Mary, over guarding her reputation.

Not everyone was critical, however. Mr. Johnson was more than pleased, and William's mother was ecstatic her son had finally married and sent them eggs as a gift, a symbol of fertility. She wrote in her letter of congratulations: *May the union be fruitful. Would you like me to buy you a featherbed?* In closing, she expressed hope the marriage was a sign her son had come back to God.

And Iris, who cried when Mary told her the news, said she hoped she was not losing a friend. "I'm thrilled. Though you can imagine my utter shock when I received William's note referring to you as Mrs. Godwin," she said to Mary. Mary and William had invited Iris and Mr. Kendall as their first guests to the Polygon. It was April, and a gentle wind blew in from the surrounding fields, carrying with it the fecund smell of spring. "No one had any idea you were getting married, including me. I do so regret that you did not confide in me."

Mary and William exchanged glances. Ensconced in a worn leather side chair brought over from his apartment, William reached for a book but did not open it. The two couples had just shared a dinner of stewed mutton followed by a pistachio cream, the latter an indulgence that Mary hoped would serve as an apology to Iris.

"I'm sorry we didn't tell you," Mary said, noting the look of hurt on Iris's face.

"Oh, don't mind me. I can understand the predicament you've been in. You're both so independent, I always considered you the perfect match. Though I never imagined for a minute you would take it to the altar. All of London is ablaze with tittle-tattle about your surprise marriage."

William looked annoyed, not at Iris, but at society feeling license to judge him and Mary. "Every one of us, critics alike, complies with institutions and customs we would prefer to see abolished, do we not? We each remain hostile toward marriage," he said, more to Mr. Kendall than to Mary or Iris, "and we probably always will."

"Indeed. People are always petty when something unusual comes at them. I wouldn't worry about what they think or say," Mr. Kendall said.

"Well put, Mr. Kendall," Mary said. "William and I have been outspoken critics of marriage—in its current form. We intend to and have already defined marriage differently. William, for example, has taken a room for work."

William was renting a room twenty doors away at Evesham Place on Chalton Street, she explained. He left before breakfast and returned each evening at dinnertime. In the interim, he and Mary sent notes back and forth, multiple times a day, continuing their practice of Marguerite and James Marshall serving as messengers. Sometimes William slept there if he chose.

"How deliciously modern," Iris said. "That ought to wag a few tongues."

Mary smiled at seeing some of Iris's old mischief return. Iris had declined wine at dinner, a sign that she was taking better care of herself. And she had been dabbling again in writing poetry.

"Excessive familiarity is the bane of social happiness," William said to Mr. Kendall.

Mary knew William loved her, but their unborn child was really what had prompted them to marry, and this annoyed him deep down. As for herself, Mary did not care what the reason. Her life had turned into one of bliss. She benefitted as much from their unusual living arrangement as did William. In exchange for him having dedicated space away from home, they agreed Mary should not have to assume full responsibility for the household. Servants would take care of the domestic duties. Mary occupied the study in their new home as a room of her own where she could write undisturbed.

"Are you to still go your separate ways in the evenings, then?" Iris asked, eyeing them both with open curiosity.

"We shall, and why not?" William replied. "Our arrangement combines to a considerable degree the novelty and joys of domestic life along with our respective individual social lives."

Iris raised an eyebrow at Mary, no doubt thinking of Mrs. Inchbald, who continued to think she had rights to William. Among her friends, only Iris knew how Mary loathed Mrs. Perfection.

"I'm invited to the Drury this evening," William said to Mary one morning in late April before leaving for Evesham Place. "Mrs. Inchbald has reserved a box. You should join me."

"I do not think it wise." They were at breakfast, and she picked at the edges of her toast. In fact, she thought the idea a terrible one.

"Her invitation is an indication she regrets her harsh judgment toward us," William insisted, cajoling Mary into going with him. "I believe she is ready to make amends."

Mrs. Inchbald had been among the most hostile toward them after they announced their marriage. She accused them both of a complete lack of propriety and wrote William a scathing note informing him she had found someone else to escort her about town. A thin apology followed, in which she assured William she would not snub him the *next* time he married. To Mary, she maintained a judgmental eye.

"The invitation didn't include me," Mary said, the slight a direct aim at her. And at five months along, Mary's pregnancy was obvious. They were not lying about it, but they had not announced it either.

"We can't hide forever. I'm determined for us to have our first real public appearance since becoming a married couple."

When William set his mind on something, Mary found it was difficult to dissuade him. He was growing impatient over people's unkind attitudes toward their union. They still suffered the occasional jab, and while Mary could ignore such small-mindedness, William found it harder to stomach. For a man who despised any form of governmental infringement on a person's freedoms or liberties, he had even less patience with individuals who tried to trample on the choices of others, his most of all.

"What time shall we leave?" she asked, knowing her condition was going to reveal itself soon enough. They might as well let it be known tonight. When people saw her, they would figure things out on their own. At least they would be among friends.

The evening was too warm for a cloak, leading Mary to opt for a sky-blue pelisse over her shoulders that she had found at a secondhand store. But as she and William entered the foyer of the Drury and made their way up the stairs, she wished she had worn her cloak instead. Just as news of their surprise marriage was cooling down, she and William were giving the public another morsel on which to feed. She imagined how the gossip would unfold: *Did you hear? Mary Godwin is with child.* Rather than shrink from the speculation that was sure to follow tonight's outing, she held her head high.

"Good evening," William said, his manner genial as he greeted those who had already assembled in Mrs. Inchbald's box. He led Mary to two unoccupied seats behind the hostess. "I hope we haven't kept anyone."

Upon hearing his voice, Mrs. Inchbald turned. Her smile dissolved into a frown at the sight of Mary. "I will not sit with an unwed mother," she hissed.

The widow could just as well have stabbed Mary with a penknife, even though Mary could not discern whether Mrs. Inchbald's intended reference was to Fanny, now that it was obvious Gilbert and Mary had never married, or if she was referring to the child in Mary's womb.

William's face hardened. Other guests turned their gaze away, uncomfortable at Mrs. Inchbald's lack of decorum. "Come now," William said, keeping his good nature intact. "She and I are wed."

Mary, who was ready to dig her nails into the woman, marveled inside at his patience. The entire theater seemed to go silent.

"I invited you, *not her*," Mrs. Inchbald said to William. With a strident huff, she turned her back on him but could be heard saying, "I withdraw my invitation."

William's eyes bore into her. "Your manners are inexcusable. I will not allow you to speak ill of me or my wife."

Mrs. Inchbald did not reply and remained facing the stage.

Mary understood, then, that William would stand up to anyone who sought to discredit her. Even Mrs. Perfection. Mary sat in triumph for the remainder of the evening.

"I'm questioning that stubborn part of English culture that prevents men from giving utterance to their sentiments," William said to Mary. They lingered in bed, unwilling to part and face the day. The early morning sun unfurled its rays across them. The fresh scent of clover wafted into the room through open windows.

William propped his head with one hand and rested his other on her abdomen. "Have I told you your pregnancy is a source of a thousand endearments?"

Mary burrowed into him. "Yes, but I shall never tire of hearing it."

He kissed her neck, then leaned back to gaze at her. "I'm a changed man, you know. Even what I write is changing. With each word, I think of you."

"I'm flattered. Truly." She, too, had seen a transformation in him, in his actions and his words. Whereas he had once spoken of the importance of relying on reason as the sole guide for making a decision, he now included hints of how feelings should also be considered.

"You're glowing," he said.

Mary laughed. "And growing." Her breasts were as full as her figure, which had turned round. All traces of morning sickness had passed, leaving her free to take delight in carrying William's child.

"We've conquered the devil himself." William looked pleased. "For two people who used to quake at the mention of marriage, we've taken joyous command. I'd like John Opie to paint your portrait again, one I can hang at Evesham Place so I can see you every minute I am away."

"If you wish." His request touched her. That he would want her presence hanging in constant view was yet another sign of his affection. "Shall I ask him?" John Opie had painted her after *Rights of Woman* brought her fame. While she sat for him, they had formed a close friendship despite rumors at the time that he was in love with her. She now counted him among her closest acquaintances. Mary and Opie dined regularly.

"Please. You encounter him more than I do."

They got up and began to dress. "Were you aware," she asked, brushing her hair, watching William behind her through the looking glass, "that John Opie is courting Miss Alderson?"

"Who isn't?" William buttoned his shirt. "Miss Alderson is a good deal better than Opie's former wife. I never laid eyes on the woman, but from the sounds of it she was an appalling flirt." John Opie's wife had run off with a soldier, causing quite a scandal, and they had finally divorced.

Mary continued to monitor William's reaction. "Opie tells me he was smitten the minute he met Miss Alderson."

"Hm."

"I suspect they'll marry one day."

"The next time you see Miss Alderson," William said, reaching for his own brush, "please give her my regards. And tell Mary Wollstonecraft Godwin the rumors of William Godwin having once loved Amelia Alderson were exaggerated."

So it was true. William had loved Mary and only Mary all this time. The burden of doubt she had been carrying lifted, and they strode downstairs hand in hand to break their fast together, her step as light as if she were floating.

TWENTY-FIVE

Mid-August 1797
Three Months Later

In life, as people gradually discover the imperfections of each other's nature, they also uncover hidden virtues. For Mary and William, marriage was a winding road, the serpentine nature of love something they embraced without reservation. Mary was sure no two people had ever loved so well or with such honesty. They took to staying in together in the evenings as her pregnancy neared an end, co-mingling their friends and entertaining at the Polygon. Their table was reminiscent of Joseph Johnson's weekly dinners. Tonight, Mary was pleased to have him in attendance.

"Thank you for coming," she said, squeezing his hand. She had placed him next to her at the round table she and William had purchased, a table with no head, no foot, no one person dominant. William sat on her other side, his fingers laced with hers.

"I wouldn't have missed it," Mr. Johnson said. He looked at her with the eyes of a proud father. "You've done well, Mary."

"You've been uncommonly good to me," she replied. It was only fitting for Mr. Johnson to join them on this memorable evening. After dinner, John Opie would reveal her new portrait. "I owe you much. Had you not believed in me, I doubt I'd be sitting here."

Mary often wondered what would have become of her had Mr. Johnson not taken an interest in her, had not helped establish her in London.

"You're special to me," he said, "but I suppose you know that by now. I just wanted to be sure I told you before I leave this world."

His eyes misted. His health was up and down these days. Though still churning out more volumes than most other publishers, he was toning down the political tenor of his publications. Officials were still watching him and the writers he supported. The British Crown's nerves remained thin as France continued to try to launch a working government, their efforts a series of fits and starts.

"You're especially dear to me, too," Mary said. "I can't recall having ever been happier."

"I see that." Mr. Johnson glanced around the table. "You and William have amassed quite a set of friends."

Mary swelled inside with affection at those gathered. The Kendalls were there, along with Thomas Holcroft, John Opie, and Amelia Alderson. The most special of those present, besides Mr. Johnson, was Iris. Upon the Kendalls' arrival that evening, Iris had pulled Mary aside in the foyer, away from the others, before going upstairs to the dining room, where she presented Mary a handmade book. "I am better now, thanks to you. Though I can never repay your kindness or your patience in seeing me through my darkness, I've written these poems with you in mind."

Written on the first page in Iris's flowing hand, *To Mary, whose acts of courage and kindness have helped me see there is hope in every sorrow.*

"Thank you, friend," Mary said. "I shall savor every word." She saw how Iris was slowly returning to her old self. No more looking for solace in spirits or wallowing alone in her apartment. The color in Iris's cheeks had returned. Her eyes brimmed with joy, reminding Mary of when she had first met Iris. Iris was a survivor. Like Mary, her pain would not rule her, only her will.

"Mr. Johnson has agreed to publish them," Iris said, "with me listed as the author."

Mary hugged the book to her breast and beamed at Iris, knowing the joy of not having to be anonymous. She hoped for a future where women would never need to use someone else's identity to publish.

"My opinion of you rises considerably for marrying such a creative spirit," Holcroft said to William as the guests waited for dinner to be served, drawing

Mary's attention back to her guests. "Your wife ascends you. You are the most extraordinary pair in existence."

"Exaggerating doesn't make it so," Mary said, embarrassed by Holcroft's effusive praise. "William and I are nothing but two people who found in each other the perfect other half to make each of us whole."

"Don't Mr. Kendall and I get any credit?" Iris asked, laughing.

"I won't deny it," Mary said, joining in her friend's laughter. "It was you who opened the door to us being together."

Though it was more than the Kendalls' matchmaking or chance that Mary and William were together as man and wife. Mary had aspired in life to be an independent woman in need of no one, to prove that she could educate herself and find her way alone. Her want of autonomy, however, had turned into a cage of its own. She had failed to consider how love might alter one's life. Her self-imposed exile protected her from pain, but it locked her out as well, from a world she was, in truth, desperate to be let into. Marriage, she had finally learned, could be a positive nexus between two when both partners respected and supported each other in their shared and individual interests. With William by her side, tomorrow and the next day, and the days forever after that, held more promise than she had once dared hope would be hers.

William held up his glass, and his guests followed suit. "To my wife, Mary. The one who inspires me daily."

"Here, here!"

"What do you say, John, to unveiling Mary's portrait now?" William said, his eyes dancing with anticipation. Mary and William had discarded the custom of married couples referring to each other as mister or missus. To her, he would always be William. To him, she would always be Mary. "Let's not wait until after dinner."

"If you wish." John Opie motioned at Holcroft to follow him to the parlor. Moments later they returned with an easel covered with a cloth.

Mary's nerves bundled beneath her skin as she waited. Opie had assured her she would be pleased, but she had learned from the other portraits of her that seeing one's likeness could result in disappointment. When he pulled the cloth away, however, she inhaled a sharp breath.

A hush fell over the room.

"You've captured her perfectly," William said, his voice raspy with emotion. He stood and walked to the portrait as if in disbelief.

"The likeness is truly stunning," Iris and Miss Alderson agreed.

"Your kindness," Iris added, looking at Mary, then at the painting to compare. "And your confidence. It's as I see you each time I am with you."

Mary found herself speechless. It was, indeed, a true likeness. For this portrait, as a busy mother she did not have time to fret over what to wear or how she should represent herself. She did not change the style of her hair or purchase different clothing to reflect a woman with daring, new ideas, as she had when John Williamson had conveyed her as a stern intellectual. Nor was this image like the revolutionary woman Opie cast her as in the first portrait he had painted of her. In this, she wore what she always wore: a mother's dress, a soft black hat. An air of calm registered in her eyes and in the lilt of her brow. Her mouth turned up softly at the edges in a knowing way, and her overall countenance warm and mature.

A woman in life's prime.

"Your intelligence is once again on display for the world," Mr. Johnson said. "Your cheeks are the perfect color ... and the luster in your eyes ..." His own eyes dampened. "It's the loveliest portrait I have ever seen."

Mary laid her head on his shoulder. Other than William's, no compliment could mean more to her.

After dinner, when the night was late and the last crumb of dessert wiped away, the last bottle of wine emptied, Mary and William led their guests to the Polygon's courtyard, except for Mr. Johnson, who left, saying he was too tired to stay up any longer. They gazed at the night sky, the air warm, the stars vivid. A comet was passing over London.

"It's like fireworks," William said.

Mary's neck arched alongside his to the heavens above. "Some believe comets to be an omen."

Spellbound, William's gaze fixed itself on the hazy ball trailed by a band of light. "A magnificent one, I hope."

"Word is it can be a harbinger of bad news," Mary said, equally enthralled by the spectacle that made the stars seem inconsequential.

"I don't believe in superstitions," William said, slipping a protective arm around her waist.

"Nor do I. We shall consider it a sign of good things to come." She looked forward to the years ahead, to raising children together, to learning more each day about this man she loved.

Mary cast a hopeful glance at William. "Perhaps it means our baby will be born soon."

TWENTY-SIX

August 30, 1797

Two weeks after the comet, Mary woke with small contractions at five a.m. By seven the time between them had shortened. "I've no doubt of seeing Master William today," she whispered in her husband's ear.

William sprang to a seated position and rubbed the sleep from his eyes. "How can you be certain?"

Mary giggled, shooing him from bed. "I just know. Off you go to Evesham Place. A little patience and all will soon be over."

William dressed quickly, chattering the whole time about the things he and Master William would do together when he grew older. Mary could never have foreshadowed such a burst of excitement from so stoic an individual and hid her amusement behind her hand.

Before he left, William caressed her cheek. "I will do as instructed. But give me your word that you will send for me should anything happen."

His eyes hinted at worry, but Mary did her best to put him at ease. "I will. My portly shadow soon shall be no more. Thank you for putting up with my moods." She had been demanding these last few weeks, yet he had listened to her without complaint and rubbed her feet when they ached.

"Even your moods have been scrumptious." He kissed her, long and with zeal, until she had to push him away lest he linger the whole day.

"Off with you. On your way out, please have Marguerite call for the midwife." Mary and William could not afford a stay at a lying-in hospital. Nor did Mary want to be in such a place. Hospitals were rife with infections. "And if you would, deliver me a newspaper and a novel to occupy my time. This might take a while."

"I can't get the placenta to come out," Mrs. Blenkinsop said fourteen hours later. Rivulets of sweat streamed from the midwife's harried face. "I must send for a doctor."

"I want to see William first," Mary insisted, registering the midwife's alarm. She had not the energy to lift her limbs and could scarcely keep her eyes open. The clock on the mantle read two a.m. Her baby had been born at twenty past eleven and was resting peacefully in Marguerite's arms.

"I'll go for him straightaway." Mrs. Blenkinsop rushed from the room.

Mary shifted her worried gaze to Marguerite. "Is my baby all right?"

The same fear Mary saw in the midwife's eyes were present in Marguerite's, sending tremors through Mary.

Heavy footsteps bounded up the stairs. Seconds later, William burst into the room.

Mary tore her eyes from Fanny's nursemaid and did her best to greet him. "We have a baby girl." Her voice was barely audible despite her excitement at seeing him.

"I know," William said, his voice hushed as he rushed to her side. He looked panic-stricken and delighted simultaneously, a man frozen over what to think or what to do.

"You can hold her," Mary said.

Marguerite handed him the baby. The lines on his face melted as he took the child in his arms. "Baby Mary." William looked awestruck. "Do you think it a good name?"

Mary nodded. When his eyes welled with tears, her own gushed forth. She could see how he would spoil this little cherub. Every girl should have a father who adored her, that thought her the smartest, most important person in the world. Being loved like this would make her strong, and she knew without worry that Mary Godwin would enjoy all the blessings of a devoted father.

Despite the overwhelming swelling of her very soul upon seeing William and her baby together at last, Mary fought to stay awake and heard William say, "I need to go."

Her eyes popped back open. William appeared torn as he handed the baby back to Marguerite. He sat next to Mary on the bed and felt her forehead, then her cheek, down to her neck. His touch was heavy against her clammy skin.

"Mrs. Blenkinsop is sending me to find a doctor. I'll be back as soon as is humanly possible."

"Hurry," Mary whispered. Something was terribly wrong. Her body was screaming inside.

TWENTY-SEVEN

Friday, September 8, 1797

William's image blurred, then cleared, fading away again as if Mary observed him underwater. She had lost all sense of time.

"What day is it?" she asked. She was floating.

From a chair close to their bed, William's bloodshot eyes told her he had not slept in some time. He was not wearing a coat. William would never have allowed himself to be seen in a shirt so rumpled.

"Friday." His voice was tired.

Mary shivered and could not get warm. "Where's Baby Mary?" She could not remember when she'd last seen her. Her arms ached with emptiness. More than a week had passed since she had given birth.

"Iris took her and Fanny home with her on Monday."

Mary remembered everything then. She had childbed fever. A part of the placenta was still inside her womb. Her body was on fire one minute, freezing the next. An unquenchable thirst left her mouth thick and dry.

"I feel as if I'm in heaven already," she managed to say.

"It's the wine we've been giving you," William said, his words laced with sorrow. "The doctors said it would dull the pain."

Death. The imminent stranger no one wanted to at last encounter. Mary's ability to fear, however, had somehow left her. Perhaps, during days of sleep, the inner workings of her mind had made peace with her condition before her consciousness had fully absorbed what it meant. Though she did not fear death, she was angry. Out of years of longing came a life she treasured with William and two girls she loved with fierce determination—a life she must now surrender. Perhaps it was penance for playing fast with her mortality. She had tempted death twice when frantic for an escape. Death was here now, knocking for her instead, like a predator outside the door.

"Will Baby Mary live?" she asked William, holding onto what little breath she had left. She prayed Death did not wait for her baby as well. The child was weak. Mary knew by the way everyone avoided talking about her.

William's face crumpled like Fanny's when she was about to cry. His lips quivered. "The doctors aren't sure."

Saturday, September 9, 1787

Mary's eyes fluttered open at the sound of William's voice. She judged it was late afternoon. She knew all the angles of light by now, how it changed the color of the walls, how the mood of the room shifted as the day faded.

William was speaking to her, his face pressed close to hers while sitting in the same chair by the side of their bed he had not vacated for days. His chin was shrouded in days-old stubble, masking his dimple. Mary regretted leaving him. Without her, she feared he would become closed off again. He did not know yet how to trust his feelings.

"You must tell me what you want for your girls," William repeated. He appeared older than Mary remembered.

"I know what you're thinking." He wanted her to lay out for him how to raise their girls. It was there, she wanted to say, in all their conversations, in the way they had lived their short life together, but she had not the strength to utter the words. She wanted to tell him the answer was in her writing as well, where she had spelled out in detail what society must do to elevate the status of women, what values, what traditions must change. Help them to acquire strength in mind and body. Raise them to be rational creatures and free citizens, and they will become wise and virtuous women. Teach them their humanity, and they will be kind.

"I need your guidance," William insisted, his voice coming now in gulps. "Upon my word, I shall try to fulfill every wish you've ever possessed for them." He let go of his tears then. Being unable to take him in her arms grieved Mary. How was he going to manage without her?

She reached for his hand. More than anything, she wanted him to teach Fanny and Mary about true love so they could experience the passion, the contentment she and William had found. He could bestow no greater gift on them; no greater gift had he given her.

"You'll know what to do," she whispered as she closed her eyes for the last time, "for you are the kindest, best man in the world."

TWENTY-EIGHT

Sunday
10 September 1797

My wife is now dead. She died this morning at eight o'clock ...

I firmly believe there does not exist her equal in the world. I know from experience we were formed to make each other happy. I have not the least expectation that I can ever know happiness again.

When you come to town, look at me, talk to me, but do not—if you can help it—exhort me, or console me.

—Letter to Thomas Holcroft from William Godwin

EPILOGUE

Mary Wollstonecraft Godwin died from childbed fever ten days after giving birth to her second daughter. Her family laid her to rest five days later in the cemetery at St. Pancras Church, where she and William Godwin married. William Godwin did not attend the funeral. Installed at a desk in James Marshall's apartment, he buried himself writing letters to friends, expressing his untold grief in the only way he knew how: pen in hand, alone.

END

POSTSCRIPT

Mary Wollstonecraft

Mary Wollstonecraft was a writer and philosopher best known for her ground-breaking book, *A Vindication of the Rights of Woman* (1792), now widely recognized as one of the world's first and most important treatises regarding women's rights. In it she argued women were not inferior to men, as was the accepted belief at the time. Prior to her career as a writer in London, she served as a lady's companion in Bath, headmistress of her own school in Newington Green, and governess to one of Ireland's wealthiest families. Historians have dubbed her "the mother of feminism."

William Godwin

William Godwin deeply mourned the death of Mary Wollstonecraft. With two small daughters to raise, he married Mary Jane Clairmont four years later. He continued to write, branching into other genres besides political philosophy in order to support his family, eventually opening his own publishing house with his new wife. He died in 1836. Godwin was a significant influence within the British literary community during his lifetime. He is credited with founding political anarchism—a society without government that functions through free agreement.

Joseph Johnson

Joseph Johnson was one of the most influential London booksellers of his time. His career spanned more than forty years. He was known for publishing works promoting free thinking, tolerance, religious freedom, and political reform. In 1799, two years after Mary Wollstonecraft died, he spent six months in prison on charges of seditious libel for publishing works by Gilbert Wakefield. Johnson died in 1809, at which time he left two hundred pounds to William Godwin with strict instructions to use it only for the care of Fanny Imlay. Several of Johnson's nephews, Rowland Hunter among them, took over Johnson's book business after his death but never achieved the success Johnson enjoyed. The bookshop stood for more than a century longer until Germans destroyed it in the London Blitz during World War II on December 29, 1940.

Gilbert Imlay

Gilbert Imlay largely disappeared from history after ending his relationship with Mary Wollstonecraft, leaving scant trace of himself beyond the two books he authored. Claire Tomalin, author of *The Life and Death of Mary Wollstonecraft*, posits that Gilbert Imlay died in St. Brelade in Jersey, a center for smuggling. A tombstone for a Gilbert Imlay rests there. The epitaph reads like the adventurous, restless man Mary Wollstonecraft had loved: *Transient hope gleams even in the grave ... As brightening vistas open in the skies.* For those wondering about the whereabouts of Imlay's silver ship and its contents, it remains a mystery to this day and has been the subject of continued speculation.

Fanny Imlay Godwin

Fanny Imlay Godwin grew into a shy, modest young woman. In William Godwin's eyes, she was a shadow to his own daughter, Mary Godwin, and he largely overlooked Fanny, who also never bonded with her stepmother. Only Joseph Johnson seemed to care for her interests. It was not enough. After finding life at home unbearable, Fanny committed suicide at the age of twenty-two by drinking laudanum, alone at an inn in Wales, after her aunts Eliza and Everina Wollstonecraft refused to take her in.

Mary Godwin

Mary Godwin grew up the apple of her father's eye. Like Fanny Imlay, she also never got along with her stepmother. At sixteen Mary Godwin fell in love with the married poet, Percy Bysshe Shelley, and ran away with him. Eventually they married. At nineteen, Mary Shelley wrote *Frankenstein; or, The Modern Prometheus* in response to a parlor challenge from Lord Byron to write a ghost story. Her novel launched an entire genre. *Frankenstein* is considered the first science fiction book ever written. Mary Shelley longed to know her mother and reportedly learned to read by tracing the letters on her mother's tombstone at St. Pancras. Later in life, having gleaned what she could from her father and other of her mother's contemporaries, she wrote the following:

Mary Wollstonecraft was one of those beings who appear once perhaps in a generation, to gild humanity with a ray which no difference of opinion nor chance of circumstances can cloud. Her genius was undeniable. She had been bred in the hard school of adversity, and having experienced the sorrows entailed on the poor and the oppressed, an earnest desire was kindled within her to diminish these sorrows. Her sound understanding, her intrepidity, her sensibility and eager sympathy, stamped all her writings with force and truth and endowed them with a tender charm that enchants while it enlightens. She was one whom all loved who had ever seen her. Many years are passed since that beating heart has been laid in the cold grave, but no one who has ever seen her speaks of her without enthusiastic veneration.

In Italy Mary Shelley met Margaret King, Mary Wollstonecraft's student in Bristol, who by then was Countess Mount Cashell. Mary Shelley was touched when Margaret King said she was heavily influenced by Mary Wollstonecraft. King became a feminist herself, pursuing a literary career and studying medicine. Like Wollstonecraft, King led an unconventional life. She also met William Godwin as well when he toured Ireland in the 1800s.

AUTHOR'S NOTES

At a time when society minimized women, and the law reduced them to being the property of husbands and fathers, Mary Wollstonecraft boldly disregarded stereotypes and hurdled through obstacles by relying on her sharp intellect and finely tuned instincts. Her life was not without sacrifice, and not without scandal. Yet she prevailed because of her extraordinary determination. In my humble assessment, Mary's life epitomizes the heroine's journey, as defined by Maureen Murdock in her ground-breaking book *The Heroine's Journey*, which describes contemporary women's search for wholeness. Mary's story, though centuries old, is one of healing the feminine wounds within.

If Mary were alive today, we would recognize in her the aftereffects of witnessing and being the direct recipient of abuse as a child, for she appears to have had many of the symptoms identified by modern psychology. Mary was prone to anxiety and depression, sometimes had difficulty with relationships, and displayed psychosomatic complaints, including frequent headaches and abdominal pain. Self-blame, guilt, and shame were frequent companions. Other post-traumatic anxieties Mary routinely exhibited included fear of abandonment, excessive worry, and sadness.

Fortunately, Mary also possessed critical attributes that helped her overcome the devastating effects of her early life. She was intelligent and curious. Reading was an outlet for her, one she relied on throughout her entire life, and her inquisitive nature drew her to people beyond her dysfunctional family. Despite her tendency toward moodiness, she had a vivacious, charming personality, being both outgoing and socially competent. Though such traits helped her transcend her family situation, her liabilities followed her, forcing her to find ways to manage, sometimes with less success than others. We love her in part for her imperfections and what sometimes appear as stunning contradictions.

From one biographer to the next, depictions of Mary differ, from admiring her to seeming harsh toward her. Mary to me was vulnerable, a woman in search of answers who stumbled into love, only for it to ransack her identity. Broken, she had to put herself back together. In addition to her intellectual brilliance, what intrigued me most about Mary was the powerful attraction she had for the men she loved during her short and tragic life. With Henry Fuseli, she was naïve. With Gilbert Imlay, she was a smart woman who made foolish choices. Who doesn't know a woman like that? In William Godwin, however, she found enduring love with a man who viewed her as his equal.

Solitary Walker is a work of fiction told in chronological order, inspired by Mary's unlikely writing life, and what I would call her late-blooming love affairs. Like many biographical fiction writers, I massaged dates to serve the story. Names and locations, however, are historically accurate, except for Iris Kendall, who is a fictional figure. It would have been impossible to include all the women Mary befriended. I intended Iris as a melding of them. She grew in my consciousness, ending up with her own unique story to tell. The letters Mary wrote to Iris include sentiments borrowed from actual letters Mary sent to others at approximately the same time. Norris, Imlay's associate, is also a composite figure. To avoid confusion, in one instance, I renamed an actual historical figure by taking the liberty to use the Irish spelling for little Mary King by naming her Mairen.

What also is fictional in the novel are the conversations and the day-to-day situations Mary encounters in her struggle to evolve. *Solitary Walker* is my interpretation of her as a woman, what might have been going through her mind, as well as what she and others may have said or done. The blend of fact and fiction allowed me to craft a story that would capture readers' imaginations beyond what biographies offer.

To my regret, missing in the story is more information regarding Mary's family, which was highly dysfunctional, most notably a look at her relationship with her sisters, with whom she was closer than my story would suggest. Space simply did not allow a deeper look at how Mary's family depended on, and often used her, for financial support. Also missing for space reasons are key figures who influenced Mary in London and later in Paris, people like Ruth and Joel Barlow. (Barlow was an important business associate of Imlay's.)

I owe much to biographers for helping me craft a story about Mary. Readers can find the full list of texts I referred to constantly on my website at njmastro.com. The most useful were *Vindication: A Life of Mary Wollstonecraft,* by Lyndall Gordon; *Mary Wollstonecraft: A Revolutionary Life,* by Janet Todd; and *Romantic Outlaws,* a dual biography of Mary Wollstonecraft and her daughter Mary Shelley, by Charlotte Gordon. Other essential texts were *William Godwin: His Friends and Contemporaries* by C. Kegan Paul; *Dinner with Joseph Johnson,* by Daisy Hay; and *The Life and Writings of Henry Fuseli* by John Knowles. Scholarly articles on Mary Wollstonecraft, of which there are many, were also useful for filling in the blanks and for gaining perspective regarding how readers in the twenty-first century view Mary. I also read many contemporary newspaper, blog, and magazine articles online. In those, however, I tended to find inaccuracies.

To authenticate my interpretations of Mary and her contemporaries, where possible, I used words and sentiments directly from Mary's published writings. Of particular use was *A Vindication of the Rights of Woman* and *Letters Written During a Short Residence in Sweden, Norway and Denmark.* Letters by Mary in *Solitary Walker* are based on Mary's originals, as are the letters from William Godwin, though I took the liberty to shorten them, and in some cases, modernize the language. In rare instances, for dramatic effect, I merged key points from letters she had written to different people. Sources for Mary's letters were Janet Todd's *The Collected Letters of Mary Wollstonecraft* (2003) and *Godwin and Mary: Letters of William Godwin and Mary Wollstonecraft,* edited by Ralph M. Wardle (1966).

William Godwin's memoir of Mary, *Memoirs of the Author of A Vindication of the Rights of Woman,* was yet another resource that provided much in terms of substance in seeking intuition about Mary. We can assume it is an idealized account of her. Mary was, after all, the love of his life. But it illuminates their loving relationship, along with a picture of who William Godwin really was. Sadly, when William published *Memoirs of the Author of A Vindication of the Rights of Woman,* he also published a four-volume edition of the *Posthumous Works of the Author of a Vindication of the Rights of Woman,* intended as an homage to Mary following her death. *Posthumous Works* included Mary's letters to Gilbert Imlay, as well as her unfinished novel, *The Wrongs of Woman, or Maria,* the book she was writing when she died. Friends of Mary and William begged him not to expose Mary in such a fashion, warning him it would bring scandal upon her. Surprisingly, Joseph Johnson agreed to publish both works against his better judgment. The books caused serious harm to Mary's reputation, branding her as a whore for having a child out of wedlock. Conservatives and religious members of the establishment, her primary critics throughout her career, buried her writings under moral judgment consistent with the era. William also damaged his own reputation through his affiliation with her. After he released the memoir, his contemporaries never viewed him with the same respect.

Consequently, Mary was largely forgotten for many decades. It was not until the women's suffrage movements in the middle of the nineteenth century in Europe and the United States that her writings were resurrected. Her words now back in circulation, she has become a patron saint of women pursuing liberty, rightly earning her the title as the world's first feminist.

ACKNOWLEDGEMENTS

When I first began a novel about Mary Wollstonecraft, little did I know researching and writing about her would become an obsession. I have many people to thank for helping me tell her story through fiction, which has been a labor of love and learning. Thank you to my wonderful critique partners Kathy Whipple, Katherine Kitchens, Kerry Riley Lind, Ann Fowler, Larry Keaton, Richard Lane, Susan Matsumoto, and June Peterson. Without them I can confidently say I would never have finished this book. They gave me honest feedback, technical advice, and the encouragement to keep writing. Thank you as well to my beta readers Mary Jo Schulke, Carol Schirmers, Janet Schreier, Katherine Page, Susan Larkin, Tammy Nelson, Mary Beth Gibson, Vivianne Sang, Racquel Levitt, and Leslie K. Simmons, all of whom helped kindle my resolve to finish the story. Great appreciation is also extended to the team at Black Rose Writing for believing in this story and helping shape into a novel that I am proud to share with readers. Most of all, thank you to my husband, Allan, and my son, Justin, whose never ending support continues to mean the world to me.

READERS GUIDE

1. If Mary Wollstonecraft were alive today, how would modern women characterize her? Would it be different from how supporters and critics judged her in the eighteenth century?

2. What qualities did you like best in Mary and why? Which did you not like about her?

3. Would Mary have been successful were it not for Joseph Johnson investing in her as he did with money and emotional support? Have you ever had a mentor who provided you with substantial direction in your career or personal life? How did this impact you?

4. Compare Gilbert Imlay to William Godwin. How could Mary love two such different men? What attracted her to each? Have you ever loved men or women who are complete opposites?

5. Mary was not perfect. She possessed many faults and contradictions, making her human. Which fault(s) or contradiction(s) appealed to you most and why? Which left you feeling frustrated or disappointed in her?

6. Was Mary trying to kill herself when she took the laudanum? What about when she jumped off the bridge? Was she serious about ending her life?

7. Mary appears to be a smart woman who sometimes did foolish things. Do you agree? Have you ever done something foolish and later regretted it? Or did the experience, painful as it might have been, help you grow as a person?

8. How have things changed for women since Mary's lifetime? What things remain the same? Have women achieved the kind of liberty and equal opportunity for which Mary rallied during her short life?

9. Had you read anything about Mary Wollstonecraft before reading this novel? If so, in what way did *Solitary Walker* further illuminate her as either a feminist or as a historical figure? If you've not heard about her before, do you plan to find out more about her?

10. Do you believe Mary Wollstonecraft truly was the world's first feminist?

ABOUT THE AUTHOR

N.J. Mastro writes historical fiction and *Herstory Revisited*, a blog featuring reviews of biographical novels about audacious women from the past along with a peek at the facts behind the fiction. A former school administrator, she holds a master's and a doctorate in educational leadership and spent nearly four decades in public education. Her pastimes besides writing include reading, cooking for friends, and traveling. She grew up in Minnesota, which will always be home, though Mastro currently lives in the South with her husband. She has one grown son. Learn more about her at www.njmastro.com.

NOTE FROM N.J. MASTRO

Word-of-mouth is crucial for any author to succeed. If you enjoyed *Solitary Walker*, please leave a review online—anywhere you are able. Even if it's just a sentence or two. It would make all the difference and would be very much appreciated.

Thanks!
N.J. Mastro

We hope you enjoyed reading this title from:

www.blackrosewriting.com

Subscribe to our mailing list – *The Rosevine* – and receive **FREE** books, daily deals, and stay current with news about upcoming releases and our hottest authors.
Scan the QR code below to sign up.

Already a subscriber? Please accept a sincere thank you for being a fan of Black Rose Writing authors.

View other Black Rose Writing titles at
www.blackrosewriting.com/books and use promo code
PRINT to receive a **20% discount** when purchasing.